THE UNKNOWN SOLDIER

A Novel by VÄINÖ LINNA

Werner Söderström Osakeyhtiö
Porvoo . Helsinki

Translated from the Finnish

ISBN 951-0-11289-5

Printed in Finland by Werner Söderström
Osakeyhtiö Juva 1982

Reprinted 1970

Reprinted 1975

Reprinted 1982

Väinö Linna

No other Finnish postwar writer — hardly even any other Scandinavian postwar writer — has had so deep an extra-literary influence and significance as Väinö Linna. His later novels — *The Unknown Soldier* and the »crofter trilogy», *Here under the Northern Star* — have with reason been described as an invaluable national therapy. They have captured and expressed atmospheres and trends which were in the air in Finnish society after 1945, and at the same time, through the incredible power of the characterization, thanks to the writer's unusually keen eye and burning zeal, have themselves made an important contribution to the creation of opinion and the speeding up of development in this society. More than any other writer in Finland, Väinö Linna has helped to cut the earth from under the feet of nationalistic and chauvinistic ideologies and values, and to establish the western welfare state ideal of social growth and democracy, centred on the right — and obligation — to open trial and criticism. At the same time, his books show an artistic quality of a kind and degree that raises them far above the local in time and space.

*

Väinö Linna was born in 1920, in Urjala in south-western Finland. On both sides he is descended from western Finnish crofter and farm labourer families. His grandfather was a crofter, his father a slaughterer. His father died young, leaving many children; his mother was forced for many years of poverty to support the large family by working as a servant on the same estate whose crofters the family had been.

After Väinö Linna left elementary school and spent some years in temporary jobs in his home area, he moved at the age of seventeen to Tampere — Finland's largest industrial town — where he got a job in a large textile factory. Soon after the »Winter War» between the Soviet Union and Finland in 1939—40 he was called up for military service. Väinö Linna fought throughout the war of 1941—44, when Finland was an ally of Germany, as a non-commissioned officer. He spent the first years at the front in a machine gun company, and later was an instructor at a training centre. Even in his schooldays, one of his most characteristic features was a great and varied hunger for books. During the long period of inactivity in 1942, after the Finnish-Russian front in Outer Karelia had frozen in an impasse, Väinö Linna for the first time had the chance to concentrate on reading both literature and social science. He also began to try to write at this period, and when the war was over and he returned to civilian life and the factory he had made up his mind to be a writer. He went on with his reading and writing as well as his factory work, and in 1947 he published the little novel *Goal* (»Päämäärä»).

*

As a work of art, *Goal* is very immature, tossed together in between factory work by day and fevered self-teaching by evening and night. It could best be called a spiritual volcanic eruption, a long way from artistic entity in the true sense. But as a key to Linna it is, if properly read, a goldmine. Not because it is, externally, auto-biographical in any but the most superficial sense, but in the psychological sense it is a kind of intimate diary of the thoughts and moods of the author while he was writing it. It exposes a complex of problems which were to recur in various forms throughout Linna's work.

The main character is Valte Mäkinen, a servant boy who moved to town and factory because he could not feel at home in his stagnant native milieu. Even in the new environment it is hard for him to find a foothold. He has been drawn to books by curiosity and a strong thirst for knowledge, and he devours books without plan or system. In his feelings and thoughts he describes a kind of vicious circle, where the fever increases at every turn but there seems to be no way out. The foundation is partly a strong craving for fame and a fierce need for self-cultivation, partly a sense of devastating fragmentation and a despairing desire to conquer it.

Valte's attitude to his environment, both present and past, is hostile and tinged with revolt, but in a completely individual way. He repudiates politics and ideologies contemptuously. He returns most frequently to the questions of metaphysics. If there is good and evil in the world, he reasons, following familiar patterns, then the divine will is splintered, not united. Thus men, the unwilling victims of this splintered divine will, have no responsibility. And if, on the other hand, the world is ruled by a single whole, unfragmented will, then there is neither good nor evil. There are only events.

Like Kant, whom he reads eagerly, Valte decides that metaphysics is impossible. But this does not stop him from returning compulsively over and over again to religious questions and the question of the meaning of life. He suffers as bitterly through the related ethical and moral dilemma. In a frenzy of despair he searches for the signs of goodness and guileless love among people, but does not find them, either in himself or in others. Egoism seems to be by far the most important, if not indeed the only, motive for human behaviour.

With hardwon cynicism he claims that things cannot be otherwise, but still he cannot hide his need for a firm ethical foundation.

On the edge of suicide, Valte realizes that the life-saving fear he feels despite everything is stronger than his desire for death. He cannot make himself take the decisive step. A few bewildering moments of total mental short-circuit on the bridge over the rushing rapids of the factory town have an invigorating shock effect on him. When he rouses from his state of bewilderment he suddenly sees the world, existence and himself in a new light. He feels that it is the will to live itself that is primary, and that he must build up a continued existence. One might say that he now follows Nietzsche rather than Schopenhauer in his way of looking at things. Undoubtedly one can see these two philosophers, as well as Kant, forming the pillars, as it were, on which Väinö Linna's way of thinking at this time is based. Behind the formulations in the final pages of the nebulosities of the world and the confession of the »law of events» we can distinguish the voice of Zarathustra, and again in the statement that »everything that happens is right». In a vision, Valte sees the entire world as a dizzying but consistent context where each component part has its given place and justification. He finds himself very close to Nietzsche's declaration that man implements the »meaning» of his life by assenting, with a clear awareness of self, to all that is in him.

*

The idea of the primary will to live as an ethical foundation has remained an essential feature in Väinö Linna's work. But even in his next novel, *Black Love* (»Musta rakkaus», 1948), this way of thinking becomes more subtle and from something extremely individualistic develops towards a social assent.

Black Love is a heavily-charged drama of jealousy, an Othello story in a Finnish working class setting, the story of a demonic Eros who grows to demented proportions until the tale ends in catastrophe that devastates the life of the main character. Here Linna's craftsmanship alone has developed a long way in the short period since *Goal*. But *Black Love* too has some striking artistic defects, especially the tendency to slip over into melodrama and the weaknesses in the psychological structure of the main characters.

The central problem in *Black Love* is closely connected with that of Dostoievski, especially as it appears in *Crime and Punishment*, and Pauli, the main male character, has features that are reminiscent of a rather narrower Raskolnikov. In the final analysis this is a question of guilt, responsibility, expiation and value. It could also be said that *Black Love* tries to be a graphic example of the wages of sin being death. The sin is pride and egoism, the ruin of both Pauli himself and his environment. *Goal* ended with a hymn of praise to ennobled egoism. *Black Love* ends with the bankruptcy of egoism and the self-annihilation of the egoist. Linna's Opus II is thus at the opposite pole from his first book. Here the main character's search for himself, his lack of desire or ability to look at anything other than his own navel, and his superhuman ideal of perfection, lead to disaster.

*

Six silent years lie between *Black Love* and the great war novel *The Unknown Soldier*, which brought Linna world fame. Soon after *Black Love* he began work on a novel with the working title »Messiah», where he tries to penetrate a question which then and later stood at the centre of his attention: man's situation in society and existence, the relation of the self to its surroundings. Now, too, the personally urgent questions of good and evil lay at the bottom, the problem of the contents of these concepts, of the possibility or impossibility of anchoring them in some belief, of the need for a stable ethical system and the opportunity of deriving this from rationally acceptable premises. *Messiah* was never completed, since Linna became involved in a severe personal crisis, mainly because the questions posed by the book while he was working on it weighed on him so heavily that his powers of creation were paralyzed.

The »Messiah crisis» was in summer 1952. One year later, Linna began work again on *The Unknown Soldier*, which had occupied him throughout the post-war period, and had existed even during the war in a clumsy documentary version. The new direction Linna was pressed into by the crisis was decisive for the form of the novel as a collective description and not a document in individual psychology. Since then his attitude towards his fellow men has been different from that in his earlier work. The ideal of the superman and belief in ennobled egoism are replaced by respect for the life and personalities of others, by a basic attitude that is close to the ethical principle of an Albert Schweitzer: reverence for life. In harmony with this, the writer's introspection changes, becoming more outward-turning, and his concept of the writer changes, becomes wider, epic, charged with humour.

In *The Unknown Soldier*, Linna describes a machine-gun platoon composed of young conscripts, their experiences during the long »Continuation War» — from summer 1940, when the Finnish army broke through across the border into Outer Karelia and the Soviet Union, until autumn 1944, when the armistice was concluded after fighting that was some of the bitterest in the Second World War, and after the Russians had broken through the Finnish front on the Karelian Isthmus and taken Viipuri. The group marches, fights, rests, and retreats, in a context which slowly but uninterruptedly develops. Grumbling and bickering are the everyday language of the front, where the voice of ordinary existence is heard; the voice that says that the war is an incomprehensible folly. The truth thus emerges, the war as human experience and reaction. It is a handful of ordinary, simple people — men of flesh and blood, each speaking his own language and remaining himself through thick and thin — who, in Väinö Linna, convey the picture of the everyday reality of war and make it so convincingly true and alive. The incomparable portraits of individuals, drawn with exuberant realism and broad humour, are the measure of his greatness as a describer of men and as a poet.

»I described a group of men that I tried to bring alive so that people could see just what has died», Linna has said about *The Unknown Soldier*. It is worth listening to the rest of his statement on his attitude towards the theme of this great masterpiece.

»There are many ways of seeing things. So there are many ways of seeing the Finnish soldier in his last war. The commonest is the blind way. That is, to see in him the national idea embodied, to treat him as a noble struggle for this idea. He did fight for his ideas, true — often most admirably, however dubious it is in the name of human morality to admire anything connected with war — but there was very little idealism. He tried to put up with the drudge, swearing, carried out orders with backchat and grimaces, and didn't give a damn for heroism, country and all the holy values set on them. With this pack and his kit, cap on head, rifle slung on his back, cartridges in pocket and a lump of bread in his bag he went his way through the great drama. That was what he was like, when behind a stone or a pile of earth he nerved himself to challenge the death that waited. And when he retreated in defeat, with what was left of his uniform and the memory of fallen comrades for supplies, his mouth twisted into a grin.»

In Finland, *The Unknown Soldier* has been bought and read more than any other single book except the Bible and the ABC; 345,500 copies have been published altogether, and it has been translated into 14 languages. It is the least complicated and most purely narrative of Linna's novels. The problems that are essential to Linna are there, but are kept more under the surface than earlier or later. The criticism of patent patriotic myths and of the mentality which Linna, using an expression common in the wartime Finnish army, has called »war madness», is extremely pointed but is an organic part of the artistic whole, with no sense of its being superimposed on it. The novel sparked off the liveliest controversy ever in the literary history of Finland, and made a decisive contribution to a general revaluation and shift of opinion in the view of the war as a phenomenon. Without making any deeper analysis, we may join an array of leading critics in Finland and many other countries in saying that artistically, the book represents the peak of what world literature has to offer within this genre.

In Sweden there is a man called Harry Järv, internationally renowned as a scholar and literary researcher — above all, as one of the world's leading Kafka experts. During the Second World War he was a lieutenant in the Finnish Army, with a reputation as a good, intrepid infantry officer and patrol leader. He must be considered highly qualified to judge *The Unknown Soldier* from a double perspective, both as a document and as a work of art. I shall quote his balanced and acute summary of the novel's qualities:

»Linna's book is a true book about the absurd reality of war, it deals with hardship, crudity and death, with human value in inhuman situations, with soldiers who fail in their attempts to meet the inhuman demands made of them, and often with their successes. But it is not just true, it is, from another point of view, a great literary work of art. The battle scenes are comparable with the best of their kind in literature, and Linna is also a great creator of characters. Linna attacks war and the militarism that is an end in itself, but his book is a salute to the unknown soldier in every war, the civilian who makes the best, in an unmilitary way, of a situation he is not responsible for, the ordinary, simple man who wants to live in peace but must suffer and die for the idiocies of other, more powerful men.»

The framework of Linna's second great work, the trilogy *Here under the Northern Star* (»Täällä pohjantähden alla», 1959, 1960, 1962) deals with the destiny of a crofter family and its emergence to independence as farmers. The trilogy also gives a picture of the dramatic history of Finland from the 1880s up to the period after the Second World War, as reflected in the events in a village in the western plains of Finland (in Häme). The writer has gathered and arranged a massive amount of material to make a huge fresco of the destiny of Finland from the pressure of Czarist power through the War of Independence, the Civil War, the depression of the '30s and the currents of authoritarianism and the bewilderment of the Second World War, up to the period of rebuilding and rapid development that began about 20 years ago. All the ideas current during this period are found here. They are put forward without exaggeration, without any special pleading, in fact one might say objectively. This does not prevent the author's sympathy lying with the small, the oppressed — in the gripping, brilliant description of the Civil War of 1918, for example in the »reds» — the socialist-orientated working and crofter classes in Finland who, under the pressure of privation, social injustice and the Russian revolution rose in arms, were conquered and then subjected to extremely harsh and summary reprisals from the victorious »whites» — the middle classes. But Linna does not take up his position on the ideological and political plane, but on the human. He does not defend the revolt, but he puts forward the reasons for its arising in quite a different way from the victors, in the official and officious accounts and their literature on the Civil War. Like *The Unknown Soldier*, the crofter trilogy caused a heated debate. Both the trilogy itself and the discussion it provoked have led to a reappraisal, in the name of objectivity, of the events of 1918, and have thereby laid the foundation for the healing of old wounds which have lain suppurating in the body of Finnish society right up to the last few years.

The crofter trilogy is based on a carefully thought out historical and socio-philosophical attitude which Linna has gradually worked out and which gives the work its dimensional depth and outstanding artistic power. It is an attitude that has clear points of agreement with that of Leo Tolstoy, but is so personal that we may speak of a strong influence but not of a formal discipleship.

One of the theories that Tolstoy most emphasizes in *War and Peace* is that a series of military events is never controlled by plans made in advance, however brilliant and packed with alternatives these may be. A general who thinks he is leading a campaign is the victim of an illusion. According to Tolstoy, the campaign leads the general. Väinö Linna has a somewhat similar view of the entire historical and social process. This attitude is perhaps most clearly noticeable in the section on the 1918 Civil War in the second part of the trilogy. There the events slip out of the grasp of both leaders and masses, and roll relentlessly on under their own momentum. Man does not control the event, the event controls man, high and low, leader and led, red and white. But Linna also tries to make this concept more subtle, less raw, and this seems to have grown under the influence of modern sociology and social psychology. This modification could perhaps be expressed as a belief, or at least a hope, that the relative opportunities for choice and direction increase in direct proportion to an increase in knowledge and ability. Linna does not consider the law of historical inevitability as an absolute determinism, which one might dare to say Tolstoy in fact did. Instead he thinks that an increased awareness can lead to a certain degree of increased freedom. As he himself put it in an interview: There is an idea that with every abandoned and altered theory, science comes a little closer to the truth, the final truth about the world. That the theories, as it were, converge with the truth and finally come very close, without ever actually reaching it. Linna wants to think of history in the same way: that our choices and dealings converge with an ideal situation, a »Land of Canaan», which we can approach more and more closely, but which can never be fully attained.

From this view of history and society, we come to the deepest layer in the trilogy, one that is virtually identical with Linna's old problem of personal responsibility, personal guilt and personal value. The historico-philosophical and social problems are organically combined with the question of individual free will. This question is one of the cornerstones of Väinö Linna's work. One can hardly say that he arrives at any definitive and unambiguous answer. But there is no doubt that he approaches a concept of a kind of limited and, as it were, conditional freedom within the borders of heredity, environment and period. External factors over which we have no control place us in choice situations where we can choose more or less rationally, depending on the degree of our personal development. One might say that Linna cultivates a personal responsibility where there is a measure of awareness, that he believes in a morality — or at least the possibility of a morality — where there is a measure of intelligence and ability. The lines of social and individual development that his later works show should be looked at in this light.

N-B. Stormbom

THE UNKNOWN SOLDIER

Chapter I

1.

As everyone knows, God is all-powerful, all-knowing and farseeing. So it was that He once let a forest fire devour several hundred acres of state forest on a sandy heath near the town of Joensuu. Men, as is their habit, tried their utmost to cut short His work, but inexorably He burned just as much of the forest as His plans required.

The first to perceive what the Almighty had really had in mind was a colonel. Chief of Staff of an Army Corps, he was regrouping his forces when he saw how extremely well the burned clearing would serve as a military camp site. Finland's Winter War had been fought—that war which had been the best to date, for in it both sides had won. The Finns, though, had won slightly less than the Russians in that they had had to cede territory to their enemies and withdraw behind a new frontier.

The remnants of the army had been demobilized and new age groups called up to replace them. Now the burned clearing was occupied by an infantry battalion. In warm spring weather the veterans departed, wearing their fur caps, tattered sheepskin coats, knitted jerseys and felt boots. For them there were no "difficulties of readjustment." Finnish fashion, they got dead drunk, sobered and then went to work. Had the nation's sacrifices been in vain? That was a question for those who had no spring planting to attend to.

They were, for the most part, of healthy peasant stock. So what extraordinary psychological complications could have attended their return to civilian life? They couldn't afford to make a stumbling block out of it. And as for their souls, old men with time to think of repentance may possess them, but a soldier hasn't the slightest use for such things. The eyes peering out of deep sockets above chapped and bearded cheeks reflected only the fierce determination of any wild animal to cling to its miserable life.

But now the young age group had taken their place.

There they stood, their ranks still ragged and untrained, these victims chosen by Mother Finland to be sacrificed on the altar of world history. Young farmers in heavy plain garments, overcoatless laborers, even an occasional townsman conspicuous in his topcoat, seemingly bewildered as to how he had gotten there.

Take Makinen, standing there timidly, dressed in his best, a bundle under his arm and his last pay envelope as a lumberjack still in his pocket. A photo, too, of a neighbor's daughter. He wasn't in love with the girl any more than she with him, but he had heard that in the army one looked at pictures of girls. They had been on the most casual, neighborly terms, but when he had left he had taken the photo in awkward playfulness and said:—Mind you write.

"Fair is thy death when thou fallest a hero, first in the fight for thy country." At school they had tried to sublimate the heroism that evinced itself in everlasting brawling, and guide it into nobler channels. But somehow these men failed to grasp the thought.

Such ideas were for gentlemen, and the common Finn has a low opinion of the workings of a gentleman's brain. They prefer the legends of men who leaped onto the turrets of tanks and used their rifles to knock their machine guns out of plumb. These were deeds they could appreciate, deeds in keeping with their patriotism. Indeed, in spirit they could not have been better fitted for the task for which they had been assembled.

A year had passed. Barracks now lined the clearing and the ground had been leveled and turned into a drill field where they ran, shouted, and in time were transformed into sluggishly tough veterans. Makinen was now a soldier—or was supposed to be. He was not quite what those who had molded him had had in mind, but such as he was he was ready to be flung into the maw of world history.

2.

The machine-gun company was drilling in its section of the clearing. It was a sultry afternoon and the heat, together with their recent dinner, had made the men so lethargic that drill was even slacker than usual. Even the section leaders had been NCOs such a long time that their zeal had waned, especially after they had realized that the rank of sergeant was the pinnacle of any conscript's army career. Nor could they expect even moral support from the platoon commanders idling some distance away should they attempt to extract more than a minimum effort from the men.

Orders rang out listlessly, and the manner in which the men executed their turns was even more sloppy.

Suddenly the drilling sprang to life. Voices grew sharp, movements smart; the lounging officers started toward their men. The cause of all this was a shortish officer who had come out of the headquarters barracks and was making for the company. Company Commander Kaarna was a graying Jaeger Captain in his fifties who held himself so well that he was, in spite of his small stature, a commanding figure. Always brisk in manner, he seemed now to be impelled by some special haste. He kept his gaze fixed on the company as though impatiently wishing he were there already. The result was that he tripped on a charred root and staggered, but caught himself again quickly.

Turning to look at the root, he caught his foot on another and this time only just managed to keep his balance. His pent-up energies spilled over in a soliloquy of curses.

Reaching the company he halted to draw a deep breath. Then, stressing each syllable, he shrieked in a voice that cracked ludicrously in the middle of his order.

— Mach—ine—gun—com—pa—ny — fall—in!

The men quickly faced their commander and stiffened to attention.

— At ease. . . . Platoon leaders!

The men relaxed as three officers set off briskly toward the captain who waited impatiently, his gaze flitting between the approaching men and the sky. The three officers formed before him and stood at attention. Kaarna made an effort to ignore the way Lieutenant Lammio who commanded the first platoon was standing. The self-assured arrogance of this tall thin-faced Helsinki lieutenant tried Kaarna's patience, which was never far from the breaking point. Lammio was a regular officer, spoiled for good by the Land Warfare School where he had acquired a haughty manner that made Kaarna grit his teeth. The men even hated Lammio's voice, which rose to a grating squeak as he issued commands.

The second platoon was commanded by a very young second lieutenant, a boy just graduated from a small-town school in West Finland who desperately tried to measure up to what had been expected of a second lieutenant in the Winter War by assuming an air of arrogant self-importance.

Vilho Koskela who commanded the third platoon was yet another reserve officer, the son of a small farmer in Hame, from whom he had inherited the traditional attributes of men from that part of Finland: a stocky build, blond hair, blue eyes and the habit of silence. The men had heard tales of his feats in the Winter War, but he himself never referred to them. It was known, however, that in the later phases of that war he had commanded a company while still only a sergeant. After the war he had been ordered to officers' school and had remained in the army as second lieutenant. On duty he was taciturn, a little self-conscious, but always practical, so that he managed to train his men at least as well as the others.

Captain Kaarna held Koskela in the highest esteem, and he spoke now almost as if to Koskela alone, almost ignoring the other two. Silently the company watched the protracted conversation, nurturing the hope that it meant a change from the endless drilling. At last the conference ended, Captain Kaarna set off for the headquarters barracks and the officers returned to their platoons. The company's spirits rose as the platoons marched off the drill field.

Koskela halted his platoon outside their barracks and stood as though meditating how to begin. He always had difficulty giving orders.

— Er . . . you NCOs . . . it's up to you to look after things. They're transporting the battalion by truck to new positions, so see that all extra equipment is handed in. Put a change of underwear and socks and your overcoats in your packs. And of course bring your weapons. Everything else goes to the quartermaster. Be as quick as you can.

There was something so unusual in all this that Sergeant Hietanen, the platoon sergeant, ventured a question:

— Where are we going? Way the hell out in the wilderness, I suppose?

Koskela's glance sought the horizon as he answered:

— I can't tell you. All I know is the orders. Get going now, and don't waste time.

That was all they could learn, before the lieutenant left, yet they were eager to be off. Men even asked NCO's what else they could do, a rare occurrence in any army. With Koskela gone Hietanen took over the platoon, and his booming voice rose above the din as he directed the preparations. He was a powerfully built cheerful young man who had succeeded in establishing a degree of authority in the platoon, due chiefly to his immense strength.

An eager voice spoke up:

— The boys say a messenger told them the battalion clerk said they were sending us to Joensuu as a garrison.

Hietanen knew all the false rumors to which hope gives rise:

— The battalion drivers told me it's Helsinki that we're going to garrison. We turn in all our clothes and we're all going to be issued lounging pajamas. That's what I heard, and I get to know everything.

Sergeant Lahtinen, the NCO in charge of the second machine gun was on his knees on the floor tying his pack. A big fellow from North Hame known to have Communist sympathies, he bent over his pack as he muttered:

— You'll see, boys. This means trouble. That big noise in Berlin will start it and off we'll go yapping in his footsteps.

He cast a troubled eye on the others and went on:

— Well, we'll see what it leads to. The Russians' ammunition won't run out, and there's mines on all the roads.

— I know, boys. We're going to the frontier for fortification work. The brass is afraid the Russians will drop in again if the Germans attack.

That was Hietanen's opinion, but Lahtinen frowned as he muttered:

— Why should the Russians come here? So far as I know they've never attacked any country. But there are Germans here now.

— Passing through on furlough.

— On furlough!

Lahtinen's voice rang with angry scorn. His words provoked an uproar.

— At any rate as much on furlough as the Russkies in Hanko. Or in Viipuri. Don't you start defending them.

It would have been a hopeless task. Lahtinen's "We'll see" was drowned by angry shouting, and the argument would have gone on endlessly if it had not been cut short by Hietanen's shouted "Attention!" as the captain entered.

Kaarna moved nimbly around the room inspecting the men's equipment, and talking constantly:

— Exchange any damaged equipment you have for new. If you have civilian clothes make a parcel of them and put your home address on it. The quartermaster will take care of them. Get rid of everything unnecessary.

— Not our writing pads, sir. The girls won't let us have it if we don't send 'em love letters.

Rahikainen's words gave rise to suppressed laughter, and a faint smile even flickered on Kaarna's lips as he answered:

— Listen to the Lover. Won't let us have it! Why, if a girl takes after her mother she'll never refuse, and if she takes after her father she'll ask for it. . . . Exchange those boots for a new pair, they won't stand the marching. . . . So that's what bothers him—love letters. Chasing after women with a pen . . .

He was interrupted as the NCO in charge of the Number One gun, Sergeant Lehto, suddenly asked, without even coming to attention:

— Sir, what do we have to be ready for? Will it be war?

The captain laughed.

— No, I don't think so. Wars don't break out just like that. The war's a long way off. Way down in the Balkans.

— Sir, can't it move pretty quickly these days?

Kaarna shot a glance at Rahikainen and laughed.

— If it does, we'll just have to fight.

— We'll fight all right. And if we do, we'll chase the Russkies right into Leningrad.

The captain smiled, and turned to Lehto:

— That reminds me. It looks as though you'll have to do without that coffee.

He was referring to a personal task he had entrusted to Lehto—that of moving Kaarna's family into a new flat in town. Because the captain's wife had been unable to offer him a cup of coffee during the removal, Kaarna had promised to invite him on some other occasion.

Lehto had become Captain Kaarna's favorite in unusual circumstances. It began with his overstaying his leave. From earliest childhood Lehto had fended for himself without parents or other relatives, and there seemed to be something dark and evil in him which the others sensed but could not have described. In spite of similarity in age he seemed to them to be somehow older. The hard shell under which he hid never showed the least sign of cracking, while emotion of any kind visibly irritated him. Fatherland, religion, home, family, anything at all emotional, got short shift from him.

In civilian life he had been a truck driver's helper. More about his past could not be squeezed out of him. He never tired on marches or during the most strenuous drilling, although his face grew stony with effort and his thin lips tightened.

Once, he had overstayed his leave a whole week and when asked the reason by the captain, had answered curtly:

— I didn't feel like coming back.

— Feel like it? Captain Kaarna fairly shook with rage. — Do you know the consequences?

— Yes, sir.

The captain stared out of the window for a while, drummed on the table with his fingers, and then said quietly:

— A man who takes that road should know where it leads.

For a minute or two Kaarna had put Lehto's will power to the test. Lehto's eyes stared back into his, hard and inscrutable.

— Do you know you could be risking your life? Now it's only a matter of a week or so in the guardhouse, and that's nothing. But if it came to a showdown, your desires against those of the army, with your freedom and your very life at stake, do you think you could stand your ground then?

Lehto could not see the matter in so wide a perspective, but he saw it clearly enough in concrete terms.

— I'll take my chances.

— Then you should know that all great deeds spring from such sentiments. So why waste them on petty insubordination? Bravery and self-confidence lose their value when all they result in is a negative attitude. Then they become merely ridiculous. I have no ethical right to punish you, only a right based on power. Your attitude is no more wrong than my use of power, but if you waste your talents on this kind of thing, I think it's stupid. Aim higher. The world lies open to every man. Life's a battlefield of wills and the boldest wins, but winning calls for more sense than you are showing.

After a short pause the captain became his usual brusque self again.

— All right, you can go.

No disciplinary measures were taken; instead confidential tasks were entrusted to Lehto. And one evening the captain remarked casually:

— No one's too old to learn. It's always worth while to get to know more. Start with history.

The suggestion bore no fruit, but it became known that the captain regarded Lehto highly.

Favor did not go to Lehto's head; his attitude toward the captain remained harshly noncommital, but he carried out his duties meticulously.

3.

Now at last they were moving. No one knew where, but that only made it more exciting; all the more so, in fact, because the mention of motor transport meant they would not have to endure the fatigue of a march. What could such a marvel foretell in the Finnish Army? Ride in a truck! It seemed beyond the realm of possibility.

Mattresses and blankets were borne off to the quartermaster stores, where the confusion was indescribable and the storekeeper almost frantic. Sergeant Makila was parsimonious to a degree the men would have called pathological if they had been able to make such psychological distinctions. On his immaculately ordered shelves he accumulated the best of everything, for in issuing equipment to the company he always started with the poorest materials. He spent all his time in the storeroom, endlessly checking his stocks, and was permanently at loggerheads with the company. Blustering demands for new equipment foundered before Makila's low-voiced but adamant refusal, a refusal from which he rarely retreated except at the captain's express order. Indeed, the unhappiest moments of his army life were those when he was forced to watch, flushed and angry but unable to protest, while the officers took advantage of their rank to pillage his shelves of the best they contained. After such occasions he would be heard cursing about the storeroom for hours on end, and privates would meet with a harsher reception than ever.

Unlike most quartermasters he himself wore the worst rags in his stock. And he was apt to justify his refusals to others by calling attention to his own scarecrowlike appearance.

— Who wouldn't like a new uniform? But I have to wear what's left after everything else has been snatched out of my hands.

The kind of emergency that would make Makila voluntarily surrender an article of equipment was unlikely ever to arise. As heir to a big farm in Laihia he often received parcels from home. These he would furtively carry to the storeroom to avoid having to share them with the other NCOs. Once, however, the mail arrived so late that Makila had already gone to bed, and a messenger brought a parcel addressed to him to the NCO barracks, creating a most awkward situation for Makila. He could not very well sneak the parcel away, and to keep it in the barracks meant having to share it. He temporized by muttering something about sharing it in the morning and hiding the parcel under his pillow.

In the night a faint sound of rustling paper came from Makila's bed. Instantly the light went on and Hietanen's voice boomed through the room:

— Let's go, boys! Makila's sharing his parcel.

A score of clamoring men besieged Makila's bed. Sitting up, blinking his eyes, Makila clutched the parcel, invisible under a fold of his blanket, to his bosom. Every conceivable form of pressure short of physical violence was brought to bear on him in vain. Makila stuck to his explanation:

— It's only clothes. There isn't anything to eat. It's just the underwear I wrote home for, not food.

On the other hand, Makila's virtues were duly recognized. In the machine-gun company there was none of the usual mess-hall gang's preying on the men's scanty rations, for Makila was scrupulously honest in the performance of his duties.

Now the sudden departure order put Makila in a frightful dilemma. It pained him to have to look on while the men detailed to help him made sloppy bundles of mattresses and blankets, and be unable to interfere because of his books. Even more painful was the careless way in which the men, eager to be off, dumped their equipment carelessly on the floor.

— That's Rahikainen's lot. Let's have the receipt.

Makila's face glowed scarlet.

— A hell of a state the world's in today. Throwing equipment on the floor like a dog drops dung. I won't sign for anything until I've checked it.

A man from the third platoon who had been told by the captain to get himself a new pair of boots made his request. He received a flat refusal and had to go fetch Hietanen from the middle of a game of cards to help him.

— Let's have those boots for Salonen! It's the Captain's orders.

— I've got no time for boots. What's wrong with the Captain, giving orders as though this were America where there's more than enough of everything? You're always running to the Captain for help, and he gives you whatever you're crying for.

Now Hietanen lost his temper.

— Jesus Christ, it'll always be a wonder to me, the way you hoard trash! How the hell can a man love rags and rubbish so much? Some men love pretty girls, and that I can understand— but hell, rags!

There were limits to what even Makila could stand. He stuttered in a fury until the words came:

— Take the lot! Go ahead, everybody take what they want. Bring the whole platoon and dress 'em in all the best.

— I don't want everything. All I want is a pair of boots for Salonen. There. Give him the old pair.

Salonen changed his boots and the two went off together. Hietanen was so pleased with his victory that he stopped at the doorway to shout:

— Whatever you do, don't give up! There'll always be plenty of rags and rubbish.

Makila transferred a pair of gloves to another shelf, took up a bundle of mattresses and set it down again, and groaned:

— Take what you want. What's the use of my caring?

One man pretended not to understand the real state of Makila's mind and, grabbing a blouse from the pack, began taking off the one he was wearing. Makila watched for a moment, then, his voice almost hysterical, he screamed: — Back in line!

Makila had always avoided pulling rank in any way, and usually was acutely embarrassed when he had to give an order. His action, therefore, was so unexpected that the astonished man obeyed, slinking behind the others.

At last the stores were packed and the bundles stowed on a cart. His ledgers under his arm, Makila set off after the cart to batallion headquarters.

4.

Preparations for departure were also under way in the company office. In the captain's room the bed had been stripped, and the yellowed and torn paper blinds stuffed into the stove. The orderly-room clerk and the messenger had stowed the company records in a wooden box and were now making their own packs.

Coffee was brewing on the range over a fire of waste paper. At a table against the window the captain sat looking out of the room. His sinewy hands played with a pencil, and a faint smile twisted the corner of his mouth as he glimpsed Sergeant Major Korsumaki coming slowly up the path. Korsumaki was an old Frontier Guard quartermaster who had been transferred because of his age to an infantry company. The sergeant's long trousers were stuffed into high laced shoes, leaving the red border of his thick gray woollen socks exposed. He walked slowly, looking around; then, seeing a stick of wood on the ground he bent down, picked it up and laid it beside two others in the crook of his elbow.

Soon his footsteps sounded from the porch, and carrying his three sticks he entered and made straight for the stove. As he stoked the fire with them, he remarked petulantly:

— Strewing wood all over the place. No better than children. I'll bet they wouldn't do that at home, but here they carry on as though nothing had any value.

He raised the lid of the coffee pot, saw that the coffee wasn't ready yet and seated himself at the captain's table. Removing his cap, he ran his fingers through his hair and with a glance at the telephone asked:

— Any news of the convoy?

Roused from his silence, the captain immediately rattled away in his usual voluble fashion:

— Nothing. Not a word. Nobody seems to know anything. I call it a hell of a way to run an army. They hint about special top-level orders. I guess it means men are being called up. The rumor about mobilization's probably true. They'll be creating new divisions, and if that's so, we'll be the cadre for one of them and the other two regiments will be all reservist. . . . Orderly, the coffee pot. . . .

Nothing more was said until the orderly had poured the coffee and returned to the porch where the clerk was helping him to make up his pack. Then in a mournful voice the quartermaster concluded:

— It means war.

— I don't know. They say it depends on Germany. But I'd say it depends on three things: Germany, Russia and ourselves. If the Germans attack Russia, which I don't for a moment doubt, they may demand our help. I'd say the importance of the Murmansk railway makes that likely. Then, the Russians may try to simplify the situation by attacking us first and carrying the war into our territory. They can't really believe we'd let the opportunity go by to take a crack at them. And finally, I don't believe we will throw away that opportunity.

— Of course not. But what will the outcome of it be?

— Are you afraid we'll be beaten?

The captain laughed shortly.

— We'll never have the same opportunity again. Me, I'm all for our attacking. In this world justice always follows the victor's sword. It'll be that way this time too. The defeated are always in the wrong. But no matter what we may think, one thing is certain. Finland's fate is tied to Germany's, so we must do our utmost to see that she wins. German pressure is directed outward, and when that pressure is strong, the East falls back before it and we breathe freely. When it slackens, the periphery begins to close in and our breathing space shrinks. So although we consider Britain and France to be our friends, actually they're our worst enemies. Their defeat is Germany's victory, and Germany's victory is ours. If we lose, that's the end of everything, but at the moment we have to put every ounce of energy into destroying Russia—forever.

The sergeant stared at the floor.

— I suppose I'd better let my family stay where they are.

The captain realized that Korsumaki was not following his argument at all but had been thinking his own thoughts. Old age and the Winter War had finished off any idealism Korsumaki might have harbored, and now he sighed to think of the new hardships and suffering awaiting him. Kaarna understood Korsumaki's mood, alien though it was to him. He himself hoped war would come. And a bitter war at that. His career demanded it. He had had to leave the army after the Olonets expedition as a lieutenant. The reason was readily apparent from his still hostile attitude toward his superiors. He never had a bad word for his men, but to the battalion commander he was a terror. Certainly he was a difficult subordinate, though shrewd and richly endowed by nature. Nor did he hide his light under a bushel. In spite of his superior rank the major found it difficult to assert himself against this man, who on top of everything else had a two-pound paper bag full of decorations. In the Winter War Kaarna had been promoted to captain and given a battalion. Afterwards he stayed on in the army but had to content himself with a company, demobilization having left more than enough majors and lieutenant colonels. Nor would he be given a battalion now, either. But why chouldn't he have got an infantry company? What good are machine guns in an offensive war? Well, casualties and mobilization would create openings.

The quartermaster called to the orderly for more coffee, and the captain took up the thread of the conversation where it had been dropped.

—Let your family stay where they are. We won't be falling back; this isn't the same as last time. Incidentally, the baggage trains won't join the companies until the journey's end. They're being replenished.

The companies had no transport of their own; all that had been left to the battalion.

—That's one relief, anyhow. We don't have to worry, remarked the sergeant. —But there's the smell of war in all this. First this damn haste, just to make sure there'll be plenty of time to wait later on.

5.

The local Lotta Svard, the women's auxiliary, ran a canteen evenings in one of the barracks, and when the captain's messenger arrived the place was chock-full. The standard offerings included coffee mixed with a substitute, thick crackers hard as rock, tobacco, razor blades, envelopes and writing pads. The pads bore on their cover a stylized drawing of a soldier. There he stood, steel-helmeted, his trousers creased down the middle, while behind him a Finnish flag fluttered. A wishful dream perhaps. Certainly very unlike the real thing now milling at the counter so boisterously.

— Sneak in, would you? Go on back to the tail end!

No pressed trousers here. Legs were encased, some in brown British gaiters, some in civilian trousers, others in gray army issue. The only articles all wore in common were a cap, a summer blouse and a belt.

Serving at the counter was a single Lotta. The men in the line vied with one another to attract the girl's notice, though they knew they had nothing to hope for with Lammio sitting there at one end of the long table. Rahikainen, however, would never admit that he stood no chance. Leaning over the counter with all the bravado he could muster, he began jovially:

— Now then, let's see what this girl's going to sell Rahikainen before we sorrowfully part forever. A cup of coffee, of course, and a cracker.

— You can buy all the crackers you want this time. We're selling out everything.

— There, now isn't that just what I said? It's war. You can smell it in the air. It used to be no more than one cracker to a cup. So much the worse for us. Who knows whether we'll ever again be able to look into your beautiful eyes.

Lammio listened to Rahikainen's gallantries with mounting annoyance. He could never brook rivalry under any circumstances, and he had marked the girl for himself. Who knew how long it would be before he next saw a woman? And there wasn't time for a trip to town. But if the convoy did not show up soon, he would see the girl home and try his luck.

There was, of course, all the difference in the world between a Karelian private and a Helsinki lieutenant; Lammio had no fears on that score, although he knew of Rahikainen's successes with women. His curly hair, a fine singing voice, and a tongue that could go on manufacturing gallantries forever—these accounted for Rahikainen's reputation, but they wouldn't get him anywhere this time.

— Come on, give somebody else a chance.

Lammio was suddenly full of indignation, though he himself had been holding up business for the past twenty minutes. Rahikainen, however, was unperturbed. He was not easily abashed, and for that matter it was none of Lammio's business what the men bought at the canteen.

— All in good time, sir. The farther we're going, the more provisions we need. How much of that tobacco can I have?

— As much as you want.

— Make it a whole package. And a dozen of those crackers.

Rahikainen counted out his money slowly and would have begun a new conversation if he hadn't been thrust out of the way by the next customer. He collected his purchases and withdrew to a table beside the door where the men of his platoon were gathered. Since all eyes were on the girl, his enterprise had been observed.

— She's not going to be the mother of your children, Hietanen commented. — You'd have to have stars on your collar for that.

— I'm not looking for that.

— That's a lie. Why, if we come out of this alive, I'm going to take you home to use as a breeding bull.

They were interrupted as a messenger brought the news that the trucks would arrive at 2200 hours. For Lammio this meant a chance to realize his hopes, for the others more waiting. So when the canteen closed, Lammio set off with the Lotta, wheeling her bicycle while the men drifted back to the barracks, their initial eagerness fast turning to irritation.

— Christ, I wish the brass would make up their minds. What goddamn fatheads we must have on top. Who wants to hang around empty barracks?

The wooden bunks were bare. The men had begun to look on their barracks as a home, but now with the discolored boards showing, the beds had an alien, coldly forbidding look.

They were, as a matter of routine, given a benediction before they left. And since there was plenty of time, the chaplain made a tour of the companies and held an evening service in each of them separately, a service which this time the officers and even the orderlies attended.

6.

By midnight the men were shivering with the cold, and bitter grumbling could be heard on all sides. Finally, at 0100 hours the NCO on duty gave the order to fall in. Noisy and wide awake, the men took their places with the enthusiasm and excitement an army on its way to war always generates. Of course they were not sure they were going to war, but the rumor had taken root during the night. Now when Lammio gave the order for attention, heels clicked far more sharply than usual.

They marched across the clearing to a road which led to a highway which led almost anywhere. To Lake Onega and the Svir and perhaps beyond them if it was in the men to go.

Transport arrangements had been entrusted to Captain Helminen, the commander of the First Company, who was everywhere. He moved around giving the officers their instructions until Kaarna, arriving in the rear of his company, began complaining to Helminen accusingly:

— The convoy should be here. This is the third time they've set and I'll bet it will be as much of a false alarm as the others.

Helminen tried to defend himself:

— I don't know. The C.O. told me that the second battalion was being transported to the frontier during the night. Maybe they're still on that job. By the way, some artillery passed the station. They weren't Regulars, and that surely means that we're mobilizing.

— Yes, it certainly looks like it. Well, we've been waiting here since yesterday, so maybe tomorrow will see us finally on our way.

Kaarna strode back to his company and addressed the men:

— Don't be impatient, boys. You have to learn to wait and to rest. Put on your overcoats and use your packs for pillows. Get some sleep.

— We've learned already. We've been waiting almost eighteen months to get back into civvies.

Rahikainen had not intended that the captain should hear. Kaarna did, however, though the only sign he gave was a sidelong glance at Rahikainen. Shivering men wrapped themselves in their overcoats and tried to sleep, but the cold kept them awake and, their teeth chattering, they cursed the mix-up. They were hungry, too, though that was not unusual. They had been hungry since the day they entered the army, and some of them even before that, for there are still localities in Finland where hunger often becomes epidemic.

Time passed. The night sky began to pale, and in the east the red rim of dawn glowed. Finally at 0400 hours the companies fell in once more and began the dejected march back to the clearing. This time even the officers did nothing to stem the murmuring in the ranks. But just before the company reached the barracks, it was overtaken by a messenger on a bicycle.

— Turn back, turn back, the convoy's coming.

Quickly the command was given and the company reversed itself. The murmurs ceased. The men were now convinced that they were really going somewhere, for this was the way things happened in the army. They knew, too, that from now on everything would be done with desperate haste; that also was the way it always happened.

They reached the road just as the first dusty trucks lumbered into view. The convoy leader, a sergeant major on a motorcycle gray with dust, turned in a semicircle, and the trucks swung around and halted in a line. The weary drivers took no notice whatever of the actual loading; closing their red-rimmed eyes they dozed over their steering wheels.

Gradually each of the men made himself as comfortable as possible. Koskela climbed in beside the driver, and the platoon waited for the last few minutes to pass.

— We're stuck here now. Let's take advantage of it while we have the chance. It isn't often the Finnish Army loans us a truck. The brass is all fouled up again.

The convoy leader rode along the line, feet dragging in the dust. From each truck the word came Ready! And each time he replied:

—Keep a hundred yards apart. Give the dust time to settle.

—Finally, the first truck moved off, its gears clashing and its motor complaining. Then the Third Platoon's truck lurched forward in its turn, the men swaying as the holes in the uneven road set the truck rocking. But their spirits rose as though shaken loose by the swaying. Random cheers could be heard and from one truck came an attempt at a song.

Hietanen was almost drunk with the joy of departure. Rising to his feet and clinging to Lehto's shoulder with one hand he declaimed:

— Farewell! Farewell, you asshole of the world! Goodbye forever, you old sweat-sucker. I only hope you're as tough on the next recruits as you were on us.

Cheers from the other trucks and from his own provided a fitting background. Only Rahikainen was disgruntled.

— Sending us off at this hour. There's not even one girl at the roadside to wave to us.

The truck turned onto the main road, already choked by the dust of the preceding trucks. The early morning sun flashed in the roadside trees and gilded the cloud of dust through which sped truckload after truckload of eager youths.

Chapter II

1.

A little-used wagon track, hardly more than a couple of ruts, wound through the spruce forests. Beside it a number of tents were pitched and around these the soldiers moved. In front of each tent a campfire burned in a pit, over which kettles hung suspended from poles.

Here they had set up camp the evening before, and for a while a strange solemness had possessed them after the NCO on duty made his rounds, pausing to whisper at each tent:

— No noise now. The frontier's only a mile or so away.

They were soon used to the idea; but still a note of uneasiness was apparent. To be sure, they played cards all day, having nothing better to do, but many were also to be seen staring, lost in thought, into their campfire. The conversation, such as it was, was carried on in low voices, a precaution not without a touch of the comic, for the woods echoed for miles around with the clash of axes cutting wood for the fires.

More than two weeks had passed since the battalion had left the burned clearing. They had been set down, stiff and dusty, beside the highway, and there they had camped. There, too, the suspicion that this was the real thing gradually was confirmed. Cartridge boxes were filled, each unit was brought to battle strength, and every measure taken obviously had but one aim: to put them in readiness for battle. Then came the news that the Germans were "preventing a Russian attack" by themselves attacking. "The barking dog in Berlin" had taken the initiative, and now the men waited to see when "we little puppies would go yapping off after him," as Lahtinen had put it. They did not share Lahtinen's view of the consequences. On the contrary, they were convinced that the Germans would tie down such large Russian forces that the Finns would themselves easily bring the Soviets crashing to their knees.

The evening before they had marched almost to the frontier, turned off onto a forest road and there camped. The machine-gun company's command post was nestled beside the road. Now, Sergeant Mielonen, the captain's battle runner, crawled out from under the tent flap.

— All of you who want to hear the news broadcast can come inside to listen. Afterwards, one of the big Government wheels is going to speak.

The Third Platoon's tents were pitched next to the captain's, and he derived much amusement from the conversations he could not help overhearing. Today he felt especially drawn to Hietanen, whom his admiration of everything strong and uncomplicated had always made him like. Hietanen's breezy chatter created a cheerful atmosphere that prevented the men's spirits from sinking. It was for this reason that Hietanen, and not Lehto, would take over from him if it became necessary. Lehto was certainly a capable NCO, but he lacked the qualities that make a man a good leader. He lived in a vacuum, and his harsh and surly attitude had created a barrier between him and the men. Hietanen, however, was a true comrade to them and they would follow him anywhere. And the captain also knew somehow that Hietanen would give a good account of himself in combat.

— I'd like to hear the news, but I don't give a damn what those cabinet ministers have to say. They're no help against these damned mosquitoes.

The captain laughed to himself.

— That's the kind of thing the men need. Now if only things don't go wrong the first time they're under fire! The first time has got to give them a taste of success.

Time and again that day Kaarna had studied the leaf of the map uppermost in his map case.

— There. That's where the Third Platoon will get its baptism.

The Russians' first line of defense was known to be some distance behind the frontier, screened by a protective line of outposts. After these had been dislodged, the second battalion would launch a frontal attack while their battalion undertook a flanking move on the Russian communications. That open swamp across which the Third Company must advance was, however, a weak spot. The captain had decided to put Koskela's platoon in support there and set up his own command post in its rear. God, how he hated his job! A machine-gun company commander. Furnishing support for others. Hell and the Devil. But it would not be for long. He smelled a battalion in the offing. Come to think of it, who could prevent him from setting up his command post ahead of the men . . . ?

Gradually men drifted to the command post. The faint sound of music within suddenly swelled as someone turned the radio up. Then it stopped and the news began:

— The Soviet air force has continued its activities over Finnish territory and dropped bombs on many localities. Only slight damage was done. At several points on the frontier, enemy guns continued to shell Finnish territory and in a few sectors our troops repulsed attacks by small patrols.

The news was followed by a bulletin from "the Headquarters of the German High Command:

—On the Eastern Front our advance continues. Powerful armored spearheads have penetrated . . .

A crackling voice reeled off names of cities the men had never heard of. At the end came the announcement that a member of the Finnish cabinet would speak.

— Who is he? a man asked Mielonen in a whisper.

— I don't remember his name. You'll hear it soon enough.

Mielonen was a man with a very high opinion of himself but he was otherwise level-headed. When the captain picked his headquarters squad he had put Mielonen in charge and by doing so increased his already strong sense of importance. Usually he answered the men's inquiries in an almost omniscient tone. Either "The captain and I decided" or "Why bother the captain, just do as I say." But even he knew nothing about the government.

A soft rustle of paper, a guarded whisper, a low cough, and the speech began:

— Citizens. Without an official declaration of war, Soviet forces have violated Finland's frontier. Our defense forces, while everywhere repulsing the attackers, have not violated Soviet territory. Because of these continuous breaches of neutrality, the Government now regards a state of war as existing between Finland and the Soviet Union . . .

The minister went on to describe in detail the boarder incidents and the government's countermeasures. Then he began to appeal directly to the patriotism of the Finnish people:

— The flood tide of world events has again laid heavy burdens on us. For the second time in a few short years the men of Finland are called on to defend their homes and their country. All we want is to be allowed to build our country in peace, to lift it to even higher levels of prosperity, but this our enemy's greed for power would not permit. It is not in us to want war, but neither can we surrender our freedom and independence. As unanimously as in the dark days of the Winter War, the Finnish people go forth to battle in the cause of liberty. Under the leadership of our beloved Marshal, our brave and tested army stands on our frontier, ready to repel every attack. And this time we are not alone. The mighty army of Germany has already dealt our common enemy staggering blows. Our faith in victory is unwavering, and trusting in the righteousness of our cause we go forth to battle for everything we hold sacred and dear . . .

—Hey . . . the guns are coming . . .

From the bend in the road came the snorting of horses and the shouts of drivers. Then the lead gun, a three-inch cannon drawn by a foam-flecked team, came into sight. The gunners were mostly reservists, many of them middle-aged. They tried to help the horses by pushing from behind, but at the speed the gun was traveling they were themselves being hauled along. In the rear trotted a little old reservist. Rivulets of sweat streaked his grimy face, the peak of his cap was awry and his belt sagged under the weight of his cartridge pouches. His breeches were much too long for him, and his boots were of the ordinary laced kind. He had stuffed the ends into his stockings, making them full to bursting point. When the team put on speed in order to get a start for a hill he broke into a run and chased after it, looking neither right nor left, blind to everything except his own despairing effort.

Here and there the late afternoon sun filtered through the spruce onto the road, where the dancing clouds of insects scattered as the guns drove through them.

The guns rumbled, horses snorted, drivers shouted, and the member of the Government spoke on:

— . . . brave men of Finland. Free we were born, free we have lived, and now with heads erect we go to meet those who would wrest from us our freedom. Our path lies clear before us. Our forefathers blazed it for us by their great deeds, the noble heritage they left us.

The machine gunners standing at the roadside no longer listened but gazed admiringly at the guns. They were an inspiring sight, even though the desperate struggle of the old reservist to catch up with his comrades moved many of the men to a rough pity.

— It isn't right to send men like that out here, someone muttered.

Private Salo, however, had fallen wholly under the spell of the guns. Standing with a cigarette dangling from his lips, his hands thrust deep into his pockets, he burst out:

—My God what guns! When they begin to have their say, Ivan'll run for his life.

Lahtinen's self-assurance had been shaken a little by recent events on the Eastern Front, and any reference to the subject seemed to pain him. He still, however, tried to curb all too extravagant enthusiasm.

— It takes more than one battery to support an army, and they've got some of those on the other side, too. If the Russkies do run, all the better. But I'm afraid we'll meet with all the guns we can stomach.

— I don't know anything about the weapons they've got, but it doesn't look like it at Bialystok. They can't seem to hold their ground.

— It's easy to advance when the other fellow's completely unprepared. . . . All I meant was don't be too cocksure. . . . Things aren't always going as they're said to be. . . .

— Oh, I don't know. They say up north our boys have had to be practically tied to trees to keep 'em from setting off too early. . . . We'll show them what they get for picking on those smaller than themselves the way they did in the Winter War.

The dispute was cut short by the crash of falling trees as the gunners began taking up positions.

The men looked at each other, and their mood was hushed as they returned to the campfires.

All seemed in order; nevertheless, everywhere men could be seen fiddling with their equipment. They stayed up late that night, and news kept trickling in which increased their preoccupation. Reserve regiments had camped along the main road. Someone reported big concentrations of artillery in newly prepared positions. A patrol was said to have come back two men missing.

2.

— Wake up, boy! It's started!

The tent sprang to life. Hands snatched up caps and belts, and everybody tried to get out at once, some with their packs already on their backs.

Off to the right guns were firing singly, each report followed a little later by the crash of a shell exploding across the frontier. As they mustered, the men listened in silence. In the forest about them all was still except for the occasional twitter of an early bird in a treetop. In the wan light of the summer night faces took on a ghostly tinge. At last the silence was broken by a whisper:

— It's artillery.

— Shelling the main road.

— Aim's way off. Can't even hear the shell.

— It doesn't need to shift much to fall here.

It was an incautious remark. Some of the men stirred restively, a few felt for their trench-digging tools as Koskela emerged from the CP. Private Riitaoja, darting fearful glances around him, went up to him and in a low voice asked:

— Sir, if they shift their range, will it land here?

Koskela paused:

— Shift what?

— The artillery. They're firing at the road now. But if they shift their range a bit, won't it hit us?

— I don't think so. They're keeping the road under interceptive fire. They won't fire into the forest blindly.

Riitaoja relaxed, his relief so great that his eyes were laughing as he said jovially:

— That's what I thought, sir. Let them shell the forest! They don't know we're here.

Koskela's arrival made the others easier in their minds.

— The guns are singing already over there, Hietanen said to Koskela, causing Vanhala who was the platoon humorist to laugh.

— Singing! Ha! The guns sing and the bullets play a tune. Ha, ha!

—They've been making too much noise, said Koskela. —Driving cars up too damn close. Asking for bloody noses when they've no reason to do so. All right. We leave in half an hour's time with the third company. And remember, if you tie two ammunition boxes together with a belt, you'll be able to carry them round your neck. It'll keep your hands from cramping, too.

Koskela lapsed into silence, but the men guessed rightly that he hadn't finished.

— Maybe I'd better explain a thing or two, since I've been through it before. There's really nothing much to it, but you've got to keep cool. Hurry when you have to, but too much haste causes trouble. Being afraid won't help any, but that doesn't mean keeping all you've got on sale all the time. Ivan'd be only too pleased to buy. Aim at the belt buckle. A bullet in the belly will stop them every time—they're just as human as you.

Private Sihvonen, who hailed from the same parish as Rahikainen but unlike him was a fighter, said:

— Cool, that's the word. Above all, keep cool.

— All right. Let's get those tents on the carts.

In a remarkably short time all was in readiness. The machine gunners were continually hefting their guns and tripods on their shoulders as though to accustom themselves to the burden, while the spotters and ammunition carriers tied ammunition boxes together as Koskela had advised. The squad leaders carried the reserve barrel, a water can and one ammunition box. Thus equipped these human mule teams were ready foı a journey which might run to hundreds of miles. Many, of course, would not get that far, but no one wasted a moment's thought on that.

The rifle companies moved off, each followed by one platoon of the machine-gun company. Slowly the First and Second Companies vanished into the forest amid the clink of equipment and an undertone of muted orders.

As the Third Company marched past, Koskela called softly:

— Double file. Let's go!

They passed a battery that had taken up positions the evening before and noted that the guns were fully manned, the gunners conversing in low voices, shielding their cigarettes with their hands. A little farther on they left the path and plunged into the forest. The rumble of gunfire in the south had ceased now, but the silence was even more ominous.

They advanced slowly. Stops were frequent, and the men, breathing heavily, listened intently to the stillness and the thudding of their own hearts.

— Halt.

The rifle company ahead spread out in extended order, and men armed with tommy guns raced forward a score of paces to form an advance guard while the machine guns, divided into half-platoons, stayed an equal distance behind the firing line. Soon the company commander's messenger brought the message:

— The frontier's just ahead. Keep your mouths closed now. A patrol from the First Platoon's on the border, so don't fire without asking for the password.

The talking stopped. The men began to smoke—at least, those who had tobacco did. Most of them had run out days ago, for no tobacco rations had been issued yet and there was nowhere it could be bought.

Rahikainen, however, had plenty, thanks to his lavish purchases at the canteen. He had already sold his crackers for a good price and was now asking fantastic prices for a single cigarette. But since most of the men had no other resources than their small pay, customers were confined to those with means of their own. When one of these fortunate beings threw a butt away, it was immediately pounced on and, at the risk of scorched lips, thrust into the finder's mouth. One man begged for credit until next pay day, only to be scornfully refused.

— Who knows who'll be signing up for the next pay? Who'll guarantee that I get my money?

Koskela coughed and broke in:

— I haven't any money either, but if anything happens you can have my field glasses. They're my own, and you can easily get money for them. There's plenty of buyers.

— I trust you . . . I trust you. . . . It's not so much that I . . . with money, you never know . . .

Shame and a sense of injury were in Rahikainen's voice, but he parceled out his cigarettes. The men noted that Koskela spoke to Rahikainen as an equal; henceforth he would speak to all of them the same way. It seemed strange at first to be on such terms with an officer, and many found it difficult to answer in the same tone; to a few it never came naturally. It was indeed rare in a regular regiment such as theirs, where officers tended to keep their distance as a means of retaining their authority. Some of them succeeded in maintaining it right to the end, but in these cases the tone of voice they employed had nothing to do with it. Koskela's gesture, however, was not without its effect. Feeling closer to the man on whom they depended for the answers to all the problems ahead, the men lost some of their anxiety.

From the rear came a dry cough and the sound of low voices, and then Kaarna appeared with Mielonen a shadow at his heels.

— All right, boys, let's keep it quiet. Where's Autio?

— Over there with the Second Platoon.

— Good. Hietanen, what men are these?

— Men of the best damn machine-gun company in the army, sir.

— That's the spirit.

The question was an old one which always had to be answered in just those words for to Kaarna his own company was a cut above any other. And it would not have mattered even if it had not been true, for he knew the value of self-confidence. He was perfectly aware that machine guns were declining in importance, especially in offensive operations, but he continued to hammer pride in their weapon into the men's heads. And always he stuck up for his own men. Officers from other companies had better not come complaining to him about them. An officer candidate had once tried it after a private had neglected to salute him. Kaarna had told him coldly that his men never failed to salute, so there must be some mistake.

— And what's more, you're not standing properly at attention. Let's see you stand correctly for an hour.

The private was duly punished, but the talebearer took care never to come face to face with Kaarna again.

The men knew all this, so Kaarna's words brought a smile to faces which had been far too grave. It is often said of an officer that he has "the unbounded admiration of his men," but actually it is never really true. The officer whom a Finnish soldier would boundlessly admire has yet to be born. Nevertheless, the men's attitude toward Kaarna was exceptionally admiring. Yet even so there was nothing comradely in their relations with him. They had no doubt whatever that he would be down on them if they did not do as he ordered. What they respected was Kaarna's complete fairness toward them.

Now, too, they smiled as they watched him go off in search of Lieutenant Autio, who commanded the Third Company.

— You'll see, boys. His command post won't be far behind the firing line, said one of the men, and the others nodded their assent.

After the subdued voices of the captain and Mielonen had died away, silence reigned until it was suddenly shattered.

— God damn . . .

— Down!

There was a loud rustling of grass and a clatter of equipment as they flung themselves down in a panic. Close behind them, a series of sharp explosions rent the air. Baroom. Boom. Boom.

A piercing shriek swept over the treetops, and the men, their eyes bulging, hugged the ground. More crashes followed, not quite so evenly spaced, and more whistling shrieks. From the other side of the frontier came distant dull thuds.

Koskela, sitting on a hummock, laughed.

— Get up, boys. It's our own guns. And don't shake those boxes so much.

Slowly the men rose to their feet, glad that they all shared in the shame. Lehto alone had not budged. He sat where he had been all along, a contemptuous smile on his face. Hietanen was one of the first to recover, along with the gunner of the Number Two machine gun, a short fellow from the northeast called Maatta.

Vanhala had flopped down hastily only after seeing the others take cover. He was the last to get up, a smile twinkling in his eyes.

— That's the way to obey an order, he chuckled to his neighbor.

The battery fell silent, but the uneasiness they felt subsided very slowly. The second lieutenant commanding the platoon in front of them was also nervous, for they could see him pacing behind his line. His tone, when he spoke to his men, was casual, but his irregular breathing betrayed the fear in his heart. Finally he walked over to Koskela:

— I hope we'll hear from you when the time comes. Autio promised me one of your machine guns.

— We'll see, Koskela said quietly, sending the second lieutenant angrily back to his men. The machine gunners knew this blond, new young lieutenant. Kariluoto, his name was said to be. In camp he had been too comradely with his men, with the inevitable result that they did not take him seriously. He made a practice of telling off-color stories, but it was easy to see that this sprang from a false conception of manliness for they didn't seem natural coming from him.

— He talks about what a girl's got as though he'd once had a feel, the men would say scathingly.

They waited in silence half an hour before orders came. Then, from the right, the word passed down the line: — Forward.

Through the dim spruce woods gray shadows moved noiselessly toward the frontier. Men with tommy guns crept first, sharp eyes probing the forest, hands gripping weapons so tightly that the knuckles stood out white. They reached the boundary, an open corridor cut through the forest and doubly fenced with barbed wire, which made a grating sound as it was kicked down.

The cautious advance continued. Every tree and bush presented the threat of Russian guns. None, however, opened fire. Not even from the far side of the meadow they crossed, fully expecting the enemy to be entrenched there. On their left the tiny meadow broadened into a ploughed field with a gray house on one side. They knew from their briefing that the frontier skirted the house, leaving it on the Finnish side, and as they watched they saw a few men moving there and recognized them as men of the Second Battalion advancing toward the road.

As they watched, a frightened horse plunged and reared, and they saw men run to stop it. One of the Second Battalion's companies had been unable to wait for their food before setting out. Finding them gone, the driver of the field kitchen had driven up to the frontier after them. He caught the advancing company just as the battalion commander, troubled at the slowness of their deployment, arrived on the scene.

—God damn it, man! bawled the commander. —Take that thing to hell out of here! Of all the damned fools.

Instantly the startled driver lost his head, jerked at the reins and the horse bolted so that it took several men to get him under control and turned back. The men of the First Battalion who witnessed the incident from a distance never thought of connecting what they had seen with the subsequent legend that out of sheer bravado the Second Battalion had sent a field kitchen to head the advance across the frontier. This story circulated widely, gathering new details as it spread. The battalion commander was nicknamed "Wild Kalle," and the legend attached itself to him. Young officers who had never set eyes on Kalle spoke of him as though they knew him intimately, and before long the mother of one of these officers was informing her friends that her son and a certain "Wild Kalle" had been the first to cross the frontier, riding on a field kitchen. The Russians had mistaken it for a tank and fled without firing a shot.

The truth was that the battalion commander had raged like a bear with a bullet in its backside while the kitchen was being sent back to the rear. The advance was not progressing according to plan, the companies were making mistakes, and the confusion grew as Kalle, beside himself with rage, started issuing orders to platoons, thus going over the heads of the company commanders.

With pounding pulses, the First Battalion waited. The sun had risen and the men sought to warm themselves in its rays, lying in the dewy grass. Mosquitoes whined, an airplane droned somewhere, but aside from that all was still. At last they saw the men who had been moving around the house disappear from sight, but still no order came. Then they froze into immobility and listened as off to their left a tommy gun rattled. At once a crackle of other arms broke out. An automatic rifle set the forest echoing and then a machine gun hammered out a long burst. They listened in silence until a man said:

— A whole belt in one burst.

— Must be something happening over there.

For the first time in their lives they heard a bullet ricochet. Vow-eeeee . . .

— What are we standing ground here for? Sihvonen asked anxiously. —They'll encircle us.

— Shut up, Koskela said calmly, brushing mosquitoes from his face with a leafy branch. — At the most that was only an outpost. Pretty soon you'll hear what gunfire really sounds like.

The firing died down, and again they waited. Later they resumed their advance only to be halted again when firing once more broke out on the left.

—We're not getting anywhere, a man said. —Something's gone wrong.

— No, it hasn't. This is war. A couple more days and you'll understand it.

By five in the afternoon they had advanced about a mile. On their left the firing was now continuous. They realized that the Second Battalion had come up against the main Russian positions.

3.

Before them lay a swamp behind which rose a wooded ridge. The swamp was dotted with stunted pines and the men tried to peer between these to the forest on its far side. Nothing remarkable could be seen, yet they knew that their enemy lay there.

Lieutenant Autio of the Third Company came from the rear to speak to Kariluoto. Autio was a young regular officer who was reputed to be a good commander, but Kariluoto could not make sense of what Autio was saying.

— The guns will lay a barrage in front of the Second, along with the trench mortars. When the shelling stops, advance without waiting for further orders. Don't let the advance bog down; your impetus must carry you forward. Above all don't let the men take cover under fire. You, Koskela, support him with both your machine guns if the attack slows down, but not before. And all of you be sure to set off as quietly as possible. They know we're here, of course, but let's still try for a surprise. I'll be right behind the Second Platoon. Is everything clear?

— Yes . . . it's all clear. Wish us luck.

As Autio left, Kariluoto confusedly repeated to himself scraps of his instructions. No taking cover under fire . . . try for a surprise.

Behind him, Koskela gave his men his own instructions:

— We'll follow right behind the line and if it's pinned down we'll take up positions at once. Remember, Finnish lives depend on how quickly you open fire. Don't all get bunched up behind the machine guns. Two men only, the gunner and his mate.

They all nodded, though hardly one of them had any idea of all that had to be done in combat. They all knew how to shoot, but not one knew whether he could stand up under enemy fire. It was easy to insert a belt and to press the trigger, but not so easy to conquer the fear of death which gnawed at their hearts.

They heard guns speak from beyond the frontier; it was the battery that had given them their first shock in the night. But from still farther back came a deep-toned rumble, followed by evil shrieks and violent explosions which set the earth quaking. Between crashes they could hear the weaker cough of trench mortars.

When the explosions stopped, a furious rattle of small-arms fire began, and above it they could hear confused shouting.

— That's the Second Battalion attacking, a man whispered.

The platoon next to them was already advancing when Kariluoto rose from behind his hummock and in a choking voice shouted:

— All right, here we go!

He forced himself forward, and the men followed. But they had not gone far before a fierce crackling and whistling began in the stunted pines.

Pee-uh-pee-uh . . . pee-uh.

Frightened, the men looked about, then threw themselves down. Kariluoto ran on alone for a few paces, then he too took cover behind a tussock. Breathlessly he shouted:

— Forward! Get up . . . Don't lie down under fire. . . .

Not a man rose, and Kariluoto lay where he was, completely paralyzed. Dimly he realized that the firing had spread all along the company's front, and that his entire platoon had taken cover in the grass. One searing thought passed through his mind, increasing his helplessness: I'm no good . . . the men won't follow me . . . I've done just what Autio told me not to. . . .

— Machine guns—take up positions!

Koskela knelt behind a pine, pistol in hand. His men too were lying down farther back, and only Koskela's voice could have induced them now to rise to set up the machine guns. Lehto, seeing Koskela kneeling, rose to his knees and in a strangled voice shouted:

— Get moving, get moving! Get the guns set up. Quickly.

Koskela watched as the machine guns were set up, then gave the order: —Fire!

— Fire! echoed Hietanen, and Lehto and Lahtinen repeated the cry.

Private Kaukonen, Lehto's gunner, yelled "Fire!" and pressed the trigger. Lahtinen's gun had already gone into action with Maatta, his face devoid of all expression, at the trigger.

Kaukonen felt his weapon vibrating under his hands, his stinging eyes saw the belt move jerkily through the breech and his sights hop against the rim of forest. The smell of burning powder and the sickening stench of sizzling grease filled his nostrils.

Their own fire kept them from hearing the rattle in the pines. Then suddenly a shell exploded against a tree trunk, followed by another which ploughed into the forest ahead of them.

Crouching down, Koskela thought for a moment of taking command of the platoon, but he could not quite bring himself to do so. He could imagine the young lieutenant's agony, but he knew that Kariluoto had to win his own victory over himself.

The belt ran out of one of the machine guns, and Vanhala, who had been feeding it, turned and shouted:

— Ammunition! Quick!

Riitaoja, lying behind a hummock with the ammunition boxes beside him, did not stir. His eyes were dilated with terror and he answered Vanhala's shout with a hideously distorted smile.

— Bring a belt! screamed Lehto, and when Riitaoja still did not move, reached him in a couple of strides. Quickly he threw Vanhala an ammunition box and then, seething with rage, bent over the prostrate Riitaoja.

— You damned fool! I ought to throw you into the swamp.

Riitaoja blinked in terror and made no answer. Instead he shrank deeper behind his cover, leaving Lehto to crawl back to the machine gun.

— Leave him alone, said Koskela who had observed Riitaoja's terror.

— We're all scared, but that shouldn't keep a man from even moving a hand.

Then, as if to point the contrast, Lehto rose to his knees and emptied his rifle at the forest opposite.

As he did so, two men came walking toward the swamp. It was Mielonen. Mielonen, a few paces in the rear, was saying:

— They're using an anti-tank gun, captain.

— No, they're not. It's a tank. You can tell from the muzzle report.

They reached the swamp, and Kaarna at once burst out:

— What's this? Come on, boys, that isn't the way to fight. . . . Let's cross this little swamp now. The others are almost through to the Russians.

The men raised their heads, except for Kariluoto who let his sink deeper. A bitter sense of shame held him paralyzed. But now Kaarna was beside him saying quietly:

— Let's try again. We can do it.

The captain walked on straight as a ramrod. Then he turned to look at them over his shoulder as he roared:

— Let's go, men of the North!

Something exploded, and the men sensed rather than saw the captain and Mielonen collapse. Mielonen, however, rose instantly and sprang to where the captain was lying motionless, his body strangely twisted. He knelt beside him, deathly pale, calling in a shaky voice:

— First aid, first aid . . . quickly, quickly. . . . He's bleeding . . . quickly!

Carefully he turned the captain over on to his back, and the men saw that one leg was bent unnaturally to the side. Kaarna had taken direct hit in the hip, and only the tattered cloth of his breeches kept the leg from falling off altogether. Dully Mielonen mumbled as if to himself:

— Got me in the arm, too . . . got me, too . . . stretcher bearers . . . where the hell are they . . . stretcher bearers!

A pair of stretcher bearers came up and with their aid Mielonen, his hands trembling, tried to dress the captain's wound. It was a hopeless task.

Get him to the field dressing station. . . . He's moving his hand . . . he's alive. . . .

Kaarna stared up at Mielonen. His hand moved slightly, then his jaw dropped and the whites of his eyes showed. They laid the corpse on a stretcher and the strenuous journey to the rear began.

4.

The realization that the captain was dead stunned Kariluoto. His eyes filled with tears, and his hands clawed convulsively at the ground. Then he heard other cries for stretcher bearers and tried to rise to his feet. In some recess of his mind pictures formed and flashed before his eyes. His father and mother speaking proudly of him to their friends. Comrades rejoicing with him at the prospect of war. The wrongs done Finland would be righted.

The thought was overwhelming. A bare ten seconds after Kaarna had been borne away Kariluoto was on his feet and heard his own frantic cry:

— Let's go, men of the North! Forward . . . at 'em, boys!

He was conscious of Koskela racing along beside him, while on his other side Private Ukkola, yelling like a madman, fired from the hip as he ran.

Kariluoto's spirits soared. He emptied his pistol at the trees ahead, overcome by a desire to come to grips with the enemy. He did not even notice that the firing from the forest had stopped. He did not look back to where a man was swaying on his knees, his hands pressed to his stomach.

— Help me, help me!

The cry was lost in the ferocious yelling and the crackle of tommy guns. The machine-gun crews, panting and stumbling under their burdens, followed the infantrymen.

They found the Russian positions deserted. Kariluoto caught a glimpse of a solitary brown-clad figure running for shelter in some bushes. Lahtinen caught up with the firing line in time to take a shot at it with his rifle, but missed. Their breath coming in loud sobs, the men threw themselves down on the ground. Now a man was shouting excitedly:

—Jaakko's hit, sir . . . Jaakko's hit . . . Vuorela's back there, sir.

—Two of you go back to see to him, shouted Kariluoto. —All the rest, forward! The road's near. Let's get to our objective.

His wild fury had passed and been succeeded by a surge of joy. He pressed on boldly, holding himself erect and exhorting his men onward. And there in front of him was the road, the one from which they had turned off into the forest that morning. On the left all was quiet; but on the right, in the First Company's sector, the firing was still heavy. Above it could be heard the roar of a motor. The road showed the imprint of a caterpillar tread and the roadside moss had been ploughed up by a tank turning.

They halted on the road, and gradually the firing on the right died down as the Russians took to the forest to detour around the road block the First Company had established. Not until then had they been able to consider what had happened that day.

— We lost the captain and Mielonen.

— Not Mielonen. I saw him by the captain's side.

— Christ what a racket! The barrel's still hot. Feel.

— And not a single Russky done for, said Hietanen. — Not one. I didn't even see one.

Koskela wiped his forehead with his sleeve and stared at the ground:

— A tank got Kaarna . . . He walked right into it and let himself be killed.

But the men did not understand Koskela's meaning, and soon his face regained its usual stolid expression. But he remained silent all that evening, looking into space.

Kariluoto paced to and fro on the road, cursing his inability to relax. Then, seeing Lieutenant Autio approaching from the left, he hastened to meet him.

— Well done, boys, that was a good beginning, Autio said. — Well, what was it like?

— All right, once things got going. I couldn't get them moving at first. Then Kaarna . . .

— Yes, I heard.

Autio's expression did not change. He had been through the Winter War and was used to this kind of thing.

— I didn't know they had that tank, or I'd have given you an anti-tank rifle. Still, all things considered, you made a good beginning. Any casualties?

— Vuorela, a tommy-gun man.

Kariluoto had forgotten all about the first phase of the attack until Autio had reminded him of it. His face reddened and he avoided looking Autio in the eye. But Autio's reference to the tank helped to restore his self-confidence. It was all that damned tank. No man could be expected to attack a tank with his bare hands. His spirits rose again as the burden of shame lightened.

5.

Kariluoto returned to his men, once again the sturdy lieutenant who had drilled them on the burned clearing. He thought of Sirkka and the remembrance of her filled his bosom. Sirkka was very dear to him. And now his mind was made up: he would go to the altar with her a captain, or, who knows, a major, in Finland's army. At the very first opportunity he would enter the Land Warfare School. No studying law for him. Kariluoto could already imagine himself as a regular officer. Smiling, he drew a couple of cigarette packs from his map case and called out:

— Who wants a smoke? Here's one for every one of you. Orderly, hand them out.

As the men clustered about the orderly, a strange-looking party approached from the direction of the swamp. Two men were carrying a third whom they had bound with three belts to the trunk of a birch sapling they had cut down with their knives. A fourth man staggered behind under the burden of several packs. It was Riitaoja, and the man strapped to the pole was the wounded Vuorela.

— How is he?

— Dead.

They had not even been able to treat his wound, so furiously had Vuorela threshed in his death agony. He had not even recognized who they were. In the end they had cut down the sapling and bound him to it. Finding Riitaoja cowering in the swamp, they made him carry all their packs.

The bearers set down their burden as Kariluoto, still under the influence of his dream, said almost too solemnly:

— Well, Vuorela was the first to go. Is there anyone here from his part of the country?

— I'm from the same parish, but the other side. I didn't know much about him at home, except that his people weren't well off.

— I'll write his family. It's always a good thing to send a few lines.

The dead man's blouse was stiff with blood; a belt had been passed around his waist, another about his ankles and a third around his neck. But it was his face they looked at. Beneath the tan and dirt the skin showed a horrible yellow. His gums were bared in an ugly grimace. A man retched, making them all turn away.

— Take him over to the roadside.

They were glad when Vuorela's body was no longer among them. Now the machine gunners turned their attention to Riitaoja who stood apart from the others, an idiotic smile on his face. No one had the heart to say anything to him. Even Lehto only scowled at him and grunted contemptuously.

In the back of their minds they dimly realized there had been nothing unique in Riitaoja's terror. The cheer with which they had charged, and of which they were now so proud, had been wrung from them by fear and by the hatred they had summoned up to cover their fear. But now no one felt like boasting, for no one knew what tomorrow might bring. Rumors had reached them of fortifications ahead, but it was better not to think about that. Food and tents were on the way to them, and between now and tomorrow lay all the time in the world.

6.

— Here's one over here.

— Where?

— Here in these bushes. An officer. He's got shoulder tabs.

The men crowded around. Lying on his face in a clump of juniper bushes was a Russian Lieutenant. His mouth was set in the same grimace Vuorela had worn, but its effect on them was not the same. They felt only curiosity.

— See how far he's dragged himself. Look at the way his nails are all torn and bloody.

— They don't seem to take much care of each other, leaving him to crawl around like that.

— He was a tough son-of-a-bitch, dragging himself all that way with his fingers.

They inspected him solemnly until Rahikainen, tapping the dead man's helmet with the barrel of his rifle, called out:

— Halloo there! Is it cold in a Russky Hell?

Vanhala glanced at the others, but seeing that few smiled held back his own laughter. But now Rahikainen had bent down and was busily stripping off the Russian's badges.

— He won't need these.

— Hey, give me one.

— Not so fast. There aren't enough on one little fellow like this for all of us. Wait till we've knocked over a few bigger ones.

The others protested, but the insignia were already in Rahikainen's pocket.

— Tell me whose bullet brought him down and I'll give that man one. Nobody else.

No one, of course, claimed the hit, and Rahikainen kept the tabs. Now, however, the awe that was their first reaction had worn off. A man grabbed the dead man's fine new officer's belt, then his pockets were turned inside out, yielding a leather pouch containing a toothbrush, a manicure set and a bottle of toilet water.

Hietanen sprinkled a generous quantity of this latter on their filthy blouses, making them all roar with childish glee. One of the men took a few mincing steps, his lips pursed.

— Form a line. Only two hundred marks each.

The manicure set was divided, though it was rare for a man to clean his nails. What was the use? The dirt peeled off without any trouble when there was enough of it.

— Here's his wallet.

— That's his I.D. card with his photo. Look, there's his birth date. 1916. Four years older than me.

— Look at the rubles.

— What's it say on this copper coin? Koneck. Koneck. What the hell kind of a word is that? How much is it worth?

— It means kopek.

— Well, whatever it means it's nothing a man can understand.

Troops marched past on the road. The Third Battalion was on its way to take over from the First.

— Better have a good rest if you want to catch up with us tomorrow, a voice shouted from the ranks.

Most of the men in the ranks, however, were quiet until a nervous voice asked:

— How far is it to Ivan's positions?

— Keep going. You'll find 'em.

They left the dead Russian in the bushes. Lieutenant Boris Braskanov, born in Vologda on May 6th, 1916, lay on his face, beltless and badgeless, his pockets inside out.

At last the baggage train arrived with tents and food. The platoons assembled and the machine-gun company could count its casualties. One dead in the First Platoon; no casualties in the others. Many heard with genuine regret that Kaarna had fallen, and all of them already felt his absence as a loss, if only because his successor was to be Lammio.

That evening Kariluoto wrote three letters. The first was To Vuorela's family:

. . . He was one of my best men and it was a heavy blow that he should be the first to go. Our country's lot is hard and our sacrifices great, yet they must be borne. I say this with the hope that you may find consolation in the knowledge that his life was sacrificed in the cause of the loftiest and noblest of human ideals, the freedom of one's country and its people. And now that Karelia is being liberated and a new day is dawning for Finland, may you hear in your sorrow your son's voice proudly rising above the battle in the song: "O beloved country, Finland . . ."

To his own father and mother he wrote:

. . . I am proud of my mission. My mind is at last made up—I have decided to become a regular officer. In times like these no other career seems worth while. Soon we shall see Karelia free. Out of the depths of the despair Finland will rise to greatness. And today it finally became clear to me that my life is not my own but belongs to Finland. I know things are not going to be easy, but I see the road clearly marked before me and shall do my utmost not to stray from it. I am indebted above all today to a Jaeger captain, for he taught me how to tread one's path fearlessly even though it may lead to death. Such sights create a standard it is our duty to maintain. After a man's baptism of fire he doesn't talk big, but as I said I now know what my mission is and that knowledge makes everything easier. . . .

To Sirkka he wrote:

. . . Today I feel able to say things which at any other time would be difficult. Certainly I confess that when we last met I hadn't the courage. Today I smile at my timidity. What a child a man is before events make him search his own soul in earnest! I speak my mind, therefore, although I'm not sure of you. But be that as it may, and however hard a blow your refusal would be, I shall try to fulfill my duty. After today I owe that to those who have already fulfilled theirs . . .

Vanhala was on sentry duty. He paced between the tents, his eyes puckered in laughter. Hey, is it cold down there in Russky Hell? Rahikainen's question still amused him, and now that there was no one to object, he gave full vent to his mirth. Without a tremor he heard the battery open up and send shells shrieking over the camp. From the flap of one of the tents a startled face protruded, only to relax when its owner's eyes fell on Vanhala's smile.

The sun had set. A mist rose from the swamp and in the forest the dusk deepened. An occasional rumble of guns came from the south and north. Somewhere a tommy gun chattered and was answered by a slow-firing Russian machine gun.

A cart appeared on the road. It came from the direction of the front—its burden four bodies over which a canvas tent flap had been spread. The First Company's casualties.

Chapter III

1.

They sat at the roadside and waited, chewing the bits of bread they had saved. Occasional sounds of firing came from the front line, and farther away they could hear aircraft motors humming, the sound fading and rising again to a crescendo in which the crackle of machine guns mingled.

—Dog fight, a man said, his eyes searching the sky.

—Let 'em fight, answered his neighbor in the condescending tone of a man bored with the remembrance of battles too numerous to count.

Lieutenant Kariluoto paced restlessly to and fro on the road. He had posted his letters that same evening and now, in the morning, wished he could get them back. The mood had passed. Desperately he tried to rid himself of the tension the expectation of combat aroused in him by joking too loudly with the men. But even to his own ears his humor sounded forced.

Nevertheless it helped. The news that they were to attack had revived all his former fears, and he could not convince himself that this time he would not behave as he had before. What if the victory he had gained over himself was not a lasting one? No. Never again would he behave like that. Never.

As he worried, Lieutenant Lammio came striding up from the rear, Mielonen a few paces behind him. The change of commanders had hit Mielonen hardest of all. No more arguing, for now orders came in stiffly formal tones which left nothing to dispute.

Lammio had no real business here, each machine-gun platoon having been subordinated to a rifle company, but he wandered around filled with his new importance. He was hardly out of earshot when Rahikainen said:

— That's a strange one they've put over us. It's a wonder he didn't want us to get up and salute him.

Maatta drew deeply on his cigarette.

— It's one thing to want and another to get. My elbow doesn't bend that easily.

Coming from Maatta it was a surprising speech, for he had always been one of the meekest and most willing men in the platoon and had never grumbled. They had all taken note of his cool courage and almost complete indifference to danger during yesterday's fighting. They had noted, too, that not once had he asked to be relieved of the burden he was carrying. Short as he was he seemed able to carry a machine gun forever without tiring.

Maatta puffed away at his cigarette. It was obvious that he was not merely being brave behind Lammio's back, but from whence this defiance sprang, they could not have said. Actually, the answer was simple. The boy whom everybody tended to forget because he was quiet and never asserted himself had realized yesterday that in battle he was as good as anybody else. He had looked at death and had not found it terrible.

It was hot in the sun, and they were weary and bored. Can't the Third Battalion make any headway . . . they'd better send us up to open the road for them.

Their musings were interrupted by a dull rumbling sound from the Russian lines, and they all sat up to listen. The low roar continued, and then was lost in a rising shriek.

The first shell exploded on the roadside ahead. — Cover! a voice screamed, but the warning was unnecessary. All of them were already flat in the ditch. Thought had fled from their minds; they were conscious only of a world that was all terror and waiting. The earth quaked, successive blasts pressed their clothes to their bodies, splinters whined and buzzed in the air and fell to the ground amid a rain of stones and clods. After a couple of very long minutes the shelling stopped. But the last echo had not yet died away when a cry of distress rang out:

— Stretcher . . . Stretcher! Quickly!

A team of stretcher bearers came racing from the rear. Farther up the road a man could be seen endeavoring to rise.

— Air . . . air . . . help me . . . !

Two men knelt beside the wounded man. —Don't, don't scream like that, they implored him. The stricken cry cut through their defenses and so upset them that they were incapable of doing anything to aid him. The man's shoulders were badly mangled, and the stretcher bearers tried to dress his wounds only to be hampered by his violent efforts to get to his feet. And through it all he went on screaming:

—Help . . . Shoot me, somebody . . . a-ah . . . a-ah . . . God damn you, shoot me . . . you cowards. . . .

A soldier came up, pale and nursing a bleeding hand.

— Dress it, will you, he demanded.

The stretcher bearers looked up at him, worried and haggard. One of them was holding the struggling man down while the other tried to dress his wounds:

— We can't take care of everybody at once. Where the hell is the medical NCO . . . can't he come himself . . . ? We've got to be everywhere.

The man with the wounded hand sat down by the side of the ditch, and a determined look came over his pale face as he said:

— Holy Christ, I can put a rag on this myself. It's nothing. Ylitalo there has half his head blown off.

Smoke and dust still hovered in the air as Kariluoto shouted:

— Scatter! Don't bunch up. His face was pale, but there was a resolute glint in his eyes. In a moment of defiance he had raised his head during the shelling to test himself, and it had been easy. He knew once again the feeling of victory that had swept over him after the fighting yesterday. Not with the same exuberance, however, for both the wounded men belonged to his platoon.

Lahtinen climbed out of the ditch smirking:

— I thought you were on your way to the Urals, boys. What's stopping you? Let's get going.

— Oh, shut your face, said Hietanen angrily. — Of all the goddamn lies. They say you can tell from the sound whether a shell's going to fall near you. The one that came down almost on top of us didn't even whistle. One whoosh and it burst beside the road. How the hell can people tell such stories? They said that on the Western Front you had time to listen and then take cover.

Maatta was still puffing at his cigarette.

— What's the difference whether you hear it or not? he said as Lammio came up to them.

— Spread out. Didn't you hear the order?

— Keep your damn mouth shut, Rahikainen muttered from the ditch.

At that very moment the Russian guns opened up again, and the earth shook as the men dashed for cover. Lammio did not stir however, and Koskela, who had also remained seated, called:

— They're way over us.

Lehto, Maatta and Hietanen arose at once as the shells passed overhead to burst far in the rear.

— Our artillery's getting it, someone observed.

Lammio, standing in the middle of the road, smiled nastily:

— You'd do better to do as you're told. They might have our range next time.

His courage made him more hated than ever, for it deprived the men of the opportunity they would have had to despise him if he had shown fear. Rahikainen, for example, was livid with hatred as he whispered:

— Stop baa-ing, you misbegotten turd.

And Sihvonen muttered angrily:

— Go on, make some more noise. Stand around waving your arms. Be sure they see you from that observation tower over there, so they can blow us all to bits. Why the hell did we have to stop here to give them a target? But what else could you expect from those pissheads upstairs.

The badly wounded man had lost consciousness, and the perspiring stretcher bearers lifted him onto the stretcher. Now they were free to put a dressing on the man with the wounded hand, but he would not let them, instead growling angrily:

— Go to Hell!

— None of that shit, said the stretcher bearer. I've been there and I'm not going again. Bandage it yourself if you want.

The soldier set off for the rear, waving his good hand.

— So long, boys, I'm going home on leave.

Silently they fell in again, their anxiety to leave the spot apparent in the way the column tended to bunch up. Someone had covered the dead man's head, but pork fat could be seen oozing from his rations pouch where a shell splinter had pierced his emergency-ration tin.

2.

— The Russians are about three hundred yards up ahead in prepared positions. Our scouts reported at least two bunkers. We'll have a five-minute artillery barrage, then two minutes before we shove off the trench mortars will join in. We take off at ten forty-eight.

Kariluoto spoke in a low voice, and the men listened intently, their eyes glued to the barricade visible between the trees. Along a steep slope the trees had been felled in a belt about forty yards wide. They could not see any wire, but earlier reconnoitering had disclosed the existence of several machine-gun positions behind the obstacles, two of them in Kariluoto's sector.

An advance guard about ten yards ahead whispered hoarsely:

— There's something moving behind the barricade. Shall I take a crack at it?

— For God's sake, no! Lie still.

On the right an artillery observer was speaking into a radio telephone, his low mumbling sounding like an incantation. Mosquitoes sang in the morning-damp forest, and the spider webs which were everywhere between the blueberry bushes stuck unpleasantly to hands and to wrists in which pulses raced. Here and there men cautiously edged ammunition boxes into place as NCOs whispered their last instructions. Belts were tightened, cartridges stuffed into pockets where they'd be readily available.

— Have your hand grenades ready.

The artillery observer went on whispering figures into his phone. Over on the right, in the Second Company's sector, shots rang out every so often. The Russians obviously scented an attack and were jumpy.

Watch hands pointed to 10:43. And on the second the earth seemed to open behind them in a tremendous crashing and howling. Sharp-voiced field guns, low-pitched howitzers and hollow-sounding heavies raged as though trying to outshout each other.

The men pressed themselves to the ground as salvoes of shells swept over them with a sound like passing express trains. In the Russian lines smoke, soil, stones and trees erupted in the air. Flashes of flame lit the dull gray storm clouds.

— Jesus! Can human beings stand that? a man asked, raising his pale face.

— It's their turn now, jeered another voice.

— They're a little off, said Koskela, on his knees watching the effect of the gunfire.

Kariluoto's watch ticked on. 10:44 . . . 45 . . . 46 . . . 47 . . .

Kariluoto waited nervously until the watch hand pointed exactly to 10:48 and the last shell whizzed overhead.

— All right, men. Here we go!

He set off swiftly, running half-crouched, and the men followed. Ahead of them the scout ran silently. Then suddenly the Russian trench mortars opened fire, the shells whistling over their heads and exploding in their rear.

— Let's go, the men exhorted each other. The scout's tommy gun crackled and at once drew answering fire.

Kariluoto raced onward, whipping himself into a fury to keep up his courage. The platoon was still advancing at a crouch with only a man here and there halting to take cover. He prayed he could carry the men with him in a charge that would not stop until it had overwhelmed their objective. At that moment the scout dropped his tommy gun and sank to his knees, his hands pressed to his face. Blood spurted between his fingers.

— My head . . . I'm hit . . . my head.

— Can you look after yourself?

— I think so . . . I'm still alive . . . It can't be very dangerous. A head wound that kills, kills right off . . .

The shock had dazed the scout, and, babbling to himself, he crawled off toward the rear on all fours. Meanwhile the others continued to advance, although the sight of the wounded man had sent a few more of them to cover. Ahead lay the slope and its fortifications, from which came a continuous rattle of infantry fire.

Halfway up the slope the Russian fire began to tell, and the men flattened themselves to the ground. A few still advanced in short dashes while others crawled forward, but most of them had stopped and were exchanging fire with the enemy. Kariluoto, however, crawled forward on his hands and knees shouting:

— Let's go, boys . . . keep up the pressure!

A voice shouted: —Look out for that stuff!

— What stuff?

— Those things hanging from the logs. It's TNT.

— The barricade's mined! Look out for wire!

Hanging from the defenses were TNT charges looking very much like cakes of soap. Actually they were not particularly dangerous unless a man happened to be right over them, for since they were not enclosed the greatest danger was from the concussion.

— Take them off carefully.

No engineers were attached to the company, but they had been lectured on the subject of mines and were expected to look out for themselves. But the men were afraid of the wires, and the attack halted.

—Now we're stuck.

—Goddamn those things.

—They won't hurt you. They're not dangerous. See? Kariluoto released a wire snare and the men near him gingerly copied his example.

Baroom! The explosive went off.

Kariluoto rose to a crouch.

— Be careful not to touch the rest. Let's go!

The firing grew hotter until it billowed left and right in waves. From somewhere came the sound of shouted commands and the cheers of men charging. Shells crisscrossed in the air as the artillery on both sides dueled. Bullets whistled, ricochets whined. From the platoon next to them came frantic cries for stretcher bearers.

The boulders and the little hollows of the ground offered some protection to which the men gratefully clung. The Russian machine guns were not firing bursts now but were letting fly with whole belts at one clip. Fighting was going on as far on each side of them as they could hear. The regiment was storming the bunker line, while far to their right other regiments could be heard attacking. The summer air quivered with the endless echoes. Thousands of barrels glowed red hot, thousands of hands loaded and fired, thousands of men crawled or dashed forward. And thousands of other men sought to halt their advance, holding stubbornly to their positions until death claimed them. Men died in scores and hundreds, and hundreds more were wounded.

On both sides there were abundant exhibitions of craven fear and reckless courage. For more than a year the thought of revenge had smoldered in the minds of the Finns, but the defenders were no less determined. Finally Kariluoto had to admit that a further charge would only result in the decimation of his platoon—if, that is, the men could be induced to charge. They were now creeping forward.

— Our damned artillery's no use at all, a man sobbed.

Kariluoto was in despair. He could feel the will to fight ebbing from his men, but the realization only spurred him to greater effort. He had banished his own fear to some secret recess of his mind and managed to keep it there until at last a conviction that he had finally overcome it enabled him to ignore it altogether.

— Keep crawling. Use all the cover you can find.

Kariluoto was nearly ten yards ahead of his men when the NCO nearest to him ordered his section to fire, and under cover of the resultant volley, dashed toward Kariluoto. But as he reached his side, he suddenly slid to the earth and rolled over on his back. Between his eyes, right in the center of his forehead, was a bluish hole. His hand clutched at his collar button and stayed there as his mouth opened and shut a couple of times like that of a fish out of water.

Kariluoto cried his name and edged nearer, but the man was dead. At the same instant a bullet pierced his own cap. Desperately he called to another man to take over the section.

A few more yards gained. The men, however, were losing heart.

— I'm hit!

A man set off rearward at a crawl.

— Stretcher bearers!

A minute or two later still another man creeping along the ground screamed as he was struck by machine gun bullets.

Again a bullet made a hole in Kariluoto's equipment, this time in his holster. The strain was telling on him, but he refused to give in. When the platoon was at last level with him, he resumed his advance. Privata Ukkola, who had raced to his side the day before, again followed him, and they tried hand grenades which overshot their mark because their prone position made throwing difficult. Immediately the Russians retaliated with four or five grenades, but these too were well off their mark.

Abruptly Kariluoto started as he heard someone calling his name. Autio was lying a little ways in his rear. Slowly he crept back to him.

— Can't you keep 'em going?

— I've tried my best.

Kariluoto's voice was tinged with a despairing anger.

— I've lost three men and my best section leader. There'll be nothing left of the platoon if . . . but we'll give it another try if you think . . .

— No. Forget it . . . The whole battalion's at a standstill. The Second Company has heavy losses . . . Two platoon commanders. I've lost a dozen wounded in my company. I reported the situation to battalion, but they ordered me to keep on trying.

— How about a new barrage to soften 'em up?

— If we pull back we'll never get a new attack going . . . If you can force a foothold you can bet you'll get your reward. And it'll be the making of you if you break through.

Autio understood Kariluoto and knew that he planned to remain in the army. And it was this knowledge that dictated the pressure he was bringing to bear. Kariluoto of all his platoon commanders could least afford to admit that he could go no farther.

— I'll see what I can do . . .

— Try. Mind, I'm not ordering you to. But it'd be too bad to call off the attack after all our casualties.

Autio crawled away, and Kariluoto crept back to the head of his platoon. The firing had slackened a little; it seemed impossible that it had taken them more than an hour to advance fifty yards. And they were exhausted, their lips cracked with thirst.

A turf-roofed bunker was now plainly visible. From its black apertures machine guns fired steadily. Beyond it the Russian line made a bend which marked the beginning of the Second Company's sector. There, men had been withdrawn from the firing line to help the stretcher bearers, for the fighting here at the pivotal point of the attack had been costly.

The shelter arranged for the wounded was crowded with dead and wounded, and more were continually arriving on stretchers sticky with blood. Amid the groaning and the delirious cries a lone medical corpsman worked busily.

— Damned if I know how I'm going to get them to the rear. If it keeps up, half of the company will be carrying the other half.

3.

During most of the battle Koskela and his first squad had been inactive for the machine guns could not be brought up in support until the line had gotten close to the bunkers. It was no use, Koskela realized, exposing such an easy target as a machine gun to the Russian fire until it could be used for a direct attack on a bunker. Some of his men were glad to be out of it, but others found the inactivity difficult while fighting was in progress. It was their first real battle, and they were not yet inured to such situations. Thus when Koskela .saw that the firing line had been halted before the bunkers, he decided that their time had come.

For the first time his men experienced the full misery of a machine gunner's lot. Riflemen had sometimes taunted them: — You sure have an easy time bringing up our rear. But for that doubtful privilege they paid dearly by having to carry heavy equipment. And inaction keeping under cover was always a problem. Now they tried to work the tripod up the slope, crawling sideways with it, but it was slow going.

At last, after much perspiring effort, they got the gun into the firing line and found cover for it in a tiny hollow under a fallen birch tree. Kaukonen attached the barrel, and Koskela saw that if the machine gun could keep the fireports in the bunker under fire, Kariluoto and his men might be able to make it to the trench.

— Fire at the loopholes! Koskela ordered, and Kaukonen obeyed. Instantly Kariluoto rose to a crouch.

— Let's go, boys!

The trunk of a fallen birch beside him began to crackle and he dropped to the ground again. Immediately Vanhala burst out laughing.

— I do believe Ivan's trying to put holes in us. He can't take a joke.

— You keep your eyes on that belt, Lehto said in a surly voice, and Vanhala quickly shut up.

— Keep it up, Kaukonen. You're doing fine.

Heartened by this praise, Kaukonen raised his head to get a better view, only to duck down at once. Now again Kariluoto set off at a crawl. A few men moved after him but quickly gave up the attempt as a burst of fire riddled a submachine gunner and wounded his mate. The terrifying gurgle from his pierced throat effectively killed any desire those near enough to hear it had to leave their shelter.

— What's the use? We're being sent to be butchered, a man said. — Where's the brass hiding?

— Shut up and get moving! Kariluoto. He knew that the word

"brass" was not meant for him, for he had been ahead of his men all along, but still he felt insulted. Now Koskela crawled to his side:

— Don't go on, you'll be killed. . . . The men won't follow . . . you'll be throwing away your life for nothing.

— What else can I do? I've got to keep going. . . .

— I know one thing we could do. Let's try to get one man up close with explosives. It'll be easier for one man with all the rest supporting him.

— I'll go.

— No, you'd better not. I'll do it.

— It's my job, not yours. Whoever heard of a machine gunner spearheading an attack?

Koskela was irritated by Kariluoto's excessive touchiness. Nevertheless he explained calmly:

— You can't go. Someone has to get the men moving, and that's your job. If they don't, the whole thing's wasted.

Kariluoto instinctively recognized the logic of this and shouted for explosive charges for Koskela. A few were handed up from man to man, and Koskela deftly fastened two charges together with a fuse, his mouth tightening with each twist of the fuse. Finished at last he turned to Lehto:

— Now listen! Once I start off you've got to keep up a covering fire the whole time. And Kariluoto, I want your men to do the same, but look out you don't put a hole in me.

Koskela studied the ground carefully. The men were all watching him.

Kariluoto was overcome with hesitation. He feared that Koskela would be killed in the attempt or that the explosive charge would prove ineffective, in which case Koskela would also certainly die. It would be the second time a man had lost his life for his sake. The memory of Kaarna's death swept over him again.

— What if the charge doesn't work? he said nervously. — I think I'd better try it myself.

Koskela did not even glance at him. He was staring at the enemy's positions, and when he spoke he was a man completely preoccupied with a problem:

— Only one layer of logs and all the rest turf. Two charges are bound to do some damage. At the least it'll give you the time you need.

He was off, dragging the explosives behind him.

— Watch Koskela and keep up that fire! Kariluoto was resolved to charge, if need be alone, the instant Koskela fell. The men stepped up their fire, and the machine gun shook and rattled until the water in the barrel boiled. Then Kaukonen raised his head in order to aim the stream of lead better. As he did so a strangled sigh escaped his lips and he slumped forward, his face striking the grips as he collapsed over the weapon.

— Kaukonen! Kariluoto shouted. Lehto turned white as a sheet but there was no awkwardness in his movements as he dragged the dead man from the machine gun, took his place and resumed firing. He saw the upper part of a man's body bob up out of the trench and send a hand grenade flying towards Koskela. Quick as lightning he turned the machine gun and saw the tracers bite into the Russian.

— Koskela . . . look out! he screamed.

The hand grenade exploded a few yards away from Koskela. His cap was gone and his hair stuck out in all directions above his angular face as he shouted over his shoulder:

— Keep it up! I'm going to try to get closer.

Swiftly he worked his way from cover to cover, the tall grass and the enemy's error in placing the obstacle too close to the trench proving a great help. About ten yards in front of the bunker was a boulder, and he made for that. The men held their breath, realizing that if he reached its shelter he might succeed in his enterprise. As they watched, he arrived unhurt and calmly settled into a good throwing position. A jerk of a string and in a flash he had jumped to his feet, spun round and the charge was flying through the air. In the same movement he dropped flat behind the boulder, his hands pressed to his ears.

As the charge fell on the roof of the bunker and exploded, a roar of triumph broke from all near enough to witness it. Through the smoke a log could be seen standing on end.

— Let's get at 'em!

Kariluoto dashed forward and unhesitatingly the men sprang after him.

— They're running. . . . I got that one!

— There goes another . . . Shoot! They're running! Don't let the bastards get away.

Kariluoto was already in the trench. One after the other he threw two hand grenades into the bunker and stood aside as

Ukkola added a burst from his submachine gun. The entire platoon was now in the trench and the men, drunk with excitement, began to work their way along it. It was not a difficult task, for the shaken enemy was abandoning his positions without a struggle.

As soon as the trench was secure, Kariluoto sent a message to Autio, asking that the reserve platoon be brought up into the gap to turn the Russian positions facing the Second Company. His own men began to spread down the trench in their company's sector, leaving the machine gun and a rifle squad to secure the other flank. The Russian resistance was rapidly collapsing everywhere: the platoon nearest to them was also in the enemy's positions, and on the slope behind them, fleeing Russians were being picked off before they could reach the sheltering forest.

The men securing Kariluoto's flank saw the enemy abandon the other bunker and took possession of it as the Jaeger Platoon sent by Autio arrived and began the mop-up in that direction.

Koskela sat on the ground shaking soil out of his hair and holding his still-ringing ears.

4.

The dead lay scattered along the trench, many with their pockets turned inside out, as the machine gunners turned back for a last look at Kaukonen. His body had already been placed on a stretcher.

— Where did he get it?

— In the neck. The slug went right through his windpipe.

— A quick end's a good end, said Lehto with a malicious smile.

— Let's get going. We'll be left behind.

Above all they wanted to get away from the scene as quickly as possible; for they had lived with Kaukonen for more than a year. Although they were still under the influence of their recent experiences, the memory of his yellowish face, one eye closed and the other bulging out in a glassy stare, lay heavily on them.

— You go ahead. I'll be with you in a minute or two.

Lehto set off towards the rear.

— Riitaoja!

A man emerged from the bushes and stiffened to attention.

— Sir! he said obediently, a silly smile spreading over his face.

— You devil's turd, what are you grinning at?

— I'm not grinning, sir. Riitaoja's smile faded. Still stiff as a ramrod, he peered furtively around him.

—Sir. Sir. You won't get around me with your Sirs. God damn it, if I weren't ashamed to hit a man like you, what a beating you'd get!

Riitaoja drew back a step. Shakily he stammered:

— I'm frightened of all that noise, sir. It's the whistling sound they make.

— Go on, you'll be weeping soon, you bastard. Lehto was angry and disgusted. He hated Riitaoja's terror with the hate that weakness of any kind aroused in him.

— Go over and bring two boxes of ammunition from the cart. Wait for the Third Company's stretcher bearers and come back with them. They're moving the dead to the rear. And see you don't loiter or try to hide.

— Yes, sir.

Riitaoja, only too glad to escape, hastened off, leaving Lehto to set out after the company. Reaching the trench he was about to jump it when his eye fell on a mess tin at the bottom, half full of a paste of bread and water. Beside it lay a dead Russian with black hair and slanting eyes whom the attack had apparently interrupted in the middle of a meal. Nimbly Lehto dropped into the trench and with one kick sent the mixture flying into the dead man's face. Laughing harshly he went on his way.

He caught up with the advancing company in the forest. The men were joking, laughing heartily on the slightest pretext. For more than two hours they had lived with death, and they were still alive. That was reason enough for laughter.

Abruptly their talking ceased as the advance scout called back a warning and cast himself down on the ground.

— Look, across that meadow—houses. It's a village.

— What village is it?

— Who knows. Get down!

Pee-oo pee-oo pee-oo.

— There the bastards go again.

— Take cover.

From beyond the village came the echo of muzzle reports. Seeing his men throw themselves down, Koskela, still unable to hear, also dropped on one knee. Shells burst loudly in the forest behind them.

— Ought to be our turn to stay in reserve. We opened the way for everybody. The rest were all lying waiting.

— Reserve? Not a chance. The brass want some medals.

— Come on, machine guns. Quick. Russkies on the right.

The sight made them catch their breath. To their right a meadow sloped down to a pond. About forty Russians had emerged from the forest and, unaware of any danger, were making their way across the field toward the village.

— Get your sights on them, but wait for the machine guns to open up, ordered Kariluoto. Eagerly he took a rifle from a private's hands.

— Let me have a shot . . . my pistol won't carry that far.

Still the Russians noticed nothing. Lehto was handling his machine gun himself and he laid his sights on the largest group. His jaws moved as though he were chewing something. Maatta, calm and expressionless as always, sighted the other gun.

— Let them have it! cried Kariluoto, aware despite his eagerness of the horror of the situation.

Bullets strummed into the men in the field. Some crawled into the ditches between the plots, but a dozen or so lay motionless. Unfortunately the ditches lay open to the raking fire, and through the bursts despairing cries could be heard.

— That's the way, boys.

— I got that one for certain!

— I've got two.

— Listen to them hollering!

— Keep pumping lead into 'em and they'll stop.

The man whose rifle Kariluoto had taken kept tugging at his neighbor's sleeve.

— Let me have a shot. Just one.

— Stop shoving me.

Lehto was completely absorbed in his gun. He shouted to Maatta, and as always when excitement got the better of him his voice rose to a squeal.

— The ditches, Maatta! The bottom of the ditches!

Maatta also was enjoying himself. He inserted a new belt and aimed, his face puckered in concentration. But at last there were no more targets and the firing slackened until only occasional stray shots were heard. Now the moaning of a wounded man floated across the field.

Only then did the men realize that they themselves had been

under fire from the village. Rising to his knees, a man cried exultingly:

— I bagged four of the bas— . . . uhh!

There was the smack of a bullet. The others heard it clearly, followed immediately by the man's faint groan.

— Stretcher bearers!

— No, don't bother. He's done for.

Quickly they crawled under cover and returned the fire.

5.

Pillars of earth and smoke erupted from the village, and the ground shook beneath the bursting of six-inch shells. When the barrage ceased, they were surprised to hear the sound of fighting beyond the village, but before they had time to puzzle out its significance Kariluoto's shouted command sent them forward.

They encountered only weak fire. There was no organized opposition; the remnants of the troops defending the village fought for their lives, scattered and leaderless. Encircled, they were trying to break out of the ring into the forest singly and in small bands. Hard fighting had been going on all day behind the village where the Second Battalion had already established itself on the road that morning after a long detour through the woods had brought it behind the Russian positions. The First Battalion had heard nothing of this fighting because of the sound of its own battle.

In the yard of the first house lay a team of dead horses, a forsaken field kitchen, and a trench mortar with a few corpses lying around it.

Through the open square of the village they advanced cautiously, crouching low. An occasional burst from a tommy gun indicated that one more defender had fallen.

Autio's messenger brought word of the Second Battalion's presence behind the village and a warning to be careful lest they shoot their own men. Immediately the tension relaxed, for the news meant that the situation was well in hand. More and more of the men slipped away to do some looting, and the officers had considerable difficulty getting the whole of the village mopped up. Rahikainen emerged from a house staggering under the weight of a big sack.

— What have you got?

— Sugar. Chunks the size of your fist.

— Come on, let's have a share.

— Give, give—whenever I get hold of something, the whole regiment's after me. This is for my own boys. If you want sugar, look for it.

— What's the matter? Koskela looked on inquiringly, still too deaf to hear ordinary conversation.

— A sack of sugar. He says only his own boys get a share.

— You know you're not supposed to take anything. But I guess this time we can keep it quiet. If the whole platoon gets a share, that is.

— Oh, all right. But damned if I'll carry . . .

Rahikainen broke off in mid-sentence and dropped to the ground with a thud. A burst from an automatic rifle whined over their heads.

— There's another one who wants a share, said Rahikainen, peering over the sack. — There he goes, into those bushes.

In the middle of a field lay a heap of stones partly overgrown with willow bushes.

— Don't shoot. Let's take a prisoner.

They scattered and approached the bushes in a semicircle.

— Look out he doesn't escape.

— Come on out, *tavarits*. We've got some sugar for you!

In the bushes all was silent until a sound emerged which they recognized as sobbing. They exchanged glances, and one man shouted harshly:

— Shoot him, someone! The devil himself couldn't stand that noise.

Bolts clicked, but the next second the crash of a hand grenade came from the bushes.

— Who threw that?

— No one. He blew himself up.

— Jesus!

They closed in cautiously on the bushes.

— There he is with his guts all over the ground. He must have held it against his stomach.

A few stayed for a better look but most were satisfied with a brief glimpse.

They combed the far end of the village, interrupted occasionally by the sound of a shot, for the Russians were not surrendering but even in the most hopeless situations were trying to fight back.

— They're just scared to death. Who's going to surrender knowing your family'll be shot for it?

Then from the rear of the last houses came shouts: —Don't shoot. We're Finns!

— What outfit?

— Fourth Company.

The men of the Fourth were lying on the ground, sullen and silent. They had fought hard all day to keep the Russians from breaking out of the ring and to prevent the arrival of reinforcements from the rear. Now not even the knowledge that the day had been won could lift their spirits. They answered questions surlily.

— Did you cut the road?

— Yes.

— We stormed a bunker line.

— You don't say.

— Lost nearly one man in three.

— Well, thank God you weren't one. You don't need to come boasting to us about your corpses. We've got a row of our own under those trees.

— Got any bread?

— No.

— Neither have we.

— What's that supply sergeant got in his sack?

— Nothing.

— Nothing? It's stuff you've stolen.

— Listen to him. First he asks, then he tells us. If a man knows something, why does he have to ask?

— Don't wag that jaw of yours so much, sarge.

— I'm goddamn glad I can still wag my jaw.

Hietanen was losing his temper and a fight might have started if Kariluoto hadn't arrived.

— Come on, boys. It's all over and food'll be along any minute.

The two groups parted, for the companies were falling in, and soon their spirits started to soar. Now the lighter side of their day's experiences claimed their attention. Hardly anyone seemed to have a thought for the dead. They had survived; nothing else could compare with that all-important fact.

While the platoons were still forming on the road, Kariluoto sought out Koskela:

— I haven't had time to thank you yet. If it hadn't been for what you did, we wouldn't have got anywhere.

Koskela smiled momentarily, then mastered himself again and said seriously:

— No, your platoon did a real job today. They're good boys. You wouldn't think they were new at it.

Now it was Kariluoto's turn to smile with pleasure. Praise from Koskela meant more to him than anyone could have guessed. During the past two days his respect for the silent lieutenant whom he, in common with many of the other officers, had regarded as clumsy and ineffectual, had been growing along with a recognition of his own inferiority. And Kariluoto could afford to acknowledge merit in others, for he had not done badly himself.

He hastened back to his men in high spirits and thanked them warmly.

— I want to tell you, boys, that the battalion succeeded today only because of you. That's the way, boys.

The men were pleased, and for once they did not wax sarcastic about the stupidity of Kariluoto's ideas.

6.

Food was being served from a field kitchen. It was no worse than usual, but the men had envisaged their meal as a victory dinner and the sight of a few peas swimming in a greasy soup aroused their wrath. Thus the cook doling out the food got curses instead of thanks for his trouble.

— Half-cooked! And you've had a whole day to cook it, said Rahikainen peering into his mess tin.

Makila, standing beside the kitchen, spat.

— What's the use of complaining? We're all in the same piss. They've been shelling us all day. One of the first company's cooks was killed.

But Makila's attempt to defend himself was received with derision as a sarcastic voice spoke up: — Why the hell did he aim at the wrong kitchen?

Vanhala alone did not complain. Instead, he asked humbly for more. Amid the general contempt Vanhala's humility shone all the brighter, and the cook filled his tin, scooping his ladle along the bottom of the pot. Vanhala could scarcely keep back a smile as he hurried off to enjoy his good fortune in some quiet spot.

Even Lammio's arrival could not check the grumbling until he said:

— If the food isn't good enough for you, leave it. You aren't ordered to eat it.

There were no more comments after that, but a low murmur voiced still stronger feelings:

— There's one bastard who won't live long if he gets near the firing line.

— Look at that freak of nature. Looks like a grasshopper on a fish hook, and talks as though he was someone.

The Third Platoon went into seclusion in a dense grove of alder, and the sugar was shared out with Hietanen counting the chunks.

— Let's agree that if one of us gets killed before he's eaten his share, only the men in his own section get it, suggested Lahtinen. — Then there won't be any quarreling.

Through the crunching, voices could be heard assenting.

— At least we won't have to fight for a while after the job we've done.

— Don't be too sure, said Lahtinen. — Nobody got off easily today.

Lahtinen always seemed to be trying to cast a pall over any general optimism. Actually he did not want to belittle the men's achievements, but it had become a habit with him to be pessimistic.

— Anything left over is mine, called Rahikainen. — I found the sack.

— Was that all there was?

— No, there were a couple of corpses and a sack or two of cabbages. But what good was cabbage to me? It takes too damn long to cook.

They rolled themselves cigarettes from the tobacco they had found in the pockets of the Russian dead. Lying in the grass the whole world seemed to be at peace, the war nonexistent. Flowers of all colors grew in the unsown fields, and the tall hay had a sweet smell. They drew the fresh evening air into their lungs. In the sky an advancing army of clouds cast a deepening shadow over the earth. Rain was imminent.

— Boys, look. Lottas!

— And the C.O.

The battalion commander was taking a walk on the road, accompanied by his adjutant and two Lottas. They had been inspecting the battlefield, and the adjutant had taken snapshots of the Lottas standing beside a captured trench mortar. They had even looked at some Russian corpses and the Lottas, shivering, had cried: —How horrible! when they saw a dead man whose brains had been splashed over the ground by a shell splinter.

Lotta Raili Kotilainen felt that as a woman it was her duty to say something feminine, but actually she was too happy to feel any real pity. Her thoughts were centered on the adjutant, a very handsome and polished officer. Highly cultured, too. He knew four languages. Was he to be the answer to the dream that had brought Raili Kotilainen to the front?

— The Germans are advancing very fast, she said, remembering the news bulletin. —I don't think even the greatest optimists dared to hope for so much.

—Perhaps not the optimists. But the planners certainly did. The German High Command has one valuable tradition. It doesn't hope, it plans. But the Russians have one sole trump card. They're as stubborn as elephants. Let's hope stubbornness isn't enough since war's become so technical. And as technicians the Germans are supreme.

Major Sarastie was forever talking about "scientific" warfare. He had read a great deal of military literature and his mind was in tune with German thought. And his scientific approach was to some extent genuine, for he was an active thinker and liked to look at matters from an abstract angle, and to generalize. He walked with the lumbering gait of a big man. His neck and face had the ruddiness that bespeaks health and vigor, and he carried a willow switch with which he was forever rapping on his calves.

The machine gunners sitting by the roadside tried to avoid seeing him so as not to have to salute, for just ignoring the salute did not yet come naturally to them. The major, however, stopped to speak to them.

—Had your rations?

—Yes, Major. Salo rose to attention to reply.

The major knew perfectly well that the men had eaten, but under the circumstances it was a commander's duty to ask some such friendly question. He had been under a tremendous strain himself all day, the stream of reports reaching him at first auguring none too well for the outcome. Casualties had mounted and still the Russian line had remained intact. The battalion's losses were upward of a hundred killed and wounded, heavier than he would have cared to report if the road on which he now walked had not been opened. It had been, however, and therefore he spoke good-naturedly to his men.

—Good. And you've got tobacco too, I see.

—Yes, Major, replied Salo.

—Well, have a good rest. We'll need all the strength we have.

—See those hips, said Rahikainen. —Ah, what treasures those girls carry! But what can a poor private do about it? He just has to get along without any loving. That's another thing that hasn't been shared fairly. Some have more than they can use and others get nothing.

—If I was a general I'd have all that stuff put into one big whorehouse and rationed on tickets issued on paydays.

Immediately Rahikainen seized on the idea enthusiastically.

—There's good money in those tickets.

—Ha-ha! I can see Rahikainen doing business in them. But he'd be buying, not selling.

Riitaoja had arrived with his ammunition boxes in time for his rations. Blushing like a child he said:

—There were a lot of bodies beside the road at the field dressing station. Kaukonen was there. And dozens of Second Company men. The chaplain was taking off their identification tags. The shells even killed some of the horses. And the cooks lost a lot of men. One of the wounded men kept crying out: "Forgive me—Forgive me." I wonder why?

Lehto turned away from Riitaoja angrily, but the others looked at him pityingly. Such childishness did not even provoke sarcasm. They were saved from further embarrassment, as Mielonen approached, calling loudly:

—Get ready!

—Ready for what?

—To move on, of course, to move on.

—Move where? Where to?

—After the Russkies. Where'd you think. Home?

—Jesus! Are we the only battalion in the army?

—We've done our share. Let the rest do theirs. Where are all those reserve regiments we saw lying beside the road?

—I'm only a sergeant, I don't command regiments. The order came from higher up.

—That damn major must want a promotion. The son of a bitch must have begged to be put in the first wave again.

Hietanen was as angry as the rest, but he felt compelled by his position as second-in-command to smooth things over a bit.

—Get ready to die for home and country! Pick up your packs. The Finnish Bear wants to get moving again.

Lehto's section uttered not a protest as they saw him sling his rifle in silence. It was useless, they knew, to argue with him. And Hietanen, seeing that his words had provoked a smile on some faces, went on:

—Go on, get moving. What have you got to grumble about? Your bellies are full. We're Finland's revered heroes. They're going to sing songs about us to our grandchildren and their children. Isn't that worth marching to the end of the world if need be?

—You sure must want another stripe badly.

—Fall in on the road. Double file.

The sky was now overcast. Guns rumbled in the distance, and flickers of light on the dim horizon identified muzzle flashes. The first drops of rain fell as the column wound on into the deepening dusk.

Chapter IV

1.

—Watch your intervals . . . Are we still in contact on the left?

—I can see something out there.

Puffing and panting, cursing and staggering, they advanced in double file through the dark forest. The gloomy spruce and the low blanket of rain clouds made even the northern summer night dark. Water sloshed in their boots, and their wet clothes clung to them until the heat of their bodies made them steam. Weak with fatigue and hunger, swaying unsteadily, each man kept his gaze fixed on the gray phantom stumbling along in front of him. They had no thought of where they had come from or where they were going; they were too fully occupied in finding enough energy for the next step.

From somewhere came the thunder of battle, but they took no notice of it. All they hoped was that the enemy was far away and moving ever farther. All the way to Hell.

Was it possible that only twenty-four hours ago they had been in that village?

During the night they had pried the Russians from their positions, but of that clash in the darkness they retained no clear memory. The crash of grenades, the whine of bullets, muzzle flashes, cries for stretcher bearers. Not until morning did they learn that the neighboring platoon had lost a half dozen men.

They had seen a few Russian dead. Dark as it was and raining, they still stopped to take the tabs. All day they had moved forward, halting every now and again, completely unaware of what was happening all around them.

They had not eaten since yesterday. Having learned from experience that there was no telling when they would get their next meal, they had divided their bread into two parts: one to eat, one to save. Then they would break off a bit of the saved part, a little while later another bit, and soon it would be gone. Later they would ask: —Has anybody got a piece of bread? I'll give half a cigarette for it.

—I had some yesterday, but I've eaten it.

They had turned off the road into the forest in the evening and were still pushing forward, ignorant of where they were being led and for what purpose.

—Let's shift loads.

—I carried it longer than this last time.

—Christ, I'll be damned if I'll go on carrying the thing!

—Stop grousing all the time! Hand over the tripod, I'll take it. The speaker was Lehto.

A spruce branch sprang back into someone's face.

—Holy Christ, can't you be more careful, you pisshead?

—You watch your goddamn tongue!

—Think I'm going to take any shit from you?

The battle of words never led to a fight or even to bad feelings; with the disappearance of the exhaustion and nervous tension which was its cause, the quarrel was as completely forgotten as though it had not occurred.

No one thought of cursing Koskela, for he was never without a burden. While the others spelled each other, he handed back one piece of equipment only to take another man's burden, helping each of the machine-gun crews in turn. Some of the men objected to letting him carry for them, but they did not persist in their refusal for they were actually grateful for his help. And Lehto did not want to appear in a worse light, so he too carried continuously.

—Where's Number One gun's barrel?" Koskela asked.

—Maatta has it.

—Where's he?

—I saw him walking over there a minute ago.

—Keep moving. We can't stop to look for anyone.

—You've tried to keep out of Maatta's sight so you wouldn't have to take the barrel, and now you've let him get lost, growled Hietanen.

—Oh, keep your mouth shut, Sihvonen said angrily. —We've all done our share of carrying.

Prrrrrr.

A long chattering burst from a tommy gun put an end to the conversation and sent them tumbling to their knees, their hearts hammering.

—What was that?

—Russkies, what else?

—Machine guns—stations!

Wearily they dragged their weapons into position. The barrel of Number One gun was still missing, and Lahtinen wanted to go back and look for Maatta, feeling himself responsible for his disappearance. But Koskela forbade him to go.

—You'll never find anyone in these woods. The firing will tell him where we are.

The Russians were banging away perfunctorily from the darkness now, as Koskela whispered:

—We're supposed to be covering one flank of a general advance. We may have a long wait ahead of us, so we'll stand half-hour watches, and let those not on guard try to get some rest.

Guards were posted and the rest withdrew to the shelter of some tall spruce standing a short distance in the rear. Raindrops dripped from the branches and the wet blueberry bushes and ferns soaked their already sodden boots. But the sky had paled and now they could dimly see each other. They were an ugly lot: faces covered with dirt and stubble, eyes empty and expressionless, mouths grim and set. Could this still be only the fourth day of the war dawning?

They wrapped themselves in their overcoats, but the cold made sleep impossible. And each time the desultory firing grew sharper, they would start to a sitting position and look about questioningly until it slackened. Then the tenseness left their faces and they sank down again.

Soon the rain stopped and the sky became still brighter. A breeze shook little showers of water from the branches, and their wet garments collected litter from the carpet of needles under the spruce. A bird broke hesitatingly into song, and far away guns rumbled.

Rahikainen stood leaning against a tree trunk, staring at his waterlogged boots and humming softly to himself until Lehto, glancing at his watch, declared that Vanhala and Salo had to be relieved.

—Is it my turn already? asked Rahikainen.

—It sure as hell is.

—God damn, I might have known. They'd never get to Moscow without me.

Grumbling, he slung his rifle and went off with Sihvonen to the guard post. Their footsteps had hardly died away when a rustling sound came from the forest. The men seized their rifles and listened.

—Halt! Give the password!

—I've forgotten the damn thing. But I'll give you the day before yesterday's if that's any use.

—Is that you, Maatta?

—It's me. Is the gun there?

They were overjoyed to see Maatta back, although they had actually worried very little over his disappearance, knowing that he would master the situation somehow. Maatta was dripping wet but as unperturbed as ever as he stood looking around him in silence as though taking stock of how things might have changed in his absence. In general he tried to get along without asking questions, and now again he left the initiative to the others.

—Where have you been?

—Lost.

—How did you find your way here?

—I guessed where you'd be from the shooting.

Sitting under a spruce Maatta began taking off his boots. He squeezed the water from his socks before remarking casually to Koskela:

—There's a hell of a lot of Russians in the forest. Maybe we ought to let the battalion brass know. In fact, maybe we ought to take a look around ourselves.

—Where?

—Over that way a mile or so. It's hard to guess distances.

Hurriedly Koskela sent a messenger off to carry Maatta's news to headquarters, and shortly received a reply saying that the Second Company would comb that area. They felt better after that but still they kept their rifles ready. And as their tension waned, their hunger grew. Soon the talk turned again to the subject of food.

—You know I'm hungry?

—How can you be when you ate only yesterday morning?

—Jesus, how I'd like to be back in civvies!

—Civvies! I'd be satisfied with a piece of bread, and I can't even get that.

—I wonder how long the brass thinks a man can keep on his feet on the rations we're getting, said Vanhala.

Lahtinen snorted with bitter contempt.

—Think? They don't think, they know. They've counted the calories in your rations. Go complain and they'll lay the figures down in front of you to prove you can't be hungry. As a matter of fact, it'd take a bold man to complain after what they did to Isoaho.

Isoaho was a First Company private who had taken a visiting inspecting general's query as to whether anyone had any complaint, too literally. Afterwards he had been put through the mill until he was nearly driven out of his mind. Three times a day he was weighed on a scale and no sooner had he gotten back from one medical examination than he was ordered to a new one. All this plus the way the officers and NCOs picked on him made him bitterly regret that he had ever opened his mouth.

Hietanen slapped the wet knees of his trousers as he said:

—I don't know anything about calories, but my belly tells me there aren't near enough of 'em.

—Mm. Your stomach may tell you that, but do you think the brass understands what your guts say? Soldiers' bellies have been growling for so long that the brass have forgotten what the rumbles mean. Especially since their own bellies are full.

Lahtinen spoke in all seriousness, but Hietanen only burst out laughing:

—You know, boys, I've heard that you can learn to throw your voice so it sounds like it's coming from your belly. We ought to learn, so that every time the brass goes by our guts can holler "food."

Vanhala rocked with laughter. Lahtinen's attempt to indoctrinate his companions had had no more effect than on a thousand previous occasions. And his failure well illustrated the difference between grousing and revolt. The men were always ready to deride their country's upper class, but all attempts to lend political significance to their mockery met with laughter, for their criticisms were never more than half serious. Similarly they fought shy of flag waving patriotism. "Damned preacher" was how they described any Educational Officer who was prone to such talk.

Vanhala was so overcome with mirth that only with an effort could he speak:

—All our bellies talking, khee-hee! What would the brass say to that?

Lahtinen was in the vicious mood which these clashes always aroused in him. He knew he ought to hold his tongue, but his present physical misery increased his bitterness to such an extent that he went on:

—What would they say? They'd throw you in jail and give you a Bible to read so you could see that there's something holy in hunger. And you can't deny that hunger has been turned into a tradition in Finland, a tradition the rich have made the poor believe is sacred. Our army has gone into battle half-dead with hunger for six or seven hundred years, always with a bare behind showing through its rags. First it was the Swedes we had to make history for, and now it's our own gentry's turn. Rich old men and women need something to shed a few tears over, so they're glad there are poor people they can help to show their own goodness. That's the way it is with us too—if we had bread and decent clothes, where would the heroism be?

The conversation came to an end as all eyes turned toward Lehto. He had taken out his emergency ration and was busily opening the meat tin with a knife.

—Don't you know that's forbidden? demanded Hietanen.

A smile hovered on Lehto's lips.

—So's killing. The Fifth Commandment, or one of them anyway. Opening a meat can's nothing when skulls are being blown open all around us.

As one man they looked at Koskela, who had been listening in silence, as though waiting for his opinion before making up their own minds. The talk had greatly amused him, but he was a man with whom laughter never went beyond his eyes, leaving the rest of his face stolid and expressionless. Now he felt uneasy as he saw all the men looking to him for a decision for he hated making decisions of any sort for others, and this time he was faintly contemptuous of the men's inability to open their emergency rations and eat them without all this fuss. He looked away now as he said in a toneless voice:

—It's all right with me. You're not likely to get any hungrier than you are now. They say the edge goes off after the first twenty-four hours. If that's true, then this must be the emergency the ration was meant for.

He was aware not only of the lameness of his explanation but also that the men knew it to be lame. Nevertheless it served to cast a cloak of official sanction over the matter, and that was enough for Koskela.

The repast over, the men rolled themselves cigarettes of mahorka leaf and an atmosphere of content settled over them. Maatta picked his teeth with a match and when they asked him to tell them more of his adventure was only slightly more informative than usual. He belched comfortably and began slowly:

—The Devil almost got me that time.

—How did you get lost?

—I got behind, and when the line seemed to be bearing to the right, I thought I'd take a short cut. And then there I was, alone in the forest. I guess you must have turned to the left. I kept on straight ahead, though.

—And then you saw the Russkies?

—Yes, I heard noises so I thought I'd take a look to see who it was. Then I saw them, about a dozen of 'em. I was so surprised that I'd called out "Hello, boys" before I noticed their helmets. They hollered something, but I didn't feel like stopping to answer. I just ran like a rabbit. They took a few shots at me, but I was dodging and twisting, and they missed.

—Damn it, we shouldn't be making so much noise. For all we know there might be more of 'em roaming around.

2.

—Down, everybody!

Koskela drew his pistol and signaled with it that someone was approaching. The men cautiously worked the bolts of their rifles, and the barrels swung in the direction Koskela's pistol was pointing.

—Open order. Advance silently.

They crept forward from tree to tree. A twig breaking under a man's foot sounded like an explosion and provoked angry head-shakings. Then a shot rang out.

—What was that?

—There he goes.

A brown-clad figure dashed toward a tree for shelter. He tripped and fell, but was up at once and dodged behind another tree.

—*Ruki veer! Ruki veer!*

Hesitatingly the Russian emerged from behind the tree with his hands up, his glance fleeting from face to face as he took a few steps forward. The dirt on his face could not conceal his extreme pallor, and although his eyes rested in turn on the faces of those nearest to him, he seemed to see nothing. He was obviously frightened half to death as he stepped forward expecting to be killed yet hoping that by some miracle he might yet be spared.

—Search the bushes. There may be more of 'em.

They found no one, however, and were soon gathered around the prisoner who had calmed down noticeably. Though he still kept his trembling hands raised, he tried to smile as if seeking instinctively to win over his captors. He looked about thirty and his face bore the same signs of fatigue and hardship as their own. He was dressed in a brown blouse and breeches and wore laced boots and black leggings.

—His belt's only canvas.

—You'd think they could do better than that.

—Any other *tavaritsi* about?

The prisoner shook his head.

—*Tavaritsi, tavaritsi. Panimai?* Are there any more of you? Don't you *panimai?*

—*Niet tavarits,* the man muttered indistinctly.

—Anything in your pocket? Pocket, *vintovka*. This, see, *vintovka*.

—Why ask him? Look, said Lehto and began to search the man's pockets. He found a hand grenade in one of the pockets of the prisoner's blouse.

—Jesus, what was this for?

—Going to blow yourself up?

—He's not that kind, can't you see that? said Koskela. —It takes a different sort of man to do a thing like that. Of course he'd have a hand grenade. Haven't we?

—Where are we going to put him?

—I guess he has to be, taken to the CP. Koskela looked inquiringly at the men. —Who'll take him?

—I will, said Lehto. —Let's get going.

Lehto signed to the prisoner who, hesitantly, as if afraid he might have misunderstood, set off at a walk. Lehto walked behind him, his rifle ready, and the others turned to go back to their resting places. But Lehto and his prisoner were hardly out of sight when a shot rang out from the direction in which they had gone. It was followed immediately by an anguished cry and a second shot. Startled, they all rushed to the scene. The prisoner lay face down on the ground and Lehto was calmly ejecting an empty shell from the breech of his rifle.

—What did he do?

—Died. Lehto's lips were two thin lines.

—Did he try to escape?

—He tried.

Koskela cast a suspicious glance at Lehto, and although his voice was not directly accusing, his meaning was clear as he said:

—That wasn't necessary, you know. He wasn't one of the bad ones.

Lehto laughed with the grating note that always jarred on their nerves. —Hell, who's going to sort them out?

—You shot him in the back, Hietanen said angrily. —He wasn't trying to get away. Hietanen had been shaken by the prisoner's cry for, simple man that he was, he had warmed to the prisoner's frightened smile. The Russian had really been a human being to him, not an animal to be casually shot without any pangs of conscience.

—In the back, the infuriated Lehto snarled. —It's just as good as from in front. He's better off this way. Go on, cry, God damn you. Say a prayer for him.

Riitaoja withdrew trembling to a distance. He could not bear to look at the body with the two bullet holes between the shoulders. But Hietanen had turned his back on Lehto:

—All right, shoot the lot of them for all I care. I'm not the Provost Marshal. But that man had suffered enough already.

—Why all the fuss about one man? Lahtinen let his glance range over them. —Over there a man pulls a lanyard, and three miles away another man gets his head blown off by a shell without being able to do a thing to avoid it. That's war. But you mustn't shoot an unarmed man! That's all a pile of shit. War's so senseless in itself that it's insane to make it even more idiotic with a lot of polite rules.

—All right, let's get back.

For the first time they detected a note of irritation in Koskela's voice as he walked away. Some of the men blamed it on Lehto, others on Lahtinen, but actually Koskela's anger was directed at all of them. The incident had aroused feelings in him he thought he had buried for good in the snow of the Winter War. To keep his peace of mind he had thrust the thought of death, his own as well as that of others, from his mind. The resultant inner peace he had guarded jealously, but now he had allowed it to be touched and his sense of security was shaken. War had not hardened him to the extent that deep in his mind he did not recognize its senselessness. He fought better than the great majority of soldiers, but something within him would not countenance unnecessary killing. He had tried always to do his duty and forget war's insanity, and now he had been reminded that he could not forget. So he strode along rapidly, keeping well ahead of his men, wanting to be alone. Gradually, however, as the shock wore off he became his usual self. The senselessness of Lehto's deed which he had felt more than the others ceased to trouble him within a few minutes.

Nevertheless, for a time all the men's spirits were at low ebb, while Lehto was sullen and, if anyone happened to catch his eye, stared back in aggressive defiance. Then without being told, he went to relieve the guards, whose tour of duty had been prolonged by the recent incident. Ignoring the bullets that still occasionally whistled through the forest, he stood erect behind the machine gun, drawing fiercely at his cigarette. Even when Kariluoto called to him to take cover, his answer was only a contemptuous smile.

Rahikainen and Sihvonen joined the others after they had been relieved.

—You've been at your emergency rations while we've been away, Rahikainen accused at once.

—Well, go ahead and eat yours.

—I did, while we were still on our side of the frontier.

—We should have guessed that.

—Why didn't you, then? Who shot the Russian?

—Lehto.

—That'll teach them to try to get away.

—But this one was half scared to death, said Hietanen to whom the prisoner's obvious fright evidently dictated the humanity with which he should have been treated.

—Of course he was scared, said Salo. —Don't they tell them they'll be shot if they surrender?

—Well, wasn't he? He had a reason to be frightened, offered Rahikainen.

One after another they burst into laughter as they grasped his grim humor.

Their laughter was interrupted as Lehto returned to tell them that the infantry were moving on and that they too had to leave at once.

—Pack up, said Koskela, leading the way to their positions. The men followed and began at once to gather up their possessions. Their inoculation against humanity had proceeded one step further.

3.

The rain clouds dispersed swiftly and a golden brilliance lit the gray dawn as the sun broke through the clouds. The wet forest glittered, and although the grass still held so much moisture that moving through it was like wading in water up to their knees, walking became a pleasure. In the warm sunshine the moisture soon evaporated from their clothes, and the beautiful summer morning drove from their minds the gloom left by the rainy, wearisome night. Now and then they heard shots, and from far off came the humming of a motor.

—There's a road up ahead, boys.

—*Ruki veer, iti suta. Iti suta.*

A man stepped out of the bushes carrying a white rag, and then others followed until there were a score of men in sight. They belonged to the same broken units wandering lost in the forest as had the prisoner Lehto had shot and the men Maatta had seen. From their surrender the men, little though they knew of the overall situation, gathered that something decisive had happened. The enemy must have been driven back, for during the night the sounds of gunfire had receded until it seemed very far ahead.

They reached the road and stepped out on it cautiously, still not convinced that it was safe. The sun had already dried the road's surface, which was scarred by the treads of caterpillar tracks. And no sooner were they on the road than a bicycle troop rode up from the direction of the frontier.

—What regiment are you? Rahikainen demanded.

—Jaeger Battalion. Are the Russkies far off?

—There's a bunch of them over under those trees.

—Don't be funny. Where's your company commander?

The steel-helmeted Jaeger lieutenant dismounted, his helmet, the rolled-up sleeves of his blouse and the tommy gun hanging from his neck making him look very military. His men, too, were completely unlike the disreputable-looking infantry, and, indeed, seemed themselves to think that they were some kind of elite troops.

Soon Kariluoto came hastening to the scene, and gave the lieutenant an enthusiastic salute.

—What's the news? What's your objective?

—Lake Onega, eventually. But right now it's a place called Loimola. Are you the company commander? I was told I'd find your regiment hereabouts and ordered to contact you.

—No, I'm not, but you'll find him around that corner with the other platoon.

Kariluoto was in a very good humor, and felt strangely friendly toward this lieutenant whom he had never seen before. This morning was one of the happiest of his life. He knew that the Russian defenses had been breached and that the advance into Karelia was under way. As a result, he fired off such a stream of questions that he failed to notice how somber the lieutenant was. But ignoring his reticence, Kariluoto tried to imbue him with some of his own enthusiasm.

The Jaegers leaned on their bicycles, eying the infantrymen lining the road. And soon Rahikainen went over to see whether anything was to be had.

—You've got no use for field kitchens, I see.

—What do you mean?

—You've all got your own pots on your head.

—Haven't they given you helmets?

—Hell, all we've got are empty stomachs. I'll bet you've even got bread.

—A little. We drew rations last night before we left.

Rahikainen fished in his pocketbook.

—How many pieces of bread will you give for a Russky badge?

A Jaeger thrust his hand into his pocket and brought out a handful of red stars.

—What do you think we are? Recruits?

—That's some handful. But how about an officer's tabs? How much for them?

—I've got plenty of my own. The triangular ones.

—Bah. They're only noncoms badges.

—I'll trade you two triangles for one officer's.

—No you won't. What's an NCO compared to an officer? But throw in three pieces of hardtack and it's a deal.

—I'll give you two.

—Show them to me.

The Jaeger drew a piece of hardtack from his pouch.

—Thin stuff, Rahikainen said disparagingly, pretending to lose interest in the matter. It'll take three pieces of that at least.

—All right, hand it over.

After the exchange had been made, Rahikainen stood staring at the bread as though regretting the trade.

—I let it go too cheaply. Oh well, worrying won't help. I'll just have to get me some more.

Now the men were questioning each other about their battle experiences.

—Where were you?

—Over there. We broke through a bunker line.

—There were the same kind of bunkers across our road, too.

Lahtinen hauled himself up to a sitting position on the side of the ditch and, eying the Jaegers as though to measure the effect of his words, began to speak:

—They talk about the miserable life of the Russian people, but so far we've had to kill nearly all we've met in their holes. They're a tough lot—at least, those we've had to deal with.

The Jaegers, for their part, gave no sign of disputing his opinion, but Rahikainen saw a chance to brag about his exploits and at the same time turn the tables on Lahtinen.

—It wouldn't matter so much if you only had to kill 'em once, he said. —We've been fighting the kind you have to kill twice. That shows how tough they are. But any poor cat's said to have nine lives, although I can't guarantee it to be true.

The Jaegers took up the challenge, and a battle of wits began. They joked and laughed, and soon some of them were giving away part of their bread for nothing. But they could afford to do so at the moment, having just received their rations for the next few days. So the men's spirits revived in the morning sunshine. It had only taken a few days to teach them the value of casting off all worries during any brief halt on such a fine, fresh summer morning. Minutes become precious when each hour may be one's last.

When their lieutenant returned and gave the order to mount, the Jaegers faces turned grave again. Adjusting their equipment, they waited in silence for the order to move on.

—All right, let's go.

The cyclists moved off and soon other troops were streaming past. Cyclists, tanks, mechanized artillery.

Kariluoto watched, delighted. It was almost like watching German elite units. Why hadn't his regiment been issued helmets? What strength they lent to the face! And yet Kariluoto knew that if his men had had steel helmets, last night they would all have been hurled into the forest. To be an officer in the Finnish Army, the best army in the world, was something to be proud of, but it had its drawbacks. There was little or no military spirit. That was not quite true of the Jaegers who had just passed, but certainly his own men were far slacker. And the reservist regiments were even worse. The sunlit road stretched invitingly ahead into Karelia. But where were the disciplined iron-gray ranks of Storm Troops? That was what Kariluoto longed to see that morning—the colors of his beloved country borne onward by speeding detachments of an army as hard as steel, an army marching in perfectly closed ranks or rattling past him on heavy wheels.

Instead he saw a band of ragamuffins absorbed, like a bunch of foodtramps, in puzzling out means of cadging a little more food—

men who cursed and complained and joked at the most sacred things. They did not even stop at poking fun at the noble and stirring language of the Marshal's Orders of the Day. They were almost as bad as Communists—gobbling their emergency rations the first time they happened to be a little bit hungrier than usual, and forever singing filthy songs.

Streaming along the road now were infantrymen as the high common troops poured more and more through the breach in the Russian defenses. Most of them were reservists, proof that Finland was trying her utmost. Worn and bent laborers, keeping up only with difficulty, their faces showed their agony. Kariluoto noted their downcast appearance but was not disheartened. On the contrary—this was a nation in arms.

Kariluoto no longer bothered to write letters to the families of those who were killed. As the war ate deeper into his sensibilities, gestures of this sort seemed less important. This morning, however, his former idealism was again in full tide. He drew himself erect, straightened his blouse and strode toward his men. In spite of his fatigue his step was elastic.

Jalmari Lahti, unskilled laborer by profession, marched among his comrades, his unshaven face deeply furrowed by fatigue. He did not even have the energy to be bitter, all he felt was a hopeless weariness. The ditch-digging job he had been working on was still unfinished, and although the farmer had promised to give his wife the money, it would be a miracle if the old skinflint paid honestly for the ditch he had dug. And who was to cut the hay? Even if someone could be found to do it, there wasn't any money to pay him. —What possessed me to take along that eighty marks when I didn't really need them? If only the boys would help their mother—but then, what could the brats do to help? The oldest was already in the army—a Jaeger, riding along this very road to Lake Ladoga. Or at least, that was what old Lahti believed. Actually the boy had ceased to be a Jaeger two hours ago. A direct hit by a shell from a tank hiding behind a bend in the road had made a tangled mess of youth and cycle. This, however, Lahti did not know. Becoming conscious that the men around him were not members of his platoon, he hobbled on faster, cursing because he never seemed able to keep up with the others. And that old pain in his back was coming on again.

Shock troops on the march.

4.

Between the new troops the First Battalion marched up to rejoin the rest of the regiment which had been sent forward along another road. It seemed strange to the men to catch up with the regiment after having left it behind, but there it was at a crossroads about a mile ahead of where they had been. During the past three days of fighting they had had very little idea of what was happening beyond their immediate surroundings. But now they heard vague reports that the Russian defenses had collapsed completely. That very morning Jaeger units and the division that had been next to them had penetrated deep into the enemy's rear. They were glad to hear this, believing that now they would be allowed to rest out of the lines as a reward for three days of ceaseless effort. And the sight of their own field kitchen aroused almost the same rapture in them as Kariluoto had felt at the sight of the advancing Jaegers.

—What are we eating?

—Grits.

—Suffering Christ!

Grits was a porridge of wheat grain boiled whole which the men hated but often had to eat. Once again the cooks and Makila had to take the blame for their country's poverty and the army's primitive supply system. The language the men used was so filthy that Sergeant Korsumaki almost lost his temper. Realizing, however, that there was more than a little justification for the men's indignation, he tried to console them with the news that their cigarette rations had at last arrived. They would also be receiving their pay—and at the increased rate that reservists were getting, a raise dating from the date of mobilization.

—That's good news, boys, said Hietanen. —And they're sure to keep us in reserve for a while. They ought to be able to do without us, with all that bunch we saw going up.

—You'll see. When they get stuck, we'll be thrown into the line, said Lahtinen. —That's why good troops are always left in reserve. —Christ! You mean you really think we're good troops? I never thought you'd admit it.

—Well, I do. We're young and we'll go wherever any pisshead tells us. You can't trust those reservists with any important job that comes along. And there's no getting away from the fact that if we're in as bad shape as the condition of those reservists indicates, we shouldn't be trying to make a Great Power of ourselves. They've scraped up every man who can walk and drag a rifle. If you want to see the real heroes, go have a good look over by the roadside. That's where they are, though they don't look so wonderful to me.

Sihvonen pointed to the prisoners, and Salo went even further:

—They've got belts made out of threshing-machine belting. And leggings of sackcloth dyed black. And they've been driven into battle by force.

Lahtinen stretched out on his back.

—I don't know. Let's hope all goes well. But you don't fight with belts. I mean, they're tough and to me they don't seem to be fighting against their will.

—You sure ought to be on the other side, Lahtinen, said Hietanen with a mischievous smile. —If I found all this as hard to stomach as you, I wouldn't be here grousing about everything. I'd go over to the Russians and give us hell. But Lahtinen's a radical. He wants to give everybody land and money so no one would have to work for more than what he needs to feed his own face. That's what a radical is. Christ, sometimes I'm surprised at how much I know! Why, I even know all about radicals.

Vanhala laughed and thus set them all laughing, except for Lahtinen, who turned his back on them in disgust.

They disliked the porridge of grits so much that in spite of their raging hunger enough of it was left over for the prisoners to be fed. Huddled close together on the ground, the Russians took turns eating, for many of them lacked eating utensils. Those waiting their turn watched with hungry eyes while their comrades ate, and a ring of curious onlookers soon formed around them.

—See them putting that slop away, a man said.

—They must be starving, said Salo, who had come up for a sight of the Russians.

One of the prisoners, a fair-haired youngster, smiled and said suddenly in Finnish: —Three days without food.

—You speak Finnish?

—Sure. Good, pure Finnish. I'm from Ingria. A place called Raapyva.

—But how is it you speak Finnish?

—Why shouldn't I? My mother hardly knew a word of Russian.

More questions were fired at the man than he could answer at once. Gesticulating and grimacing, he described how the company he belonged to had been dispersed. A second lieutenant had collected all the stragglers he could find, intending to lead them through the woods to a road. But in an encounter during the night the officer had been killed, and not knowing where their own forces were they had surrendered.

—But weren't all the Ingrians taken to Siberia and put into prison camps?

—Why should we have been? We hadn't done anything wrong.

—Is life better in Russia than in Finland?

—How would I know that? I've never lived in Finland.

—Have you ever seen Stalin?

The man spread out his arms. Then he said something to the other prisoners in Russian. They nodded slyly to each other, and one of them struck the earth with a stone.

—Stalin, Stalin, he said, pointing to the earth at which he was striking.

—Go and blow them all to Hell, said the Ingrian. —We were forced into the army.

No one except Salo was taken in by this clumsy attempt at deception. One man asked what they called Finns, and after a moment's hesitation the Ingrian said: —*Tshuhna,* and set all his comrades laughing. Vanhala laughed with them, shaking all over. He repeated the name to himself over and over again, sizing up his companions as though to see how the name fitted them. Suhna. Suhna. Hee-hee . . .

When the prisoners realized that the word could freely be laughed at, they gave way to mirth, repeating the word and nodding their heads. —*Tshuhna. Tshuhna.*

—*Russki, Russki,* countered Rahikainen, who had just come up.

The men were so elated at the thought of being left in reserve that they couldn't sleep, tired though they were. —There'll be time for that later, they had been told. The blow was therefore all the more stunning when Mielonen went through the bivouac area shouting for them to prepare to move out.

—Don't screech, you bastard.

—Won't someone kill that son of a bitch!

—Fall in on the road. Double file.

—Let's go. Forward, double time, march!

Chapter V

1.

They marched on for day after beautiful day through Karelian villages with yards full of summer flowers. A blue mirage shimmered on the horizon, and the muted rumble of artillery came from somewhere far away, while the humming of invisible aircraft was borne to them on the air. High up in the deep blue sky battles were fought, the distant rattle of machine guns coming to them like the chattering of insects on a hot summer night.

—They're ours, they heard an officer say as they watched fighter aircraft skim along the horizon. —Covering the advance . . . The Russkies aren't finding things as easy as in the Winter War.

The men, however, no longer cared about the Winter War, or this one either. Their feet full of blisters, exhausted and irritable, they dragged themselves onward with little thought of what was going on around them. The first day they had been full of lusty enthusiasm and a spirit of adventure. Then fatigue had come to dull their senses.

This was an army whose individualism had never been equaled. Other armies may on occasion have resembled it while retreating in headlong flight, but never at any other time. Advancing or retreating, it looked the same, moving like a scattered horde. In the morning the companies formed in a column, but an hour or two later they had disintegrated into separate little gangs making their way along the road in their own fashion, asking nothing of anyone and listening to no one. Rifles they carried any which way. One man would stroll along the roadside grass in his bare feet, his boots slung across his shoulder. Another sunbathed as he marched, the upper part of his body bare, his blouse under his arm. On the first day of the march some men had carried not only their packs but also many extra objects picked up on the battlefield or in the villages as souvenirs.

By the second day these were all lying in the ditches along with many necessary articles. The officers even had to take back the men's gasmasks for fear they would otherwise be thrown away. And always they searched for food wherever they scented a possibility that some might be found. In the village there had been a pig-breeding collective whose stock had been let loose. An automatic rifle had proved to be an admirable weapon for a pig hunt, but only the first companies to arrive had enjoyed an unexpected ration of pork, for the pigs were soon under official lock and key.

Some of the villages had still been inhabited. There were floral arches in the lanes, and decorations fashioned of moss and stones everywhere.

—What are all the decorations for?

—Some kind of harvest festival.

Few things failed to arouse their ire. Cars drove past carrying laughing Lottas and officers of the comet's tail of staffs, canteens, laundries, hospitals, etc., that follows any army. They grimaced at the cars, the epithets hurled at the Lottas would have made most women drop dead of shock, and a general's car stirred up a storm of fury and invective that would have made a stranger think that tomorrow at the latest the army would be in open revolt.

—That's it, blow dust in our eyes, you bastards! There's no gasoline shortage when you and your whore want to go for a ride.

Parish after parish was left behind. By every road Finnish troops were streaming into Ladoga-Karelia. Dust clouds hung in the air overhead mingling with the blue smoke of forest fires, and through the smog the sun shone hot and red. And men in other places, in other lands, men whose feet were not blistered, whose collarbones were not frayed by pack straps, rejoiced wholeheartedly: The Finns were on the march. They were taming the Russian Bear.

2.

Lehto, Maatta and Rahikainen did little marching. Every morning they dropped out of the column, and every evening they turned up again, having gotten a ride from some passing convoy. They were reticent about what they had been doing all day, but the others could easily guess. However, they brought food with them every evening, and so long as they shared it no one saw any reason to complain about the ease with which they were making the march.

Then one evening Rahikainen showed up looking more pleased than usual.

—Lehto has a pound of butter and a sack of flour in his pack. We're going to have pancakes.

—God, it can't be true!

—Let's see it.

—God bless them, it's true, boys.

—Get a fire going!

They forgot their fatigue as they fried the batter in mess-tin lids and ate the pancakes while the silence of the summer night descended on the world. The sun, a red ball, sank behind the Karelian forest, and a blue mist softened the rough contours of the landscape.

—Take it easy. Don't just gobble them down. Let me tell you, they weren't easy to come by. It took eight different trades before the last one brought this. Why, at one time I had a bottle of vodka and didn't drink . . .

—You'd have drunk it if I'd let you, interrupted Lehto, thus disclosing whom the platoon had to thank for the provisions they had been getting.

And still the march continued.

—All right, boys, here we go again.

Koskela scrambled to his feet, slinging his pack on his back. Slowly, cursing and muttering, the others rose from the ditch in which they had been lying with their feet propped up on the bank. Using their rifles as crutches, they limped the few steps necessary to make the blood return to their feet. But nothing seemed to bother Koskela. Hour after hour, always at the same pace, he led the way.

—Learn to walk right, he told them. —Don't stride along all stiff and tense. Each step has to be loose and effortless, the way a tramp walks. It may look as though you were loafing, but it's far less tiring. Swing your legs from your hips.

Riitaoja brought up the rear, silent but childishly happy not to be under fire. He would have been willing to march to eternity, enduring any fatigue, if it meant he would never have to hear the spiteful whistles of Death seeking its victims again.

On the afternoon of the fifth day they began to notice that the road had begun to deteriorate. Before long it had become a mere forest track, and soon afterwards they arrived at a strip of land which had been cleared of all trees.

—Hey, it's the old frontier!

The news swept down the line, cheering the men visibly. Hietanen, from his place in the column, called out:

—We're in Russia, lads!

But Lahtinen, limping along sullenly, glowered at the others:

—So we are. And we've got no right to be here. We're no better than a bunch of bandits.

—Bandits! snapped Sihvonen. —When we cross a frontier we're bandits. When the Russkies do, they're taking measures for their security. Bandits . . . Hah!

Hietanen was busily examining their surroundings.

—There doesn't seem to be much worth stealing. Even the road's not as good as on our side. But the forest looks the same . . . You know, boys, this part of Karelia is supposed to be a land of song.

—There'll be cause for plenty of sad songs over here. Lahtinen took a swig of water from his canteen: —From now on we're on Russian soil, so they'll really try to stop us. I think up to now they just figured, well, since you're always crying about it, take back that little bit of Karelia and welcome. But you know what happens when you go poking a bear in its lair. . . .

—Not if you have a rifle to defend yourself with, said Salo. —We aren't depending on spears this time.

—Hah . . . You and your rifles . . . a lot of use they're going to be. . . .

—And there's lots of other troops ahead of us. We won't be thrown right back into the front lines.

—You know, we may have done our share already, suggested Salo. —A sergeant told me the reservists had been told it would all be over in three weeks and they'd be back home in time for haymaking. And more than a week is gone already.

Lahtinen laughed in savage contempt. —Latest bulletin from the Latrine News Agency. The brass launched that rumor because the reservists groused at crossing the old frontier. I know them. We're out here to build a Greater Finland. The government's so hot about it you can see the steam coming out their ears.

The flicker of interest the old frontier had aroused died out and they plodded on in silence. To their surprise the march came to an end that day earlier than they had expected, and they camped on the bank of a brush-covered brook. After they had eaten they rushed to bathe their feet in the cool water. A few even tried to swim though the water came only up to their knees. Somewhere ahead guns were booming again, and through the reverberations now and again the faint yammer of machine guns could be distinguished.

—Here we go again, boys. They're expecting us.

—Of course they are. To open up the road. Sihvonen was washing his socks, standing in the brook with his trousers rolled up. —And there comes that turd, God knows what for.

Lieutenant Lammio was walking toward the camp site. He had had time to wash himself and put on a clean uniform. Then, knowing that the regiment would be resting for a while, he had decided to utilize the interval to improve the low standard of discipline in his company. For Lammio felt that discipline was the backbone of an army and that only by maintaining discipline could a commander win the respect of his men. His ideal officer was a well-groomed, white-gloved professional soldier who led his men with cool courage and pride, and whom his men humbly admired and obeyed out of respect. This ideal officer would himself be a shining example of military obedience.

There was a Divisional H.Q. in the neighborhood with some pretty Lottas, and thus Lammio now wore a clean shirt under his blouse. He came to a halt, tapped his cigarette holder with his forefinger to shake off the ash, and began shrilly:

—Now listen to me. The sergeant major will be giving you your pay, so keep inside the camp area. And after that remember no one is allowed to leave the camp without a pass. I suggest you take the opportunity to wash your clothes in the brook, have your hair cut and shave yourselves. I don't want to see a man looking untidy after noon tomorrow. Another thing. The fact that we're at war doesn't justify any relaxing of discipline. I want no repetition of the things that occurred the past few days. You looked more like a bunch of tramps than an army unit. I don't hold with the idea that veterans can be as sloppy as they like and I will not tolerate any such attitude. This regiment has played a decisive part in the corps' operations and we've earned a reputation already, and I want every man to see that he behaves in a manner in keeping with that reputation. And let me warn you that if any complaint is made about your behavior, I'll make you regret it. I hope I've made myself clear to every one of you? All right then, carry on.

Hietanen sat on a rock, soaking his feet in the brook. All the time Lammio was speaking he had been watching his comrades, and now that Lammio had gone, he spoke out:

—I trust you all heard those fine sentiments? I only hope you understood them.

Hietanen feigned seriousness and stared disapprovingly at Lahtinen who glared back at him contemptuously:

—He meant be like the Germans. But what it really shows is that the fool has lost whatever brains he used to have.

—Wash clothes, hah! . . . Can't you see us washing clothes between battles. A Finnish soldier has to possess many skills.

Vanhala laughed, then turning serious, pointed behind them:

—Look!

They turned their heads in the direction of his finger just in time to see Lehto, Maatta and Rahikainen jump out of a truck that had stopped on the road.

—By God, they're caught this time! said Hietanen, waving his arms to attract their attention. Unable to shout it, he tried to convey a warning by gestures.

The three comrades saw their peril too late. Always, before, they had ridden a little past the camp and then approached it through the forest. Success, however, had made them careless, and now they found themselves, incriminating cardboard cartons under their arms, face to face with Lammio.

The lieutenant paused for effect before asking:

—Who gave you permission to ride in that truck?

—No one, said Lehto. Seeing no escape from their dilemma he saw no reason not to be his usual surly self.

—What's in those cartons?

None of the three made any attempt to reply until Rahikainen, realizing that the others were not going to speak, said:

—Why, just crackers . . . and jam.

—And where did you steal it?

Rahikainen smiled innocently. —We didn't need to steal them. There's a depot down the road manned by some lads from my village, and they gave us this stuff.

—You're lying. And for that matter, you had no right to accept government food in addition to your rations. Do you mean to tell me you didn't know they had no right to give you food?

Rahikainen still feigned ignorance. —Maybe they had no right.

But when they gave it to me without my asking, I thought, well, they must know what they're doing.

—Don't try to excuse yourself. Are you stupid enough to think I'll believe that stuff? Lehto, don't you know that you're not allowed to leave the company without permission?

—Yes.

—Well I'll be damned! You certainly must think well of yourself. What if I turn you over to a court-martial? You'll lose your stripes and spend six months at hard labor. Or what did you think would happen?

—It's no use asking me. I should think a lieutenant ought to know such things without any help.

In the mood Lehto was in he would have let himself be cut to pieces rather than grovel. Lammio's tone had wounded him to the very depths of his soul, and from that moment on Lehto felt nothing for Lammio except implacable hatred. Up to now his attitude toward the lieutenant had been one of cold contempt, but now he gritted his teeth and only Lammio's inability to read another man's mind prevented his realizing the peril he was in.

—By God . . . !

Lammio was about to start shouting when he remembered that a good officer would never do that but would always act with cold correctness. So instead he called in his most official voice:
—Lieutenant Koskela.

—Yes . . . ?

Koskela emerged from his tent, and Lammio began to reel off the punishment the culprits were to undergo in a voice intended to indicate to Koskela that it was all his fault since he had not maintained better discipline in his platoon.

—Sergeant Lehto and Privates Maatta and Rahikainen are each sentenced to twenty-four hours close arrest. The punishment is transmuted to two hours at attention with rifle and full field pack beginning on the next hour. Reason: absence without leave from a company on the march, theft of food and, in the case of Sergeant Lehto, insubordination to a superior officer. Have you got that?

—I've got it, said Koskela, withdrawing into his tent so that Lammio had to shout after him:

—The stolen provisions are to be given to Makila to forward to the battalion's stores.

Lammio stamped off and the three convicted criminals followed

Koskela into the tent. Inside Lehto threw himself on the ground angrily:

—I can't see myself standing for two hours.

Koskela was embarrassed, and as he always did when he was, he cleared his throat noisily, before speaking.

—Well, I'm not casting judgment, but I think it might be best if you did that standing.

—By God, I'm not afraid of that shrimp . . . They can stand me up against a wall for all I care.

Lehto was livid: —I hope he never knows how close he was to landing in a hospital and me in a prison.

Koskela busied himself with his pack. —It's not a question of being afraid or not. It's just the easiest way out.

—All right then, I'll stand for a couple of hours. But I sure as hell won't put anything in my pack. And if that bastard ever has the bad luck to run into me again, I'll knock his teeth down his throat whatever it may mean for me.

—The packs don't matter. The main thing is the standing. But I'll have to send that grub to Makila.

—Not all of it, said Rahikainen. —He never thought of looking to see how much there was, so we can leave a little in the bottom of each box and eat the rest. I lay waiting for a good half hour with my heart in my mouth before I got a chance to get at it, and the damn sentry almost shot me. I'm not going to stand at attention two hours for nothing.

Less than a third of the food was finally sent to Makila. But Koskela, though he did not interfere, refused to accept a share.

3.

The sergeant major doled out their pay, and groups of men went wandering off to gamble as soon as they got their money, for the first time at the new higher scale. The three delinquents, anxious to start their punishment so as to get it over with, were near the head of the line, and Korsumaki grinned at them.

—At least you don't have to worry, about keeping it in your pockets for a couple of hours.

Hietanen had been ordered to supervise the carrying out of the sentence and he started them on their way, although Rahikainen kept eying all the men with their pay longingly. The other two were already on their way when Rahikainen finally followed, dragging his rifle behind him. Hietanen led them some distance away from the camp, for they had no intention of obeying the order to the letter. Then the three culprits lined up.

—You certainly look handsome standing there, said Hietanen, settling himself on a boulder for a smoke. —Stay there a while, but we're not going to waste two hours. The lieutenant went to HQ for a look at the Lottas and Koskela'll be asleep soon.

—All right. But who do you think Lehto is, putting him in the middle. Jesus? He's the one who tempted us. Enticing two innocent, inexperienced soldiers into a life of crime.

They were barely at attention, having discovered that by resting the butts of their rifles on their belts they could keep them up without having the weight on their arms. Hietanen was a sympathetic observer, for although he was usually inclined to submit to discipline he had once suffered the same punishment. While still a recruit he had flared up at a corporal who had bullied him too much, and taking the man's nose between his forefinger and thumb had given it such a twist that the cartilage broke.

They had kept up this pretense for half an hour when a low humming began to be heard in the east. The sound grew, and soon they could make out black specks in the sky.

—Bombers.

—Maybe they're ours.

—Coming from the east. No . . . one, two, three, four . . . by God, boys—eighteen! Ours don't fly in such big formations. There's more . . . nine fighters behind 'em for protection.

The humming swelled, the motors roaring with a rich organlike sound above which, however, could be distinguished a regular beat: vow, vow, vow, vow.

—They're Ivan's . . . there goes the flak.

They heard the knock of the light anti-aircraft guns, but their red tracers fell far behind.

From the camp came cries: —Air raid! . . . Shelter.

Koskela, popping out of his tent, shouted to Hietenan:

—Take cover!

—Into the woods! Hietanen cried to his charges, but Lehto remained standing:

—I'm not going anywhere. I'm undergoing punishment.

Hietanen smiled at first, thinking Lehto was joking. Then he saw that he was in earnest.

—Don't be crazier than you are, said Rahikainen, nervously eying the bombers.

Lehto didn't even glance at the sky.

—If you're so damned afraid, go ahead. I'm staying.

—I don't mind staying either, said Maatta, making things difficult for Rahikainen who was not of the stuff of which heroes are made. Nevertheless, though darting fearful glances at the sky, he said:

—All right then, we'll all hang together.

—Don't be crazy, what's the sense of this? said Hietanen, eying the approaching peril.

—Ask Lammio, said Lehto. —This isn't my idea.

—Do you think I'm such an oaf that I can't see what you're aiming at? You want the guard to run off and leave you standing here. Well, if you stay, I stay too . . . hey, look at that! I saw the bombs start falling. . . . By God, that'll put a stop to any clothes-washing.

The roar of dozens of motors set the air quivering. The bombers glittered in the evening sun and the men could clearly see the bombs as they began their descent. The first had already hit with resounding crashes, and pillars of smoke and soil rose above the treetops.

—This next lot's for us. They're headed this way.

The bombers were overhead now except for the last flight which was a little behind. They knew that by the time it reached them the bombs would be exploding. An ear-piercing screech grew to a crescendo.

—Stay where you are . . . don't run! shouted Lehto, pale but determined. As the screech grew louder, Rahikainen pulled his head between his shoulders and screamed.

The first bombs burst on the other side of the road. Then came a whole series of tremendous crashes followed by blasts of air which nearly knocked them flat. The nearest bomb, however, fell a safe distance away among the tents. As it exploded Rahikainen fell to the ground, but he was up so quickly that in their breathless excitement the others hardly noticed it. They were white-faced, but as soon as they realized that the last bomb had fallen and they were still unhurt, a smile spread over their faces.

Abruptly the smiles faded. The fighters had begun to strafe the forest as though trying to sow lead in the furrows ploughed by the bombers. At the same time confused cries came from the tents:

—Help, somebody . . . help me! Jesus, help . . . I'm dying . . . help me . . .

The cry was drowned in the crackle of machine guns and the roaring of motors. Lehto's face was grim.

—Don't move . . . not until our time's up. . . .

Actually they were not in great peril, for the fighters were shooting up the road, which was some distance away.

—Somebody's hit . . . we ought to go help, suggested Hietanen. But still Lehto refused. —Well then, by God, I'll go alone, said Hietanen and set off at a run toward the tents. Rahikainen and Maatta would have followed, but Lehto restrained them.

—Why trouble yourselves for nothing? We've got to finish out our time . . . Hietanen'll do whatever can be done. There's Koskela, too, and the stretcher bearers are coming up the road.

They stayed, for the last fighter had gone and a number of men were running toward the tents.

—Wonder who it was, said Rahikainen. —It sounded like Salonen's voice. . . . Hell, you talked me into this damned foolishness . . . for the first and last time.

Lehto laughed harshly. He had gained revenge, and they could do nothing to him. Death was the worst they could inflict on him, and he was not afraid of that.

Now that it was over Rahikainen tried to pretend that he had not weakened halfway through. He essayed a joke in his usual manner:

—We'll see what class Liberty Crosses we get when the bastards hear of our heroism. Hietanen deserves oak leaves with his for staying with us when he wasn't being punished.

In the camp, card and clothes-washing parties had quickly broken up when the aircraft were identified as Russian. Koskela had ordered everybody into the forest, but a few men stayed near the tents. —They'll aim at the tents, and Russians never hit their target.

Sergeant Major Korsumaki was still in the camp when the bombers came over. Though Koskela had called to him to seek shelter, Korsumaki for some reason had chosen to remain among the tents. He lay down in a little hollow between two of them, his hands to his ears, and waited.

The earth rocked under him as the explosions came nearer, until suddenly he felt a numbing blow between his shoulders and sank into unconsciousness. He returned to his senses to find himself on his knees, completely unable to recall what had happened. Only when he heard groans and saw a man stretched out on the ground did he remember. At the same instant he realized that he himself was wounded. Rising to his feet he staggered a few steps. Dimly he remembered having expected from the very beginning of the war that he would die . . . so this was what it was like.

—This is the end . . . no more strength.

He felt the earth sway and his sight grow dim. He was already unconscious when a stream of bullets from a fighter pierced his body. His last words, between sobs, were: —Don't . . . don't . . . Let me live.

Koskela and Hietanen reached the spot simultaneously with the stretcher bearers, but there was nothing to be done. Korsumaki was dead and the wounded man unconscious. Rahikainen had guessed rightly, it was Salonen, the same Salonen for whom Hietanen had procured new boots from Makila before they left the camp on the burned clearing. One of his arms had been torn off, and when one of the medical corpsmen sought his pulse, it had almost stopped beating.

Men gradually gathered on the scene, the clerk among them repeating over and over excitedly:

—I was so close. My God, if I'd stayed with the sergeant major . . . I might be dead, too.

Hietanen, shaken by the incident, turned on him angrily:

—Christ, stop your jabbering!

The clerk only pulled on his blouse and went on muttering as Hietanen felt Salonen's pulse:

—No use dressing his wound. He's done for.

Carefully they placed the body on a stretcher, all clumsily eager to be of some service. A man gently laid the severed arm on the dead man's chest.

The stretcher bearers went off with Salonen, leaving Korsumaki behind. The men gathered around his corpse were surprised to see how old he looked.

Under the fallen tent lay a third body. In the corpse's clenched fist they found three crushed hundred-mark notes and five cards.

—What did he have?

—Four aces and a queen.

—My God!

—I'd have bet my place in Heaven on that.

—Ivan went one better though.

They were all badly shaken by what had happened, but as soon as the dead had been taken away, the oppressive atmosphere began to clear. Soon they were even merrier than usual, and any remarks about the dead tended to be facetious.

They did, however, feel especially sorry about Korsumaki. No one had ever borne him any grudge, and after the actual fighting had begun he had risen in favor, especially after the men had noted that he, too, had no use for the common enemy, Lammio. They knew that when the army was mobilized he could have been transferred to a safe garrison job if he hadn't resolutely refused to go.

—To think he came all the way out here to die.

All this time the three criminals remained on the edge of the forest, still standing at attention. Not until the dead had been disposed of did Koskela remember them and ask Hietanen:

—Are those three still standing there?

—They stayed there right through the raid. Wouldn't leave, even though I told them to.

Koskela laughed and went to tell them they could quit, but they insisted on completing their punishment.

—Well, if that's the way you want it, all right, Koskela said with a smile. He had immediately grasped the humorous implications of their stand and was pleased. Lammio needed to be taught a lesson! And though Lammio, little as he cared for other people's feelings, had always avoided directly insulting him, Koskela still had no liking for him and could see the poison Lammio sowed in the men's mind by his every act.

When the full two hours were up, the three comrades returned to their tent. Lehto was taciturn, but a dark smile hovered on his lips:

—You have to be able to stick it to the end, Kaarna once told me. He knew what he was talking about, but what that bastard Lammio needs is a fist in his eye.

Even Rahikainen played the hero, though he had been the only frightened one of the three.

—It's no use running from death. If you do, you're finished. Well, our sins are wiped out now and we can start on a new lot. Since we're stuck here, we've got to see about some supplies. You'll have to do what you can to cover us, Koskela, because we're not going to starve.

4.

They were allowed a longer rest than they had expected. Nor were Lammio's plans for restoring discipline ever realized, orders having come that unnecessary fatigues were to be avoided. Rahikainen fully lived up to his promise to see to food supplies—with Koskela's blessing. The lieutenant knew well enough that the supplies Rahikainen brought had been stolen from somewhere, but he also knew that the men needed the extra food. Their rations kept them alive but fell far short of their needs, and the men were losing weight. He was also aware that the men at the commissariat were getting far more than their share, so in his heart he wished Rahikainen luck and even temporarily appointed him his messenger to succeed the fallen Salonen. Actually Koskela had found that he could do without a regular messenger, but he kept Rahikainen in that position to facilitate his movements. From then on anyone inquiring as to Rahikainen's business was told: —I'm on a mission for Lieutenant Koskela.

The whole regiment gradually learned of the three machine gunners' punishment, and the story lost nothing in the telling. Eventually it even came to the ear of the battalion commander and on his next visit to the camp he asked Lehto:

—Were you one of the ones who stood that field punishment?

—Yes, sir.

Major Sarastie smiled indulgently.

—Hum. Well, next time you go adventuring, take care you're not caught.

As he walked on he said to his adjutant, whom he delighted in impressing with the keenness of his psychological insight:

—You can see from that lad's looks that he's made of good stuff. And that he has the basic Finnish hatred of those set over him. That sort of boldness and energy is pure gold, but Lammio lets it go to waste by his clumsy handling. And there have been plenty of other times, too, when the measures he's taken weren't suited to the situation. I've told him that, but he isn't an easy man to convince, though he's a good officer in other respects. I remember Kaarna once told me this man should be trained for a commission. He felt his character was basically sound, though he tended to defy authority, and in a position where he had to exercise that authority, he'd be very successful.

The major fell silent, and a thoughtful look settled over his face. Actually he was not thinking at all but merely savoring the wisdom of his recent words. Sarastie did not consider Lammio, who so efficiently carried out his duties, his ideal of what an officer should be. Knowledge of the world was also required. Take, for example, the worldly approach with which he himself approached matters. His own thoughts were not confined to the narrow channels in which the mind of a conventional battalion commander moved.

He let his mind dwell on the decorations to be awarded that evening, and was well content with the cross he was to receive.

Later in the evening the battalion turned out on parade; the regimental commander himself having arrived to distribute the decorations in person. He began by inspecting the battalion, looking at each man as though he were trying to divine the inmost thoughts of his mind. It is one of the greatest of military achievements to be able to walk down ranks of men staring at each one with knitted brows and encountering vacant stares in return without laughing.

That finished, the colonel made a speech, trying to lend a comradely tone to his voice.

—Men. This is the first opportunity I have had since the outbreak of war to thank you for what you have done. There is no need for me to recount your achievements, for you know them and the world knows them. You have been given difficult tasks and have carried them out brilliantly. The regiment has already made its proud mark on the glorious pages of Finland's military history. And I know that you will continue to add new and noble chapters to that history. I thank you for the devotion and courage you have shown. The admiration and respect of our friends and the fear our enemy feels prove what a Finn is capable of when he takes up arms to defend his home and his family.

—I have been entrusted with the task of distributing, in token of the nation's gratitude, the following decorations to those who have specially distinguished themselves.

He read out a list of names. Officers received crosses, while enlisted men got medals. Each man named stepped forward to receive their decorations from the colonel's hand together with his congratulations. Some stretched it out, extracting the last ounce from their moment of prominence; the majority, however, hastened back to the ranks almost on the double, as though ashamed of being rewarded for something they did not know they had done.

Such decorations were, of course, trifles, especially in the eyes of the unfavored. The most curious aspect of the matter, however, was that no one seemed to have the slightest realization that it was the best killers who were being singled out to be rewarded—not even the chaplain who officiated at the service which brought the occasion to an end. A sorry affair it was, the presence of the colonel aggravating the chaplain's chronic stage fright to such an extent that he was unable to summon up even the very small gift he possessed for preaching.

Afterwards they returned to their tents where the two dominant themes of conversation that evening were the decorations and, for the undecorated, the number of undeserving who astonishingly had been deemed worthy. Koskela had been awarded a Fourth Class Liberty Cross; Hietanen, Lehto, Maatta and Lahtinen Second Class Liberty Medals.

A sarcastic remark about medals by Rahikainen made Lehto throw his at Rahikainen's feet.

—If you want one so badly, take it. I don't want the damn thing.

—Hell, neither do I.

Lehto's medal stayed on the ground, while Lahtinen examined his, muttering:

—Are they trying to bribe me with colored ribbons? I wouldn't kill a man for one of these things. Or go and be killed. Any shooting I do is to save my own life, and not for a ribbon and a hunk of bronze.

Maatta turned his medal in his fingers, studying it closely from every angle.

—For bravery, it says. But what's bravery? I'll be damned if I know.

—Bravery is when a soldier is afraid only of God. And doesn't bare his head except in church and a court of law.

—Well, at last it's clear to me. Of all the . . . I thought it must be something pretty remarkable to be engraved here so handsomely.

Maatta truly had no use for his medal. He tied it to the string of his pack, and it soon dropped off, never to be seen again.

The distribution of the medals made them suspect that their rest spell was about over. Lahtinen said so openly:

—They don't give ribbons away gratis. It won't be long before we'll be somewheres where we'll have to pay through the nose.

August had come, and a darker shade had crept into the green of the landscape. Everywhere the countryside revealed that the first flush of summer was over. During the last evenings they spent resting they were able to admire a magnificent August moon. On such nights many foolish letters were written, and even the sentinel walking his beat in the moonlight saw visions of women. And his ear caught scraps of conversation from the tents:

—They're always talking about how small the nation and the army is, but they won't let us go home on leave.

—If they'd give me two weeks, the class of 1941 would be a strong one. I'd sire them all the recruits they wanted.

—Shut up and go to sleep. . . .

Hietanen's words did not, of course, put an end to the dreaming. Ever more glowing pictures were evoked of a coming leave; pictures in which the fact that they stood small chance of ever realizing them did not interfere with their dreams of the women they would love and sleep with.

Their reverie ended only when the flap of the tent was lifted and two faces appeared in the opening.

—Which tents are your officers in? The question was spoken in a rapid Karelian dialect.

—One of 'em's here. A man pointed to Koskela.

—I want the company C.O.

The strangers were told the way to the CP tent and set off. Lammio was sitting in the rear of his tent, listening to a broadcast, when the two new comers crawled in on all fours.

—Are you the company commander? We're your replacements. I suppose the major telephoned that we were coming. Here's our papers.

Lammio examined the men in the light of his lantern.

—All right. You a sergeant?

—Yep. They gave me my stripes in the Winter War, though I don't know what for. I hadn't done anybody any harm. . . . But listen, Lieutenant, fix it for us to be in the same squad or at least in the same platoon. We're neighbors and we stuck together in the Winter War.

Lammio was offended: —This isn't a reserve regiment. It's not our custom to give superiors advice or we'd have the conscripts forgetting their discipline.

The man regarded Lammio out of the corner of his eye, a barely perceptible smile hovering on his lips.

—Is that so? Well, how could I have known that? You see, we happen to be reservists.

His tone was slightly apologetic, but the next minute he was again his free and easy self.

—But listen, sir, Lieutenant, all I wanted was for me and Wolf's Paw here to be in the same bunch.

—You and who?

—Wolf's Paw.

—What's your name, you?

—Wolf. Private Wolf, sir.

—I see. And yours?

—Me, I'm Rokka. Antero's my given name, but I've been called Antti all my life and that's what I call myself.

—Sergeant Rokka, then. We've no place right now for a section leader, so you'll be the reserve leader. Report to Lieutenant Koskela in the Third Platoon. Is that clear?

—Sure. Now if you'll just tell us how to find this Koskela, we won't need you any more.

Lammio was not quite certain what attitude to take toward the man's manner of addressing him. It seemed so natural, however, that Lammio hesitated to make a fuss over it, though he was certain it was against regulations. He indicated where the Third Platoon's tents were, and Rokka said:

—Why, we've just come from there. Let's go.

They headed back while the hitherto silent Wolf held forth:

—That fellow sure thinks he's somebody. If there are many of his kind, Antti, I'm not going to like it.

—We'll manage. Don't you worry, Paw. He's still young. I think all the officers here are regulars, and they're always too damn military. But we've come through worse things.

—We have, admitted Paw, and let the matter drop.

The peace of Koskela's tent was disturbed again when the two friends crawled in.

—We hit the right place the first try. The C.O. says to us, go to Koskela's. And I'll bet you're Koskela. We're your replacements. I'm Rokka and this is my pal, Wolf. Now, where are we going to sleep? Oh well, there's room here. Come here, Paw. You there, shove your pack a little more that way. . . . Any idea when we move out, Lieutenant?

—Soon, I guess, if we're being brought up to strength.

—It's a sure sign. You must have lost some men or they wouldn't have sent us here.

—A few. An air raid just took a couple. You string along with the first squad for the time being. We'll see later where you're needed most.

—As long as you keep the two of us together. We're neighbors at home, you see.

Rokka fell silent and almost instantly was sound asleep.

5.

They awoke in the morning to the sound of Rokka's voice. He had apparently been up for some time.

—Tea, boys. I took some mess tins and fetched it from the kitchen. Listen, Lieutenant, we're leaving today. I poked about a bit to see what was doing, and they were loading stuff on carts at Battalion. That means a move for sure. Why, you're all still children. Wolf and me, we're over thirty. We've got wives and kids.

—None of us has a wife, said Hietanen. —We're Finland's juvenile heroes.

—Heroes is what we are too, Paw and me. Hell, listen to that gunfire. That's where we'll be soon.

—Have you been at the front before? Koskela asked.

—In the Winter War. We did our trembling at Taipale. We're from the Isthmus. They took our farms, the devils. Didn't get our lives, though they certainly tried. I wanted to be sent to the Isthmus; I've got a few things to settle there with Ivan.

—What's it matter where we do our bit? said Salo. —There'll be houses to be had all the way to Moscow.

—I don't know a thing about Moscow. Those Germans sure are getting a lot of praise. They'll do all right, but on the way here I watched a bunch of 'em and there was too much heel clicking and arm waving. That's not the way to get things done. But what do we care—we don't give a damn for Europe. We'll take Karelia and then go home.

—You know, boys, said Hietanen. —I think that if there were thirty million of us, we'd take a crack at the whole world.

Rokka began to pack his equipment, humming a tune of his own.

—Start collecting your things, boys, we're moving. . . .

Rokka was not a man to behave as if he were among strangers, shyly until he had adjusted himself to them and they to him. From the very first he seemed to assume command. Nor were the men offended, for instinctively they saw that his self-assurance was based on something solid. Now he was certain that they would be moving out, and acted accordingly. Twenty minutes later his belief was given official confirmation as Mielonen appeared on the road shouting:

—Get ready! We're leaving in an hour.

There were none of the usual comments this time, for they realized that now it was their turn.

They set off, their spirits drooping as they marched toward the crashing guns. But gradually they acclimated themselves to the atmosphere of a battle front. Artillery fire once more became a reality as they passed dead and wounded victims of a barrage which had surprised the battalion preceding them.

They, however, had better luck, for they passed through the danger zone during a pause in the shelling. Just behind the front lines they left the road and bivouacked in the forest. There they spent the whole of that day speculating on what lay ahead and listening to the desultory firing from the front line positions about a half mile away along the bank of a river.

That evening Rokka, who had been missing for some time, turned up and informed them:

—We're going try our hands at fighting on the water for a change. They're bringing up pontoons and assault boats.

—Then we're really in the piss.

—That's us. Finland's brave heroes—always in the worst possible place. Sihvonen's voice sounded aggrieved.

—It doesn't make any difference to me whether we die on water or on land. The airplane pushers are all heroes, but I'll be damned if I can see that it matters how far you fall when you die.

—Let's stop all the talk about dying, said Hietanen with a feigned shudder. —You'll have me crapping in my pants soon.

Nearby, Rokka sat on a tussock gnawing a piece of hardtack and looking around as though seeking something on which to expend his energy. Finally he spied Kariluoto's platoon and shouted to him:

—Hey, you over there . . .

Kariluoto turned, not a little astonished: —What do you want?

—We'll soon be crossing the river.

—I know it.

—Well, that's all right, then.

Rokka waved his hand in dismissal and turned to Koskela.

—Listen, Koskela. How are we going to make the crossing? Shall we put the guns in the boats or use them for fire support from the shore?

—We'll be getting detailed orders. We'll use both ways, I expect.

—That's the way I see it, too. Part in the boats and the rest giving Ivan hell. That's good strategy. You know, in war you've got to use strategy. The Russkies would've been in our trenches lots of times in the Winter War if they'd had. But hammering straight away all the time like they did, they never had a chance. You've got to think first before you try to do something. That goes for a man or a regiment . . . Get some rest, you can't tell when you'll have a chance again.

Rokka fell asleep at once, but the others could not. Excitement and fear of what lay ahead had won out over their fatigue. They had swelled with pride when they had heard the reservists at the roadside say: —Here come the regulars, now things'll open up. But now they were apprehensive.

They did indeed regard themselves as superior to the reservists, and their officers continually took advantage of this to say: —All right, boys. Let's show them how real soldiers fight.

Some of them even felt eager for action after their long inactivity, and when the order came to fall in, few needed to be awakened. They assembled a short distance away from the river bank near where the pioneers and the men of the Bridge Company had dragged the boats. Here they were assigned their tasks. One half of the Third Platoon was to supply covering fire from the shore, while the other half was again detailed to help Kariluoto's platoon, which was to be the spearhead.

Each detachment was given its own craft and shown the route by which it could best be rushed into the water. The machine guns were set in the bows where they could be kept firing, a measure Rokka declared to be useless since there would not be time for them to fire more than a couple of bursts. The dispute over this matter was the first in what was to become a running war between Rokka and Lammio. Even after Lammio had forbidden Rokka to criticize his orders, Rokka refused to be silenced.

—Hell, man, you can see for yourself that it isn't worth while mounting a machine gun for that little trip. It'll only hold us up on the other side when we have to dismantle it again.

—Now you listen to me. I'm your superior officer and you'll do what I tell you.

—The hell I will! At the most we'll put the barrel in the bow without the tripod.

Lammio did not reply, but after Rokka had moved off he took the order as his own:

—We'll only put the barrel in the bow. There'll be just about time for a couple of bursts.

At four o'clock they were ordered to get ready. Silently the men ranged themselves beside their boats, trying to ignore the pictures that kept invading their minds of machine-gun bullets piercing the gunwales and spreading death among them. Softly they discussed the chances of swimming in their heavy equipment and decided they were nil until Kariluoto's tense face rose above the first boat.

—Don't talk rubbish.

He had barely spoken when the world seemed to explode behind them. Oo . . . ee . . . ee . . . rooommm.

Shell after shell ploughed up the opposite bank. Then after five minutes, smoke shells began to fall and they immediately started hauling the boats down to the shore. The smoke screen soon hid the far bank of the river from view, and a voice said in relief:

—They'll have to aim by ear through that.

—Get moving!

The motors of the boats were started and the men began to push them into the stream.

—Let's go!

The propellers churned the water and the boats sped toward the opposite shore as the second wave of the attack moved down to the bank. Stray bullets whined through the smoke screen, doing little if any damage.

Rokka lay in the bow of his squad's boat, firing into the smoke. Then, with a soft scraping sound, they touched, and the men sprang ashore. Here they suffered their first casualty as a man of the Bridge Company staggered and fell back into the water, which began crimsoning where he lay. Alarmed, the men were about to seek the shelter of the low bluff, but Kariluoto drove them onward, helped immeasurably by Rokka, who pushed on through the smoke, the machine gun on his shoulder, shouting:

—Let's go, boys, or Ivan'll make things hot for us! Remember we've got our backs to the river.

They ran through the smoke up a sloping meadow toward the Russian lines, with Kariluoto calling constantly to his men to maintain contact, for visibility was still poor although the smoke was clearing. The Russian positions were on the edge of a forest. Now the smoke screen had thinned so much that it was no longer any protection, and one of Kariluoto's men was hit. Despite Rokka and Kariluoto's protestations, the rest threw themselves down and returned the fire. At once Koskela ordered the machine guns into position to silence the enemy's automatic weapons. Actually the order was unnecessary, for Rokka had already opened fire without waiting for the tripod, supporting the barrel on a stump. Maatta fed the belt into the breech, carelessly exposing himself to show Rokka that he had no monopoly on courage.

—There the devils are, Rokka said calmly. —See 'em? Machine gun . . .

Rokka saw three heads behind the machine gun, but the Russians had also seen them, and bullets whistled past their ears. Lahtinen, hugging the ground beside them, got two holes in his rolled-up overcoat. Then Rokka took aim, quickly but accurately, and two heads vanished while the third sank over the machine gun, which did not fire again.

Kariluoto roared the order to charge. As he heard it, Rokka handed the machine gun to Maatta: —I'm going with the boys. . . .

The Russians had abandoned a section of the trench in front of them, or rather all the defenders had been wiped out, and Kariluoto leaped into it followed by a few of his men. Here Rokka joined them, and Kariluoto had no time to protest as Rokka snatched his tommy gun out of his hands saying:

—Let me take it . . . you use your grenades. . . . Jesus, I sure wish we'd had a few more of these in the Winter War. . . .

Then Rokka was gone, racing ahead, hugging the wall of the trench. Quickly Kariluoto collected a half dozen grenades from the men behind him and went after him. As they reached a bend in the trench Rokka stopped and motioned him to throw a grenade around the corner.

—As soon as it explodes, I'll go in and clean up. Then we'll take the next bend and so on. We'll really mop them up that way. . . .

Kariluoto lobbed a grenade, and as it burst Rokka stepped quickly around the corner. Two Russians lay dead in the bottom of the trench, while a third, blood pouring from a wound in his head, feebly attempted to raise his rifle. Quickly Rokka riddled him with a burst from the tommy gun.

Around the next bend three more Russians fell as Rokka fired quickly and accurately, all the while shouting instructions which the others obeyed instinctively. Even Kariluoto did not seem to notice that Rokka and not he was leading the platoon. Instead he threw the grenades as Rokka directed and admired the man's speed and unerring judgment. Rokka's courage enabled him to think clearly and thus avoid mistakes, while his common sense told him that as long as they pressed forward the enemy was helpless. The continuous fire prevented the Russians from themselves throwing grenades, and Rokka's tommy gun did the rest.

On their right the company which crossed after them had joined the battle and easily penetrated the Russian positions, for Kariluoto's advance along the trench had paralyzed the defense. Thus when they established contact with this company's left flank Kariluoto's men made their way back. Meanwhile part of the Third Company cleaned up in the opposite direction, for the Russians were everywhere retreating. Only Rahikainen was missing from the section, having taken advantage of the opportunity to search for souvenirs from the Russian dead.

Kariluoto came up to Rokka as soon as they had consolidated their newly won positions:

—What's your name?

—Rokka. I already reported to Lieutenant Koskela.

—That's all right, I just wanted to know. The way you cleaned that trench up was something to watch.

So great was Kariluoto's enthusiasm that he had all but forgotten how Rokka had ordered him about. Rokka wiped the perspiration from his cap and laughed. He had an unusual way of looking at people out of the corner of his eye, and usually there was a laughing twinkle in his glance. His speech, too, was rarely more than half serious, except when he would lecture the men like a schoolmaster on the real meaning of things. Now Kariluoto's praise brought a smile to his lips.

—Don't go praising me, Lieutenant. You're young and still believe in heroes, so you want to perform heroic deeds. Me, I don't give a damn for such things. Advance when you're ordered to, and the rest of the time keep under cover. When we were attacking a while ago you kept walking around to set an example. That's fine, but examine the situation before you do it. We're not here to die but to kill.

Here Rokka seemed to realize the exaggerated earnestness of his speech, for he laughed and went on:

—Somehow I'm just not afraid in this war. It's child's play compared with Taipale. Wolf here remembers how we lay surrounded by corpses in the snow and men went mad. And every night we dragged half our number to the rear, dead. That was real war! . . . Now I'm going to see what sort of men those were who tried to put holes in me with that machine gun.

Chapter VI

1.

Now there was rarely a lull in the fighting. The second phase of the offensive launched by the Army of Karelia was in full swing, and unrelenting attacks were in process all along the front. The company was, of course, as ill-informed about the rest of the Army of Karelia as they were about the different stages of the offensive. They knew the number of their regiment, but a division was something they had difficulty comprehending, to say nothing of a corps or an army. A car would pass with a general inside whom they recognized from his picture, and they would comment: —What the hell's he doing nosing about here? A general was a creature from another world. Their world was one of toil, danger, hunger, weariness and innumerable other inconveniences, to all of which they had become accustomed.

On and on they struggled for mile after mile while from north and south of them came the incessant thunder of artillery. Overhead air battles were fought, and they would occasionally stop to watch an aircraft fall flaming from the sky.

Every time they dislodged their foes, they hoped that now the road was open for a swift advance. But always they soon ran into new resistance. Day by day they grew more silent and irritable, and quarrels broke out over trifles. Their eyes sank ever deeper into their heads, their cheekbones jutted out more prominently; smooth young faces became furrowed in a matter of weeks. Rahikainen had given up gathering Russian insignia; tent cloths and food were now more in demand.

And all the while Koskela and his platoon were growing ever closer together. The taciturn second lieutenant's authority over his men had become so absolute that he had only to hint at a task for it to be done. In combat he was quiet and tenacious, deliberate and calculating. And as a result, his platoon had very few casualties. Not once did he expose a machine gun to danger unless absolutely necessary, and when he did so, he was there himself to instruct and advise. But above all else the men knew he was one of them because that was the way he always acted. When the platoon was not in action, no one would have taken him for an officer unless they happened to see his stars, so completely did he identify himself with his men down to the smallest detail.

Lehto's moods, however, grew ever darker. Once a shell landed right beside him, leaving him unhurt but temporarily deafened. And he was still deaf when he shot a wounded Russian on the grounds that the man's cries got on his nerves. But no one took any notice of the incident this time, for their education as soldiers was complete. Another time, forced to withdraw from a captured hill, they left a wounded man behind. When they retook the hill, they found him lying dead, bayoneted in the stomach. In retaliation one of Kariluoto's tommy gunners coldly shot down three prisoners. Two days later a shell cut him almost in two. Death had ceased to be a moral issue.

Rokka alone seemed to thrive on war. He never showed any signs of fatigue, but on the contrary was always trying to infect others with his own good humor. His reputation spread, but commanding officers were compelled to admit that he wasn't always the model soldier they would have wished him to be. He showed no respect whatever for rank, however high. In combat, however, he showed unmistakable genius; he killed in cold blood, and often when the machine guns were not engaged he would voluntarily accompany the riflemen. —Hand-to-hand fighting is something you don't get in a machine-gun outfit, and I want to find out what it's like.

Vanhala, too, had proved himself a good soldier and Lehto had begun to single him out as the member of the squad in whom he could confide.

And so it was with the rest of the men in the platoon; each of them showed the psychological effect the slaughter had on him. The strong were made stronger by the fatigue they endured, while the weak became even weaker. Riitaoja, fox example, began to babble incoherently, and Lehto demanded a replacement for him. But Riitaoja was not sent back; every man was needed.

Kariluoto had developed into one of the best platoon commanders in the battalion, and Autio entrusted all the most difficult missions to him. And usually Koskela went with the machine guns detailed to support Kariluoto, for he preferred to handle difficult tasks himself. The ties between these two went deeper than was customary. Kariluoto always tried to adapt himself to Koskela's moods, and Koskela tried tactfully to avoid any appearance of his assuming the leadership. He knew that every time Kariluoto boldly exposed himself in an attack, he did so to atone for his cowardice on the first day of the war.

And he was certainly succeeding. At every obstacle Kariluoto would repeat the order: —Forward! And each time his voice was steadier as he scourged the uneasy feeling under his heart and drove it ever deeper into the depths of his being. Now he shared with Koskela, Autio and Lammio the reputation of being the bravest officers in the battalion.

Mentally Kariluoto underwent a change also as sentiment gave way to a strong sense of duty. Before long he was the most popular man in his platoon. Not that the men had ever disliked him; his idealism had merely made them think him childish. Now they seemed to feel it was their duty to keep up with him.

One event had shaken him to the core and decisively affected his state of mind. He had chosen a young volunteer, a couple of years younger than the others, as his messenger. The lad showed great bravery, but it was a childish courage, happily oblivious to how closely death had often passed him by.

There was a hill being defended by the Russians with even more than their usual stubbornness. Four times the attackers were thrown back, and in the process lost more men than the battalion had lost at any one time before. Kariluoto's platoon shrank to little more than half its normal strength. But he had decided on one more desperate attempt. An order had come forbidding further useless assaults, but he was convinced the next charge would succeed. The capture of even the smallest sector of trench would be enough, so in order to avoid heavy losses he determined to try a limited assault with only a few of his best men.

He succeeded in inducing a few men to follow him, but no sooner had they set out than his young runner was hit in the stomach, putting an end to the attempt. Ignoring the bullets flying about him, Kariluoto dragged the boy behind the shelter of a big boulder. The youth was in agony, for the wound had been made by an explosive bullet which had torn his intestines to shreds. Even Kariluoto could not suppress a moan when he uncovered the dreadful mess in order to apply a dressing. He said gently:

—Don't move . . . it'll make the pain worse. We'll wait until the stretcher comes.

Blood-flecked foam gushed from the boy's mouth.

—Death . . . not the stretcher . . . coming. I'm going to join father . . . aah . . . aai . . . burning, I'm burning . . .

Kariluoto wept openly.

—You won't die . . . The stretcher bearers'll be here soon and then they'll operate at the field hospital.

The boy, however, was overwhelmed by a childish fear of death and tossed about until Kariluoto had to hold him down.

—Pray for me, sir . . . I'm too weak . . . oh, it hurts . . . Jesus . . . I'm dying.

Kariluoto hardly knew what he was doing as, in answer to the boy's wish, his lips mechanically formed the words:

—Our Father . . . which art in Heaven . . . hallowed be Thy name . . .

The boy moved his bloodstained lips: —Our . . . Father . . . Our . . . Father . . .

He arched his body, his back completely off the ground in an agonized movement. Then his face turned blue, and his body stiffened, leaving Kariluoto to wipe his eyes and crawl back to his men.

Once again he wrote a letter. It was the first since the one he had written when Vuorela was killed.

. . . I know words mean nothing to you and cannot help you in your sorrow. We cannot change the sorrow losses cause us,

> but must endure it alone as best we can. I write to you because I sent him into the battle in which he died—not from a sense of guilt but because I am aware of my responsibility. I write not because I wish to evade that responsibility but because I want to bear the burden of it. . . .

This time Kariluoto was not ashamed of his letter. But the naïve patriotism filling the letters he got from home completely nauseated him.

Days grew into weeks, then time lost all meaning for them. A man would say: —Isn't today Sunday? and after thinking a bit, answer his own question: —Why, damn it, so it is.

They measured time by such events as: —That time the Second Platoon lost six men; the day the column of trucks was destroyed; the tank battle.

The nights grew darker, rain fell often, and now the feel of autumn was in the air. They captured village after village from most of which the inhabitants had been evacuated. Their hopes centered on rest and food, and of both they got all too little. One day, however, they captured a field kitchen full of newly cooked cabbage soup.

—Don't touch it. It might be poisoned.

Rokka filled his mess tin.

—You're a lot of fool kids. Shells and bullets whistling all around, and you're afraid of poison.

Rokka ate his fill and since he showed no sign of dying, the others ate too. Lahtinen was loud in praise of the soup, comparing it with the inferior stuff their own cooks made.

—These Russkies sure are being fed pretty well, although for the past thirty years people have been expecting them all to starve to death. I wonder how it's all going to end.

—Who knows, said Rokka with a smile, licking his spoon clean. —Looks bad, doesn't it? There's one comfort, though. Ivan's lost that good soup. And if victory depends on that, we're that much to the good. Have another plateful and make victory certain.

Even Lahtinen had to laugh at this sally, and when they set off again they were in slightly better spirits. Now Hietanen would often stop to laugh at Communism on the basis of things they saw in East Karelia, and Lahtinen was hard pressed to defend the poor roads, the rotting buildings, and the ragged clothes the native population wore.

On the other hand they had to admit that the defenders seemed to like what they had, for they died at their posts amid piles of expended cartridges.

Barrages thundered, automatic weapons rattled and men died. In the act of dashing forward a man would drop, while another would be standing still when he let his rifle slide out of his hand and fell quickly to the earth. Men died groaning and laughing, cursing and praying.

Mile after mile of the muddy, twisting Karelian road leading towards Petrozavodsk, was purchased with the lives of such men.

2.

Curls of smoke rose reluctantly from the campfire into the gray drizzle. A howitzer battery boomed close by and ammunition convoys roared by on the muddy road, but the men in the tents slept on undisturbed. They had been sleeping like logs for twelve hours and showed no signs of having had enough.

Rahikainen was on guard, and to pass the time he was playing poker by himself, dealing two hands and talking to himself:

—What's he got? Three whores. Not bad.

He threw the other hand angrily on the pack, glanced at his watch and then went to the sleeping Hietanen.

—Hey, wake up! It's your turn.

He poked and pummeled Hietanen for some minutes before he succeeded in getting him to a sitting position. At last Hietanen ran his fingers through his hair, his eyes open but unseeing.

—Come on. It's your turn.

—All right. Hietanen sank back on his bedroll, obviously not having understood a word. But Rahikainen shook him violently until he woke again with a start.

—What's the matter?

—Guard. You're on guard.

—Hell. I was dreaming the war was over.

Hietanen looked out of the tent. On the road lay the ruins of three tanks while a few dead Russians were stretched out by the roadside, mute evidence of the counterattack that had been thrown back there. Hietanen drew up a leg of his trousers and carefully examined a small wound in his thigh. It showed a promising scab. A shell from a tank had landed close to where he had been lying and a splinter had lodged in his thigh. He had sterilized a knife blade with a lighted match and dug out the splinter. Wrapped in paper, it now lay in his pocket.

Outside Hietanen thrust a couple of sticks into the fire and sat nodding beside it. The howitzers still boomed, and from the front where another regiment had taken over for them yesterday came the sound of small arms fire. Hietanen listened, almost asleep. Machine-gun bursts came at short intervals, and an automatic rifle fired singly. Hietanen guessed it to be Russian from the sound, which was different from that of one firing away from you. Pa-ku, pa-ku, pa-ku.

Hietanen's head gave a jerk, awakening him abruptly. He knew he would fall asleep if he continued to sit beside the fire, so, throwing his overcoat over his shoulders, he crawled out of the tent. After putting more wood on the other squad's fire he wandered aimlessly about the camp site. A gray drizzle oozed from the low clouds, spreading a gray melancholy over the forest. Tens of thousands of men were locked here in battle, invisible, their existence revealed only by the sounds of war. A cart carrying a big soup kettle trundled past on the road, its driver huddled beneath the overcoat he wore like a hood.

Hietanen saw Mielonen emerge from the CP and at once his mind filled with gloomy suspicions. Their rest period must be over. It was of course possible that Mielonen was out on some other errand, and torn between hope and fear Hietanen refrained from asking.

—Well, what are you thinking about out here at this hour?

—I was just thinking that war's a miserable business. Hunger, cold, death, no sleep, and to crown it all, lice in your clothes.

—You're right. There are plenty of houses in the villages, but no, we've got to sleep out here. I was talking to a couple of ambulance drivers over there. They said they've got more cargoes than they can carry. Men falling on every side. I hear we're attacking on the Isthmus now, too.

He hasn't any orders for us, Hietanen thought with relief. He still feared, however, to come right out and ask whether they were about to return to the front. He was about to say something else to carry on the conversation, when Mielonen went on:

—We're shoving off, too. Wake up the Third, will you? I haven't the heart to tell Koskela.

—You wouldn't have.

—That's right. So get them going, will you?

The blood rushed to Hietanen's face:

—You son of a bitch, I ought to shoot you!

—Now, now, friend. Shooting me won't change anything. To do that, you'd have to bump off men a lot higher up.

Mielonen had long ago ceased to take seriously the outbursts of fury his arrival with unpleasant orders provoked. Always as he moved from tent to tent at reveille, calling out: —Time to get up; come on, let's go, heads appeared from the tents cursing so bitterly that Mielonen's indifference would have amazed a stranger.

Now Hietanen stood between the tents bellowing angrily:

—Let's go. Wake up, you lazy good-for-nothings. Up with you and show the world what a terror a Finnish soldier is! Up, Finland's fearsome lions.

From the tents came sleepy voices raised in a medley of curses.

—To hell with them! Tell 'em we want at least three days' rest before we budge. It's easy for the brass to get going. Nothing to carry and orderlies looking after 'em. Give the bastards a pack on their backs and they'd never leave camp.

Koskela gathered up his equipment quietly, ignoring the men as they voiced their feelings. He knew that when he slung his pack on his back and left the tent the men would follow. And if he tried to put a stop to the men's complaining, their grievances would be left to rankle in their minds. He, too, was dissatisfied with the brief duration of their rest. Fatigue was not only unpleasant, it was dangerous for it led to tasks being done badly and thus resulted in unnecessary casualties.

The grumbling continued, but Koskela knew that when the sharpest discontent had worn off, a reaction would be set in motion by Hietanen and Rokka. Rokka, in fact, already was sounding off:

—You're soldiers, aren't you? Then what are you complaining about? The only way to end a war is by fighting. We've got to move in some direction—who the hell would want to spend his life in this forest? Don't worry, lads. The big villages lie ahead, and the Russian women are waiting for us. They can't wait to see us Finnish heroes.

By degrees they calmed down and coarse bantering was filling the air when Makila called them to come and get their food. He issued their dry-rations for three days, thus indicating to the men that they were off again on a special job.

—Don't eat it all at once. It's got to last you three days, Makila warned them.

—It'll have to if you're not going to give us any more.

—There isn't any more.

—Well then, steal some from somewheres.

Makila shut up abruptly, knowing that they were baiting him. But then Rahikainen asked for new boots.

—These aren't going to last me all the way to the Urals.

—They're still in good condition.

—They're in the same kind of good condition as I am. Look.

By placing one heel on the edge of the sole of the other boot Rahikainen made his toe stick out of a hole, and Makila was forced to issue him a new pair.

The field kitchen doled out oatmeal porridge specked with chunks of meat which had a most unsavory look.

—What is it?

—Horse meat.

—Horse meat?

—Yes. An old horse. Hietanen took the gristle he had been chewing out of his mouth. —And the signs all point to it being a gypsy's nag. I can see the whip marks.

—Let's have no grousing about the food. The meat is absolutely up to standard.

The voice belonged to Sinkkonen, the new sergeant major who was on duty for the first time, for since Korsumaki's death Makila had been acting sergeant major. Sinkkonen was a regular NCO, a man well over forty, and his first words showed him to be completely incapable of handling men. He wore a smartly cut uniform, the rim of a white collar showing at his throat, and he was shod in beautiful new high boots. He could not have created a more unfortunate impression. Hietanen regarded him glumly for a minute:

—Who in hell asked your opinion?

—I'm your new sergeant major, and I'll tell you right off that endless grumbling is not worthy of a Finnish soldier. Under the circumstances the food is good.

Lehto was eating from the lid of his mess tin, and as Sinkkonen came near he looked stonily up at him:

—Under the circumstances you're full of shit.

Sinkkonen's neck began to turn red, and the flush deepened when Rahikainen added:

—Yes, complaining is beneath us, but in war you have to make allowances. And actually, you can't blame a horse for getting tough as it grows older.

For the first time in his life Sinkkonen, who had a considerable reputation as the terror of new recruits, found himself rebuffed. The shock was immense, the men's contemptuous jibes agitating him so deeply that he could only stammer:

—Those who complain loudest are the worst cowards in battle. The better the man, the more he does his duty without complaining.

Rokka shook a spoon at Sinkkonen. —You listen to me. You've got something wrong with your head. You make jokes as if you were really serious. In this bunch you have to be happy all the time. We're comedians, we are.

Sinkkonen fled, leaving Rokka as well as Rahikainen and Vanhala helpless with laughter.

—What do you think this is, a circus?

Lammio had come up behind them unnoticed. Quickly their faces became serious, and Rokka explained:

—Our new sergeant major was feeling low so we thought we'd bring a little happiness into his life. But he left. I'm afraid he has too many things on his mind.

—Stop your clowning. I want the company ready to leave in one hour. Those of you who don't own white handkerchiefs get hold of a piece of white paper. The quartermaster will give you some. Carry on.

The order was so unusual that no one even thought of joking about it.

—I can guess what's in store for us, said Rokka. —We're in for a night attack.

—That means we're in the piss again.

—When are those goddamn Germans going to take Moscow?

3.

Twilight was falling. It was still raining, and a melancholy sense of autumn pervaded the wilds as company after company trickled from the road into the forest.

—Here we go, boys. The whole regiment's on the move.

Every man had a white handkerchief or a piece of paper pinned to his back, and talking had been forbidden after nightfall.

Pioneers moving ahead of the companies blazed a trail and laid log bridges across brooks and bogholes. Soon the ground turned swampy for good.

The men were more heavily laden than usual, for they carried a double issue of cartridges. But the heaviest burdens fell to the machine gunners, the trench-mortar squads and the anti-tank men, for in addition to their own equipment they had to carry their heavy weapons.

They covered the first stage of their laborious journey in silence. Then, as darkness fell, the pace slowed. Already the weakest were beginning to show signs of exhaustion. A foot would sink in a boghole and, wearily incapable of keeping his balance, a man would fall headlong. Gasping for breath he would rise and plod on. At intervals, whispered contact reports passed along the file.

The spearhead was wading through swamp miles ahead when the last man turned off the road—nearly three thousand men advanced in single file through the swampy country in fog, drizzle and darkness. It was a desperate gamble for high stakes. Who could guarantee that the file would not break at some point?—it was only as strong as its weakest member. Someone might go astray and lead those who followed him God knows where. And that was only the beginning. About ten miles ahead lay their objective, the heavily defended Russian road-and-rail communications. It was into this wolf's den that the regiment was to thrust, relying solely on the ammunition and supplies it could carry, alone, unsupported, its only link with the rear a single thin telephone wire which was certain, sooner or later, to break.

At regular intervals the C.O. sent a telephone message to Divisional Headquarters:

—Point so and so. All's well so far.

And received an answer:

—Situation unchanged. Proceed as planned.

The colonel, in a black raincoat, strode along, nervously sucking his mustache. Any second he expected to hear a fusillade from his point, for it seemed impossible that the regiment could reach its objective unobserved. But with every minute that it moved on unchallenged the chance grew that it might. What if the dead-tired regiment was to run into organized resistance? The colonel needed a smoke badly, but still he hesitated to break his own order.

About midnight the strain began to make itself felt on the men.

They had covered many miles in the untracked wilderness until they could do little more than stagger along. Groans and whispered curses were heard, as with increasing frequency men stumbled and fell. There were loud splashes whenever a man sank to his hips in the swamp. But not a man dropped out. It was not a matter of discipline, patriotism, honor or duty. Something mightier than any of these flogged them on. The fear of death.

It was impossible to drop out, for to do so meant certain destruction. And it would be even more certain if they threw away their ammunition and weapons; for every man knew that his survival would depend on them on the morrow. At each rest stop they dropped in their tracks and lay panting, oblivious to the wetness and cold of the swamp.

Koskela carried four ammunition boxes, having taken Salo's when he seemed on the verge of collapsing. Hietanen had Riitaoja's boxes, Lehto carried the tripod and Vanhala the barrel of their gun without even asking to be relieved. Lahtinen and Maatta did the same with their gun, while Rokka helped Sihvonen and Wolf's Paw, both of whom were ready to drop. Finally Rahikainen had to take Riitaoja's rifle when it became obvious that the man could go no farther.

They were lying resting when three men approached from the rear. A cigarette glowed between the palms of the leader, and Hietanen observed it. He too hungered for a smoke, and it was largely for this reason that he called out angrily:

—You damned pisshead, don't you know you're not allowed to smoke? I suppose you're such a big cheese you think you can light up whenever you like.

The man put the cigarette away without a word. One of his companions, however, said reprovingly:

—Have a care what you say and to whom.

—No, no. He was absolutely right. In fact I was testing to see whether my orders were being obeyed. What's your name and company?

—Sergeant Hietanen, First Machine-gun Company, Colonel, sir.

Hietanen rose nervously to his feet for he had recognized the regimental commander. Now he tried to calm himself with the thought that he had acted correctly, even though he had been prompted by his own desire for a smoke.

—All right, Sergeant Hietanen. Keep up the good work.

Turning to the others the colonel asked:

—Well, boys, how are you getting on?

With an effort Salo pulled himself to attention:

—We're doing fine, Colonel.

—Good, that's the way a Finn should talk. Be tough and the devil himself can't stand up to you.

The colonel turned away and Salo, shaking with weariness, dropped into a puddle, as happy as it is possible for a completely exhausted man to be.

—Which of the two is the biggest fool? Lahtinen whispered to Vanhala, who laughed gleefully.

—Kee-hee . . . kee-hee. Stand up to the devil! What a thought! Hee-hee.

—All right, men, let's get moving!

Night was fading, and it was becoming easier for them to distinguish each other. Fatigue was giving way to mounting excitement, for the advance guard could not be far from the road that was their objective. Every few minutes an order to observe the greatest caution passed down the file.

Then Riitaoja fell again and lay on the ground, unable to rise. The others went on, but Lehto stayed with him.

—Give me your pack and get up.

—I can't go any farther.

—Do as I tell you and get up.

Riitaoja wept, the remnants of his strength dissolving in his tears. He was limp, incapable of any effort. In addition he was in such mortal terror of Lehto that he tried to sink even deeper into the swamp. Lehto was almost beside himself with rage at the sight of Riitaoja's tears. He kicked the prostrate man, hissing:

—You son of a whore! I'd give anything to be set free of you by a Russian slug. But you never come near the shooting, you bastard.

—I can't go on . . . don't hit me . . . oh . . . oh . . .

Riitaoja squirmed and sought to escape Lehto's boots. He moaned and shouted for Koskela, by now far away at the head of his platoon. The units filing past them were unfamiliar, and all so preoccupied with their own laborious progress that the idea of intervening did not even occur to them. What did anything else matter? When at last one man was moved to say something, it was due to sullen rage at his own sufferings rather than to indignation at Lehto's cruelty.

—Stop kicking that man around! Someone ought to put a bullet through your kind.

The speaker was more concerned, however, with keeping his place in the file than with Riitaoja, and he made no reply to the challenge Lehto, foaming at the lips, shouted after him:

—Try it, you whoremaster, and we'll see who ends up full of holes!

Just then news came flying along the file:

—Viipuri's been retaken . . . pass it on . . . it was in last night's broadcast.

—Viipuri's been retaken . . .

—Viipuri's retaken . . . pass it on . . .

—Viipuri's retaken . . .

Lehto took a firm hold on Riitaoja, jerked him to his feet and began to drag him along. —Viipuri's been taken, he hissed, forgetting to change his tone with the result that the man in front of him received the news in a voice that seemed to imply that for Lehto it was the worst catastrophe that could have befallen them.

Lehto succeeded in setting Riitaoja in motion, and soon Riitaoja was walking unaided, impelled perhaps by Lehto's threats from behind:

—You lie down again and I'll take a rifle and beat your brains out. Haven't I enough to do without having to haul along a pile of shit like you?

Even in peacetime Riitaoja had been afraid of his section leader, for Riitaoja had never been able to shake off the dread aroused in him by his first experiences in the barracks. He went on saying "sir" long after the others had become accustomed to telling an NCO to shut his mouth. After fighting had broken out, his fear had altered in character. Now the gloomy and violent Lehto had come to represent a vague but dreadful force that at any moment might destroy him. Koskela had ordered Lehto to cease torturing Riitaoja, but he could not always be present. Then, too, Koskela understood Lehto's venom, for Riitaoja not only left his tasks for others to perform, but had to be helped along like a child. Even Lehto's bravery was a source of terror to Riitaoja; it made him think that a man for whom death seemed to have no meaning would not scruple to kill him if he ever wanted to do so. Now he staggered on through the swamp, afraid to let the despairing sobs that rose in his throat escape his lips.

A new halt was called, but this time they all guessed why.

—Road ahead. Every man on the alert.

They started at the sudden crack of a rifle ahead. A tommy gun rattled a reply: prr . . . prr . . . prr . . .

Slowly they began feeling their way forward again. Now the battalion was deploying, the machine-gun platoons placing themselves behind the infantry companies to which they had been assigned. The Third Company spread out to the left, the Second to the right, while the First lay behind in support. Koskela divided the machine guns between the rifle platoons, just as Lammio arrived to order the transfer of one gun to the Second Platoon of the Third Company, which was farthest out on the left flank.

—Which of you wants to go? The other guns are already placed.

Koskela looked at Lahtinen and Lehto, and they in turn regarded each other. After a brief silence Lehto said:

—We'll go.

—Of course we've got to hit all the worst places, muttered Rahikainen.

Lammio took out a map and a flashlight, and Koskela and Lehto got down on their knees beside him, spread an overcoat over their heads, and in this improvised shelter studied the map.

—The Second Platoon is to advance from the edge of that meadow to the road and then turn west. There's a path from the northern tip of the meadow to the road, see it? The platoon's to advance along that path. A patrol reported a barn in the meadow, but even without it you'll find your way. It's about two hundred yards in front of where we are now. If the platoon's gone, follow the path to the road, and you'll find them there. Any questions?

—No. It's Sarkola's platoon we're to join? Right?

—Yes. If the Russkies defend the road, there'll be fighting and you can find your way by the sound . . . And we're pretty sure to run into something since we must have been observed on our way here. We aren't certain of that, though, so keep your eyes open. Take care of yourselves. Carry on.

—I don't want Riitaoja with me. Lahtinen can give me another man, he's got a bigger crew.

—That's true, said Koskela. —Give him one of your men, Lahtinen.

—All right. Sihvonen, you go with them.

—Jesus, I have all the luck.

Sihvonen was indignant, not only because he had no liking for this special assignment, but because he knew Lahtinen naturally gave up the man for whom he had least use.

—Never mind the grumbling, said Lammio. —And Riitaoja, you'd better carry out your duties. If this shirking doesn't stop, I'll have to stop it. A man your age should damn well have enough self-control so that he can at least carry ammunition.

Riitaoja stood up and guiltily gasped:

—I'm all right. I'll do my share.

Poor Riitaoja didn't know which he feared most, the enemy or Lammio, and he was so distressed that he felt no shame at this public rebuke.

Lehto's crew set off, but no sooner were they out of hearing than a violent quarrel broke out.

—You goddamned hero, you just had to volunteer! Go ahead by yourself if you like it so much . . . trying to find somebody in this pitch darkness . . . God knows where they've gone.

Rahikainen fumed at Lehto, who, all his senses alert, replied in a brief whisper:

—Keep your trap shut and your eyes open.

—Who knows yet what'll develop? Listen to that firing on the right . . . they've reached the road. And that roaring's a tank. What are we going to do without anti-tank guns?

—Shut up. There's the meadow and the barn. If we skirt the meadow we can't miss the path . . . It starts in that hollow if the map was right.

It was a little lighter in the open than in the forest, and after cautiously skirting the meadow they found the path to the main road. But there was not a sign of Sarkola's platoon. The firing was all on their right, and according to Lammio's account of the situation that was in the First Platoon's sector.

—Let's go back, said Rahikainen.

—No. Let's find the road. You heard the order as clearly as I did.

—What if there's no one there? Rahikainen insisted. —I don't believe half what that bastard says.

—He knows what's happening . . . and we're going on.

—We're not going, are we, Vanhala?

—Going? Sure. And while we're at it, let's make it all the way back to Finland. All the way home and tell them we lost our way, khee-hee-hee . . .

—You think you're funny, always laughing. Go ahead with that maniac and there'll be two of you.

—The two of us fighting tanks, hee-hee. It'd mean a sleeveful of stripes and a chestful of crosses . . .

Angrily Lehto ordered them to stop talking and follow him. Releasing the safety catch of his rifle, he began to make his way along the path, guiding himself by the narrow streak of pale sky between the black treetops. Mud squished under his boots, but in the damp dark forest all was still.

Lehto knew that he must be near the road, but he was beginning to worry. Where was the Second Platoon? He stopped to listen, and the others caught up with him.

—Let's go back, repeated Rahikainen.

The suspense was making Lehto increasingly irritable, and he whispered angrily:

—For God's sake stop that croaking! We'll at least take a look. The lieutenant isn't going to get a chance to chew me out for coming back without at least seeing where we were supposed to go, by God. I'm going on a ways. If anything happens, one of you go back for help. But remember, they'll be on the road now and not where we left them.

Lehto went on alone. A choking fear made him catch his breath for a moment. What lay out there in all that darkness and silence? If there were Finns out there, why wasn't there any shooting? What was that tank doing, clanking around on his right?

Sweat streamed from his body, and overcome by a feeling that something was wrong, he stopped. No sooner, however, had the idea of going back entered his mind than his fear gave way to hate. No, never. Never. They would never have that pleasure. To Lehto "they" was a vague entity. It consisted not only of Lammio, but of everything he had rebelled against since his childhood. And there was little he had not been against. To Lehto there were two kinds of people only: enemies, and the indifferent. As far as he could remember he had hated people since that time during the great Depression when, living like a stray dog in Tampere, he used to take a rusty tin to the Workers' Building for a share of the soup they were doling out free there. He hadn't even been able to join the Communists, for he couldn't bear to let anyone become close to him. Only two men had ever aroused any feeling of respect in him, Kaarna and Koskela; but even with them, woven into the feeling was a proud assertion of his own individuality and superiority.

Driven onward by this omnipresent hate he advanced step by step, trying to pierce the darkness with his eyes, his ears alert for the faintest sound. The forest thinned out and he knew he could not be far from the road. At the same moment, a pungent alien smell came to his nostrils through the damp night air and drizzling rain. He raised his rifle and was about to move off the path when a voice cried out almost at his feet. He saw a bright flash, felt a paralyzing blow in his chest and with a sharp cry fell senseless to the ground.

4.

As the Russian lines opened fire, Vanhala, Rahikainen and Sihvonen dropped to cover beside the path, but Riitaoja again abandoned his ammunition boxes and raced off in panic. Rahikainen had discarded the tripod, but Vanhala still clung to the gun itself.

—Let's go, boys, gasped Sihvonen. —Ivan'll be attacking soon.

—What's happened to Lehto? For once Vanhala's voice was serious.

—Happened? Didn't you hear him holler? I'm not staying here to get shot. I warned him . . . but he had to go and get himself killed.

Rahikainen started to crawl away as the Russian fire ceased. Now the silence was doubly terrifying, the darkness seemed saturated with danger. The others were already withdrawing after Rahikainen when Vanhala whispered:

—What if he's only wounded? We ought to find out . . .

—How can you find out? And even if he is, you won't bring him out of there alive . . . under their very noses. It'd only mean more men killed. And besides, he told us to go back for help.

—Yes, one of us . . . Where's the tripod?

—I left it there on the path . . . and the damned thing can stay there. Try dragging it away and they'll hear you and make hash of us.

—The officers may ask for it, said Vanhala. He was of two minds. He had his fear under control but it was hard for him to oppose another man's will, for he was not a leader. Still, to leave matters as they were seemed somehow unfortunate.

—You take the barrel, and I'll get it.

—Go ahead, said Rahikainen. —I've done all I feel like doing tonight.

Rahikainen and Sihvonen crawled away, leaving Vanhala to creep noiselessly along the path toward the tripod. He reached it and began cautiously to pull it to one side. But inevitably it clinked against a stone on the path, and a burst from an automatic rifle lashed the ground around him. With an oath he snatched up the tripod, hoisted it on his shoulder and, heedless now of noise, dashed to cover beside the others. And no sooner had he got his wind back than he began to giggle. His successful venture had given him so much self-confidence that now he would not leave Lehto to his fate but decided he had to find out what had happened to him. And the only means he had to do that was shouting, so he yelled as loudly as possible:

—Leh-to—oh!

An automatic rifle replied angrily, but they heard nothing else.

—Jesus, don't yell like that! Why won't you believe me that he's dead? Why else would he keep quiet?

—What was that noise over there? whispered Sihvonen.

They listened intently, but the sound was not repeated. After that, however, they made haste to get away from the place. There was something about Lehto's loss that had made them feel more helpless than usual. They had certainly never had any great liking for their section leader, but his courage and savage determination had made them trust him. He had seemed to them bigger and more to be feared than the Russians, and thus invulnerable to harm from that source. But now he had fallen before an automatic rifle fired blindly at a sound. They had seen many men die, but Lehto's death was all the more horrible because of the loneliness in which he must have died. Left out there alone in the darkness, almost at the enemy's feet. His cry still rang in their ears, full of warning, surprise and lamentation.

All this while they had given no thought to Riitaoja, knowing that he must be lying terror-stricken some distance in their rear. But now as they withdrew they called him guardedly, but got no answer. Reaching the meadow they stopped to search for him, still softly calling his name.

—Who knows where the damn fool went? said Sihvonen.

—He'll have to head back to the company, said Rahikainen. —Anyway, it's no use looking for a man in this darkness.

Setting a course by the sounds of firing, they headed for the road by a long detour which they guessed would bring them back behind their own firing line.

5.

Lehto regained consciousness only to become aware of agonizing pain and sink back into merciful blackness. His great strength, however, was not so easily overcome, and soon he was again conscious. But he had no memory of anything and could not recall where he was and what had happened except that sharp, burning pains were racing through his chest and stomach. Then gradually it all came back to him.

He felt his body, pain sweeping over him at every movement. His stomach was wet with blood and his back too was moist and warm. Each movement was as though someone twisted a knife inside him. His legs were numb; and dimly he realized the lower part of his body was completely paralyzed.

He knew then that all was over for him.

Moaning softly he gave way for a moment to despair. For the first time in his life he let go of himself, only to be brought back to full consciousness by the excruciating pain. Even now he did not grasp at the hope that leads men to believe against all the laws of probability that a chance of salvation still exists. He considered his position with the same brutal frankness that had been his attitude toward everything else. He knew that the machine-gun crew had been with him, but he did not call out for help at once as another man would have done. That, he knew, would merely prolong the agony, for he was convinced that at the best he had no more than a few hours to live. On the way here they had discussed what chance the wounded would have on this expedition where the corpsmen would have to rely solely on a shot of morphine, luck and the prayers of a weak-kneed battalion chaplain.

When he discovered that several bullets had pierced the upper part of his stomach he knew for certain that he would die. He was aware also that the Russians were all around him, for he could hear low coughs and whispers from the opposite side of the road. Everything pointed to one decision, but where was his rifle?

He groped about him but failed to find it. Like the other machine gunners he had not taken any hand grenades with him because of the weight of the extra cartridges they had to carry. For a moment he thought of his sheath knife, only to discard the idea as too taxing in his present weakened condition; instead of inflicting a mortal wound, he might merely make a bigger mess of himself. He went on groping, but the least movement cost him so much extra agony that soon he again lost consciousness.

When he came to, he felt weaker but was in less pain than before. A groan rattled in his throat, and certain as he was that his companions had fled, he spat the blood out of his mouth and shouted hoarsely:

—Vanhala . . .

—Pa-pa-pa-pa-pa-pa . . . pa-pa-papa.

—Rahikainen . . .

—Pa-pa-pa-pa-pa-pa.

—Vanhala . . . aah . . .

—Pa-pa-pa-pa-pa.

The burst flew over him, for he was lying in the shelter of a bank beside the path. If only he had dropped flat the instant the Russian had cried out, the bank would have saved him. Now it only prolonged his agony, and calling up all his strength he shouted with some of his old fury:

—Lower . . . lower . . . you goddamned squint-eyed whore's son . . . aim lower!

—Pa-pa-pa-pa-pa-pa-pa.

—Don't you hear me, you damn pissheads? Lower . . .

—Pa-pa-pa-pa-pa.

Lehto wept with pain and rage. The sound was that of an animal in its death agony, a blend of curses and tears. Aah . . . aa . . . ah . . . haa. Can't you bastards kill a man? Throw a grenade . . .

—Pa-pa-pa-pa-pa-pa-pa-pa.

Lehto turned on his side. The pain made everything go black, but he had had time to catch sight of something that restored his courage. A couple of yards away the breech of his rifle glittered.

He began an agonizing journey. Scrabbling at the mud with his nails, he pulled his paralyzed body along, inches at a time. His nails bent double and pain made him bite his lips until they split. Twice he fainted, though for no more than seconds. His mind held only one thought—the shining object lying so near and yet so terribly far. He struggled toward it, and at last his fingers closed on the strap. He drew the rifle to his side, raised the barrel and put its muzzle in his mouth. He bit as hard as he could on the cold steel, smelling of gunpowder, then he turned his head until the barrel pointed to his palate. Straining, he slid his hand down until his finger was on the trigger. Slowly he squeezed the trigger.

The report startled the Russians. An automatic rifle chattered, a hand grenade thudded on the ground beyond the path. Then silence descended.

6.

Riitaoja crouched beside the tumbledown barn in the meadow, sobbing quietly. At first the building had given him a sense of security, for at least it was the work of human hands and amid all the darkness and danger it had seemed to breathe a human warmth. Then its gloomy silence began to frighten him. Maybe it was occupied by the Russians. This was a night of ambushes.

To the extent that his paralyzing fear would let him, he began to consider plans of escape. Over there where the firing was going on must be where his comrades were. But Lammio was certainly there, too, and he had thrown away his ammunition boxes again. It was a case of leaping from the frying pan into the fire. And to the right lay instant death. For all he knew, the whole of Number One crew might be lying dead there right now.

A breath of wind caused a rustle at the corner of the barn and set the grass swaying. Riitaoja swallowed and set off slowly toward the spot where the path began. If he could find his ammunition boxes, he could return to his unit. He was but minutes too late; Vanhala, Rahikainen and Sihvonen had only just crept away from the meadow when he reached the path.

Dark and ominous, the path lay before him. Shaking with fear, Riitaoja walked on, stopping every now and then to whisper the names of the members of his crew into the darkness. His legs would hardly obey him. He had no idea whatever of the distance from the meadow to the road and expected every minute to hear shots ring out and feel the slugs tearing through his body.

Then, dead ahead of him, he heard Lehto shout: — Vanhala . . .

When the automatic rifle opened fire, Riitaoja threw himself down on the ground and lay trembling, incapable of answering Lehto. Then when Lehto went on calling Vanhala and Rahikainen, Riitaoja was misled into thinking that they too were somewhere in front. In his panic he failed to understand what had happened even when he heard Lehto's groans and curses. Then came a long silence, and Riitaoja was emboldened to crawl a little closer on all fours.

Suddenly the burst of firing provoked by Lehto's shot rattled around him. Then when the hand grenade exploded, he sprang to his feet in terror and began to run blindly, screaming:

—Don't . . . don't . . . !

The bullet splintered the back of his head, so that he was spared the knowledge of death.

Chapter VII

I.

The platoon Lehto's section was to join had been unable to extend its front far enough to the left without losing contact with the First Platoon. Hence no other course had been open to Lieutenant Sarkola than to amend his orders on his own initiative and advance a hundred yards to the right of the path. But, good soldier that he was, he had reported the situation.

When Koskela heard of the enforced change of plans, he at once sent a messenger to warn Lehto. But the messenger had not gone far before he was met by Lehto's men returning.

Koskela was on his knees in the roadside ditch peering into the darkness, from which came the sounds of a Russian tank, when Rahikainen crawled to his side and reported:

—Lehto's dead. . . . There was nobody there.

Koskela stared into the darkness. Then, after a long silence, he said, as though it had taken him all this while to digest the news:

—Yes? . . . So no one was there.

—No one but the Russkies. They didn't seem to care for us.

Rahikainen was still upset and his voice was surly as though he expected to be criticized. He misinterpreted Koskela's long silence as unvoiced criticism and went on in an aggrieved voice:

—Christ, what else could you expect! We were creeping along the path when an automatic rifle opened fire . . . Lehto was hit right off . . .

—Ah . . . And you left his body there?

—You bet we did. We were right under the Russkies' noses. We had a job getting the gun away.

—Where are the others?

—Back there. I don't know about Riitaoja, though. Hasn't he turned up here?

—We haven't seen him.

—He disappeared somewhere. We looked for him and shouted, but when he didn't answer, we thought he'd come back here.

—He hasn't, and I can't spare anybody to look for him. Rokka!

—What's the matter?

Rokka crawled along the ditch to Koskela's side.

—Lehto's dead. You're in charge of Number One gun from now on. Send Sihvonen back to his own squad and take Wolf in yours.

—All right. How did he get it?

—They ran towards the enemy defenses in the dark.

Koskela stared into the darkness:

—They shouldn't have been sent straight in. Why didn't they go around by the flank . . . ?

—Well, there's two kinds of luck. Some's good and some's bad. Lehto's just turned bad . . . Damn that tank. Why doesn't it come nearer? We've mined the roadside.

—Take up your positions on the left. If the tank misses the mines, don't mess with it, but see that the infantry behind it doesn't get through.

The road had been cut and Russian reinforcements had been rushed to the scene. Both sides were preparing for the inevitable battle on the morrow and the sporadic firing along the front was the result of the jumpiness of the advanced posts. Rokka's squad lay concealed beside the road, careful not to reveal its position by firing, for the tank rumbling a little ways ahead was still occasionally firing at random into the dark.

—Don't shoot unless you have to, boys, whispered Rokka. —Damn you, come a little closer. Just a little . . . The bastard isn't coming. Have I got to go and put a grenade down its vent? Jesus, here it comes, here it comes . . . that's the way . . . now!

The ground shook and a flame lit up the night as a mine exploded under the tank's caterpillar track. Immediately a furious exchange of fire broke out, only to weaken and die away again. A tongue of flame licked one side of the tank, and soon it was blazing like a torch, making the waning night bright as day.

Rokka whispered joyfully: —He drove over a mine. Jesus Christ, that's one bastard we won't have to worry about again.

—Don't crow. You don't know yet how it'll turn out.

Rahikainen was still under the effect of his recent shock. Vanhala, however, was exuberant. Rokka was a man after his own heart; Lehto had too often cut short his merriment with a curt: —Stop your damn snickering. But Rokka was himself always joking, and to Vanhala the future was bright.

The tank burned amid a great many explosions as the heat set off the ammunition inside. Rokka watched for an attempt by the crew to escape, but they had apparently been knocked unconscious by the mine, for no one tried to leave the tank.

They watched the blaze, its reflection making their faces shine in the darkness. Rokka was in high spirits, for the destruction of the tank materially reduced the danger they were in. Wolf regarded the burning tank for a long time in silence and then said in a voice that was little more than a whisper:

—That's a hell of a way to die.

—Don't you start pitying anybody. This isn't a Sunday School. You've got to kill or be killed in this game. I've told you we aren't here to die but to kill. It's the only way to keep alive.

Paw raised his rifle to his cheek, fired into the darkness and ejected the spent cartridge:

—I wasn't thinking of that . . . And those men in the tank aren't the only ones.

2.

Dawn brought a wretched gray morning. It had stopped raining, but everything was wet. Water dripped from the branches of the spruce trees, and their wet trunks loomed black in the pale light. The men were soaked to the skin, for the slightest movement released a cold shower from twigs and leaves.

The men shivered in their wet clothes, trying to forget their misery, and indeed it was gradually submerged in their realization that soon they would again experience the greatest excitement possible for a human being, that of meeting death face to face.

The Russians had withdrawn a ways to avoid being caught in a trap when daylight came, and the men were encouraged by their retreat, the more optimistic taking it as a sign that the road would fall without a fight. They were blissfully ignorant of the true situation. They did not know that Russian troops were swarming in their rear, that their telephone communications had been cut and that their only contact was by radio. Nor did they know that the division had been unable to advance far enough along the road to give them artillery support.

They had to enlarge the foothold they held quickly, for it was far too small. The battalion therefore moved forward on both sides of the road. Reaching the spot where the path from the meadow met the road, they found the bodies of Lehto and Riitaoja and realized what had happened. The back of Lehto's head was blown almost completely off.

—He shot himself through the mouth. Three bullets in his chest. See how he dragged himself along . . . his nails are in shreds.

—So Lehto was dead, was he? said Hietanen, looking at Vanhala and Rahikainen. Vanhala nervously shuffled his feet, but Rahikainen spoke up angrily:

—I don't know; he didn't answer our shouts. You've got no reason to look at me like that.

—I'm just surprised. We seem to have a real mystery here. How could a dead man shoot himself? No, by God, it just doesn't seem logical.

Rahikainen swore and slung his rifle violently over his shoulders. Koskela gazed silently at the bodies, then, to put an end to the argument, said:

—It looks like he regained consciousness later. What difference does it make? One thing's certain: they couldn't have brought him away. Anyone who tried it would only have been killed too. It's a good thing it was Lehto. He was better at facing that kind of death than I'd have been.

Mystery also attached itself to Riitaoja's body. Vanhala insisted that it had not been there when they left, pointing out that the corpse lay on top of the tracks which the legs of the tripod had made in the path when he dragged it away. It was Koskela who drew the obvious conclusion that Riitaoja had returned to the spot later. This the others found difficult to believe, for it would have meant he had done so voluntarily.

They laid the bodies out side by side beside the path, and Koskela spread their overcoats over them. The men's faces were strangely solemn. Carefully they extracted the cartridges from the dead men's pockets, for they were too precious to be wasted, and then hastened to catch up with the company.

After advancing some three hundred yards the battalion made contact with the Russians anew and took up defensive positions. Around a bend in the road a large tank trundled into view, then another. Strong Russian infantry units were obviously deployed to attack behind their protection.

—Dig in.

—With what? Our fingernails?

—Where's your goddamn entrenching tools? See what happens when you throw stuff away!

The supply of entrenching tools tended to vary widely. In combat it grew as the men took them from the Russian dead, but during even the briefest march they were sent flying into bushes. There were, however, a few, and these were kept well employed. Other men tried to throw up some sort of protection with their bare hands, for the ability of a man to deceive himself grows in proportion to his need to do so. A man would take cover behind a tussock on which he had laid a rotting branch and a few handfuls of moss. It would not stop a rifle bullet, and they knew it would not, but somehow it made them feel protected.

For the most part the men were calm and determined, for there was something irrevocable in the situation. And there was no escape, a fact which greatly simplified matters.

Kariluoto and his platoon defended the road with the help of two of Koskela's machine guns, one on each side of the road. Now Kariluoto came crawling along his firing line on all fours, exhorting the men to stand firm:

—Remember, boys, I don't want anyone pulling out. Every man stays put. No matter what happens.

Behind them a Finnish trench mortar was trying to lay down a barrage with its scanty stock of shells. The men cursed its inadequacy and then went on to curse the mortar crew for firing at all as the Russian artillery opened up in retaliation for the few shells.

—Damn fools . . . looking for trouble. See what you've stirred up!

Shells were crashing behind them, for luckily the Russians' range was a little long. When it stopped, brown-clad figures could be seen flitting through the trees and a long, nerve-wracking cry went up:

—Uraa . . . aaa . . . raaa . . . aaaaa . . .

It was like a signal. An incessant rattle set in which deafened the men. And always, mingling with it, rising and falling, was that uraa . . . aaaa . . . uraaaa . . . aaaa . . .

The tanks crawled toward them. Obviously aware that a force which had driven through such swampy terrain could not have brought along heavy anti-tank weapons, they drove brazenly to the edge of the minefield the pioneers had laid, and stood firing as if they were on the practice range.

Hasty cries went up along the firing line:

—Anti-tank men . . . Anti-tank men.

An anti-tank rifle squad crawled along the ditch where a pioneer lieutenant was lying trying to make himself heard above the din:

—You can't stop them. Hey . . . you there . . . that rifle's not heavy enough . . .

But the anti-tank men crept on their way, oblivious to the officer's shouting. Now three of them were crawling forward with the rifle while the others remained in the ditch. They fired two ineffectual shots, then the muzzle of the tank's cannon turned on them like the eye of an avenging god, and rifle and crew vanished in the smoke of an explosion. When the smoke cleared three mutilated bodies lay in the ditch, the twisted barrel of the rifle sticking up in their midst.

New cries came from the firing line:

—Engineers . . . explosives . . .

They knew that when the tank commander overcame his fear of mines and ventured to advance along the shoulder of the road it would be the end of their defense.

The Russian infantry was now only a hundred yards away. A man would suddenly appear running crouched over, flit for an instant among the trees and take cover again or drop in between, hit by a bullet. The platoon fired until their barrels were too hot to hold. Wordless, dazed with excitement and noise, they loaded and fired, loaded and fired, and each time a hand groped for cartridges one thought ran through their minds: —Is that all I have left . . . ?

Here and there voices shouted: —Stretcher bearers! In the act of aiming, a man would realize that the man next to him was no longer firing, and turn to see him lying motionless. But he could not afford to pause for long. Nor were they able to follow what was going on around them. Pale, tight-lipped, tense-faced, shouting in voices hoarse with excitement, they fought for their lives.

The Russian advance was visibly slowing down now, and gradually the two sides became locked in a bitter exchange of fire. The two tanks, however, were still in constant action, and an icy fear gripped the defenders' hearts at the prospect of their turning off the road.

Hietanen lay behind a boulder on the left-hand side of the road with Rahikainen close behind him, Rokka having sent into the firing line the members of his crew not actually needed to operate the machine gun. Some distance ahead was a cluster of juniper bushes behind which Hietanen thought he saw something moving, possibly a machine gun being put into position. Soon a stream of bullets proved that he had guessed rightly.

When the burst rattled around them, Rahikainen ducked and fired without aiming, his rifle almost upright. Hietanen screamed at him wrathfully:

—Aim, God damn you! Don't fire at clouds. Those bushes are crawling with men.

Rahikainen fired again, his head still ducked behind the rock. As with most brave men, Hietanen's own fear expressed itself in a restless need for action, and made Rahikainen's attempts to hide seem all the more contemptible. Hietanen knew that failure to contain the attack spelled death for them all, for it would be easy for the Russians to wipe out a scattered, fleeing horde. The thought made him furious, and he yelled:

—Jesus Christ! Stop wasting cartridges.

An old dislike of Hietanen revived itself in Rahikainen's mind. Nor had he forgotten Hietanen's remarks beside Lehto's body.

—Don't order me around. Do you think you're a goddamned general?

—I'm enough of a general to make you take aim when I tell you to. Fire at that bush. There's a machine gun and its whole damn crew there.

Rahikainen deliberately raised his head, fired and retorted:

—You keep your trap shut. A lousy sergeant! Your stripes must have gone to your head.

Hietanen was so angry that he almost rose to hit Rahikainen. A Russian shell made him duck his head again, however, and he went on firing, though he continued to give vent to his feelings as he did so.

—Just shut up so I won't have to shut that muzzle of yours. A bastard like you . . .

No answer came from Rahikainen. The lead tank had turned off the road and was approaching them, while the other tank stepped up its fire to the limit. A new cry burst from the Russian infantry, and again men were seen flitting between the trees. The defenders' fire slackened, however, instead of increasing. Obviously, it would not take much more to send them fleeing in panic. The pioneer lieutenant who had been lying in the ditch half-rose and set off at a couching run toward the tank, a mine dangling from his hand. He had covered only a few paces before he spun around and fell a few feet away from Hietanen.

3.

Hietanen could actually see the bullets strike the lieutenant, for with each impact the man's blouse fluttered. For a second he hesitated. With death before his eyes it was even harder to summon up nerve for what he knew he had to do. In his brain was the frozen awareness that unless he did something the tank would crush him, and that if he fled, he would be shot in the back. The second alternative, however, offered to postpone the fatal moment briefly, and thus tempted Hietanen. In those two seconds he was weighed in the balance.

The tank was twenty yards away, but between it and Hietanen lay the torn-up roots of a fallen tree. It was for this shelter that the pioneer lieutenant had been running. Making up his mind, Hietanen crawled swiftly to the dead man's side and snatched the mine out of his hand as bullets flew around his feet and angry hisses sounded in his ears. Then he was on his feet, running for all he was worth for the shelter of the fallen tree. As he did so, he heard Rokka calling:

—Cover him! Cover him!

Gasping for breath Hietanen threw himself down in the blessed shelter of the fallen tree. He drew the mine close to him, and suddenly the thought struck him that he knew neither whether it was in working order nor how to work it. All he knew was that it was intended to explode under heavy pressure. And it was too late to learn more now.

A picture flashed before his eyes of a caterpillar track churning beneath its armor. —There . . . right there . . . swiftly he rose and made his throw. The weight of the mine made careful aim impossible, and it was with a prayer on his lips that Hietanen ducked down again. He flattened himself behind the fallen tree, opened his mouth and pressed his palms tightly over his ears.

He sensed the explosion not as sound but as a stunning concussion that wrenched the breath from his body and left him unconscious. —When he came to his senses, he saw that the tank had stopped almost sideways to him, still partly hidden in the smoke and dust. He saw too that the men nearest to him all had their mouths wide open but failed to grasp why for he was unable to hear their ecstatic yells. His brain seemed benumbed, and he was incapable of thinking what to do next as he lay looking now at the tank, now at the men.

Suddenly he saw a foot come into view beneath the tank, then another, followed by a pair of legs. Then the man gave a jerk and moved no more. Hietanen glanced behind him and saw Rahikainen's excited face, but his deafened ears could not hear him shout:

—Get under cover! I'll take care of the rest.

Only then did Hietanen's brain begin to function. He made a dash to his former shelter and crouched behind the boulder.

—Keep under cover. I'll finish it.

Rahikainen's tone seemed to imply that a good half of the destruction of the tank was his own work. Hietanen's deed had provided an annihilating answer to his taunts, and to restore his own self-esteem now he adopted a protective and patronizing attitude toward him.

Hietanen, however, merely lay in the shelter of his rock shivering as if he had a chill. As his brain began to function again, his terror grew. With trembling fingers he dug out a cigarette and thrust it in his mouth. He managed on the fourth match to light one side of the cigarette and drew on it nervously.

His shivering gradually abated, and he began to hear firing and shouts. Then, abruptly, a wave of laughter swept over him, releasing him from his terror and bringing with it a fierce joy that he had come through safely and that he had dared to perform a deed that had marked him as the savior of the battalion.

Meanwhile the situation had altered greatly. Left alone, the second tank had withdrawn in confusion and the Russian infantry abandoned their attack. Soon they no longer returned the platoon's fire. Men rose cautiously to their feet and discovered that they could do so in safety. The Russians had retreated.

Koskela at once hastened to Hietanen:

—Are you all right? You ought to get a furlough for that.

Hietanen heard Koskela's voice but not his words. He stammered in confusion:

—I don't remember anything. Not a single goddamn thing. I threw it, and that's the last I know. Thank God that lieutenant had time to set it. Jesus, I was scared. I didn't think a human being could be as frightened as I was.

—I've finished it off, said Rahikainen, joining them. But although he might have succeeded in deceiving himself, he did not fool Koskela who ignored him. The three of them approached the tank warily.

Hietanen climbed up on its turret and with considerable effort managed to lift the heavy lid. He thrust his head inside, then withdrew it:

—They've all had it!

—This one I got's a lieutenant, Rahikainen called from beneath the tank, where he was cutting off the dead man's insignia.

Hietanen had already forgotten their quarrel. He stared at the tank in genuine surprise:

—By God, I'm a hero. A goddamn hero! Now if only that buzzing in my head would stop. You don't think anything's wrong with it, do you?

—What's there in it to go wrong? asked Rahikainen. The bantering words were an invitation to let bygones be bygones, and Hietanen, accepting it, laughed.

Soon a score of men and officers, all full of praise for Hietanen, had gathered around the tank. Even Lammio was there nodding his approval. Then the circle parted as Major Sarastie arrived on the scene and proudly shook Hietanen's hand.

—I guess I know best of all what you've done because I know how bad things were. First of all, thanks. There'll be a Liberty Cross for you, and we'll put a recommendation in for your sergeant's stripes right away.

Hietanen flushed with embarrassment, and now Sarastie went on to matters of more import.

—From all reports this new tank is a great success. But even the most skillful designers haven't been able to devise protection against Finnish courage.

A moment before, the major had been praising Hietanen, but now he shifted the praise to himself. Like most military leaders he identified his troops' every achievement with himself. The failures, of course, were due to someone else's cowardice or to insurmountable difficulties. It was, however, true that the major had been under a greater strain than his men, who had not known how truly critical their situation was. And all battalion and company commanders had received special orders forbidding their moving their command posts to the rear no matter what happened. The implication was clear that in case of defeat, they were to die at their posts.

The situation was now no longer so serious. The failure of the Russian attack had strengthened their morale, and a report had just been received from Divisional HQ that the artillery would at last be able to lend support as soon as the batteries had taken up positions.

Shortly before, however, Sarastie had lived through some anxious moments. Many of the heavy infantry weapons were running short of ammunition, his last reserves had been committed, and his flank facing the swamp was almost completely unprotected.

Sarastie therefore had good reason to feel pleased. The importance of the operation was such as to guarantee that it was being watched with interest all the way up to GHQ. Why, at that very moment the Marshal might be listening to a report: —An attempt to break through from the west was foiled by Battalion Sarastie after hard fighting. Other attempts to bring relief from the north and east on a smaller scale were also repulsed.

4.

Lahtinen and Maatta could not afford to waste time marveling at tanks. They were collecting cartridges from the enemy dead, for they had almost exhausted their own supply. Lahtinen was in the act of turning a dead Russian on his back in order to get at his pockets when he heard the major's loud voice from across the road.

—Listen to that big noise! Christ, we're lucky we're still alive. Those bastards are a tough lot—coming at us bolt upright even after I'd let them have four whole belts.

Maatta was not impressed. —Count your blessings. It's easier to hit 'em if they're not all crouched over. . . . It's a good thing we use the same caliber. I'm glad someone had the sense to make sure of that.

—Ho . . . what was sense about it? It all started with the rifles we stole from the Russkies during the 1918 rebellion. That's the original reason.

—I thought you said it was the Germans who armed the bourgeoisie.

—Sure they did—with the rifles they'd taken from the Russkies on the Eastern Front. Jesus, look at this son of a bitch still clutching his rifle. Come on, let it go. You won't? By God, I'm still a match for any dead man. One measly cartridge! Let's take a look over there. Ivan had a machine gun there.

They found the gun still standing amid the bodies of four dead Russians. Beside it were five full ammunition belts and in the block another one only half fired. Lahtinen gathered up the belts happily.

—The belt I used on these bastards wasn't wasted. Nearly six for one is a good trade. Six? No, there's two hundred and fifty cartridges in their belts and only two hundred in ours. We'd better share these, we won't be able to carry them all.

—There's plenty there for the others. Say, that one there looks pretty old. They must be running short of men.

—Don't you believe it!

Lahtinen's dissent was strictly routine; he was too pleased with the haul of ammunition to argue. His face wore a self-satisfied smile as he slung the ammunition boxes on his shoulder and turned to go:

—We've got to switch these to metal belts, these canvas rags are no damned good. No, the Russians won't run out of men. They've got plenty of them and all the equipment they need. Right now they may be a little hard up, but that stands to reason. They've tried to see to it that the people have at least something to eat and haven't sunk everything into ammunition for loafers. They used to fire the people's money away into the four winds. Sundays running around the forests with rifles on their backs and then promoting each other in the evenings. Although it's no better now. If the Russians run out of men they still have fifteen million women soldiers. Everybody's trained over there. Even the old women.

—And where's all that been going on?
Rokka had heard only the last part of Lahtinen's speech and was grinning slyly as he asked the question.
—In Russia. If you need any ammunition, help yourself.
—Let's see what you've got. I picked up some but we could use some more. The boys are all hunting for bread and insignia and don't give a damn about cartridges. But what's all this about our being attacked by all the women in Russia?
Lahtinen was annoyed, guessing what would follow. Nor was he mistaken.
—At least we'd know where to aim! And knowing where to aim, we could even use Rahikainen.
—We'd see some real close fighting, khee-hee. That's when Rahikainen'd earn a Mannerheim Cross.
Their bantering was ended by Koskela and Hietanen's arrival with the news that they would be moving on immediately. Koskela had ordered Hietanen back to the field dressing station until his hearing was normal again, but after his exploit nothing so tame would suit Hietanen. He was too restless to keep still anywhere. And nobody envied him his sincere self-satisfaction, for always his boasting was done with a note of humor which in the eyes of these men redeemed anything.
—Get moving . . .
The talk and laughter stopped, and their carefree mood disappeared as quickly as it had come. They trudged on silently, their faces tense and restless.
After advancing about a half mile they again encountered resistance. But now they had artillery support and succeeded in driving their foes ahead of them for another hundred yards. On the outskirts of a village, however, they were brought to a halt. They made one more unsuccessful assault before nightfall, and then exhaustion and darkness put an end to the battle. Grimly Sarastie decided he would have to wait for the morrow even though that meant leaving the wounded without proper care for another twenty-four hours.
The battalion spread out in positions along the edge of the village fields. Before them lay a potato field and under cover of the darkness Rokka and Rahikainen stole out into it. Rahikainen, however, did not stay long, for when the Russians heard their digging they came under heavy fire. But Rokka only took cover in a ditch

until the firing stopped, and eventually came back with such a large load of potatoes that there were enough left over for Kariluoto's platoon.

They dug a pit behind their positions and built a fire in it to cook their booty, but when it began to draw Russian fire they quickly extinguished it, and squatting down in the darkness and drizzling rain, wolfed down the raw and unwashed potatoes. They had finished the last of their three days' dry rations that morning, and the potatoes tasted good. As soon as they had finished, the men not on guard duty stretched out under spruce trees and despite the old rain fell into an exhausted sleep.

But as deeply as they slept, fear was awake within them. If the rhythm of the desultory firing increased, a sleeper would jerk into a sitting position, listen tensely until the firing slackened and then drop back again, asleep before his body touched the ground.

5.

The field dressing station's tent was full to overflowing even though the unconscious who were sure to die and the lightly wounded had been carried outside. The orderlies sprawled in a stupor which served to isolate them from all the surrounding misery, and the medical officer was also worn out and nervous. It tortured him to see men dying when an immediate operation would have saved them, but all he could do was dress wounds and give morphine to relieve the pain.

One of the badly wounded was dying. A bullet had struck him in the stomach the previous night and he had been in great pain until, as the day drew to a close, unconsciousness had mercifully brought him relief. Now, as the medical officer bent over him, the man opened his eyes. Bright with fever they stared up at the tent wall on which a powerful gasoline lamp cast the doctor's shadow, dark and shapeless.

—Well, how are you coming? whispered the doctor as he saw that the man was conscious. The man stared without answering at the shadow on the wall. Then his lips moved and he tried to raise his head, but he was too weak. Again his lips moved and this time the doctor caught a few words:

—D-death . . . On the wall . . . Lord . . . Jesus.

The doctor laid his hand on the man's shoulder to stop his desperate attempts to rise.

—Take it easy. There's nothing there. Close your eyes and try to get some rest.

The man relaxed and lay back, his eyes now glazed and unseeing. Knowing he could do no more for him, the doctor sighed and crawled out of the tent on all fours. Outside he spied the chaplain huddled under a tree:

—Eerola's dying. You ought to try to do something for him. He's in pain, and I can't go on giving him shots of morphine endlessly. He's vomiting enough as it is. Oh God, why can't they get that road open!

Even as he spoke, the doctor had his doubts about the wisdom of sending the chaplain to speak to the man. Would a wounded man enjoy hearing a dying man being prepared for his departure while he himself waited, with fear in his heart, for his own hour to strike? The doctor cursed the Third Battalion to whose field dressing station he had had to lend his other tent because of their larger number of casualties.

—We half killed ourselves carrying the goddamn tents and then we have to give them away. Why in hell do we have to just sit here?

—The C.O. said the men were too exhausted to attack before morning. Did Eerola ask to see me?

—No, but he's afraid of dying and I think he was praying. See what you can do for him.

The chaplain took off his black rubber raincoat and hung it on a tree. He cleared his throat and laboriously got down on his knees, for he was in the habit of praying before embarking on anything. Indeed, it had become so much a habit that it was hardly a prayer at all, but as perfunctory an act as the few strokes of a whetstone a haymaker gives his scythe before starting on a new swath.

Finished, he crawled into the tent, shielding his eyes with his arm until he became accustomed to the light of the gasoline lantern, and gagging as the stink of sweat, blood and disinfectant came to his nostrils. An orderly nodded half asleep beside the stove, paying no attention to the moans of the wounded men lying wrapped in blankets along the sides of the tent.

The chaplain made his way to Eerola's side. Eerola looked up at him, his eyes glassy with approaching death, and the chaplain noted the big drops of sweat standing out on his face. It was an infallible sign that he had little time left.

—My son, are you in pain?

The man said something, but the words were unintelligible.

Eerola's dirty, ravaged face had assumed a yellowish cast. He was only twenty, a slightly built lean youth who had been undernourished since infancy. He had grown up working twelve and fourteen hours a day on a farm on which his father was a common laborer, a position than which nothing was lower on the social scale save vagrants and poorhouse inmates. Hard work and poor food had left their stamp on his body, yet the toughness acquired through day after day and year after year of hardship refused to give in to death.

The chaplain watched as life ebbed from the boy's features. As had the doctor before him, he put his ear to the boy's lips and listened to the hoarse, rattling whisper:

—Jesus . . . Jesus . . . will take . ... from here.

—Be calm, my son . . . be calm. He will help you. Jesus will not forsake you. You are His. He has redeemed you and all of us . . .

The troubled breathing became more regular, and the chaplain whispered in the dying man's ear:

—Jesus has forgiven you your sins. He will give you rest and peace everlasting.

A brief shudder shook the dying boy's frame, and he sighed softly. Carefully the chaplain pressed his eyelids shut with his fingers, whispering:

—Amen.

Across the tent another wounded man drew his blanket over his face and beneath its protection sobbed softly to himself. The chaplain was about to go to him when the man next to Eerola, drugged with morphine, groaned in a thick guttural voice: Jesus . . . Jesus . . .

The chaplain bent over him, believing that he was praying. The man was young, large in body and broad-faced. His mouth was open, revealing teeth blackened by tobacco.

—Jesus, Jesus, repeated the man.

The chaplain's voice was imploring.

—My son, shall we pray?

—Jesus, Jesus, the man repeated to himself and then suddenly broke into a tortured screeching cry.

—Quiet, quiet, whispered the chaplain, but the man went on screaming, foaming at the lips, the whites of his eyes showing. The man who had been sobbing under his blanket shouted from beneath it:—Stop it, stop it! Then he began weeping hysterically.

—A-ah . . . oh, oh. Stop it. For Christ's sake stop it!

Hurriedly the doctor entered the tent and went to the weeping man's side to try and soothe him, while the crestfallen chaplain turned to leave the tent. As he emerged he heard a corpsman say:

—Why the hell does he want to go getting them all upset? Can't he at least let them die in peace?

The chaplain took his raincoat from its branch and crouched on the ground. Half weeping he prayed to God to open the road and save the lives of the wounded. Behind him the weeping and screaming in the tent subsided; the doctor had succeeded in calming the men. Soon two orderlies came out carrying Eerola's body, and laid it at one end of the row of bodies behind the tent.

Rain poured from the heavens. Around the field dressing station sentries stood in the darkness, guarding the gloomy stand of spruce in the heart of which the price of victory was being paid in pain.

6.

During the night the Russians withdrew through the forest past the place where the road had been cut, leaving behind all their heavy equipment. Of the two tanks that had been engaged, the undamaged one had been driven into a swamp and abandoned. Skirmishing was still going on along the road when the first ambulances drove through to evacuate the wounded, many of whom had been waiting twenty-four hours for treatment. Unceasing pain, the slow torture of waiting, and the fear that the regiment might not be able to hold this salient in the enemy's rear, had been their unhappy lot. Their hearts constricted every time they saw the body of another comrade who had not been able to endure carried out to join the long line beneath the trees.

The arrival of the ambulances was greeted with hysterical joy. Even the weakest among the wounded demonstrated their relief as much as their strength permitted. The agonies of the past hours were forgotten, now all minds were bent on the future.

When daylight came, Sarastie's battalion combed the surrounding area. Kariluoto's platoon together with Koskela's men were sent to search the village before which the attack had halted the evening before. The ambulances had already driven through it, but the buildings had still not been closely searched.

Only one inhabitant had remained—an old man who was only a burden on others and had been left behind. From the window of his tiny cabin on the outskirts of the village he watched the gray-clad soldiers moving between the houses. He was badly frightened, for he had heard how the Finnish devils treated captives. Then he sighed with relief. The soldiers had dropped their packs and rifles and were running toward the potato patch.

When they had dug up all the potatoes they could carry, they washed them in the brook while Rokka brought a table, a couple of chairs and a bench from a house and broke them up for firewood. Soon potatoes were boiling in mess tins over three or four fires.

Major Sarastie came strolling along the village road, gazing at the houses. He knew that he ought to be impressed by the beauty of their gable ornamentation, though actually he knew nothing about art or architecture. But the major was essentially a conformist and since every writer and journalist who visited the area went into raptures over the local architecture and those ornate gables, Sarastie felt it was not for him to ignore them.

Then his eye caught something that really interested him. Around the corner of a house stalked a rooster. Sarastie was about to shout for his orderly when a stick whirled through the air and caught the fowl in the neck. The rooster squawked and squirmed helplessly on the ground as a soldier dashed into view and, seizing the bird by the legs, broke its neck with one jerk.

—Hey, soldier!

The man started, saw the major and stiffened to attention, the dead bird in his hand.

—What's your name?

—Private Rahikainen, sir."

—Don't you know that it's against regulations to lay hands on the property of the local population?

—Yes, Major. But there isn't any population. We looked.

—Then you ought to know that everything belongs to the government. You've been told often enough.

Rahikainen, still with the fowl hanging from his hand, spoke slowly in an effort to give himself time to concoct a plausible lie.

—Of course we know that, Major. And we haven't touched anything. But there was something wrong with this bird. It limped.

Maybe it was hurt in the fighting. It was bound to die, so I thought it'd be a waste to leave it to die by itself.

Sarastie smiled to himself. The man had his wits about him. He cast a wistful glance at the fowl, then, amused by Rahikainen's air of injured innocence, said:

—Keep it this time. But don't do it again. Let's say that you threw that stick so well that I'm giving you the bird as a prize.

Rahikainen played his part to the end with a perfectly straight face:

—Thank you, Major. I'd better go pluck it right away. We can't let it spoil.

Rahikainen speedily withdrew from the major's sight and made his way back to the platoon. The men welcomed him warmly, and soon the rooster was boiling in a bucket they had found.

Finding that no one had any salt, Rahikainen decided to see whether any had been left behind in the village. The third house he visited proved to be inhabited. Sitting on a bench was a badly frightened old man. Rahikainen was startled to come on him, but relaxed when he saw how old he was.

—Hello, what are you doing still here?

The old man looked at him but said nothing.

—Come and see, boys. There's an old man here who must be over a hundred.

The old man blinked his eyes at the men crowding into his cottage.

—Hello, grandpa, said Rokka, seating himself beside him. The oldster nodded to him.

—Greeting, greeting.

—Left you here, did they?

—They left me here.

—Did they leave you any salt? asked Rahikainen. —We need some for our stew.

—They left me nothing.

The old man kept crossing his legs nervously as he looked around him.

—Didn't they leave you anything to eat? asked Salo, drawing closer.

—They took everything. Left me all alone . . .

—Here's some bread . . . I haven't any more, but the service gangs are on the way. You'll be able to fill your belly for a change.

The old man took Salo's bread with trembling fingers, looked at it doubtfully and seemed to be on the point of handing it back, but instead thrust it into the bosom of his padded coat.

—Do you know whether there are other people here, old man?

—There's no one else. Everybody went away.

—They needn't have, said Salo. —Everything's going to be all right now. Did they treat you badly?

The old man looked at them as though uncertain what to say, then nodded:

—Badly. Very badly.

Rokka was examining the room, paying no attention to the old man. The rest wanted to know all kinds of things about life in East Karelia, and as the talk was about simple matters they had no difficulty in understanding the old fellow's dialect. For his part, he volunteered no information, contenting himself with answering questions, trying hard to guess what answer his interrogators wanted him to give. Salo did most of the asking:

—Did you have priests here?

—There was a priest earlier at Priaza. . . .

—Didn't they kill him?

—Yes, yes, he was killed.

—Have you any children?

—Two sons. They killed one, and put the other in prison. . . .

—Why did they kill him?

—He wouldn't join the collective.

—Did you have a farm?

—Yes, a farm. They took away everything.

The old man had noted that his questioners seemed to want to hear that people had been killed or ill-treated so he answered every question in the affirmative:

—Yes, killed, killed. They killed everybody.

—Never mind, you'll get your farm back. And the churches won't be used as stables any more. They'll be a new order.

—What about that salt? Rahikainen was vexed, for none had been found.

Rokka watched the old man for a time, then he patted him on the shoulder and laughed:

—You're a smart old buzzard. Go on lying to them. Why the hell should they be so inquisitive?

—That's what I think too, said Hietanen. —The old bastard's fooling us.

Salo protested angrily: —You're crazy. He's had a hard time, but now there'll be better days ahead for him.

Rokka crossed the room to the stove. On a stool beside it stood a basket over which a sack had been thrown. Rokka lifted the sack and looked at the old man, who rose to his feet in alarm.

—Well, now, old man. You've been speaking ill of the Russkies when you had no reason to. They've left you a whole basketful of bread. See for yourself. Maybe they forgot to tell you.

The old man began to tremble, but Rokka soothed him:

—Don't be frightened. We won't steal it. But if you have any salt I'll take a little of that.

Shaking with fright, the old man pointed to where some salt, brown and coarse, stood on a shelf.

—I'm taking this much, see. And in return we'll give you some stew. And tobacco. Give him some, boys.

The men thrust tobacco into the old man's trembling hands as Rokka looked at Salo and laughed:

—Let him keep the bread you gave him. He earned it for amusing you.

Salo tried to save face by joining in the laughter. With a forced guffaw he said:

—He's a clever old fox. He knows what's up.

They left the old man in peace and went back to where the rooster was stewing. A convoy was passing, causing Sihvonen to exclaim eagerly:

—Fresh troops! Now we'll get a rest.

Their hopes had centered for some time on the arrival of fresh troops. Any unfamiliar squad was eagerly questioned as to their regiment. After so many disappointments, however, most of the men had lost hope. But now Sihvonen ran to the roadside.

—What company do you belong to?

—We're the machine-gun company's transport.

—Which company?

—The First. Don't you know your own company's drivers?

—Hell, I can ask, can't I?

—Sure. What are you asking?

—You go to hell.

Then Mielonen came from the command post:

—Here we go, boys. We're attacking again.

Not a word was said, but their heads drooped dejectedly. The stew had not even had time to be more than half cooked, so they tied the bucket to the end of a pole and shouldered the pole. Perhaps there'd be time to cook it during their next rest stop.

Chapter VIII

1.

—Is it still that far to Petrozavodsk?

A dirty, black-rimmed finger hovered over a map of East Karelia.

—That's Matroosa, there. And that's Polovina, and then Vilka.

—Once we get to Petrozavodsk, I'll be damned if I'll even move for a week, said Rahikainen.

—The war won't end there, said Rokka. —Do you think it's such an important place that Russia'll fall on her knees when we capture it? Don't. There's a lot of Russia beyond Petrozavodsk.

—Who cares? We won't go any farther.

—You're damned right we won't.

—No.

—No.

—No.

Po-pow-pow-pow . . . uuuuu . . . uuuuuu . . .

—Here we go again . . .

Pa-pa-pa-pa-pa-pa-pa-pa . . .

—Stretcher bear . . . er . . . ers . . .

Pa-pa-pa-pa-pa-pa-pa . . .

Their clothes hung in shreds, their boots were mere wrecks. The lines in their faces had deepened, while the hair sprouting from their chins and the dirt encrusting their faces gave them a dark complexion. They had become inured to almost everything. They rarely complained or murmured as, gloomy and silent, they listened to their orders for their next task, their muscles still shaking with fatigue from the one just completed. Somewhere ahead lay Petrozavodsk. That was their goal, and gradually it had come to them that all their problems would be solved as soon as they arrived there. But whether they were solved or not, they swore they would not under any circumstances go any farther. So they put all their strength into their tasks. Petrozavodsk, Petrozavodsk, golden city. Like pilgrims to a holy place they struggled on, submitting uncomplainingly to any strain and suffering.

To their minds, their regiment had earned the privilege of being quartered on the town after its capture. Yet probably all the regiments fighting their way toward it, felt the same way, and for the same reasons.

—We've been in all the toughest fighting, and besides, our strength is just about gone.

The nearer they came to the town, the stiffer the resistance they met. The wearier they became the more was demanded of them, and the better they performed. But it was evident that they were cracking under the strain. On some days they would retreat before even the weakest counterattack. Their frayed nerves were often unequal to a situation they would earlier have regarded as but a skirmish.

Four miles from the town Lieutenant Autio, who had commanded the Third Company, fell, riddled by a dozen bullets. His was one of the bravest deaths they had witnessed. The men had begun to waver while warding off a counterattack. A few had already stolen away from the firing line when, to instill new courage in them, Autio rose to his feet:

—Remember who you are. Not a step backward!

An instant later his body was falling as a burst from an automatic rifle hammered into it. Now, Kariluoto was in command. Autio's death reminded him for the first time in a long while of Kaarna, and this repetition of that earlier incident was a challenge to him to show how different things were now. Bullets were flying about his head, but he rose and shouted:

—God damn you, I'll put a bullet through the first one of you who takes a step backward!

An infantryman near him was, however, more frightened of the Russians than of the usually mild-mannered Kariluoto. Scuttling like a crab, he set off on all fours toward the rear.

—Halt, damn you, halt! Kariluoto was livid.

The man kept going without even a backward glance. Once again Kariluoto cursed and screamed at the man to come back. Then, abruptly, he turned, snatched the rifle from the hands of the soldier next to him, aimed and fired. The bullet took the fugitive in the small of the back. He screamed, pitched forward, tried to rise once and then slumped to the ground dead. Without another glance Kariluoto handed the rifle back to its owner and turned his attention again to the front.

On the evening of the last day of September they reached the outskirts of the town. They lay in the twilight before the Russian's positions, looking at the bunkers and the wire.

—It's going to cost a hell of a lot of lives to storm those.

—Yes, but not ours, said Koskela. —We're not in on the attack here. There's other troops coming up for that. We're turning north.

—Jesus, no! Aren't they going to let us into the town?

The thought was bitter to their minds, and nothing more was said. The men hung their heads. Despite all their hopes, this was not, after all, to be the end of the fighting for them.

Late in the evening Finnish guns began shelling the town. The men listened to the shells howling overhead and heard them burst in the town.

—How will the people ever rebuild all that damage? said Lahtinen.

—I don't know, but it's a damn shame.

—The pissheads, sneered Rahikainen. —Blowing everything to smithereens. It won't even be worth while going in there.

—Our offensive progresses, khee-hee! Our brave gunners carry the fight to the enemy, chuckled Vanhala. He sat on a stump chewing a piece of hard bread he had found on a dead Russian. He had cut off the bloodstained parts.

2.

The morning of October 1st dawned fine and beautiful. The cloudless sky was a limpid blue so that a man looking upward and away from the autumn landscape could easily imagine it was still midsummer.

They advanced through scraggly brush, following an overhead power cable. They had not been sent north after all, but were driving to cut the roads leading north from the town. A rocky wooded ridge ahead of them now hid the town from their view, but its proximity was evidenced by the footpaths which crisscrossed the underbrush, and the scraps of paper, bits of wood and other rubbish which lay everywhere.

The first man to climb the ridge was Viirila, a foul-mouthed loutish private who was the despair of his officers, and who in peacetime would have spent most of his time in the guardhouse. In war, however, he had displayed an insensate, almost insane courage and would volunteer for any scouting job, no matter how dangerous.

As he reached the top of the ridge, he stopped.

—Hey, guys! I can see Petrozavodsk. It's all afire and the boys are plundering for all they're worth.

They all scrambled hastily up the ridge. Below them lay an airfield and beyond that clusters of houses on the edge of the waters of Lake Onega which stretched to the blue horizon. Pillars of smoke were rising from the town and bursts of desultory firing could still be heard from various quarters.

—There it is!

—What, all this trouble for that bunch of hovels?

They were astonished at the dilapidated look of the town. Amid a motley collection of shanties stood a few whitewashed brick buildings. That was all there was to the town, and the men were hard pressed to hide their disappointment. The landscape, however, was beautiful. Blue with smoke the air shimmered over the gleaming lake, and in the distance blue-gray headlands loomed above the water.

—Ha—alt!

The company dispersed and sat admiring the view. There it lay, the goal to achieve which they had endured such hardship and suffering. Now they were at their objective. Would it really mean the end of the war for them? Perhaps because they wanted it to so badly, they were actually able to believe in the possibility.

Rahikainen was impatient. —Why are we stopping here? The best pickings will all be gone.

Rokka leaned on his rifle. —It isn't worth a damn to me. Now, if that were Käkisalmi . . .

—Don't mention that name, sighed Wolf, his voice full of the wanderer's longing for home and loved ones.

Hietanen lay sprawled in the sun, his rifle propped on his knees. For a long time he said nothing, then at last he burst out proudly:

—There it is, the goal of all our hopes! I wish all the boys were alive to see it. Well, here we are, despite all they did to stop us. Boys, we've made history! Soldiers will tell about this a hundred years from now. Our children will sing about how we fought our way to Petrozavodsk. Things like this don't happen every day. There lies Finland's newest town. . . . I hope there are decent saunas there. I haven't had a bath in so long my skin itches like hell. Every time I run my fingers through my hair there are a dozen lice in 'em.

—Lice! You should see mine, Rahikainen said disparagingly. —I've had one crawling around on my belly for a week. His name's Oscar. Honestly, he's nearly a quarter of an inch long and has a Liberty Cross on his back. But what are they keeping us waiting here for? I'll bet we'll be sent to Suoju after all. They say some of the reservists have refused to go any farther. That'd really put us in the piss.

—By God, here's one man who's not going to Suoju!

Maatta was sitting on the bare rock, looking thoughtfully down at the town.

—Ha, you'll go if you're ordered to, said Sihvonen.

—Not while I'm alive.

—Did you hear that, Koskela? They're going to mutiny. What are you going to do about it?

Koskela lay on his stomach on the rock prodding a couple of ants with a twig. —Not a damn thing, he replied, his face lit with his strange smile.

Kariluoto came over to them, the wind tumbling the hair on his proudly erect head. Unconsciously he felt that this was how a conquering knight of old must have felt looking down from the walls of the castle they had just taken. This was one of the supreme moments of his life—as a commander of a Finnish infantry company he was privileged to see the blue cross rise over the tallest buildings of Petrozavodsk. Whatever doubts he might have occasionally felt on the way here were forgotten. He swallowed to clear his throat, hitched up his belt and began to speak:

—Well, boys, there it is. The Jaeger Brigade and the First Division have occupied the town. We weren't given that honor, but no matter who set foot there first, we opened the road for them. History will always acknowledge that. They're still cleaning up some resistance there, but that won't take long. For the moment we're to stay here to make sure no one gets away. Take it easy, but keep your eyes open.

—Will we get a rest?

—I don't know, but I hope so. Well, boys, we were the first to set eyes on the town—at least, of the troops advancing from this side.

—Aye, and I was the first of all to see it, Viirila said, breaking into a coarse, grating laugh.

Kariluoto smiled wanly. He could not deny that Viirila was the boldest man in the company, yet he could not overcome his dislike of the man. It seemed somehow blasphemous to think of that big-headed ape in this context.

Time passed, and now the firing had ceased in the town and people could be seen moving about.

—You'll see, boys. We'll be left licking our wounds. Everything'll be gone by the time we get there.

Rahikainen stared gloomily out over the airfield.

3.

It certainly seemed as though they were not to be allowed to enter the town. Evening, however, brought a messenger with orders for them to proceed there at once as part of the garrison. A huge barrel of vodka, perhaps left behind on purpose, had been found in the town, and the first occupying battalion was roaring drunk and busy plundering as the second battalion marched in. Every now and then they had to break ranks and take cover from a hail of bullets as drunken soldiers fired indiscriminately in the streets in celebration of their victory.

At one street corner they passed a captain and three privates. Two of the privates were holding the captain erect, for he was so drunk he had lost the use of his legs, while the third marched in front playing a mandolin. The captain's feet dragged along the ground, his head was sunk on his breast, but occasionally he would raise it and bellow out something.

—Damn you, try to walk a little on your own two feet, said one of the privates. —You've had no more than we had and you're drunk as a fish.

—Play, Hessu, spluttered the captain. —Play "From the White Sea to Ladoga Our Sword Shall Carve a Frontier . . . Whate'er our fate we shall not falter" . . . tralala la la . . .

—Try to walk a little . . .

—Walk? You walk. Tralala la la lay. The captain threw back his head and bellowed: —Whate'er our fate we shall not falter . . . We'll close the gate in the invader's face . . . And drive him into the sea . . . Hello, hello, who are you?

He now noticed the men marching past and roared:

—Welcome to the Young People's Association! Hey . . . who are you? Me, I'm Captain Usko Antero Lautsalo . . . the terror of the Russians . . . Play, Hessu, to let them know Lautsalo's coming. . . .

Lammio bade the captain's escort take him somewhere out of sight, but was answered with abuse.

—You go to hell! We don't take orders from any lousy lieutenant.

The soldiers were obviously taking advantage of the fact they had been drinking with an officer, and Lammio was helpless, for he couldn't very well arrest a captain. But it was a bitter pill for him to swallow.

The captain's eyes turned towards Lammio. He tried to balance himself on his own feet, a smirking air of self-importance on his face.

—Lieutenant . . . I ask you . . . I, Captain Usko Antero Lautsalo, that's who I am . . . I ask you by what right you give orders to my men. . . .

The captain's head slumped, he hiccuped, and, forgetting his own importance and Lammio, he bellowed:

—May there, hic . . . always be, hic . . . in mighty Finland . . . courage and resolution. . . .

—I took the liberty of pointing out to your men that their behavior was unseemly, said Lammio stiffly.

—Hic . . . hic . . . I give the orders here. . . . Forward, my brave lads! We've still got half a bucketful of vodka. . . . Forward!

The bellowing voice and the music of the mandolin died away as the quartet rounded a corner.

Next the battalion saw their first civilian—a woman, fearfully lugging a mattress somewhere. She was stout and matronly and appeared to be wearing all the clothes she owned in the world on top of each other. She walked by hurriedly, for a drunken soldier had turned when his eye fell on her and was walking at her side, addressing her in what he believed to be Russian:

—*Maatuska . . . maatuska . . . russki maatuska . . . yepatnaatsa . . . Liepuska . . . vinski Liepuska . . .*

Fear made the woman quicken her pace, but she could not shake off the man, who now tried to take her arm and pat her backside.

—*Russki maatuska . . .*

Abruptly she darted into a house, leaving her pursuer standing bewilderedly in the street. He was a big bony man with a reddish growth of beard covering his face. His dirty blouse was unbuttoned from top to bottom and one knee of his trousers showed a big rent. He thrust his enormous fists into his pocket and set off at a staggering walk, singing drunkenly.

Kariluoto had taken a few steps toward the man when he saw him seize the woman's arm, only to stop as the woman escaped into the house. He felt angry and ashamed. Bastards like that . . . where did they spring from?

The woman made him think of Sirkka for the first time in days. Even though the East-Karelian woman had been middle-aged and so wrapped in clothes that she looked like Father Christmas, just thinking of her as a woman made him remember Sirkka. His memory of her was beautiful, but it filled his heart with a painful longing. When would leaves start?

Kariluoto turned to look behind him to where the company marched in double file. How often in his childhood had he heard his father discuss East Karelia with his friends . . . a kindred people groaning under an alien yoke, their liberation was Finland's duty—a duty never to be forgotten. A Finn had to remember it while eating, while working, before going to sleep, and then in the night dream of it. Now it was an accomplished fact.

Karelia was being liberated.

At a street corner they encountered a noisy group of men laden with bundles and boxes. In his reverie Kariluoto hardly noticed them; the battalion had not yet taken over the policing of the town, and thus it was not their business to round up drunks.

Shots and cries sounded somewhere, and ahead of them fires were still blazing, painting the autumn evening sky blood red. Evening descended on Petrozavodsk's first night as a part of Greater Finland.

4.

Being an army of occupation was fine. They had time now to examine the town at leisure and see all kinds of interesting things. They rounded up the lunatics a drunken soldier had released from the local asylum with the idea that when the intent was to liberate, one set free everybody behind locks and bars. In the streets they were surprised by the number of young Russians walking about, clad, to be sure, in civilian overcoats but still wearing uniforms underneath. These were men who had strayed or deserted from their units and by their own leave become civilians. Nor did the Finns object to this, for it was what they would have liked to do themselves.

They had strict orders to guard the houses from looters, but what did it matter who owned the old phonograph records, the instruments, the crockery and all the other trash that lay everywhere? There was nothing of any real value left in the town. The inhabitants had to be protected, but once the vodka barrel had been emptied and most of the troops moved elsewhere, things quieted down of their own accord. They made friends among the local population, who were soon on very free-and-easy terms with them. One and another had found himself a woman, Rahikainen, of course, being the first to do so. His stay in town was a story in itself; a captured town with its goods, its hungry inhabitants, its women, its large army stores, was made to order for him. He was soon in business in a big way, not so much for profit but because it came naturally to him, and he was bored if he had no scheme hatching. His main occupation was obtaining food for hungry civilians, mostly as payment for the services of young girls. For an art-loving officer he ferreted out several icons, although he himself was of the opinion that a man who paid good money for them was a fool. Bashful soldiers could confidently leave their sexual affairs in his hands; he already knew every female in the place who was prepared to sell herself for bread. In fact he sold the mother of his own seventeen-year-old favorite to a sergeant for two packs of cigarettes.

They enjoyed life. Except for rare intervals of guard duty, they were free. And an order which arrived bidding them to clean out the Russian barracks for their own use indicated that this bliss would continue.

The town had been renamed Aanislinna. A Finnish field gun now stood where a statue of Lenin had previously stood, and in many other ways the change of ownership was emphasized.

Rokka, Hietanen and Vanhala walked the streets side by side, regularly forgetting to salute the officers they met. Indeed, the town was soon full of all kinds of occupying officers whose behavior in many cases was such that the men would sooner have gone to prison than acknowledge them as superiors. They had passed several officers without incident one day when a captain came along who, when they spotted him at a distance, seemed already to have his eye on them. When they gave no sign of having seen him, the captain stopped abruptly:

—Just a minute, you. Why didn't you salute?

He wore shiny new boots and spurs, and his visored cap was pulled down over his eyes in an effort to produce a very military effect.

Actually his air of importance and bravado made the comrades even less compliant than ordinarily. They regarded him blankly without answering, until the captain asked again angrily:

—Why didn't you salute your superior officer? Answer me!

Rokka smiled the sly smile he always wore when he was being sarcastic:

—We didn't notice you.

—What are you grinning at? You didn't notice me! If that's true, your offense is all the greater. An NCO failing to see an officer in an empty street—how would such a man be able to see the enemy in the field?

Rokka stopped smiling:

—Well, I guess it has something to do with an eye for color. I can't see gray properly. Brown's another matter, and that's why I manage all right with the Russkies. But our officers wear gray and I always have trouble seeing 'em. Still, I see bright things well enough, so don't worry. Now that I've noticed those spurs of yours, I won't miss you again.

—Your unit—what's your unit? Give me your names! Choking with rage, the captain was incapable of deciding what to do. —Your unit, your unit!

Vanhala was not usually inclined to insolence; but this time, provoked by Rokka's example and the more than usually tempting situation, he said the first thing that came to his lips:

—The Latrine Orderlies Battalion, kee-hee-hee.

—You're all three under arrest! I'm taking you to Headquarters—march!

—Run for it, boys!

Vanhala was carrying a phonograph and a bundle of records, and Rokka snatched the records to lighten his load. With Hietanen and Vanhala galloping after him, Rokka darted into a convenient alley, leaving the captain shouting in the street:

—Arrest them, arrest them . . . Stop!

Swiftly they ran through the alley, crossed the next street and after rounding a couple of corners decided that they were safe. Puffing, Rokka paused to rest.

—It's shameful to run from a man like that, but I'd be more ashamed to go to prison because of him. He'd have raised such a row that we'd have got at least a month in the guardhouse.

Vanhala laughed happily. For the first time in his life he had dared to make fun of an officer.

—What are we going to do about him?

Hietanen pointed to a lieutenant colonel riding toward them on a handsome stallion, obviously enjoying his splendor.

—Let's not make an issue of this one, Rokka said, and slipped into a doorway. Hietanen and Vanhala followed, and all three watched the lieutenant colonel ride past. Once in the street again, they found themselves walking behind two army clerks and a chaplain who were engaged in conversation.

— . . . The wisest course would be to let the Orthodox Church die out, considering how far Bolshevism has already brought it on the road to decay. The revival of religious life should be along Lutheran lines. We'll start by baptizing all the infants as Lutherans. Of course, they'll scream religious persecution, but actually it's just letting things take their natural course. . . .

— . . . The Russians will have to be moved out. That's a problem which could be solved by transferring some of the population after the Germans have taken over Russia. . . .

The chaplain and the clerks turned off down a street, the building on the corner of which housed an army office of some kind.

Suddenly, as one man, the comrades stopped. Approaching them was a squad of Finnish girl students, members of a volunteer group who had arrived to help clean up the town. They walked along in brown overalls and stocking caps, singing in clear young voices.

The three men stared at the girls yearningly, Rokka as interested as the others, for all his three children.

—Come on, Rokka said at last. —It isn't as if we hadn't already found girls of our own.

The comrades had their own harem, unfortunately still a most innocent one, for the girls had not, as yet, permitted any intimacies. They had met three girls, one Russian and two Karelian, who lived together in town. Almost nightly the three would call on them, Vanhala's phonograph under one or another's arm, and the girls would dance Russian dances for them until they were bored to tears, then send them packing home. Still, they were girls.

—Before we go anywhere, I want to go back to the company, said Hietanen. —I've got some rations I saved to take to Tanya and Alexei.

Tanya and Alexei were two children who lived in the same house as the girls and whom Hietanen had taken under his wing. He took them food as often as he was able to obtain any, and the children always ran to meet him when they saw him coming. It had gotten to the point where he hated to disappoint them.

It turned out that Hietanen had less food set aside than he had thought, so he set out to ask Makila for his next day's ration. At the quartermaster's they found an argument in progress between Rahikainen and Makila, who was loudly accusing him of stealing sugar.

—Why should I bother to take your sugar? Rahikainen protested angrily. —I've got plenty of places where I can get all I want.

—Maybe you can, and maybe you can't. But I've got witnesses.

—Hey, stop it a minute, Hietanen interrupted. —How about giving me tomorrow's bread ration now? . . . I need it.

—You know this isn't when I issue rations. And there's too much bread going out into the town as it is.

—Maybe there is, but all I'm asking for is my own ration.

Makila muttered something about bread and women in an insinuating tone, but nevertheless handed Hietanen his ration. Rahikainen, however, saw fit to make the matter his own.

—If you're jealous of what Hietanen's getting, I'll help you out. I know just the woman. She only speaks Russian, but you don't need to talk. Breasts . . . you never saw anything like them before.

Makila disdained to answer. Clearing his throat, he withdrew behind his piled-up supplies, insulted. Seeing there was no profit to be made here, Rahikainen hurried after Hietanen:

—What's yours like?

Hietanen winked slyly. —By God, there isn't another one like her in the world. She was a real somebody here, too. One of those young collectivists or whatever they call 'em.

—She sounds good . . . I've got one too. But what I told Makila's true. If you want a real good piece or know someone who does, let me know. I won't charge you much either. She's fat, but oh, those breasts. Like two little pigs with their bottoms in the air.

—It sounds fine . . . but I've got all I can handle, Hietanen lied. He left Rahikainen deep in thought of other possible business transactions, and ran after Vanhala and Rokka.

When the three men approached the house where the girls lived, Tanya and Alexei ran shrieking out to meet them. Alexei was eight and Tanya six. Their father had been killed at the very beginning of the war and now they lived with their mother in a single room. They kept their eyes on Hietanen, waiting for him to put his hand in his ration pouch. They knew Hietanen would keep them in suspense for a time; it was a game they played. This time, too, he waited until they were in the yard before giving them the bread. They thrust it inside their shirts, having of course been told by their mother to bring home anything they were given. Hietanen waved to them and shouted:

—Alexei . . . Down with the Russians!

—Down with Russians, echoed Alexei in Finnish, laughing, though he did not know what the words meant.

In the yard was a third child, a boy of about six dressed in a man's blouse and trousers which had been rolled up to keep them off the ground. On his head was a Red Army cap. The boy watched them intently, silently retreating as they came nearer.

—Alexei and Tanya.

Hietanen called the two children back just as they were mounting the steps to the house.

—Let's give him a little of that bread. I'll bring you more next time.

Again the children did not understand what he was saying, but guessing that it was about the boy, Alexei pointed to him and said: —Grisha.

—Come here, Grisha, shouted Hietanen. The boy, however, continued to stare at him with frightened eyes. Not until Hietanen held up a piece of bread did he sidle nearer. But as soon as his fingers closed on the bread, he spun around and set off running as though for his very life, leaving Hietanen laughing heartily.

They went in to visit the girls whom Hietanen had discovered his first morning in town when he had entered the house to search it, his rifle at the ready, and been overcome with confusion to find a pair of beautiful female eyes fixed on him.

Vera was an East-Karelian teacher who, when the Finns had taken the town, had taken in two of her teacher friends. From the beginning Hietanen had been extremely shy in her presence. Indeed, he could not bring himself to visit her alone but always brought Rokka and Vanhala along to lend him moral support. But Vera was a girl in whose presence most men would have felt uncertain of themselves. She was, firstly, an extremely beautiful woman, and, secondly, her manner was invariably reserved and proud. Her attitude toward the conquerors was friendly but condescending, partly because she was a devout Communist but also certainly because she was aware of her intellectual superiority to the three with whom she had become acquainted. Nevertheless she would converse merrily with them and enjoyed dancing. Little by little she had shown that Hietanen was her favorite, as actually he was also with her two friends.

While the girls made tea, Vanhala dug dirty lumps of sugar out of his pockets and offered them to the girls. They were gratefully accepted, for when the Russians had abandoned the town, the girls had been left almost without food since they had made no preparations for anything of the kind and their own small supply had been exhausted in a couple of days.

Vera hardly spoke a word, but sat in one corner, while Hietanen stared dumbly at her profile. She was so beautiful that he felt afraid. Up to now he had caught glimpses of her sort of women only on the rare occasions when an expensive car had driven past him while he was carting milk to the dairy.

—What's making you sad, Vera? asked Rokka, who hated to see anybody who was not happy. —Dance for us, that'll send your sorrows flying.

—Don't disturb her. She's grieving for her sweethearts, said Hietanen and blushed.

—Verotshka has no sweetheart, said Nina, one of the Karelian girls.

Vera smiled, then her face grew solemn again as she said:

—Why did you have to come? Why couldn't you leave us in peace?

—Why did we come? repeated Rokka. —You people started it. You took my farm from me. You say we bring destruction, but go look at the state the Isthmus is in. We wouldn't be here if you'd left us alone.

—Ha, listen to him . . . Who came marching into Russia? Hitler, that's who . . . but he's marching to his death.

Vera spoke out boldly, and never showed the slightest humility nor concealed her political beliefs. It made Hietanen feel distinctly uncomfortable. He disliked arguing with Vera, for he knew that as a Communist she was a victim of propaganda, so he chose a middle path, admitting that the Germans were the aggressors, but denying that that was also the case with the Finns.

—Then why did you point that rifle at me that first day? Vera asked with a smile.

—How did I know who I'd run into? said Hietanen. —I'll admit war is hard on both sides, no matter which one starts it. It causes suffering among people who've never done anyone any harm—the children, for instance.

—You brought them bread, though, said Rokka. —You call us wrong doers, but Hietanen here took his own bread ration for tomorrow and gave it to Alexei and Tanya.

Hietanen blushed to hear Rokka sing his praises to Vera, but he became utterly confounded when Vera, without a word, got up and kissed him on the cheek. He tried to laugh as Vanhala giggled and said:

—What a caption for a newspaper photograph! Our brave Finnish soldiers give away their own food rations to the children of our racial brethren who have starved under the yoke of Bolshevism. . . .

Hietanen hadn't had time to say a word before Vera flared to his defense:

—You don't give anything to children! You're nothing but a fat idiot who gulps everything down himself.

—Fat idiot, did you say? asked Rokka, for although Vera spoke Karelian Finnish, her dialect occasionally made it difficult for them to understand everything she said.

Vera's reply was to make a circular motion with her hands to indicate how fat Vanhala was. And this gave Hietanen the chance he had been looking for. He laughed louder than any of them. Vanhala, however, was the most amused of all as he repeated the words over and over as if trying to impress them indelibly on his memory:

—Fat idiot . . . hee-hee . . . the fat idiot.

To calm things down, Hietanen loudly demanded music, and at last Vanhala opened his phonograph.

—What'll it be?

—Let's hear *Yokkantii,* said Rokka, naming his favorite record.

—To hell with that, play *Armi Batalyoon,* called Hietanen, who was fond of martial music.

Vanhala said nothing but the phonograph began to grind out *"Yokkantii."* It was a quick-moving Russian song to which the girls often danced, which was why Vanhala had put it on. Already the first bars had caused Rokka's whole body to come to life and move in time to the music. Smiling with pleasure, he turned to the girls:

—Vera, you dance it. The way you do it, it's a wonder.

Vera hesitated, then at last began to dance. At first she went slowly, then faster and faster until in the climactic movement she whirled so wildly that the three soldiers could hardly follow her movements. Vera danced as if she were performing for her own pleasure alone, her body responding to every nuance of the music. The three comrades were astounded, not by the beauty and artistry of Vera's dancing which they were incapable of understanding, but by the sheer rapidity of her movements.

When they left later that night, Hietanen lingered at the door which Vera had come to close. In pretended play he loosened from her blouse the Komsomol badge she wore over her breast. For a fleeting moment his fingers thrilled to the touch of her firm body, and in alarmed confusion he said, trying desperately to appear casual:

—You'll let me keep this to remember you by, won't you?

—Take it if you like.

The next second Hietanen was overcome with shame at the clumsiness of his courting and, blushing, turned to go. And as he did so, Vera gave him a long look in which he divined a warning against further advances. As he hastened after the others he dimly realized that Vera was somehow above his reach and that circumstances were against him.

He caught up with his friends in a gloomy frame of mind. —You've got to admit that the women here are wonderful . . .

—At least they know how to make you keep your distance. Why did you run away? It would have been a uniting of the tribes, the scattered children of Mother Finland.

Hietanen was so immersed in his own feelings that he hardly heard Vanhala. But even without hearing he made an effort to indicate that he admired Vera only because of her dancing, lest the others should taunt him about the way he was attracted to the girl.

—I don't know how a human being can spin like that. At home

the girls I used to dance with made me feel like I was pushing a plough around.

—Listen, laughed Rokka. —We can't bring Hietanen here any more. He'll be so heartsick he'll be invalided for life.

Hietanen blushed and immediately began to protest against the thought that he had fallen prey to any of the higher emotions:

—Don't you get any ideas I'll get caught. To hell with it . . . I'll take what I càn get where I can get it, and you and every woman in Karelia can go to blazes.

He said no more, believing he had now convinced them all that he had never done anything so shameful as pity hungry children or feel more for a woman than the desire for a few minutes in bed.

Near their billets a number of small boys were begging for bread and tobacco. The comrades threw them a few cigarettes, and were rewarded by a string of Finnish swear words which the boys apparently had been rewarded with cigarettes for learning until they had come to regard them as a form of payment. One little fellow who had had bad luck in the scramble even ran after them, trying to arouse their generosity by shouting as he ran:

—Bastards . . . bastards . . . bastards . . .

5.

The following day a formal victory parade was held, but the battalion was concerned only to the extent that it was responsible for maintaining order in the town. And though a few of the battalion actually marched in the parade, none of Koskela's platoon did. They did, however, come in for both promotions and decorations. Koskela was made a first lieutenant, while Hietanen got the extra stripe Major Sarastie had promised, and Maatta was made a corporal. Nearly every man got a medal, for the Second Class medal had become hardly more than a campaign ribbon.

In the evening they moved from billets into barracks which, by dint of superhuman efforts, had been made habitable. The move was unpopular because in town the men had been pretty much their own masters. Here, no sooner were they in barracks than Sinkkonen ordered the company to fall in in the hall. With barrack walls around him the old terror of the recruits was once more himself. He stalked about in front of the men, coughed and loudly gave the order to count off.

—One . . . two . . . three . . . four . . .

The men numbered slowly, and when the last number had been called no report came from the end man, though Sinkkonen could see that the third and fourth ranks were not of equal length.

—How many short? Who's asleep there?

—Who the hell's had time to count 'em all? a voice said from the rear.

Sinkkonen, his face livid, fairly screamed at the man to shut up, but another voice shouted:

—We've lost seven killed and twelve wounded but eight are back again.

—Shut up . . . What do you think's going on here?

For a moment Sinkkonen strove desperately to maintain his authority over the company. Then abruptly his self-assurance wavered and was gone, and to hide the loss he began shouting:

—Look out, you bastards. Look out! You think the army can't maintain discipline any longer. Well, you're goddamn mistaken! Now report from the end how many short.

—Two, if you must know, a voice answered, and the sergeant chose to rest on this victory. Before, he had always enjoyed standing in front of the company, his prepared speech on the subject of barracks life in his hand, for addressing the troops was one of his greatest pleasures. Now his enjoyment had been spoiled, but nevertheless he began:

—Now that the company is quartered indoors, I want to call your attention to a few aspects of barracks life. Cleanliness and neatness must be observed at all times, and all barracks regulations are in force to the letter. However, in view of the special circumstances, it is not necessary to call the room to attention for the entry of any NCO except the first sergeant. All noncommissioned officers will occupy separate quarters in the room especially assigned to them. It will be your duty to see that discipline is maintained at all times.

It was at this point that Rokka interrupted loudly:

—No, damn it, not me! Wolf's Paw and I stick together. I'm sleeping next to him or else Wolf can come to the NCOs' room.

Sinkkonen had not forgotten the way Rokka had brandished his spoon at him and what he had said. Within seconds he had lost control of himself again and was shouting:

—Keep your goddamn mouth closed! You'll go where I tell you to, understand!

Rokka smiled, but there was steel in his usually calm voice as he said:

—Don't try to get big with me. You'll end up on the short end of the stick if you do. Do you think a mule driver like you can shove me around like a recruit?

Obviously frightened, Sinkkonen rushed to the Orderly Room and seconds later returned with Lammio. Lammio stood grimly until a tense silence fell over the barracks before beginning coldly:

—Sergeant Rokka.

—Is something wrong?

Rokka spoke with such an air of injured innocence that the company was reduced to helpless laughter. Lammio cast an angry glance at the men and then, deliberately stressing every word, returned to Rokka:

—You'll move into the NCOs' room, do you understand?

—We'll see about it tonight. I'm not going to start an argument over a little thing like that. But listen, Lieutenant, when do we start getting leave? I'm a family man and it's been months since I was home. If I send in an application, how about approving it?

Once again Lammio was not sure whether or not Rokka was deliberately ridiculing his superiors. But in any case his familiarity angered him.

—Sergeant Rokka, you are addressing a superior officer and not a bosom friend. I don't remember giving you any encouragement to address me as you have been doing.

—You haven't, but I don't mind. Anyway, you can call me Antti, everybody else does. And if I'm not formal with you, why, it's just because I'm a lot older than you are.

A titter came from the men, leaving Lammio for the first time in his career with the feeling that a situation was getting out of hand. The thought of threatening Rokka with a court-martial came to his mind, but even his dull instincts warned him against going further. Rokka's arrogance was so flawless in its subtlety that Lammio had been inclined to regard it as unconscious. Now he realized that Rokka not only knew perfectly well what he was doing, but also was doing it in full awareness that it might lead to a court-martial. And then there was the fact that in Rokka he would be punishing one of his best soldiers. So Lammio concluded that the man was making capital of his record under fire, whereas if he had been a more intelligent man he would have realized that

Rokka's bravery in the field and his defiance of authority sprang from the same source.

Lammio's only thought now was how best to retreat without losing face. Grimly he announced:

—For disobeying a superior officer I hereby sentence Sergeant Rokka to orderly duty for four days.

As soon as he had finished, Lammio left hurriedly, obviously fearing that Rokka might say something that would make the situation worse. Left alone Sinkkonen gave the order to fall out, then he, too, tried to make a quick escape. But his effort was in vain for Rokka seized him by the shoulder strap with such a strong grip that he had to stop. Rokka was laughing, but that was what Sinkkonen most feared, for he divined in his imperturbable mirth a defiance of the whole world. And what protection was left for any officer once the ranks lost their customary fear of punishment?

—Did you hear what the lieutenant said? Four days on orderly duty in a row . . . after we'd spent weeks to get to this accursed place! And what do you suppose I was being punished for in the Winter War when I was kept at Taipale for three months without a break? Tell me that, now.

Sinkkonen babbled something about the necessity of maintaining discipline, but Rokka thrust him contemptuously away.

—Discipline! You can't find any better than the kind I maintain. But you go your way, and I'll go mine. We don't think the same.

Sinkkonen hurried away, relieved to have gotten off so easily. And Rokka did not move into the NCOs' quarters nor undertake any of the usual tasks of an NCO on duty, and nobody tried to make him do so. Actually the whole matter was of little import to him; it was just that Lammio by his unskillful handling, had transformed it into a matter of honor. And for Rokka, in a matter of honor there could be no retreat. So once more a Finnish soldier had won his war of independence.

The incident caused much unrest in the company in the next few days, and there was much heated talk that evening, especially since a rumor had spread that they were going to be sent back to the front. The men regarded the formality of the barracks and Lammio's attempt to restore the strict discipline of their recruit days as personal insults both to themselves and to their achievements in the field.

Lahtinen, believing he would now find a more sympathetic audience for his views than before, grumbled loudest about their prospects:

—Jesus, how Timoshenko is knocking over those SS boys at Rostov-on-Don! And it's hard times for ducks when the Tampere rapids freeze.

—You don't know, said Salo, now that a medal had come his way had begun to voice his opinions. —When summer comes the Panzers will drive the whole lot of them into the Urals.

At three A.M. one morning an order came to stand to. The men awoke and, seeing their officers moving about fully clad in the corridors, at once guessed the reason.

—All ready to move. The trucks'll be here in an hour.

Cursing and muttering broke out everywhere as the men fully awakened. Lammio heard the muttering but was careful to give no sign of having noticed it. He merely ordered the men to hurry since only a few of them were lazily gathering up their garments. The rest seemed to have no intention of going anywhere.

—Let's go, let's go! We only have an hour.

—We're not going.

Lammio could no longer ignore the matter.

—Who said that?

—We're not going.

Murmurs sounded here and there.

—That's what you think! I've got a different idea. I warn you that any man not ready to leave an hour from now will face a court-martial.

The men gathered in groups, inciting each other to refuse to go. They mentioned the promise of a long rest they had been given after the town had been taken. Actually they had been promised nothing. The principal reason for their behavior was that they had been having a good time in town and were unwilling to forego it.

The majority as usual waited to see which way the scales would swing as Lammio turned to the NCOs and ordered them to begin packing. He had no difficulty in getting them started, but their example had no effect on the men. Minutes passed and Lammio grew more and more excited.

—For the last time, get ready! Don't any of you forget that the penalty for mutiny is death.

—Hell . . . a Finnish bullet doesn't hurt any more than a Russian one.

—We want a new company commander if we're going back to the front.

—Put Koskela in command and we'll go!

Lammio was not at all taken back by this demand, for he was incapable of seeing the demand as a reflection on himself.

—This isn't the Red Guard where you can elect officers by acclamation. I'm ordering you for the last time. Then, I'll use other less pleasant measures.

All the while Koskela had been standing apart in silence. Now he walked up to his own platoon. Calmly, as though nothing had happened, he said:

—It's about time to get started. Of course the trucks will be late as always, but that can't be helped. Don't take too much junk with you, though.

Silently the Third Platoon began to put their packs in order. This calm figure standing in the middle of the room had a petrifying effect on them that erased all their desire to protest. And yet, in spite of that, the men felt that Koskela was on their side and his orders aroused no bitterness against him. They found it natural to obey when the order came from Koskela.

From the other platoons men came to inquire in whispers so that Koskela would not hear.

—Are you going? For Christ's sake don't back out on us.

—What else can we do?

The Third Platoon were uneasy at the idea of causing the resistance to collapse, but not one of them thought for a moment of opposing Koskela. And soon preparations for departure were in progress throughout the company and it was easy for the others to beat a retreat.

—What good would it do, with the Third ready to go . . . ?

Koskela was silent as he moved about, his eyes expressionless yet always watching the development of the situation in the company. He knew that the others would follow the example of the Third, and his only fear was that Lammio would open his mouth, for a few words from him might still cause a lot of additional trouble. Fortunately, Lammio said nothing.

For once the trucks were on time. The men clambered into them quickly and the battalion was soon on its way. The first snow of the winter had fallen during the night and in its pale reflection the trucks rumbled through the town and took the road south.

—Where are they taking us? a private asked Koskela.

—The Russkies are attacking along the Svir. They say they've crossed the river.

—Hey, Rokka! There's no need to fret. We're all going to be on duty all the time, and not for just for four days either.

Hietanen had forgotten all about Vera. It was as if departure had wiped her from his memory. All that remained was the Komsomol badge in his pocket. Only Rokka did not seem unhappy that their rest period was over.

—Hey, Fat Idiot! he called, how about winding up your phonograph?

Vanhala's nickname had come into general use. Now he settled the phonograph in his lap and it began to grind out a tune. Rokka clapped his hands in time, shook his shoulders and sang loudly as they sped through the dark and silent wilds.

Chapter IX

1.

—Come out of there.

The military police lieutenant's voice was harsh as he opened the sauna door and gave his order. The sentry standing to one side turned to him nervously:

—Can I go? You won't need me any more.

—Go ahead.

Hastily the sentry set off at a run as though afraid of being called back as the lieutenant stepped back from the doorway to allow two soldiers to emerge. After crossing the threshold the men, both privates, stopped and stood silently waiting in the dim light of a winter dawn. As they blinked their eyes they could see a group of military policemen, a lieutenant and an army judge standing off to one side. The chaplain had also waited there, but the men had refused to see him and he had gone.

One of the men was tall and held himself erect. His fair hair hung tousled on his forehead and he seemed to be constantly brushing it back with his palm as he stared defiantly at the lieutenant, who avoided his gaze as if unable to stand his penetrating eyes.

The other man was shorter and seemed to be in a state of shock as he stood shivering as though with cold. The tall blond soldier was obviously no more than twenty-five years old, while his shorter companion looked as if he might be in his middle thirties.

The Judge Advocate began to read aloud from a sheet of paper, and now the two men stiffened as if unable to believe the words they heard, although they had heard them the evening before at their court-martial. They shook their heads as if they could not believe their ears when they heard the official verdict that they had left their posts and refused to return to them. Of course they knew that. Because of it they had been hauled before a court and sentenced to die. The past eleven hours in the pitch-black sauna had made it perfectly clear to them what this all meant, and they were prepared. They were alive, yet they both were already dead. Over and over again they had lived through their execution in their imaginations until the actual event no longer terrified them.

When the Judge Advocate had finished, the younger man looked around, then demanded in a grating voice:

—Give me a cigarette, you bastards!

The judge and the lieutenant hastily took out their cigarette cases and competed to be the one whose gift was accepted, as if the man's curse had increased their eagerness to be of service to him. Then the lieutenant quickly offered a light.

The lieutenant was in a quandary. Should he let the man finish his cigarette or get the execution over with at once? Delay was torture; the sooner he could leave this spot the better. He had presided at several executions, but always before the condemned had been Communists or Russian spies and no problem was involved in shooting such people. But this time he was executing Finnish soldiers, his own brothers-in-arms.

The younger man released him from his uncertainty.

—All right, you murderers. Let's get it over with. It's damn cold.

The military policemen started at the harsh laugh that accompanied these words. The other condemned man was shaking like an aspen leaf, unspeaking and obviously unseeing and unhearing.

—Blindfolds, the lieutenant said to his men.

They held back.

—You do it.

—Not me!

—Damn you, don't start fighting among yourselves! I'm not dying with any rag over my eyes. I've looked into a rifle barrel oftener than you have over one.

—And you. Do you want to be blindfolded? the lieutenant asked the shorter prisoner.

The man shook his head, then stepped to the sauna wall and stood with his back to it. Silently his companion did the same as the military policemen lined up before them, their rifles grounded.

At a sharp command the rifles rose. The older man looked away and a low whimpering escaped his lips, but the younger looked straight at the muzzles of the rifles as though he were the judge and not the judged. Only yesterday he had been an ordinary youth who in a moment of unthinking defiance had refused to obey a lieutenant whom he, along with the entire company, hated for his arrogance. This morning, after eleven hours in a dark sauna with death for company, he was a man with a profound knowledge of life.

The volley crashed, the men standing before the sauna wall collapsed awkwardly into the snow, and the military policemen began hastily, with gentle deference, to prepare the bodies for burial.

2.

—Battalion, attention!

The men lined up in the snow-covered forest clearing stiffened to attention as Major Sarastie drew forth a sheet of paper and began to read. They listened, half mystified. They knew all about what had happened, so what sense was there in reading it to them? To inform them that two men had been shot for refusing to return to the post they had left? Hadn't they gone after the military policemen who had done the shooting as soon as they heard the news? Perhaps it was just as well that the M.P.'s had got away, for theirs was not the greatest guilt.

When the major had finished reading, he spoke on:

—I hope you realize from this that the army cannot afford to take insubordination lightly. And I trust this battalion will not need to hear more such papers read. But army regulations must be enforced.

Now the men understood the purpose of the reading. They were being threatened. The Finnish attack had drawn unexpected Russian reaction on the Svir front. An opponent they believed defeated had shown he was still capable of counterattacking. Now Sarastie's battalion was to deliver a new attack, and the High Command wanted no breach of discipline.

3.

Beneath a clear cold sky the air echoed with the sound of small-arms and mortar firing. The battalion was thrusting toward an enemy supply line to force the Russians to abandon a village they had taken over a month ago. Bloody fighting for possession of the village had been going on for some time, but the Russians had not budged.

The crest of Bald Hill in their left rear was under heavy bombardment. The remnants of a Frontier Guard battalion had succeeded, after three costly attempts, in securing a foothold, but the slopes were strewn with dead, for with no road open for a Russian retreat the fighting had been especially bitter. The morale of the Frontier Guards had stood up under three failures and when a fourth attempt carried them to the summit, the Russians died in their pits without a single one surrendering. But now Russian guns were heavily shelling the hill and the Guards, apathetic and with fear in their hearts, crouched among the dead.

The hill, after lying unnoticed since time immemorial, had suddenly become all-important. A blue-veined hand had pointed to it on a map, a voice had said: —We must take it if the village is to be retaken. It dominates the terrain for miles around and we can't drive past it without the risk that our supply lines might be cut and our troops isolated.

The hill's importance had thus been recognized.

Lahtinen, Maatta and Salo hauled a Lapp sled bearing a machine gun through the deep snow while Sihvonen floundered behind it with the check line. The four men had been detailed to a platoon protecting the flank but because of the sled had been unable to keep up with the riflemen. They had tried to make their way on skis, but the heavy sled had made the skis slip, and for some time they had been wading through the snow on foot. Now, despite the cold, they were drenched with perspiration as, panting and cursing, they followed the ski tracks left by the riflemen. In their benumbed state of mind the din of fighting came as one continuous confused and muted thunder that gave no clue to the position of their own troops or the enemy's.

Salo led the way while Maatta hauled away silently but effectively, and Lahtinen tugged with the whole weight of his big body. Each time the sled stuck against a boulder or a tree stump he would hurl himself against the traces, cursing through clenched teeth.

Occasionally they rested briefly, sitting on the sled to get their wind back. Lahtinen panted and puffed:

—Hell! God damn it to hell! Of all the goddamn jobs. And back home the profiteers sit in their rocking chairs counting the money from their black-market grain! I'd sure like to see someone whose brains haven't been altogether scrambled by this foolishness. Grown-up men pulling a damned sled like this up and down the forest . . .

Soon they began to hear heavy firing ahead and to their left and guessed that the battalion had reached the supply road. Dead tired, they at last caught up with the rifle platoon, which was already spread out in battle order. Lahtinen chose a position for the machine gun in a clump of trees in the middle of the firing line. It was the best possible site, and Lahtinen had spotted it immediately, for he was a good machine gunner who knew how to get the maximum value out of his weapon.

The area they had to secure was large, and the second lieutenant commanding the rifle platoon was uneasy. It was his duty to protect one flank of the advancing wedge and that meant that he absolutely had to hold his position although the Russians would undoubtedly do their utmost to open up their supply road. Now he waded through the snow to the machine-gun position, looked around and said:

—Yes, that's the best spot.

Feeling lonely in his responsibility, he had a desperate urge to talk to someone:

—We may get off easily, but if Ivan goes for us, give him everything you've got.

Lahtinen was still puffing from his recent labors as he grunted surlily:

—Of course we will. Who do you think's going to stand with his finger in his mouth waiting to get killed?

4.

The cold grew more intense and the horizon was dyed a bleak red as the pale winter sun sank behind it. Through the trees the snow took on a bluish tinge, and as the dusk thickened the silence seemed to deepen accordingly.

Lahtinen, on his knees behind the machine gun, kept his eyes glued on the ground ahead while the rest of the crew crouched about a miserable little fire. On their left an automatic rifle barked out a burst and the icy forest echoed with the sound. The artillery fire had slackened and only at intervals would a salvo of shells fly shrieking overhead.

Lahtinen's boots had frozen stiff and his snow cloak made a rasping sound at each movement of his body. A louse was biting his neck, but he did not dare to scratch himself for that would mean taking his hand out of his warm gauntlet.

The snow creaked in the forest, and Lahtinen strained to listen. Again the sound came, and again. Someone was approaching, cautiously treading on the snow.

Lahtinen's heart began to thud and he sank slowly on his stomach, his hands on the grips of the machine gun. Now the noise was louder and there were other creakings mingled with it as well as a tinkle of metal.

Turning his head Lahtinen called softly to the infantryman lying in the snow a little distance away:

—Russkies out there. Straight ahead.

The man raised his head and, hardly able to breathe for excitement, whispered in a choking voice:

—I hear them.

He sent on the whisper:

—Hey. Russkies out front.

The faint clicking of safety catches being released followed the whisper down the line.

Suddenly Lahtinen started as his eye fell on a clearing. A figure in a snow cloak was standing there—peering around him, a rifle under his arm. Now a second figure appeared from behind some juniper bushes and was beckoned on by the first. Lahtinen released the catch and placed the frozen thumb of his gauntlet on the trigger guard. The upper part of the Russian's body showed over his sights.

Lahtinen's breath came quickly as, tense with excitement, he waited for more Russians. Desperately he prayed that the riflemen would not open fire too soon, for the men in sight were obviously the advance guard of a larger body. At the same time he was torn by the machine gunners' constant anxiety: would the weapon work, had the moving parts frozen fast?

Then a shot rang out beside him and Lahtinen cursed and pressed the trigger. He almost sighed with relief as the weapon obediently hammered out a burst. The leading Russian soldier doubled up like a pocket knife while the other swayed drunkenly and fell sideways.

—Stations, roared Lahtinen to his men in the rear. No need now to whisper. A few shots sounded in the forest, but there was no further sign of the enemy. Abruptly the firing ceased and all that could be heard was the creaking of the snow.

Maatta, Salo and Sihvonen extinguished their feeble campfire with snow and hastened to the machine gun where they were joined by the riflemen from the rear.

—What was it? clamored Sihvonen as he reached Lahtinen. But Lahtinen stared ahead without replying. A hissing sound came from the machine gun. The melted grease squeaked and in the midst of all the tension Lahtinen found himself thinking of the old superstition which his mother never failed to mention whenever the kitchen range made that squeaking sound. To her it foretold news of a death.

Perhaps it was fear that caused him to remember that superstition. Yet he was not a man to enjoy conjuring up visions of fear. He glanced sourly at Sihvonen.

—Now what the hell do you think it was?

Sihvonen sank into a sullen silence, and they strained their eyes to peer into the snow-covered landscape. But they saw no further sign of the Russians. A soft shuffling sound told them, however, that they were still there, probably grouping for an attack.

The second lieutenant came from the right and met his second-in-command who had charge of the left flank. The lieutenant tried to speak calmly but he was unable to hide his uneasiness.

—There's more sounds on the right. I think we've got a tough job ahead. It's certainly not just a patrol.

The second-in-command did not even try to hide his nervousness as he said gloomily:

—You're damn right it's not just a patrol. The forest's rustling all down the line, and I thought I heard voices over in front of the next sector.

—Can't you spread them out farther?

—How the hell can I stretch the line when the men are so far apart now they have to shout to each other?

The lieutenant shrugged his shoulders in irritation.

—It's got to be extended. Post an automatic rifle at the far end and tell the leader of the fourth squad to keep an extra good eye on his flank.

—I've got an automatic rifle there now. But a hell of a lot of good it'll do. The field of fire's about fifty yards.

The lieutenant fell silent. Ever since the war started he had been preparing for a situation like this when he would be faced on one side by death, and on the other by Major Sarastie's sarcastic glance as he said: —So you funked out, eh? Now what in hell can be coming at you that's so frightening?

The lieutenant had always dreaded a situation in which he would have to take the responsibility for every decision. Would he be capable of standing his ground and setting his men an example if they began to waver?

No, Sarastie would never have reason to look scornfully at him. The positions would be held, or they would die. The lieutenant drew a deep breath to fill the empty space that seemed to have developed below his heart:

—This is where we are, and this is where we're going to stay. There's no alternative. The battalion's in contact with the enemy and it's up to us to hold this flank.

From ahead Lahtinen whispered over his shoulder:

—Shut up back there. There's a hell of a ruckus started out front.

The lieutenant fell silent as the whisper of low voices came to them from ahead, accompanied by the sound of the snow creaking beneath heavily shod feet. Lahtinen glanced grimly at the officer.

—Christ, it's not my business, but it's about time we did something. That sure as hell isn't just one company. They won't have to shoot us, we'll be trampled to death. You've got to send a messenger for help. And tell him to say right off that it's no use sending a half-wiped-out platoon.

—A report's gone already, said the lieutenant. —Only I didn't ask for help because there isn't any to send.

Lahtinen shrugged and resumed his lookout, his face set and grim. But left to themselves, the lieutenant and his sergeant decided to send a second messenger to inform Battalion of the situation.

—Tell them we can't answer for the line if no help comes.

The man set off, joyful and relieved, followed by the envious glances of his comrades.

—He's on his way out of it.

The gravity of the situation infused the officer's voice with a genuine sense of comradeship as he said to the sergeant:

—Do everything you can at your end. At least they can't really rush us. Not in this snow.

The sergeant turned to go, slinging his rifle.

—Snow won't stop 'em. Well, see you again. On the tanner's rafters.

5.

It was nearly five o'clock and already the snow-covered landscape had taken on a bluish cast as the forest faded into the wintry dusk in which the cold light of a frosty day always perished. The light reflected from the snow prolonged the day's life a little, but in brush and thicket darkness was already gaining the upper hand.

Commands rang out from where their invisible foe lay, and Lahtinen cast a dour look at his companions. Frightened though he was, at the moment he felt a kind of malicious joy surging through his body as though he were pleased with the knowledge that things couldn't get any worse. As the others stared silently into the forest, Lahtinen said, as if he had to be sure that they knew how desperate their plight was:

—We've had it. We might as well admit it.

No one answered. Maatta absent-mindedly straightened out an ammunition belt, the others did not move. And in the belief that their silence indicated that even now they did not understand or would not admit the hopelessness of the situation, Lahtinen continued his missionary work:

—They tell us we're fighting for home and religion. That means if we're lucky and they find our bodies we'll qualify for a cross on our graves.

There was no answer, only an isolated click as Salo released the safety catch of his rifle. Lahtinen wondered why they so obstinately refused to admit their peril.

—At least if we have a chance to run, we're not leaving the machine gun. Get that?

—I'll take the tripod, Maatta said calmly, as though deliberately trying to keep all emotion out of the matter. It was as if instinct warned him that Lahtinen was trying to pay them back for the many laughs they had had at his expense. And at last Lahtinen dropped the note of maliciousness from his voice and gave them straightforward orders.

—Maatta and I'll work the machine gun. The rest of you blaze away like hell with your rifles. And remember that every bullet has to count. Aim at the stomach, that always puts a man out of it. Always fire at the nearest man. And make damn certain you aim and don't just bang away blindly. When you pull the trigger, do it to kill.

Uraaa . . . aaa . . . aaraa . . . uraaa . . .

Lahtinen fired, his jaws tightly clenched, and a figure clad in white furs rose from the snow, screamed and fell, clutching its stomach. Seconds later a group of Russians carrying a machine gun were observed making for the shelter of a pine. One man escaped the storm of fire. The Russians' attacking cry sounded across an alarmingly broad front, but from the Finnish line came only a ceaseless crackle. Once a hoarse urgent cry was heard from the left:

—Automatic rifle, quick . . . over here!

Under the machine gun's merciless fire the advance stopped, and the Russians settled down to return the fire. Lahtinen began to traverse both flanks with short quick bursts.

—I can't see 'em, but it makes the boys feel better if they think I can.

Maatta made no reply as he silently fed belt after belt into the block. The machine gun was beginning to glow with heat.

On the left the noise fell away sharply and suddenly Sihvonen broke out:

—They're running! Let's get the hell out of here. . . .

Lahtinen, too, saw men in flight, but he growled at Sihvonen:

—You'll stay as long as the others stay. . . .

Even as he said it, the lieutenant came scrambling through the snow from the right, shouting:

—Get back to your posts . . . get back! Who the hell gave you permission to retreat?

Farther off, one of the men in flight paused to shout:

—They're surrounding us . . . they've turned our flank!

The officer shouted the name of his second-in-command:

—Penttinen . . . Sergeant Penttinen!

—Penttinen's dead . . . They almost blew his head off.

—Lehtovirta and Kylanpaa are dead too.

—They're turning our flank.

—The automatic rifle's gone.

Panic-stricken men streamed from the left, each with his tale of woe. The lieutenant shouted hoarsely:

—Here . . . take up positions here. . . .

A few men stopped and sought new positions, but a hail of bullets rattled around them and with a faint cry one man fell. This shook the others so much that they were incapable of repulsing the attack. Even on the right, where the pressure had not been severe, man after man joined in the retreat. Even Lahtinen began to dismount the barrel as though realizing that all that remained was to get the machine gun away. Sihvonen and Salo were already heading for the rear.

Seeing the situation was hopeless, the lieutenant was about to make his way to the left to see if anything could be done to delay the Russians' progress when a hand rose from the snow and a voice cried:

—Boys! Don't leave me. Don't . . .

Quickly he hastened to the wounded man's side, calling to Sihvonen to help him. But Sihvonen only ran on, his eyes almost bulging out of his head. Salo, however, came to the lieutenant's side and together they began to drag the wounded man away from the firing.

Seeing what they were doing Lahtinen set the already detached barrel on the tripod again and beckoned to Maatta:

—Dump the stuff out of the sled and put him in . . . I'll try to hold 'em off. . . .

Maatta emptied the sled with one heave and drew it to the wounded man's side. Quickly they laid the man in it and began to pull it into the sheltering forest. Now a few riflemen returned to help, and Maatta and the lieutenant turned their burden over to them and stayed behind to wait for Lahtinen.

Lahtinen was firing wildly, swinging the machine gun as far

each way as the frame permitted. Then, glancing over his shoulder and seeing the sled gone, he rose to his knees and grabbed the gun. Meanwhile Maatta and the officer fired at random toward the invisible enemy to give Lahtinen as much support as possible. Now the Russians had obviously observed him, for bullets were whipping the snow around him.

—Drop the machine gun and get away, the officer called, thinking it impossible for one man to carry the machine gun off alone. But Lahtinen either did not hear or had no intention of abandoning his weapon; instead he heaved the machine gun on his shoulder in one swinging movement and set off at a crouching run towards his two comrades. Halfway to them when he fell to the ground, they at first thought he had stumbled. But when he made no attempt to rise, Maatta shouted: —Lahtinen!

There was no reply from the white-cloaked figure which lay motionless, one leg of the tripod sticking up crookedly behind it. For a moment more Maatta and the officer waited for a sign of life, then they turned and began to plough their way through the snow.

The red-hot sheath of the machine gun sank hissing into the snow, sending drops of water running in a tiny rivulet that flowed slowly down into an exposed lingonberry bush. A few drops of blood stained the water red as they dripped from the tiny bluish hole the bullet had made as it entered Lahtinen's head just behind his ear.

6.

—What's the matter with you? Where'd you come from?

Rokka shook the panting man by his shoulders.

—Over there . . . over there . . .

—For Christ's sake make sense. . . . What happened?

—All . . . done for. . . . Whole platoon wiped out.

—How can it be? Aren't you alive? And there's others coming over there. What happened to the machine gun? Where's Lahtinen?

—Back there. No one got away alive.

—There's no use asking him anything, said Hietanen, leaning on his ski poles. The only reinforcements Battalion had had to send was Rokka's machine gun, and Hietanen had come along with it. They knew that they were too late as soon as this first fugitive, still too frightened to speak coherently, had come running toward them.

Rokka released the man, and turned to question the new arrivals. Finally, last of all, the lieutenant and Maatta arrived. As he caught up with his men the officer began to upbraid them furiously:

—You goddamn sheep! You've pulled that trick for the last time—running with your stinking tongues out without even a backward glance . . . abandoning the wounded. . . . If any man of you goes any farther, I'll shoot him through the belly myself and let him lie.

—Where's Lahtinen and the machine gun? Hietanen whispered to Maatta.

—Back there, side by side, Maatta said as if the matter did not in the least concern him.

—It couldn't be helped, said the lieutenant. —Maatta was one man who did all he could. It wasn't his fault. He was the only real man in the entire outfit, apart from Lahtinen.

—I don't give a damn whose fault it was. I asked about the machine gun and Lahtinen, said Hietanen sharply, angry at the lieutenant's criticism.

—Me, too, said Rokka. —The Russkies'll be here soon. Let's get a firing line set up.

Now at last the officer realized that there were more important things to do than abuse his men and began rapidly to organize a defense. Hoping to still be able to hold up the Russians and thus alleviate the sting of the recent reproaches, he called out to his men:

—We'll shove a bone down their throats yet, boys. Let's get set up here. Try to dig yourselves some kind of hole in the snow for protection.

Now the lieutenant was once again all determination and drive as he sent Hietanen to take command of the men on the right, explaining that his second-in-command and both squad leaders on the left sector had fallen, so that he himself would be needed there. Quickly Hietanen got his firing line in order, while Rokka sought the best position for the machine gun. And since he had more men than he needed now that Lahtinen's crew had joined him, he kept only Maatta and Vanhala for the machine gun and sent the rest into the firing line. Then he himself approached the officer.

—Say, lieutenant, where do you need a really good man?

In spite of the gravity of the situation the lieutenant could not help smiling at Rokka's cockiness. He knew Rokka's reputation, however, and did not doubt that it was well earned.

—The most dangerous place is at the end of the line. Take a few men with you and cover our left flank. Go a little beyond the end of the line and keep an eye on things there . . .

—Suits me. You there with the tommy gun, come on with me. But you'd better give me the gun.

—You'd do better to pick someone else, whispered the officer. —Lampinen there is still all shaken up. He was over on the left and his nerves were never too good in the first place.

—I don't want anyone good. Just someone to reload drums. Come on. I'm what they call a comedian. There's always a hell of a lot of fun wherever I am. Take all the cartridges you can carry.

Silently they set off, Rokka wading ahead, his unwilling companion at his heels. The moon was beginning to cast its ghostly gleam over the forest. Clearings glittered brightly, but the thickets were sunk in an ominous gloom.

Rokka and his companion passed the last man in the line and continued on their way. Now Rokka conversed in whispers with his silent helper.

—You ought to see the felt boots I got today on that supply line. Had a job getting them off him, though. That's how stiff he was.

His companion made no answer but looked around fearfully. Suddenly Rokka stopped, holding up his hand in warning. Before them stretched a small open swamp, and across it, sinking deep into the snow at every step, white-cloaked figures were approaching them in scores, closely bunched together. Rokka beckoned Lampinen to his side, and they lowered themselves cautiously into the snow.

—We can't do anything, Lampinen whispered trembling.

—The hell we can't! Christ, what a stratagem. They knew where we were from all that damn noise we were making and sent this bunch to take us from the rear. I had a feeling all the time that something was up.

The Russians came on slowly yet incautiously. They had no scouts out in front although they were crossing open ground. It was as if they were so confident of success that they felt no need for precautions. Desperately the two Finns wormed themselves into the drifted snow, Rokka whispering advice all the while.

—Here's the loaded drums. As fast as I empty 'em you fill 'em. But put the loaded drums on the other full ones so that they don't get mixed. Don't worry, just relax. We're not in any danger here. They're the ones who'll find themselves in a tight spot, not us.

Rokka knew the Russians would not hear his whispers, for the creaking of their footsteps in the snow hid all small sounds. They were drawing nearer now, the snow making them move clumsily, as Rokka squinted over his sights:

—That first one's an officer. When he reaches that little pine he's going to get his. After that we'll take a crack at the others. Look at 'em coming on! Waddling along like ducks behind each other. Oh, you bastards, you don't know what's waiting for you. . . . Father in Heaven, if they've sinned forgive them! But be quick about it. In a minute they'll be on their way.

The officer in the lead was abreast of the pine. He never knew what happened. He saw only the dark rim of forest and the snow glittering in the moonlight. His eyes may have registered a flash, but what it meant he never knew.

Cries broke the stillness and a few shots rang out at random, but the dominating sound was the tapping of Rokka's tommy gun as he killed with cold deliberation. Some of the Russians made a dash for safety. Others tried to escape by burrowing in the snow. A few fired blindly, for the location of the yammering tommy gun was difficult to determine.

Having mown down the spearhead, Rokka went to work on those nearest the sheltering forest, aiming always at the man closest to escaping, though whenever the situation permitted he would fire into the mob. Now some of the Russians were trying to dig themselves in and return Rokka's fire, but after a few shots the snow would seem to boil around the shooter and his weapon would fall silent.

Lampinen lay beside Rokka, his whole body bathed in perspiration as with trembling fingers he tore open the cardboard containers and filled the emptied drums with cartridges. He was almost out of his mind with fear. Reassuring as Rokka's presence was, the situation itself seemed too precarious, the odds against them tremendous. At any moment they might be surrounded. And added to his fear was a sense of horror at this bloody slaughter. Occasionally he would venture a glance at the swamp and see a man creeping to safety like a wounded animal until Rokka's merciful bullet would put an end to his sufferings. Above the crackling of the tommy gun he could hear heartbreaking shrieks and cries for help.

Suddenly Lampinen heard a vicious humming blow, and Rokka's gun ceased firing. He looked up and a cry of alarm broke from him. Rokka's fur cap had fallen off and his head rested slackly on the butt of his weapon. Blood trickled down onto his cheek from his forehead.

Lampinen let the drum fall and turned to crawl away, his self-control completely gone. Choking with fear he started to his feet and was about to run when something gripped him firmly by the ankle. Squawking with terror, his eyes bulging, he whirled to see what it was.

Rokka was holding him by the leg and smiling. To Lampinen, however, his smile was horrible. It was distorted by pain and in the moonlight Rokka's bloodstained face seemed more like that of a grinning devil than that of a human being.

—Where the hell do you think you're going?

—Nnnn . . . nn . . . nnowhere.

—Get back to your place then. I thought you'd try taking off somewhere. Damn it, you can't do that. I'd run short of drums . . .

The tommy gun resumed its clatter. The survivors were not running now, but were trying to tunnel their way through the snow to safety. Some succeeded, but they were few compared to those who lay silent on the swamp.

Then all movement in the swamp had ceased. Shots were still being fired from the edge of the forest, but the Russians seemed to have lost all desire to attack. The moon shone on the dead and dying, and now and again a low moan sounded, only to be followed immediately by the brief tapping of Rokka's tommy gun. Bareheaded, a trace of a smile on his lips, he was the cold-blooded killer reigning over his prey, alert for the least sign of life.

From the rear came the swish of skis and a Jaeger lieutenant skimmed onto the scene at the head of a file of men.

—What's going on here?

—Nothing much any more. Spread your men out along that swamp. You never know, Ivan might make another try. I suppose you did come to help?

—We did.

The lieutenant set up a firing line, then returned to marvel at the number of bodies.

—Was all that firing yours?

—Well, most of it. The little Ivan did didn't amount to much. Cut my head open though, the bastards. I was stunned for a moment.

—And I tried to run, Lampinen said humbly as though to show that he had no intention of denying that he had been scared.

Rokka only laughed good-humoredly and said:

—So you did. But put a bandage on my head, will you? It's stopped bleeding, but it's best to dress it just the same.

Lampinen applied the bandage. He was not at all ashamed of having been afraid as he said with humble admiration:

—You're sure one hell of a man . . .

Rokka smiled. —There's nothing so wonderful about it. It's just that we've got to fight or we'll have to run all the way to the sea. Those bastards'll keep after you, make no mistake about that. But if you stick where you are even though all hell breaks loose, what can they do? That's the strategy of defensive war. It's all there is to it and all there'll ever be. Dammit, don't swaddle my head like a baby. I won't be able to see or hear a damn thing. Give me a smoke, lieutenant.

—Take the whole pack. I've got another.

—Say, you're a good fellow. Thanks. Tell you what I'll do. We'll see whether all that lot were wearing felt boots, and if they were, I'll fit out every man in the platoon tomorrow.

But the corpses were not felt-shod, as they saw the next day when the Russians withdrew, since the wedge driven into their line of supply had forced them back to their original lines. On the swamp fifty-two bodies were counted, and according to Lampinen Rokka had emptied seventeen drums. His weapon looked it, for certainly its barrel was of no further use.

With the fighting over, Major Sarastie paraded the battalion and congratulated the men on a job well done. Indeed, they had fought so well that they had earned a commendation from the regimental commander. —Convey my recognition of the unflinching fighting spirit the battalion has shown, ran his message. To be sure the men themselves were not aware of having behaved any more remarkably than before, but it seemed they must have done, since they had been told so.

And had not two men been shot against a sauna wall in the next village to stimulate their fighting spirit? It would have been strange indeed if that had had no effect.

Chapter X

I.

Makila paced to and fro by the field kitchen, then seeing a potato peel on the ground he instinctively picked it up and put it in the can. But despite the fact that the sight of the paring had again aroused his anger at what he termed "that everlasting negligence," he was in an exceptionally good mood. The machine-gun company had won its long and bitter quarrel with the Third Company over pasturage for its horses and gained possession of the coveted forest meadow. The credit, as with so much else concerning the machine-gun company's supplies, was all Makila's. Sergeant Major Sinkkonen was no good at all at seeing to supplies here, where regulations were of little or no use. You had to have initiative and energy, and Sinkkonen lacked these. As a result the machine-gun company was often left without benefits other more active sergeant majors procured for their units. Only Makila's untiring activity helped to even matters, though he was often at a disadvantage owing to his inferior rank. —But somebody's got to try. Standing with our fingers to our caps won't bring in anything.

The beautiful early summer evening was far advanced, and the glitter of the setting sun had faded from the pool winking between the trees. Makila would have gone to bed if he had not been afraid to do so, for leaning idly on the field kitchen chatting with the sentry was Rahikainen. He was up to something. It never entered Makila's head that Rahikainen could be out on any other errand than to steal something, and thus he moved about to keep himself awake, afraid that the sentry might let himself be gulled.

At last Rahikainen strolled nonchalantly away and Makila, seeing him vanish round a bend in the path, went to his tent to sleep. But Rahikainen went only a short distance along the path before stopping and emitting a low whistle. An answer came immediately. Rahikainen noted the direction and soon found Rokka sitting on a rock.

—It's on the side of the field kitchen toward the pool. It won't be easy but I'll manage.

—Who's on guard?

—Sipila.

—It's all right, then. I'll start as soon as I get there. Be sure you're ready by that time.

—Take care the pisshead doesn't shoot you.

—I'll be all right.

They parted, Rokka making his way farther into the forest as Rahikainen stole back along the path. Crawling through some bushes he reached a spot a few paces from the field kitchen and waited silently. The sentry, a cigarette between his lips, stared at the pool gleaming between the trees. A short distance away stood the cooks' tent, but all was silence there.

A noise came from the forest, and the sentry turned swiftly, letting the rifle drop from his shoulder to the crook of his arm. A twig snapped, and the sentry released the safety catch. He took a few steps toward the forest and stood listening. Silently Rahikainen slid like a snake to the field kitchen, seized a large pot standing upside down beside it and began stealthily dragging it into the bushes.

Again a sound came from the forest. The sentry cried out in a voice made gruff to mask his alarm:

—Give the countersign.

From the forest there was no answer, but men streamed out of the cooks' tent dressed in their underwear.

—What is it?

—I don't know. Something's out there.

Meanwhile Rahikainen was crawling back under the cover of the bushes with the pot. Reaching the rock which had been their previous meeting place, he waited until Rokka arrived.

—Well?

—There it is. Look.

—Damn, just the thing! With the lid on it'll be just what we want.

Rokka hoisted the pot on his shoulder and they set off. Soon they came to a tent in a little clearing where a number of men were lying on the ground.

Their arrival caused a great stir. Everybody except the sentry gathered in the tent, and happy cries greeted the sight of the pot. The men crowded around it, felt it and peered inside it.

The Third Platoon was "resting," or, in other words, road building. The company had arranged for the various platoons to be out of the line for one week at a time, during which the men lived near the kitchen and worked on a road leading to the front lines. Koskela's gang had just begun their rest, and it had long ago been decided that when their turn came they would brew themselves a tubful of beer. The only problem had been to lay hands on a suitable vessel since Makila would never lend them one for such a purpose. Indeed, it is unlikely that even Koskela's authority would have made Makıla surrender one of his beloved pots for such sinful use.

Maatta and Vanhala filled the pot with water at a spring, and lugged it back. Rokka acted as brewer with Koskela giving him brief instructions. First, he poured all the sugar they had saved into the water and then added the yeast they had procured by all sorts of devious means. Finally they added the bits of rye bread they had all contributed out of their rations.

The lid was fitted on tightly and the vessel set in a corner of the tent and covered with packs and greatcoats. Joyful anticipation beamed in every eye as Vanhala pressed his ear to the vessel and said:

—It's begun to work. Hark, the downtrodden seething with unrest!

—But we can't leave it here unguarded, said Hietanen. —Someone's got to keep a lookout. Makila may guess that we were the ones who pinched his pot, and search the tents.

Koskela looked thoughtful. —We can't have anyone staying behind in the tent without a reason. Hasn't any of you something wrong with you? He could go to the casualty clearing station and apply for leave.

—My throat's sore, Rahikainen said quickly, but Koskela waved him aside.

—Not you. What we want is someone no one would suspect. Salo, haven't you something you could complain about? Nobody'd suspect you.

—I've a blister on my foot, but it's nearly healed now.

Salo smiled, not grasping that Koskela's choice was not altogether a compliment. Eagerly he took off his boot and showed the place.

—Scratch it a bit with your fingernails. And before you go in the morning, rub it to make it sore. Look worried when you complain about it.

—Tell them it doesn't hurt much but it won't stand a boot. And tell 'em you've had it a long time, but it hasn't healed because we're always on the move.

So the following day Salo showed his foot and was relieved from duty, though only for three days. Under the joint ministrations of the whole squad, however, the precious abrasion became so much worse that Salo had no need to pretend as he limped back to medical inspection and easily got another three days. Thus for an entire week he was able to guard a vessel whose absence had caused a considerable stir among the cooks. But even Makila never suspected Koskela's men for the simple reason that he had no idea of what they could use it for. Had it not been for that he would soon enough have connected Rahikainen's hanging about the kitchen with the disappearance of the pot that same evening.

The beer vat became the center around which the life of the squad revolved. Every evening, returning from their road making, they made straight for it and listened to the ferment inside.

From the front would come the sound of desultory firing, ersatz coffee boiled in mess tins hung over a campfire, and in the corner of the tent the brew bubbled.

2.

The fourth of June dawned a beautiful sunny day. It was Marshal Mannerheim's seventy-fifth birthday and everywhere that fact dominated public life. For the army the day was conspicuous for the issue of what was known as "army cognac" at the rate of a bottle for every five men.

—One thing first. When we get drunk there's not to be any row. If anyone starts making trouble, all the rest go for him. What'll we do to him?

—Grease his behind with rifle grease.

—That's it!

—Let's get started.

Hietanen shared the brandy among their field mugs, and when each had received his share, he raised his mug:

—Here's to luck. We'll drink to that first for having spared us this long.

The mugs rose, and that was the end of the brandy.

—That didn't do much good, let's bring out the beer.

—What'll he say tomorrow when he learns where his pot's been?

—To hell with tomorrow.

Hietanen filled the mugs with the home-brewed beer and to the accompaniment of much coughing and choking it vanished down their throats. No one had the heart to find fault with its taste after all the anticipation it had given them. Instead, they downed a second mugful and their talk became ever livelier, their spirits more buoyant. The poorest jokes were greeted with laughter, and the air was full of a strong sense of comradeship and brotherhood.

—Ah, that warms the pit of your stomach, said Rokka. —Why didn't you go to the CP tent, Koskela? That's where the real drinks are.

—But not a tubful the size we've got.

—You don't do much drinking with the other officers.

—Why should I? This is where I belong.

Faces were becoming flushed, and Salo was already so intoxicated that he began to lavish drunken praise on Koskela.

—Say what you like, boys, but there aren't many gangs with as good a boss as Koskela.

But Koskela paid no attention to him, and none of the others were yet drunk enough to start pouring out their hearts to whomever cared to listen. Instead they boasted of the potent brew.

—Good stuff, boys. I'm beginning to feel it.

Mug after mug was emptied, and now they were discussing the campaign and remembering fallen comrades.

—We've really been through something, boys. Men cut down like grass . . . You're right he was a tough 'un . . . That Lehto was gold all through . . . He didn't need to get himself killed . . . Yes, he was that . . . Lahtinen was one of the best . . . went in just below his ear . . . Not many men would have tried to bring a machine gun back in a situation like that.

—Say, Koskela, called Rokka. —You've got to see that Maatta gets another stripe now he's got Lahtinen's job. I don't give a damn for the bits of cloth, but it's the custom. He's a good man.

Koskela had so far said nothing. The only change the beer had worked in him was that he had begun to stare fixedly at each speaker in turn. Now he said:

—I know Maatta.

But Salo was holding forth before Koskela, waving his hands about:

—Listen, lieutenant. I'm not one of the best but I've done as well as the next man. Haven't I?

Koskela again stared fixedly at them all:

—You're good men.

—You can bet your life no other gang's going to jump down our throats, said Hietanen, by this time the drunkest of them all.

—Give me my share in a bottle, said Rahikainen. —I've got to pay a few visits.

—Across the Svir? You can't do it, said Hietanen.

—There's trucks driving across all the time. But there's a big camp right near here full of women on road work. Some of the boys coming back from leave saw 'em. What do you say, chief?

Koskela's face was flushed as he stared at Rahikainen.

—A man's got to answer for his own comings and goings. I'm not giving you permission to go, but if you take off on your own that's not my affair. Tomorrow we go back into the line, and if you're not here you'll do ten times as much guard duty in the line as the others. Keep that in mind and get out of here.

—I'll be here if I'm alive. Give me my beer.

Rahikainen's share was poured into two bottles, and with these and a blanket in his pack he set off.

—What the hell's the blanket for?

—I need something to lie on. It's no good on the bare ground.

As soon as Rahikainen had gone, Rokka shrugged.

—He'll get what he wants, too. And he'll go through this war without a scratch. He's so crooked that no bullet could hit him.

—You've got to admit, though, that he hasn't very often put himself where a bullet could get at him.

—That he hasn't, Salo said emphatically, but Sihvonen, not one of the boldest himself, did not like people to talk about courage.

—I don't know. It seems to me everybody is afraid.

—Afraid? Of course. Everybody's afraid but some hide it better than others . . . there's no such thing on this earth as a man who doesn't fear death.

All concurred as one with this view except Rokka, who smiled and said with a wink:

—Don't say that, boys. I can't fear him, since I've never seen him. But let's have some music. Come on, Vanhala, put on *Yokkantii.*

Vanhala brought out his phonograph. By now the spring was broken but Vanhala spun the record with his finger, and although the rhythm was uneven, no one paid it any heed. They heard *"Yokkantii"* and *"Armi Batalyoon,"* the names derived from the most easily distinguishable words on the record, and one and another tried to jabber Russian in imitation of the singer's words.

At last Vanhala tired of spinning records, and the men sought new ways of amusing themselves. Someone remembered belatedly that it was Mannerheim's birthday, but even then they did not drink to him for the simple reason that they were trying to make the beer last. As a result when the mugs were filled again, they had once more forgotten the Marshal altogether.

And so things continued until the beer was gone and they went outside to play Vanhala's phonograph and sing. Koskela himself did not sing but continually demanded songs of the others. Then he would listen intently as if there were something of great significance in the discordant bellowing. When he was sober he was not interested in songs and consequently knew little about them. He did not even know their names but would say:

—Give us that one about Lotta Lundgren.

At once a terrific bellowing would begin, its echoes rolling through the forest and mingling with the salutes the guns in the rear were firing in the Marshal's honor.

—Play *Yokkantii*. I'll dance it. I'll dance like Veerukka in Petrozavodsk. . . . Do you still remember her, boys?

Hietanen fished out Vera's badge from his pocketbook:

—I remember . . . haw . . . do I remember . . . Look, boys . . . I remember everything. . . . Haw.

Vanhala, conscious again, spun the record and Rokka danced, ludicrously trying to imitate Vera's pirouettes and at the same time draw attention to his own marvelous skill. Hietanen spread his arms and bellowed:

—Ha . . . Listen, everybody . . . I've got a speech to deliver . . . I'm a defender of the Fatherland. All we Finns wanted was to build our houses and saunas here in peace. . . . Hahaa . . . Blessed are the wooden-headed, for they shall not sink. . . .

Rokka gyrated faster and faster.

—*Yokkantii* and *yokkantii* . . . hey, I'm good . . . Wolf's gone home on leave . . . he'll bring me a package from my wife. . . . *Yokkantii* and *yokkantii* . . . Look, Hietanen, look at me . . .

But Hietanen was very drunk as he staggered around with outstretched arms shouting:

—Look, boys! I'm an airplane.

He banked first one way then another, keeping up a buzzing sound:

—Boys, I'm a bomber.

Vanhala's phonograph stopped playing, and blissfully he joined in the air activity.

—An I 16 circling in from the left, its motor howling papapapa. It's a terrible air battle . . . knights of the sky in the heat of battle, papapapa . . . the last nobility left in war, papapa!

The two circled round each other, buzzing and papa-ing.

—Heroes of the blue . . . Eyes keen, hands steady, hearts of iron . . . our brave airmen attack the enemy's carrion birds . . . papapapapapa . . .

Suddenly Hietanen tripped over a stump and fell. There, unable to rise to his feet, he lay stunned. Vanhala described a magnificent circle.

—Use your parachute. Your plane's falling, jump!

—Falling . . . everything's going round . . . the world's spinning before my eyes, babbled Hietanen, clutching the grass to keep himself steady. Now Vanhala was shouting in his ear:

—Tailspin . . . Jump . . . You can't pull her out.

Hietanen's machine, however, was falling rapidly, spinning and lurching as it fell. He was too far gone to jump and dropped with his aircraft into pitch darkness. There Vanhala left him, annoyed at the shortness of the air battle.

Farther away, sitting around a large boulder, Maatta, Salo and Sihvonen were discussing will-o'-the-wisps. Salo, his hair hanging wildly over his eyes, assured his hearers that their lights burned in his home parish over fabulous treasure troves.

Sihvonen turned his head away and waved his hand as though warding off insects:

—The hell you say . . . It's all a pack of lies . . .

—It's a fact. Lots of old people have seen them. And there's always two swords crossed like that over 'em.

—Shit . . . Lapland tales of magic. That's where miracles are always supposed to have happened, way up in the far north.

—But which of us is from the farthest north? said Maatta. —Why, my home's so far north that we boil our coffee on the Northern Lights.

Maatta had said very little, and the beer did not seem to have affected him much. Now he looked at the boulder.

—Now, that's a stone. What do you say we lift it?

—It can't be done . . . it's too damn heavy.

Maatta inspected the boulder from every side and then seized it at the two places which offered a handhold. The boulder was almost as big as he was, but with a terrific grunt he raised it a couple of inches. He straightened his back and dusted his palms.

—I said it could be lifted.

Sihvonen shrugged his defeat, but Salo gripped the rock and heaved. The boulder did not budge, and suddenly Salo put his hands to his back.

—I've sprained my back. Jesus Christ! If it hadn't been for that, I bet I could have done it, too.

Maatta regarded the boulder with calm self-assurance.

—It gets you in the back if you lift the wrong way.

Salo continued to hold his back, his face distorted with pain. Perhaps he really had sprained his back. Hadn't his foot actually become sore after he had first only pretended it was?

Rokka had stopped dancing, for now Vanhala was playing Stalin's speeches to himself. With a grunt Koskela rose and set off toward the CP.

—Koskela, where are you going? Rokka shouted after him.

—Moscow.

Koskela walked on with uncertain steps, beltless and capless, his tunic unbuttoned.

—You going to the CP?

—I'm going to Mannerheim's headquarters.

There were no more questions, Koskela's replies having plainly indicated that his private affairs were his own business.

He kept his balance well although his feet occasionally strayed from the path. His blue eyes stared unblinkingly at the alders and only an occasional hiccup escaped him. Then suddenly he stopped and in a roaring voice began to sing.

—Break, waves of the open Onega . . .

3.

A group of the battalion's officers had gathered in the machine-gun company's CP dugout to celebrate the day. The dugout was more suitable for this purpose than any of the other company headquarters, since it was farthest removed from the front lines. Certainly Lammio was not so popular as a host that they would have gathered there otherwise. Among them was Kariluoto, who had been made a first lieutenant in Petrozavodsk. He had entrusted his company to a platoon officer while he celebrated and by now he had swallowed a great many drinks. As a result, he was holding forth on the duties of an officer:

—The only way you can influence a Finn is by setting him an example. But at the same time you have to stimulate his ambition. A common soldier feels inferior to an officer, and you have to guide this feeling so that it inspires him to deeds that will make him feel equal to his commander. Above all, you must never show weakness. Whatever you may feel inside you, outwardly you've got to be like a rock.

Lammio sat at the head of the table in his best uniform, all his ribbons in place, helplessly drunk. A young lieutenant had stretched himself out on Lammio's bed, from where he, too, was holding forth:

—O brothers in brandy, how I'm always longing . . . longing for Helsinki . . . city of joy and bliss . . .

Kariluoto thought of Sirkka.

—Quiet . . . quiet, Jokke. Don't make us so sad . . . I remember . . . I remember . . . the tango I danced with you. Dadi deeda daa daa dee daa deedeedaa . . .

Kariluoto was a ludicrous sight as, seated, he went through the movements of a tango.

Mielonen had been banished for the time being, and on his bed sat a lean, bespectacled lieutenant who interrupted Kariluoto's dance by breaking into song:

—*Die Fahne hoch* . . .

The strains of the Horst Wessel roused Lammio. Rising to his feet and striving to keep himself erect he shouted:

—Orderly!

A soldier entered and stood at attention.

—Fill the glasses.

—Yes, Lieutenant.

The orderly filled the glasses and Lammio raised his.

—A toast! A toast to all officers everywhere. Gentlemen, our role is clear. We are the army's backbone. Finland stands or falls by us. Gentlemen, unflinchingly we shall lead wherever the Marshal's sword points.

—Backbone, muttered Mielonen behind the door. —If that's so, then your bit of it sure as hell has atrophy.

Mielonen was fed up to the ears. It had taken trench warfare to reveal to him what it meant to be Lammio's orderly. The crowning insult had been a mongrel Lammio had adopted which he had ordered the men to refer to as "Sir." Finally Mielonen and the other orderly had tied a heavy rock to "Sir" and thrown him into a pool. But the next day Lammio had ordered another dog by phone from a friend of his at Divisional Headquarters. Now they could not repeat the trick without arousing suspicion.

Mielonen stood up when he saw Koskela coming and went down the steps to open the dugout door for him. But to his astonishment, Koskela turned on him angrily:

—What kind of a goddamn doorman do you think you are?

—Lieutenant, I'm Sergeant Mielonen.

Koskela's behavior was all the more surprising because he had always been tactful and considerate, and Mielonen stared at the lieutenant as Koskela went on:

—You are, are you? Well then, don't run to open doors like a goddamn doorman.

—I won't, Lieutenant.

Mielonen was so confused that he addressed Koskela by his rank, though they had long since dropped such formalities. Pushing past him, Koskela went on into the dugout, and staggering slightly, came to a halt in the middle of the floor. His hair ruffled, his tunic unbuttoned, he bawled out in Russian:

—*Rastu* . . .

The group did not seem glad to see him, except for Kariluoto, whose face brightened as he called out:

—Welcome! Where have you been? Orderly, a glass for Ville. Here, take mine to start with.

Koskela drained Kariluoto's glass and dropped on a bench. He stared at each of them in turn silently as the orderly came, filled the glasses and left.

The bespectacled second lieutenant resumed his song:

—*Die Strasse frei, den braunen Bataljonen* . . .

Koskela focused his gaze on him. The lieutenant went on singing for a while but then, embarrassed by Koskela's staring, his voice became uncertain, and before long he fell silent.

Suddenly Koskela said:

—*Siperia polsoi taika.*

—What's that? asked the lieutenant in a strained voice. But instead of replying Koskela blurted out:

—*Topra huja!*

Now the lieutenant had lost his self-assurance altogether, and with it his temper.

—Who the hell are you to speak Russian here?

—Koskela of Finland! I eat raw iron and shit steel chain.

Kariluoto, realizing that Koskela was in an aggressive mood, offered him another drink to distract his attention from the other man, but Koskela thrust the glass aside.

—*Adin tvaa tree pyet . . . Adin tvaa tree pyet . . .*

—What have you got against me? The lieutenant's anger was rising. But Koskela went unhearingly:

—*Union soviet sosialist . . . tis . . . list . . . krepuplik . . . Holotna harasoo maatuska dievuska krasni soldier komsomolski homoravitsa bulayeva svir . . .*

Abruptly it dawned on the lieutenant that it was his singing in a foreign language that had set Koskela talking Russian.

—I can speak Finnish, too, he said. —And it might be better for you to stick to it as well.

—Stick . . . stick . . . Who uses a stick? Tara rai raa . . . Not bear-hunter Martti Kitunen . . .

Koskela sang. Faster and faster the words poured from between his clenched teeth until at the last hissed word he suddenly rose to his feet and with one blow knocked the singer, who had also risen from the bed, flat on the floor.

The others rushed to pacify him. Lammio attempted to take hold of him but was sent flying against a wall. The next second Koskela had seized the heavy bench and was brandishing it in the air.

—God damn it, don't fool with me.

—Ville, calm down, begged Kariluoto, but Koskela did not even recognize him. Then the other lieutenant who had been lying in Lammio's bed seized Koskela's hands from behind and succeeded in dragging him down on the bench, thus enabling the rest to lay hold of him. The bespectacled lieutenant had regained consciousness and sat up, spitting blood. Panic-stricken, Lammio shouted for Mielonen who came rushing in with the other orderlies at his heels.

—Take that man . . . tie him up. . . .

They pinned Koskela down. Five or six men were on top of him, but he turned and rolled under the pile like a bear. At last they succeeded in binding him with three belts, and he lay helpless. Nevertheless he went on grunting, grinding his teeth:

—I won't give in, damn you . . . I won't give in . . .

He was carried bodily to the tent, Kariluoto walking beside him, speaking so soothingly that Koskela at last asked:

—Who the hell are you?

—Kariluoto. Don't you know your old pal?

—Christ, I'm glad to see you. Hey, hey, boys . . . where are we going?

—To rest. You're a little overtired.

—Tired . . . Old woman Koskela's son never tires. . . .

Meanwhile the casualties in the tent had also been high. Only Rokka and Vanhala were still on their feet. Maatta had gone to bed on his own initiative, but most of the others had passed out. Now Vanhala was playing Stalin's speeches again while Rokka was drunkenly relating anecdotes:

—See this . . . I always have one of these little almanacs. And once when I went with my wife to visit her parents I was talking about it—it tells you the best fishing days. When my father-in-law asks: Does it say whether there'll be good fishing tomorrow? I read out: Fish on the move at this time. Will enter traps. Well, the next morning the old sinner brings home a big load of fish and was as pleased as hell. But then another day when he asked me and I read the same words he didn't catch a single fish. He was so mad that he wouldn't speak for three days. And that made my wife mad. She said I was making a fool of her old man.

Vanhala turned the record with his finger, his head nodding but awake enough to mutter:

—Nagging wives . . . nagging wives.

—My wife doesn't nag long. Do you know what to do with a wife when she gets mad?

—Take a stick to her backside, kee-hee.

—No. When I catch hold of her and toss her around in a polka, damned if she doesn't always calm down.

—Hey, what the devil's that? Why are they carrying Koskela? Have they killed him?

The two rushed to meet the procession, Rokka calling out while still at a distance:

—Why the hell are you carrying him like that? What's the matter? Did they hit him?

—Hello, lone fighter. Who hit who?

Koskela was set down, and Kariluoto whispered to Rokka:

—Try to get him to bed. He got so violent we had to tie him up.

Rokka unbound Koskela's bonds and led him to the tent. Koskela went along meekly, seemingly without any idea of what was happening as he hung on Rokka's arm and babbled:

—Hey, you old veteran of Taipale! Let's sing about Lotta Lundgren . . .

But no sooner was he in the tent than he fell sound asleep, leaving Rokka to cover him with a greatcoat. Lammio was trying to maintain a pretense of sobriety but with very little success although the recent struggle had partly cleared his brain. He looked at the men stretched out here and there on the ground, some of them lying in their own vomit:

—Beautiful! Very beautiful! . . . It explains everything. The whole platoon, too, in the same condition. What in hell did you drink?

—Beer. And what a brew! Only me and Vanhala are still on our pins. We'd have offered our guests some if there was any left.

—You're responsible for the section until Koskela and Hietanen get sober. My God, what if an order came to stand to?

—Hell, me and Vanhala'd get a gun in position and send so much hot lead flying that the alarm'd be called off. But say, we'd better not get any.

Lammio did not reply, and the officers departed. But the festive mood had been broken, and on the way back Lammio dwelt on the negative side of Koskela's character:

—It's not always true that courage alone qualifies a man to be an officer. When we were asked to report men who might be trained for commissions I thought of Rokka and Hietanen first, but then I thought better of it. And now this shows I was right.

Kariluoto hiccuped. He was suddenly feeling very low, but to defend Koskela he said in a strained voice:

—Yes, but it wasn't all his fault. That homemade beer can do the same thing to anybody.

He remembered the fire-spitting bunker and Koskela worming his way towards it, a high-explosive charge at his side. And he knew that all the honor for the breach in the Russian defenses had fallen on himself. Not that it had been his fault. He had done all he could to let everybody know what Koskela had done. His intoxication was wearing off, and in his turgid state of mind the memory of it and of all he had said filled him with shame. How distant all this was from the things that really mattered! Instead of going back to Lammio's dugout with the others, Kariluoto, without a word of explanation, took a short cut to his own CP.

Rokka and Vanhala dragged the sleeping drunkards into the tent for the night. Gnats swarmed in the rays of the setting sun, and somewhere nearby a cuckoo sang in the crown of a tall spruce.

4.

They were awakened in the morning by Rahikainen's return. Tousled heads rose from the tents, and bloodshot eyes peered about as coated tongues explored dry mouths. Hietanen looked around him, saw the pot and spat:

—Christ what a campaign! I've never been on one like it before.

—You went into a tailspin . . .

—I don't remember anything. Get the coffee boiling, I've got to drink something. Someone's been eating catshit with my mouth.

Koskela, too, rose. He screwed up his forehead thoughtfully as he asked:

—How'd it all go last night?

Rokka laughed. —Oh, all right. Except that you were taken prisoner in the CP.

—Was I there too?

—You sure were. They had to carry you away, your hands and feet all tied up with belts.

—What the devil did I do?

—You started hitting people.

—Hitting people? Me . . . ?

Koskela combed his hair with his fingers and fiddled with his pack. Then his face resumed its usual blank look as he asked:

—Well, was anyone hurt?

—Nobody worth mentioning. A lieutenant in the Second Company was spitting a little blood, I've heard, but that'll only have done him good.

—Well, if it was nothing worse, it's all right then. I've got to take that pot back to Makila. And you'd better start putting your things in order. We're moving out as soon as we've eaten.

Vanhala looked inquiringly at Rahikainen, who was preparing to crawl into his bedroll.

—Did you have any use for that blanket?

Rahikainen had been waiting to be given the attention he deserved, and now, with the smile of one who had much to tell, he answered:

—I want to catch some sleep until the grub comes. Don't wake me until then. One bottle went to a sentry, but I got some bread in the bargain.

Rahikainen drew the blanket over his face and instantly was asleep. The rest put the coffee on to boil and rather wanly began talking of yesterday. They were still at it when the flap of the tent was lifted and Makila crawled in.

—Come right in, shouted Rokka, but Makila's eye had fallen immediately on the pot and he was looking at it, clearing his throat.

—Looking for something? asked Rokka.

—Who . . . who stole that?

—Nobody stole it, said Hietanen. —The boys found it back there on the path.

—Hm. Back there beside the kitchen? Hm.

Makila examined the vessel, carefully avoiding looking any of them in the eye. Sounds of distress came from his throat. —It's dented.

—Why, so it is! But don't worry, we'll mend it. Hand me that piece of wood.

Rokka hammered out the dent with the piece of wood, Makila clucking all the while as if to say: Hammer all you like, you won't restore it to its former condition. It's ruined.

Koskela was unable to make up his mind whether to say anything or not. He felt it was his duty to attempt to explain matters, but what worthwhile explanation could he give? Finally he asked:

—You haven't needed it, have you?

Neither Koskela's rank nor his reputation spared him from Makila's scorn. Indeed, such things meant little to Makila compared with theft and drinking. He snorted angrily over his shoulder:

—Hm! I suppose we don't really need anything to carry food in when the main need is for beer.

Koskela could not help smiling as Makila, in silent rebuke,

hoisted the pot on his back and left the tent, Hietanen shambling after him, wheedling:

—How about a few pickled herrings from the kitchen? I've a hankering for something salty.

He received no answer as the pot danced steadily onward. Hietanen tried a sentimental approach:

—I used to whisper all the names of the machine-gun parts to you at NCO school. And didn't I always let you off easy when it was my turn to drill the section? You ought to give me a couple of herrings for that.

Hietanen refrained, however, from going to the crux of the matter. The real help he had given Makila was much more important. Such a reserved and pious man was bound to become the butt of many jokes, and often only friendly protection from the broad-shouldered Hietanen had saved him from trouble. Remembering this, Makila deigned at last to answer:

—Go drink some more beer. That'll cure your hangover.

—Do you know where there is any?

—Steal a pot somewhere else and make some.

—Why the hell do you keep harping on one measly pot?

—One measly pot? Makila burst out. —I've had to hang on tooth and nail to keep everything from going! I'm supposed to feed and clothe a hundred and fifty men with my empty hands. The lieutenant sits in the orderly room looking important and giving orders. But whenever it's a question of somebody borrowing something, he has no thought of trying to protect his own. If I were to look on with my finger in my mouth everything would be gone in a minute.

Cunning advised Hietanen what tune to play, and in a consoling voice he said:

—Just what I always say to myself. I know what your job's like. You've always got to watch, day and night. Me, I'd never have stolen that pot. I know you can see that. Come on and give me a few herrings, will you?

At the kitchen Makila hemmed and hawed, fidgeted and fingered this and that. Finally, he lowered himself into the underground dugout where he kept his food stores and emerged a little later with one very small, sad-looking herring.

Makila so rarely gave anything away that for him it was a truly solemn occasion. There was a kind of warm comradeship in his voice as he said:

—Don't eat it where the others can see. I'd have the whole crowd after me.

The sight of the undersized herring almost sent Hietanen off into gales of laughter, but he could guess how magnificent the gift was in Makila's eyes.

—This'll keep me going for the next six months, he said.

Makila hesitated. Then, red with embarrassment, he said:

—It isn't right for you to go on sprees like that. We're going into the line again. At four o'clock this morning a dugout up at Number Three position took a direct hit. Two lads were killed and three taken to the hospital in bad shape. Hm . . . the end can come very quickly these days. And what shape were those boys' souls in?

Hietanen had a vague idea that since the government had brought them here, the government must have also taken measures to see that a lenient view was taken of a fallen soldier's sins. Good manners, however, demanded that he show gratitude, so he said gravely:

—Yes, that's a good point. But we mustn't think too often or too long about what may be in store for us. People are funny, though. As soon as the bullets stop flying they're ready to sing all kinds of dirty songs again and swear like the very devil. Well, I must be going.

On his way back he stuffed the herring into his mouth. He scarcely had the heart to chew the poor bit with which Makila had tried to save his soul.

5.

After their meal the platoon left. Lammio took care to keep out of sight and communicated with Koskela through Mielonen, but Koskela himself had forgotten all about the clash.

They were downhearted this dreary morning. Before them lay a dugout and a stretch of trench. It was peaceful enough, for quiet had reigned along the front since the spring. In April they had repulsed a fairly large-scale enemy attack, at one stage of which the situation had been critical indeed. The Russians had penetrated deep into their flank but had ultimately been forced to withdraw, and the bridgehead on the Svir had been held.

Now summer was coming and it was pleasant to contemplate. The grass grew tall in the moist soil. The day was warm, and they would have liked to sit down and rest for a while in the sun.

But instead they marched without speaking. Hanging heads only rose a little when the rolling boom of big guns sounded ahead.

—Quiet, boys. After that next bend Ivan'll be able to spot us. Off the path with you and into the forest.

Chapter XI

1.

The dugout was just behind a small alder-covered hillock. Skirting the other side of the mound was a trench with a machine-gun emplacement at each end. On the left the trench was linked by a shallow communication trench to the next strongpoint, while on the right lay a swampy hollow beyond which positions forming part of the next strongpoint could be seen. Still farther on the ground rose, and there lay the two advance posts, "Million" and "Little Million," the latter the worse of the two. They were situated on a treeless hill, and since beyond them the lines turned abruptly to the right they were exposed to Russian fire from three sides. Even during quiet periods casualties were heavy here, and as a result the posts were relieved every fortnight. In fact, they served everybody in the sector as a sort of almanac—so and so many days or weeks yet before our turn.

In front of the strongpoint lay a swamp and beyond that a height dominating the entire neighborhood—"Devil's Peak," on which pillboxes of logs and earth could be easily distinguished. The height had twice been in Finnish hands, but as it had immediately come under heavy artillery and infantry mortar attack, it had been on both occasions abandoned. Only the lower spur of the peak on which Million and Little Million were situated was held. Actually, it did not much matter where the line ran, for throughout its length it zigged and zagged as if it had been drawn by a madman.

In the autumn of 1941 desultory fighting had gone on for possession of these slopes until both sides had grown tired and dug in where they happened to be at the time. All around the positions lay the mortal remains of several crack Siberian units. In the winter no one could be bothered to bury them, if indeed it had been possible in the frozen ground, and by the spring they had been untouchable. Now they were dry and white, and moldering skulls peered from helmets.

Koskela's dugout was lined with timber taken from the prayer house of an adjacent village, and was consequently free from the bedbugs that infested dugouts in which timber taken from houses had been used. His foresight in this matter further increased his men's respect for him: —That beggar thinks of everything.

Between the door and the window a fireplace had been built with stones and mortar. Koskela's bed was beside the window where the men had insisted it be placed—for Koskela himself would have been content with a bunk in one of the double-deckers in which the men slept. There was something revealing about his relations with his men in this, for whereas in other platoons the men were constantly complaining about every little snobbery on the part of their officers, Koskela's men actually wanted him to enjoy as much more comfort than they as possible.

This uneventful bunker warfare allowed Koskela more quiet solitude than ever. He would lie on his bed staring up at the ceiling for hours without uttering a word. When he wasn't meditating, he liked to putter about in silence. His favorite pastime was rat catching. He would lie motionless holding a wire noose suspended over a rathole, and at last when a cautious rat entered it he would jerk the noose tight. A smile would spread over his face as he held the struggling rodent in front of his face, whispering to it.

—Well, old man. What do you know?

Then he would release the rat, saying:

—Go on home. But take care you don't wander in here again.

Sometimes, as the summer night imperceptibly changed into morning, he sat outside as though lost in a dream. But such was not truly the case. All the while his eyes were alertly watching the awakening birds, and once he remarked to a sentry coming off duty:

—They talk about birds having no cares, but I've never seen a human being work as hard as they do for their bread.

The men took their turns at guard duty, talked and wrote letters. Rokka and Rahikainen had become partners in a business firm. Rokka manufactured things and Rahikainen sold them. It took Rokka a long while to make each object, but the money he earned made it worth his while even though he knew that Rahikainen was cheating him on the prices he obtained. But, characteristically, he said nothing since no large sums were involved and because he knew that for Rahikainen the real appeal of such an enterprise lay in such minor knaveries.

Rokka was well stocked with metal for ring making. While watching an air battle, they had seen a Russian fighter come down not far from their dugout. Instantly he had snatched up a pair of pliers, a metal saw and a tommy gun, and raced to the scene.

Luckily for him the fighter had crashed in no-man's-land and the Russians had had time to send out a patrol to guard the wreckage. But for that it would have been stripped by the time he got there. As it was, parties out for loot were coming back disappointed when he arrived. Rokka, however, was of no mind to return empty-handed. He persuaded a few of the boldest spirits to join him, and the rest followed at a distance. Approaching Russian guards fled after Rokka had shot the officer in charge, at the same time emitting so eerie a yell that the faint-hearted among his own party nearly bolted.

The wreck became the scene of a furious bustle. One man would be bent on securing instruments, another parachute silk; several wanted the dead airman's bloodstained leather jacket, but most in demand was aluminum for rings.

They did not have much time, for the Russians soon sent a bigger patrol, and the pillagers had to run. But before they fled, Rokka, by right of leadership, had seized the choicest prize. He returned to the dugout with a three-bladed propeller on his shoulder, shouting while still at a distance:

—Our wartime economy's not going to suffer from a shortage of raw materials. Hell, you should have seen us go! We ran like hounds with our tongues tucked into our belts with Ivan spraying us with bullets from behind all the while.

Hietanen and Maatta were the biggest gamblers in the platoon. Invariably Hietanen would lose his pay, after which he would go about loudly criticizing his play:

—Oh, what a damn fool I am! What made me draw one more card? From now on I stay with a fifteen.

Then he would take another man's turn as sentry for fifty marks, and having lost that too, would change his tune:

—No. Damned if I won't go on drawing up to nineteen. Win or lose, no staying at fifteen for me.

No one was ever left in any doubt as to Hietanen's strategy of the moment. And in the evening Hietanen would write home in his awkward hand, the tip of his tongue moving with his pen:

> . . . send meat, bread and butter. And I need a little money, too, so that I can buy my tobacco ration. With many greetings,
> Urho.

He never gambled with the money he got from home, however:
—But a soldier's daily allowance isn't worth saving. I'm not here to earn money, he would say.

Rokka rubbed the surface of the ring with a cloth to give it a polish. As he held the ring to the light from the window for a last inspection, he said to Koskela who was lying on his bed:

—Lammio's threatened to take my propeller away from me. Says it belongs to the state. Damn it, if I get hold of booty, it belongs to me! I'll make sure he gets the hiding his father never gave him if he comes after my stuff.

—He won't come after anything, said Koskela, feeling uncomfortable as he always did when any friction occurred between officers and men.

—I'm not too sure. You don't hear all the bleating that's going on about discipline. The big brass doesn't even try to run the war themselves but leave it to bastards like him. It's his kind who're supposed to restore discipline. To me the whole show's gone to pieces. There's no spirit left. The men don't know what's ahead and they're beginning to take it as a game. Soon they won't give a damn who wins. And the fools think they're going to improve matters by drilling us till our tails fall off. Sometimes I wonder whether they're in earnest or not. It's hard to believe grown-up men could be so brainless . . . setting the men drilling out here. Goddamned foolishness. They're building fine quarters in the command dugouts and competing to see who gets the best. But it's not getting us anywhere. I'm beginning to suspect we're finished.

Rokka rubbed away at his ring in silence, then suddenly swung towards Koskela.

—Do you think we'll lose this war?

Koskela stared at the ceiling a long time before answering.

—The Germans are making a lot of headway in the south.

—That doesn't mean anything. They're dashing about like a bee in a spider's web. The more he tears it, the more he's stuck. Last year I thought they'd do the trick, but by autumn my guess was that they hadn't a chance. It doesn't take much brains to see that. If they'd gone on hammering away they might have pulled it off, but this winter's spoiled it for them.

—You may be right, I don't know.

Koskela's tone seemed to indicate that he had thought about the matter and was not inclined to dispute Rokka's conclusions. But Rokka, having pursued the matter long enough, now cast all his forebodings from him.

—Well, there's no use crying over spilt milk—or singed Germans. Do you know I've sent my wife six thousand marks, all of it from these rings?

—I don't doubt it.

—Hey, you young heroes out there. Water's boiling.

They had fixed a sheet of tinplate over their fireplace to serve as a range. On it several mess tins of water had been set to boil, and now the men slouched in to brew their ersatz coffee.

—There's a lot of six-inch shells falling on Million again, said Rahikainen, sitting down on his bunk above which he had tacked on the wall a series of pictures of a naked girl cut out of a magazine.

—Not much of a place for sunbathing, commented Hietanen.

—There'll soon be an end to it here, too, if you go on making all that noise out on guard. Quit shouting at 'em all the time, for God's sake.

Koskela rose to look out of the window, for he had seen a group of unfamiliar silhouettes approaching.

—That must be the draft that should have been here before.

The door opened and four men entered. Blankly the men in the dugout stared at the man who seemed to be the leader of the group. He was a tall fellow with a long horse face and big, solemn eyes. Then curiosity gave way to surprise as they noticed the longbow slung over his shoulder. The newcomer stood smartly at attention as he gravely addressed Koskela:

—Is this Lieutenant Koskela's dugout?

—It is.

—Would the lieutenant be Lieutenant Koskela himself?

—That's right.

—Lieutenant, sir. Private Honkajoki, A. A One reports for duty with the lieutenant's platoon. The first A is for my Christian name Aarne, the second A with the One is my category. Having seen service previously in Machine-gun Company Number Two of the Fiftieth Infantry Regiment, been wounded and sent to hospital and from there ordered here, I'm now reporting firmly resolved to sacrifice my own and the fine new bottled blood given me in the hospital in the cause of liberty.

The man remained standing stiffly at attention waiting for Koskela's permission to sit down.

—Well, welcome to the platoon. There's a bench. Two of you stay here and two go to the other section. You can decide between yourselves who goes where.

—Keep the archer with us, Vanhala whispered to Koskela; he had sensed at once that they would lose a lot of fun if Horse-face went elsewhere, for he recognized instinctively that there was a strong element of the clown in the man. It was not Koskela's habit to give orders where they were not essential, however, and he left the decision to the newcomers themselves. The other three were conscripts fresh out of training camp, and as the idea of living in the same dugout with an officer seemed alarming to them, they chose the other section. So Honkajoki stayed and was finally joined by one of the conscripts who in a shy whisper introduced himself as Hauhia.

The newcomers chose their bunks and made themselves at home, Honkajoki carefully stowing his bow in the rifle rack. Instantly Rokka was after him.

—You don't trust newfangled weapons like rifles, is that it?

Honkajoki turned to face Rokka:

—Considering the rapid development of weapons and technical equipment in the last Great War, it seemed to me that the adoption of new weapons was essential if the nation was to continue to defend itself.

They all stared at this warrior from the past until Koskela broke the amazed silence:

—Where are you from?

—Sir, my mother gave birth to me in Lauttakyla, but I was still in my infancy when my parents went to live in Hameenlinna, which became the scene of my boyhood. I grew up after that in different parts of Finland, being of a mobile disposition which kept me always on the move. I ought perhaps to explain that there is much of the student and explorer in me. In actual fact I am a scientist.

—But what did you do for a living? asked Hietanen. Honkajoki turned to face him with the same exaggerated courtesy.

—Sergeant, forest management is the field in which I earned my livelihood. That, however, is only my bread-and-butter occupation. As I said, actually I am a scientist. I am interested in inventing, and at the moment I have set as my goal the achievement of perpetual motion.

—Don't you know that's impossible? said Hietanen.

—I am aware of the difficulties attached to this project, but I do not allow them to discourage me . . . However, I would like to rest a bit now. What arrangements, may I ask, have you for guard duty?

—One sentry at each of the machine guns at night, but only at one of them in the daytime, said Koskela. —You can both take one turn with the older men to get used to the terrain and Ivan's habits. It'll do you good, Hauhia, to be out a couple of times with somebody else. Take the boy with you next time, Rokka, and show him the ropes. Remember what you're told; this sector isn't as safe as it may look at first glance. What age group are you?

—Nineteen twenty-two, Lieutenant.

Hauhia rose smartly to attention before answering, but Koskela wearily waved him down:

—I see. You'll be all right. And we don't go in for rank here. We're all comrades, so just be yourself. Of course, that only applies to me. Other officers are a different matter.

—Yes, sir . . . Lieutenant. Hauhia stiffened in his seat. Fear of officers had become a natural reflex with him.

2.

After a while Honkajoki lay down for a nap. His eccentricities had at first surprised the others, but already they were getting used to him.

Hauhia, on the other hand, was unable to sleep. He would have preferred to go on guard duty immediately with Vanhala, but Rokka shook his head.

—Wait and come with me. He taunts the Russkies all the time. A sniper might get you first go.

—Have you lost many men?

Rokka looked at him for a moment appraisingly, thus giving Rahikainen time to say:

—Hardly a day goes by without someone getting his.

—Don't believe him. He's only trying to frighten you. And we won't be on Million for a couple of months yet. But don't go out alone. Remember that above everything else.

—I've been through an air raid, Hauhia offered, hastening to add: —But I know that's nothing compared with real war.

—There isn't any realer war, said Rokka with a smile. And Hauhia fell silent, believing Rokka was laughing at his stupidity. He regarded the dugout and the men. There was much he would have liked to ask, and yet he dared not. Rokka and Hietanen made him feel awkward, to say nothing of Koskela. The fear of drill sergeants driven into him during his stay at the training center was still very much alive.

Rokka stowed his ring-making equipment under his bed and called to him:

—Come along, lad. Papa'll teach you how to make war.

—What weapons will I need?

—You'll find 'em there.

They climbed out of the dugout into the communication trench, and made their way to a passage behind a bend in the trench. A bar of wood stretched across it like a perch.

—The latrine.

—Those look like Russian pamphlets.

—Yes. Ivan supplies our toilet paper.

Rokka took up one of the pamphlets which exhorted Finnish soldiers to kill their officers and come over to the Red Army.

—See what's on the back. Any man who has one of these on him when he surrenders won't be shot. Remember that. Take one with you when you go out.

They continued on their way.

—There's the second section's machine gun. There's a guard here only at night. These are the riflemen's pits. That's our sentry. Hello, anything doing?

The sentry lowered the book he was trying to read in the gloom and looked into a trench periscope.

—Nothing.

—Don't you try reading on sentry duty like Ukkola here. And get this into your skull. Never raise your head over the parapet. Nearly every single casualty we've had here had their fool heads up one second too long. Use the periscope.

—I will.

—You say that, but you don't realize Ivan can see you this very minute.

Rokka snatched the youth away from the loophole in the automatic rifle emplacement.

—I'm not joking. He might have been watching you through a telescope. This is a summer evening, but don't get dreamy. Death doesn't take time off for a smoke. Do you smoke?

—Yes. But all we got when we were sent out was our tobacco ration.

—I'll give you a full pack when we get back to the dugout. Listen, that's Ivan's loud-speakers.

—Men of Finland! Kill your Fascist officers and come over here.

The voice, distorted by the loud-speaker, came from Devil's Peak.

—The Fascists have been killed long ago. We've started on the next party, Vanhala's voice shouted from the other end of the trench.

—Men of Finland! Come over and get all the bread you can eat.

—That's the way he's always going on, Rokka said, half angry despite his amusement at Vanhala's taunts.

—Hitler's dogs have suffered enormous losses in men and material, Finnish worker-soldiers. Why should you shed your blood while the Germans are raping your wives and sisters?

—Yes, and even our mothers are getting their fair share, khee-hee-hee.

Pa-pa-pa-pa-pa-pa-pa.

The alders rattled and Hauhia flung himself down to the bottom of the trench.

—Did they hit him? he asked anxiously.

—*Ruski vintovka, hutio vintovka,* khee-hee-hee. —Hear him? Let's go send that madman away.

Vanhala was studying Devil's Peak through a rough periscope he had put together of boards and two mirrors. Because of the losses caused by Russian snipers the men had been forbidden to look out except through the periscopes. The sentries also were ordered to wear a steel helmet, but they had experimented with poking their helmets over the parapets until most of them had been shot full of holes and now lay rusting there.

—Stop that damned shouting, Rokka said as they reached Vanhala.

—Ivan started it.

—And he damn well may put a stop to it. Get out of here. What the devil are you doing with that file?

—I put a notch in the nose of a cartridge. It makes a hell of a noise in the air.

Vanhala set off down the trench laughing to himself as Rokka inspected the ground in front of the trench through the periscope and then passed it to Hauhia to do the same.

—Remember to do that every time. There are fourteen bodies lying out there. Mark where each of 'em is, so in an attack you won't mistake living men for dead.

—When did they get killed?

—Last autumn; but we weren't here then. There's only bones and worms in those rags now. See those bunkers on the peak? That's where Ivan's watching us from. With luck you can see a helmet. I've a good mind to requisition a rifle with telescopic sights and take a crack at a few of them. I did try occasionally at first, but since I began making rings I haven't had time. And don't you get any ideas about sniping yet. You've got to be damn careful because it means sticking your own head out.

Rokka went on advising Hauhia for a full two hours!

—If they start coming over, pull this string. It's tied to a bell in the dugout. And if anything does happen, don't get nervous. Take time to aim accurately. Knock off a few right at the beginning and you'll see the others slow down.

—What's it like to shoot a man?

—I don't know. All I've shot were Russkies.

—Aren't they human?

—No, they sure as hell aren't. And wiser men than I say the Russian isn't human. But don't you start bothering your conscience. Just remember that Ivan'd be willing enough to take the sin on his. Me, I never think about such things. The brass who give us our orders must know, so it's their responsibility. Antti Rokka shoots and makes rings. You follow his example.

—You won't find me worrying, Hauhia said trying to sound brave, and was immediately ashamed of his words. Certainly he didn't want Rokka to take him for a braggart. Hauhia had immediately fallen under Rokka's spell. He thought himself wonderfully lucky to have gotten into Rokka's squad, for to him Rokka was the embodiment of everything he had heard and read about a front-line soldier. He'd be like that soon he thought, for Hauhia was still under the illusion that men become brave in battle. After thinking a moment he asked:

—They say you get used to fear. Is that true?

—You don't get used to it if you let it get hold of you. Fear's a bad companion. Kick it away if it tries to come near you.

The earth shook as a six-inch shell crashed on Million. Instantly Hauhia was on his hands and knees in the trench and stayed there until Rokka told him to get up. Shamefacedly he babbled that he didn't know yet which shells were dangerous and which were not. To his surprise Rokka smiled.

—There's no such thing as a shell that isn't dangerous. They're all damned dangerous. Throw yourself down every time you hear one. There's nothing wrong with that.

After two hours Rahikainen came to relieve them. At the other gun Maatta had taken Honkajoki with him to acquaint him with the positions and the lay of the land. Honkajoki had his bow with him and a few arrows in a birch-bark quiver. Maatta was of two minds as to whether to explain anything; there was something wrong with this man. It might be better not to let him stand guard alone.

Slyly he watched the man out of the corner of his eye, and was relieved to see the care and thoroughness with which Honkajoki studied the land through the periscope.

3.

Rokka took Hauhia out with him on night duty once more, and then Hauhia was given a tour of his own in the afternoon. That morning he asked Koskela for permission to visit his two comrades from the training center in the other section.

—All right, go ahead. But go through the communication trench and don't stick your head up.

—I won't, Lieutenant.

At once he set off in high spirits to tell his friends everything he had seen and experienced, leaving Koskela staring at the ceiling, wondering how such enthusiasm for war was possible.

In the neighboring strongpoint Hauhia hardly gave his friends a chance to say a word. He could not conceive that they could possibly have gone through the same experiences.

—Jesus Christ, we're in a dangerous position. You can't raise your head, or piff! But the lieutenant's one of the best. You can see they think we're babies, but I'd have gone on guard right away by myself if they'd let me. They told me they knew I'd do the job all right, but there'd been an order that replacements aren't to go out alone. You ought to see our machine gun. Hell, it'll fire seven hundred rounds a minute and maybe more.

—That's the same kind we've got.

—Yes, but ours has fired more rounds than any other in the regiment. And we've got a top sergeant who's going to be made a Knight of the Mannerheim Cross soon. Comes from the Isthmus.

—There's some tough characters in our outfit, too.

—But this one's really the top. Yesterday he went on shouting at the Russkies even though the wood was ringing with the bullets they fired at him.

The conscripts brewed ersatz coffee and drank it together, the owner of the mess tin admiring the streaks of soot on his brand new tin and fancying they were just like those of the veterans. Then they talked in whispers in a corner of the dugout, aware that what they had to say would sound infantile to the veterans. Hauhia being on his own had the most to boast about, for no one could check up on his imaginings.

—It's a good thing machine gunners don't have to go out on patrol.

—They can volunteer.

—Catch me volunteering.

—Oh, I don't know. It might be fun to see what it's like. Old Rokka said something about taking me along the next time he goes. He's the one I was talking about. But listen, I go on guard at two. Come on over and see me at four, when I get off duty. Use the communication trench and mind you don't raise your heads. Nickel paralysis is a hell of a dangerous sickness. Bring some sugar with you, and we'll have some coffee. I'll tell Koskela, our lieutenant, that you're coming. You don't need to be scared of him. You'll only make him laugh if you are. Me, I called him Koskela right off.

—Don't worry about us. This morning I was sitting outside the dugout when the C.O. came by. I didn't even look up at him.

—Remember to come on over, then, and take a look at our dead Russkies. Fourteen of 'em. Almost in our positions. There sure was plenty of hard fighting.

—So was there here. The Russkies overran this strongpoint for two hours. The old hands say it was retaken with hand grenades. The dugout was so full of bodies you couldn't put your foot on the floor.

—They never got into our positions. We're moving to Million soon. There's men getting killed all the time there. Well, see you later.

Hauhio did not realize that he had even begun to imitate Rokka's gestures and voice. Arriving back in the dugout he kept glancing uneasily at his watch, regretting having given his friends the impression that he was on such intimate terms with Koskela. They would be watching him. He tried several times to open a conversation with Koskela in order to get used to addressing him, but the words died on his lips. But finally he timidly began to question him:

—Lieutenant, have you had this platoon a long time?

—Had it already in peacetime, Koskela answered briefly.

—You're a regular officer, aren't you, Koskela?

—On extra pay. That means a reserve officer in regular service.

—Were you in the Winter War?

—Yes.

—A platoon commander?

—Yes. First I was a section leader. Then a platoon leader until I dropped to company commander.

—Dropped? How? . . .

—Well, there were only sixteen men in the company at the time. In the platoon there'd been more than twenty.

—Did you get any tanks, K-k . . . ?

—A couple that had been sunk into the ground at Lemi. But Hietanen there blew up a Klim Voroshilov.

—With a grenade, Hietanen? That name already came easily to Hauhia's lips.

—With a mine. Don't believe all the tales you hear about men fighting tanks. Those who tell 'em have usually never even seen a tank. I was so scared when I let fly with that mine that I don't know even now how I did it. And for ten minutes I shook so hard I couldn't keep a cigarette butt in my mouth. I still dream sometimes of that caterpillar track running right over me. And every time I wake up in the damnedest sweat . . . I only hope I'll never see a sight like it again as long as I live.

Koskela laid aside the newspaper he had been reading.

—You can take your turn alone now. But if you're the least bit unsure of yourself, say so and I'll come with you.

—No-o-o. I'll be all right.

—I know that. What I'm afraid of is that when you find everything quiet you won't remember how dangerous it is. Don't raise your head. Look through the periscope. And not a single goddamn shot unless you have to. Even if you see something, don't shoot. Only if they start coming over. Keep an eye open. They're tricky as hell at snatching a prisoner. There've been cases where a man was snatched away in broad daylight. And if something does happen, don't get panicky. The first shot's half the battle. And don't get to thinking that it'll be all right because that rifleman sentry's on the lookout. He may just be thinking the same thing about you. I'll be around later.

—I'll manage, said Hauhia sturdily and went off a few minutes before his time, unlike the old hands who always tried to shorten their tour by being a few minutes late when relieving.

—Remember what I told you, Rokka shouted after him.

—There's nothing more to say there, remarked Koskela. —He's been told everything.

Hauhia relieved Vanhala in high spirits.

—All right, Vanhala, off you go.

—You're on your own now. There's a sniper's rifle one of the infantry boys left behind in the shelter, but don't use it unless you have to. Ivan'd soon make a hero of you.

Hauhia twisted the periscope and peered out at the bunkers outlined against the smoky afternoon sky. A sleepy peace seemed to have descended over everything. Even the muted rumble of guns from Bulayevo in the distance did not disturb the drowsy quiet of the front. The silence was absolute. Not a twig moved.

After looking his fill Hauhia drew a pad of notepaper from his breast pocket and began to write. He felt a little guilty about doing so, and sought to dispel this feeling by glancing into the periscope after every two or three words. Each time he examined the corpses and counted them, afraid a living man might have crept among them and be lying there waiting for his opportunity. Hadn't Rokka warned him of precisely that?

The sudden crash of a shell on Million sent Hauhia sprawling on the ground, but, remembering yesterday, he rose at once. About ten shells fell at half-minute intervals.

Soon Hauhia finished his letter and began to examine the machine gun. Idly he wondered at the story it could tell if it only were capable of speaking, and he tried to imagine that story, relying mostly on the false glorified descriptions of battles served up to an inexpert public by the war correspondents. He saw no distorted faces behind it, heard no hoarse cries, no nervous cursing and abuse, nor the moan Kaukonen had uttered as his head sank on those very grips. He knew nothing of the wet and dark autumn night on which the machine gun had lain in the muddy path where Lehto and Riitaoja had died.

—A fine piece of equipment. I wonder if there's water in the jacket.

Hauhia looked into the periscope and a sound escaped his lips. Beside one of the bunkers a helmet was moving. Now it had stopped. Hauhia snatched the sniper's rifle from the splinter-proof shelter.

—I'm not going to shoot, but just in case . . .

He looked again. The helmet was still there. For a second the hunter's instinct in him fought with his fear of disobeying orders. Then he stepped into a rifleman's emplacement and cautiously raised his head:

—Must do it quickly . . . can't give him time . . .

He put a sprig of juniper into the loophole, thrust the muzzle of the rifle through it and, his hands trembling with eagerness, tried to get his sights on the helmet. He had time to feel a stunning blow on his skull and see sparks flash in his eyes before he sank into a void and his body rolled off the firestep.

4.

A new spring had been procured for Vanhala's phonograph by one of the men on leave, along with a supply of new records. A popular war ballad, "Life in the Trenches," was playing as Rahikainen, lying on his back in his bunk, sang in competition with the record:

O flaxen-haired darling of mine,
Come and care for him who is thine.
Do not leave me to perish in no-man's-land
For you know the great pain I am in—

Abruptly he stopped in the middle of the song:

—No, I've got to start trying the neighboring sectors. Ours is worked out. How many have you ready?

—This is the eighth. What shall I engrave on it? Svir–1942? What about inventing a new model, Rahikainen? We could sell a few more in our own sector. There's always buyers for something new.

—Let's sink a Finnish lion into 'em.

—We could take the lion from a five-mark piece. But that'd raise the price that much.

—They'll pay if you make a good job of it.

Rokka was preparing to extol his workmanship when the cow-bell hanging from the ceiling began to clatter.

—Something's happened to the boy, Koskela said rising.

—Let's go!

Immediately a feverish commotion broke out as boots were hastily donned, rifles snatched from the rack, and the men dashed into the trench. Honkajoki seized his bow and arrows but took a rifle with him too.

Once out of the dugout the men saw immediately that no attack was imminent, for the infantry platoon had not fallen out. Obviously whatever had happened concerned their post alone. Their first thought was that Hauhia in his inexperience had panicked and sounded the alarm. Then they saw that the rifle platoon's sentry was not at his post.

—Something's happened, repeated Koskela, immediately fearing the worst. The expression on the rifleman's face as he came to meet them on his way back to his post told them everything. He was pale as a ghost as he said:

—Better post a new sentry and take the old one off your ration list.

—Sniper?

—Yes. He had the rifle out. The cartridge is still in the barrel. There was a helmet showing but it was sticking so far up that it had to be a trap. Then when I heard the shot I knew he must have stuck his head up so I went to look. When I saw, I sounded your alarm.

—The damn fool, doing a thing like that! And after I'd spent four hours explaining to him all about that very thing. If he were alive I'd take a stick to his behind.

—He shouldn't have been sent out alone.

—No one can say that he wasn't warned.

—None of the rest of us got as much advice.

—We sure as hell didn't.

Hauhia lay huddled at the bottom of the trench, a little blue hole in the middle of his forehead. There was no blood at all where the bullet had entered, but there was no longer any back to his head. It was a familiar sight; yet this chance death affected the men more than any of the other deaths that had occurred in the platoon. Most of them were only a year or two older than Hauhia, yet he had seemed almost a child to them.

Rahikainen remained on guard after extracting a promise from Koskela that the balance of Hauhia's turn would count as a full tour for him. The others carried the body to the dugout. Tenderly they laid it down in the entrance passage and covered it with a tent half. Koskela reported what had happened to Lammio and Kariluoto and called for a barrage on Devil's Peak. Artillery support except in case of an enemy attack had been forbidden without permission of a commanding officer, so to secure Sarastie's consent Koskela lied about the heavy Russian movement that had been observed on the peak. And Sarastie trusted Koskela so absolutely that he gave the required permission.

—Now we'll let that damn sniper worry for a while, said Koskela, stretching out on his bed. —The ration cart can take the body to the rear.

They waited, and soon the dugout window rattled as guns spoke a few miles away.

—It's the heavies on Itavaara.

—Or those at Korvenkyla.

—No, it isn't. The Korvenkyla guns fire on the right of that pine over there.

—Hit the sons of bitches, growled the usually silent Wolf's Paw.

For once they really hated the Russians. Hauhia's death had done even more to stimulate the men's fighting spirit than the execution of the two men shot by the military police.

The bombardment was still thundering when Hauhia's comrades arrived. They had noticed the canvas-covered corpse in the passage, but had not bothered to look at it closely. There were four of them, two now in the infantry, the other two with the machine guns. They rushed into the dugout, frightened looks on their faces, and the foremost stood to attention as he said:

—Lieutenant, we came to visit Private Hauhia. We all were in the same group at the training camp.

Rokka idly polished the ring he was holding. The others lay silent. And since nobody wanted to break the news, it fell to Koskela to do so:

—Hauhia's dead. He stuck his fool head up and a sniper blew the back off it. That's what's left of him there in the entrance.

The youths shuffled their feet self-consciously, awed by the presence of an officer. The two in the rear moved tentatively to the door, but Koskela stopped them with a motion of his hand.

—Remember, you've got to learn from those who've been up here awhile. By the time you learn from your own experiences, you may be dead. Believe me, the man who thinks this is a lark up here is damn close to his grave.

—We'll remember, Lieutenant.

—Can we see him?

—If you want to. But make sure you cover him up again.

The youths didn't take long in the passage. Then with glazed eyes and yellowish complexions, they took their leave to return to their own platoons.

In the evening Vanhala took out his phonograph, but Koskela motioned him away.

—Suppose we forget it tonight.

He had found Hauhia's unfinished letter and was wondering if it might not be better for the boy's parents not to get it.

10. 8. 42.

Dear Family,

I'm up here in the front lines at last. The noise is deafening. We got here yesterday evening and I'm now on duty as a sentry. I forgot to ask the Loot our field mail number, but I'll put it in afterwards. There are corpses lying all over the ground. They were killed not so long ago, but they're all worm meat now. Parcels take a long time to get here. The Russians have just started laying a barrage on the positions next to us. We're to take over there soon but don't worry, I'll be all right . . .

Cahpter XII

I.

How long will the slaughter continue?
Until the people have achieved their liberty
There the fiends who thirst for human blood
With the carrion birds can drain their cup of gore.

Vanhala was again in a singing mood. He had volunteered for a patrol, or rather he had traded four tours of guard duty to a willing rifleman for one patrol, only to return with a bullet in his ribs, looking very pale. But now he was back after having been in a base hospital long enough for the others to have had time to realize how much his good-natured joking meant to them. As they recognized him from the dugout window the men came pouring out to meet him, shouting their welcome. Vanhala's face, rounder than ever after his convalescence at home, was split by a huge smile.

Honkajoki still worked at his perpetual-motion machine, still on the verge of completing it. Rokka had substituted lampstands for rings, and Rahikainen still was selling for—and cheating—him. Maatta had received his promised second stripe, but in all other respects the life of the platoon had been largely uneventful. Even their turn on Million in the autumn had been completed without casualties.

As the new year was born, the propaganda from Devil's Peak grew in intensity. Stalingrad was surrounded and now instead of wheedling exhortations the loud-speakers brayed out intimidations in tones of supreme confidence. One thing had happened though: Honkajoki's bow had become famous. It had caught all eyes, and he went from dugout to dugout lecturing on its use.

Slowly, by degrees, the idea of defeat had begun to take root in the men's minds. And no steps had been taken to dispel it except for a few minor and quite senseless measures. The men in the trenches seemed to know what was coming but deliberately refused to worry.

Kariluoto had been ordered to the Land Warfare School and

after completing his course was promoted to captain. His engagement kept him in a dream world where he escaped all the underlying currents of despondency, and a woman by the name of Sirkka became as well known as any movie star in the Third Company's command dugout. Anyone who would or could be made to listen was treated to endless monologues on the virtues of this marvelous girl.

Lammio, too, was now a captain. He had not changed, at least not for the better, for he still fancied that everything could be set right by stricter discipline. But Koskela had not been promoted since there was no higher vacancy for him in the battalion, and Sarastie refused to part with him in spite of several veiled suggestions from the regimental commander. Instead he was rewarded with several decorations, and Sarastie salved his conscience by repeatedly declaring that the first vacancy at company level would be his.

Koskela did not seem to mind. He was determined to leave the army as soon as the war was over and thus had no desire for promotion. He lay on his bed and took part in the platoon's somnolent existence as before.

Slowly the winter passed and it was summer again. The fact that Germany must ultimately go down to defeat was becoming ever more obvious, and now only Salo still believed she would win. Even the new invasions in Italy failed to shake his faith. The others sometimes made fun of his optimism and after each new setback someone would ask:

—Isn't it about time to put the secret weapons to use?

Salo, his gaze fixed over the questioner's head, would answer:

—All in good time, all in good time . . . They're letting them come nearer so they can destroy them completely. I've heard that a lot of eight-inch guns have been brought up back there. That'll give Ivan something to think about if he starts attacking.

—Jesus, is that so . . . ? Then there's no danger at all.

This last was from Rokka, and even Salo wasn't sure whether or not he was speaking in earnest.

A growing bitterness was becoming evident in Rokka's comments as he gradually realized that all the money earned by his rings and invested in the new house on the Isthmus had been for nothing. He would never live in it. And as this conviction grew in him, he spoke ever more sarcastically of the competition among the commanders to have the most elegant dugout.

—They're having armchairs made for themselves out of tree trunks. I guess they think we'll be sitting here for the rest of our lives.

It was in the summer of 1943 that Rokka was caught by a colonel in the act of carving decorations on a birch lampstand while on sentry duty. At least the colonel thought he had caught him in the act, for actually Rokka had seen him coming and disdained to hide the article. The colonel was an inspector of some kind out on a typical inspection tour set off by some little incident which would eventually result in a report for the high brass, which would then be distributed to the troops and perhaps even read by someone before being filed.

The colonel was a typical officer, so that all he could do was to bluster:

—What's this, what's this? Who do you think you are?

—A sentry, and a sentry's no man to pick on . . . he's got his duty to perform.

Rokka flung his answer back at once, for the colonel's tone had angered him. Not even rising from his seat as he carved away at his lampstand, he paused every few seconds to peer into the periscope.

—What's that you're doing?

—Carving a lampstand. Can't you see?

—Don't you know you're on guard?

—Of course I do. Why else would I be here?

—What's your name?

—Rokka. Antero Rokka.

—You'll hear about this.

The colonel departed angrily, leaving Rokka to his carving, and back in the dugout Rokka never thought to tell anybody about the matter. Indeed, he himself, hearing no more about it for a couple of days, began to think that the colonel had not carried out his threat. On the third day, however, Koskela received a telephoned order from Lammio to send Rokka and his section to clean up around the command post and mark the paths with stone borders. Koskela could not quite grasp the meaning of the message; even from Lammio it sounded too stupid. So he answered:

—All right. I'll pass on your order.

"Passing it on" meant that Koskela would not associate himself with it. And it was in such a tone that he informed Rokka. Rokka was silent for a moment before he answered softly:

—Whoever wants to can go. Me, I'm not going.

—Not without an officer to lead us, Rahikainen said promptly. —How could we simple soldiers manage it by ourselves?

Vanhala laughed and gave no sign of intending to go, while Wolf's Paw did not need to say anything, for he would of course follow Rokka's lead.

In due course Koskela informed Lammio of the section's refusal, and Lammio angrily ordered Rokka to the CP. With a shrug Rokka set off, but soon paused along the way to refresh himself with wild berries, with the result that it took him two hours to cover the distance. By the time he at last walked into the dugout and seated himself Lammio was literally seething with rage.

—See here, Rokka, he burst out. —You seem determined to flout discipline whenever possible.

—What do you mean by that? Speak simply, now. I'm a poor farmer and I don't understand fancy words.

—You act as though discipline was everybody's concern but yours.

—It isn't any of mine.

—It will be soon.

—Not enough to set me sweeping up with a broom.

—I'm your company commander, and I'm going to make you realize you have to obey orders if it's the last thing I do!

—The hell you are if it means me sweeping the grass and laying borders to paths!

—You've been reported as being insolent to an inspecting colonel, and I've been asked to punish you. You have your orders and it's up to you whether you obey them or not. But if you don't, I shall take the matter to a higher level. I included your squad in your punishment since all of them are like you. Your example has borne good fruit; you've succeeded in making every man in the unit disobedient and impudent.

—Do you think I'm afraid of you and your threats?

—Not at all. I appreciate bravery, for I'm a brave man myself. But you ask too much in return. I've given in far more than I ought to have, and waited too long for you to come to your senses. If you behaved the way a soldier, and especially an NCO should, I could promise you a Mannerheim Cross as surely as I could offer you a cigarette. I know that last winter you saved the battalion from a situation that might well have led to its complete destruction. I admit that as a fighter you are better than any man I've ever seen, and I have seen some pretty wild fellows. But don't keep thinking that can cover all your sins. Your insolence is more dangerous than Honkajoki's making mock of army equipment, which, by the way, I also intend to stop. Now I'm giving you a chance to put everything right by bringing your section and carrying out the task I assigned you.

—No!

—It means a court-martial.

Rokka's cheerful nonchalance had vanished and his voice shook with anger:

—Now you listen to me before you start playing any games. You thought you'd get the best of me, but that's something you'll never do, nor will anybody else. Do you know that my wife is pregnant and still has to farm our place in the Isthmus without any help? And you, you half-witted puppy, you'd set me to laying stone borders to your footpaths. Over yonder they're fixing up top-notch command dugouts and then photographing 'em for the papers to show what the boys of one unit have done for their "beloved" commander. Of course they've done it! They were ordered to. But I'm not going to touch that kind of job, and you'd do well to realize it. Can't you see where we're heading? Do you think Ivan's going to say to us: Sit there and be comfortable as long as you like? Hell, no! Before long we'll be in a hell of a mess. Half of us'll die yet, but you and your sort go on chattering about discipline. Go on the way you're going and soon you'll be shooting your own men. When it comes to fighting I'll do what has to be done, but I'm not going to play games. So do as you like. Have me court-martialed, so long as you bear in mind that I'm not going to die like a dog. You shot those two fellows back there against a sauna wall. Before I'm shot that way, a few others'll die first. Think that over. I'm going.

Rokka snatched up his cap and left, leaving Lammio feeling uneasy. For a moment he felt a sense of helplessness; to pursue the matter after all that had been said seemed useless. Then he began to suspect that Rokka had been play acting, and little by little, he became convinced of this. The man was a daredevil, but this time he was trying to bluff his way out of a dilemma.

So it was that Lammio went to see Sarastie and laid his case before him. At first the major was disinclined to act, but after Lammio had given a highly colored description of the affair and stressed the necessity of maintaining discipline, he finally agreed to call Rokka to battalion headquarters the next day and set an official inquiry in motion. Sarastie, too, was aware of both the positive and the negative side of Rokka's reputation. The man was famous for his impudence; the encounter with the colonel was only one instance among many; his refusal to obey orders was becoming legendary in the army. He set a dangerous example. But he was also the best soldier in the battalion in battle, and that, too, was becoming legendary. Surely it was foolish to set a man of his kind to ditch digging in a swamp for a few weeks. Perhaps he would have his stripes taken from him. But how would that affect the men's morale?

Sarastie was angry with himself for having allowed Lammio any say in the matter. But Sarastie had also sensed a slight to his own authority, which was why he finally gave in to Lammio. He wanted no visiting inspectors sending in reports reflecting on his battalion.

2.

All the while the platoon was serving its tour on "the Millions," this time on the right-hand strongpoint, or Little Million, which was by far the worse of the two. Geographically they were one and the same fortified position, their separateness consisting mainly of the fact that each was always manned by its own infantry platoon. Both were on the same hill with Little Million on its right-hand slope, which ran down to the narrow inlet of a lake. The inlet marked the end of the position, and from there on contact with the next strongpoint was made by patrols moving along the shore. Here the Russian positions were but a hundred to a hundred and fifty yards away. Behind them the ground rose sharply and from its highest points guns fired into the Finnish positions at point-blank range through open sights. Enfilading fire also came from beyond where the lines swung sharply to the right, and it was this crossfire which made the positions so dangerous. Owing to their proximity to the Russians, the positions here were very crudely constructed. There was no wire at all, and the trenches were low and unshored and thus always caving in under shellfire. But here, too, there were quiet periods, although in general both sides were far more on their toes than in the other positions.

After his visit to the command dugout Rokka was silent and morose all afternoon. All he would say about what had gone on was:

—Nothing special. He said what you'd expect of that sort of man.

That night Rokka had the watch from midnight to two. Promptly at twelve he relieved Vanhala, checked the hand grenades and made certain the tommy gun was working. To his left an infantry sentry coughed heavily. The machine-gun emplacement was on the extreme right of the position some forty yards from the inlet and was thus the limit to which the platoon's patrolling extended.

The August night was almost pitch black as thick clouds blotted out the moon. A gentle wind rustled the grass in front as Rokka listened and looked, all his senses alert. After half an hour he took the pistol from the niche in the trench wall and fired a flare. The blue light flickered in the air for a time, and by its light, he examined every little rise or hump on the ground. Shellholes, a few bodies and farther back the vague outlines of the Russian positions, nothing more. Then he ducked, knowing the consequences a flare always had. First Ivan would fire a few bursts and this would cause the sentry next to him to become restless and send up a new flare. And if they answered the Russian bursts with the automatic rifle, the consequence would be Russian shells crashing around the trench.

A twig snapped in the communication trench, and, the tommy gun under his arm, Rokka turned in the direction of the sound. In the darkness the men were very close to him before he could see them, and he held the tommy gun in readiness.

—Who's there?

—Friends . . . Ah, Vanhala's been relieved.

The men from the next strongpoint had become well acquainted with Vanhala. Of course they knew Rokka, too, and stayed a few moments to talk. But Rokka was unusually reticent and the visitors soon began their journey back to their own trench.

After they had gone Rokka turned over in his mind an old plan he had worked out for blowing up one of the Russian bunkers. He had studied the ground and planned the route along which he would crawl several times, intending to utilize the exploit to earn leave home; for he had no intention of risking his life for the fun of it. Now the plan seemed merely futile.

—They'll put me in prison, that's all the leave I'll get. . . . If the bastards do that, I'm through with them. I won't do anything. And seeing as I haven't done anything wrong, why the hell do they keep on questioning me as though I were a criminal?

Rokka was worried after all, being well aware of the trouble that Lammio could create for him. But he had made up his mind not to give in. —Not if they shoot me. And damn it, I'm not even going to think of the whole foolish business any more.

He confirmed his resolution with a shrug of his shoulders as though to cast off an annoying burden, and began to concentrate on the task in hand, on keeping watch. Actually Rokka was a man who always lived in the present. The night, the rustling grass, the sounds made by the neighboring sentry, the noises wafted from the Russian positions and the shots occasionally echoing through the night: these were the only real things in life. Lammio and army discipline were something of distant and secondary importance that had nothing to do with guard duty.

Abruptly an explosion startled him and a brief red flash lit the bend in the trench. Only after that did he hear the muzzle report. Swiftly Rokka thrust himself into the shelter dug into the trench wall. A second shell exploded ten yards away, and splinters hummed through the air and struck the firestep.

The slow shelling went on for about five minutes, then ceased. Almost at once Rokka came out of his hole, sent up a flare and moved on to the next lookout post. The ground in front was empty. New shells began to come over more often. Then came a pause, followed by more shells.

When this firing also stopped, Rokka listened, holding his breath, but he could hear nothing out of the ordinary. Then in the communication trench behind him a clod of earth fell with a tiny thud.

Holding the tommy gun at the ready, Rokka took a couple of steps toward the communication trench. The patrol might have come again, but the extreme caution they were observing seemed unusual. The men were not wont to pick their way with such care.

Rokka was hardly more than a step away from the bend in the trench when a new sound came from beyond the angle.

—Who's that? Give the countersign!

A tall figure appeared in front of Rokka, and the things which happened during the next few seconds were many and confused. Rokka meant to shoot at once, but the idea that it might be the patrol returning had cost him a valuable tenth of a second. And in that split second his tommy gun was thrust violently aside. From then on, however, Rokka acted instinctively, having grasped in a flash that he was being taken prisoner. He did not try to regain possession of the tommy gun, but instead let go of it and thrust the hand holding a pistol at him aside. The pistol went off as Rokka shouted:

—Help! Give the alarm . . . Russians in the trench . . .

As he shouted he clasped his opponent in his arms, but his situation was extremely tenuous. The man he was holding was at least as strong as he was, and his first movements showed him to be quick and resolute. Behind him Rokka saw more men, but fortunately the trench was so narrow that they were held up by the man in his arms. He realized that so long as this situation prevailed he could be neither shot nor struck down, for the man he held served as a shield. Again the pistol barked, but the bullet flew wild for the Russian's wrist was squeezed between Rokka's arm and his ribs. Rokka knew he had to gain possession of the pistol, but he knew too that if he loosed his own arm he would at the same time be releasing his foe's arm, and that would mean certain death. The patrol would surely have realized that it had failed in its surprise mission and would be anxious to finish him off with all speed.

—Sentry . . . help . . . !

A tommy gun chattered about twenty yards away, and over his opponent's shoulder Rokka saw that it had engaged the attention of at least the man immediately behind. Grimly he struggled with his opponent while the Russian vainly hissed instructions to his companions.

Rokka saw he would soon have to risk letting his foe's arm go free, for things could not continue as they were for long. Already the Russian behind was raising his tommy gun to shoot him down regardless of the danger to his own comrade's life.

Abruptly, then, Rokka let go of the man and seized his right hand and the pistol it held. The gun went off a third time as he tore it from the Russian who struck out blindly with his left hand, only to have the blow land on Rokka's shoulder. Still Rokka could not fire, for the pistol was the wrong way in his hand, but the blow he aimed at his enemy's face had behind it all the strength of his will to live. The butt of the pistol landed with a crunch, and at almost the same second he gripped the Russian and threw him against his companion in the rear. The flash from the tommy gun's muzzle almost singed Rokka's eyebrows as the second Russian fired, but the next moment he went down under the weight of the man Rokka had thrown at him. Now Rokka had time to reverse the pistol, and the third man died instantly.

Quickly Rokka shouted to the neighboring sentry, bidding him fire along the communication trench:

—I'm in the main trench. You won't hit me.

The sentry, however, failed to grasp Rokka's meaning. And for that matter he could not have fired if he had, for there were still two bends between him and the Russians. He had not had time to get any closer, for the struggle had lasted only a few seconds.

The man behind Rokka's assailant started to get up at once, but Rokka's boot caught him under the chin and he collapsed again. Rokka was consumed with a fury born of despair, but his fury was far from blind; his least movement had a purpose. In the part of the trench leading to the machine-gun emplacement there were no other foes, but Rokka guessed that beyond the bend other Russians were covering those who were to have seized him. Thus he could not run, for that would mean climbing the parapet and exposing himself. But neither could he keep still and wait, for once it dawned on the covering party that their comrades were dead, a hand grenade would fly from behind the bend. It was but a question of seconds, and therefore Rokka did not even bother to seize his own tommy gun, which lay a couple of paces in his rear, but took the one belonging to the Russian he had knocked out with his boot. And as he leaped over the man he kicked him once again to be on the safe side.

Beyond the corner of the communication trench a figure loomed and hesitated a second, uncertain whether the figure coming at him was friend or foe. Rokka had delayed for the same reason a few seconds before, but the Russian's luck was poorer and as he realized his mistake, he died. Beyond him Rokka heard thudding footsteps and guessed that the rest of the patrol had drawn the correct conclusion. Not having succeeded at once, they had failed in their mission. To remain and fight would have only meant death for them.

Now at last the next Finnish sentry came rushing around the corner. He was about to fire when Rokka yelled:

—Don't shoot, dammit, don't shoot!

—Where are they?

—Gone. On their way back . . . Look, you take care of these

two, though I think one's dead. The other one only got a kick in the head. . . . Don't kill 'em, I want a prisoner.

Rokka set off after the fleeing Russians, half afraid that the converging sentries would run into them. The Russians, however, were gone. The reeds on the lake shore crackled under their flying feet, and Rokka urged them on with bursts from the tommy gun. But suddenly a cry rang out from the Finnish patrol:

—Halt! Give the sign!

—Dammit, what was it? It's Rokka . . . Christ! Now I remember: Karelian.

—Bear, the countersign came.

Quickly Rokka told the men what had happened, and bade them stay and keep watch for a while on the lake shore.

—That's the way the bastards came. Hell, they sure knew their business. It's not their fault that they didn't take me with 'em.

When Rokka returned to his post the positions were fully manned, the riflemen's sentry having given the alarm. Rokka was completely his usual joking self again.

—You missed the international wrestling match. Finland versus the Soviet Union. I won by a fall. Maybe I did break some of the rules, but there's too damn many of 'em.

—Won on a fall . . . ha-ha . . . This one here lost on points. He's dead.

Rokka was alarmed at the thought of death cheating him of prisoners:

—The devil he is! Is the other alive? I only gave him a taste of my boot.

Rokka calmed down when he heard that the man was indeed alive. In fact the Russian was already sitting up, spitting blood.

—This man's got to be well taken care of. I need him. Say, Koskela, don't report this little mix-up. And you, Lieutenant, don't you report it either. We'll keep it for a little surprise for tomorrow. They've promised leave to any man who takes a prisoner. I'm going to take mine to Battalion tomorrow—in person.

Koskela could guess why Rokka wanted the prisoner, and the lieutenant commanding the rifle platoon also promised to keep the matter quiet until Rokka had handed him over.

They threw the dead men over the parapet, and in the shelter of the dugout inspected the prisoner with more care. The man's lips were badly swollen, but he looked them straight in the eye, apparently resigned to death. His tunic was without shoulder straps but there was something about him that made them suspect him to be an officer. At last Rokka brought him water, and the man washed his face. Koskela's men were sure that he was a more valuable prize than any ordinary prisoner, since a patrol sent to grab a prisoner would consist of picked men.

A soldier who could speak Russian was brought from the neighboring positions and the prisoner was questioned. At first he refused to speak. Finally, however, he identified himself as Private Baranov, but when the interpreter opined that he was lying about both his name and his rank, and said as much, he at last confessed to being Captain Baranov.

In the end he admitted being the leader of the patrol, but no sooner had the interpreter begun to question him about the military situation on the Russian side than he shut up tight. On the subject of the patrol he was, however, more communicative. The man Rokka had killed with the pistol butt was an NCO specially trained for this kind of duty. It had been his task to seize the prisoner. They had failed, said the captain, because Rokka had heard them coming and turned to face them.

—He's wrong there. Tell him it was just because it was me on guard—they'd planned the raid damn well. Tell him I know all they'd been thinking. They've been watching night after night to see how often and by which routes the gap between the positions was patrolled and laid their plans on what they'd learned. That shelling was to drive the sentries under cover. While it was going on they crept through the reeds . . . he's still wet. They thought sentry'd take them for our own patrol. But I'd thought of creeping through those same reeds to their side, and that's why I suspected that they might try it. Koskela, remember me saying that there ought to be one more guard post on the shore? We're not using enough men to patrol a place like that. . . . Come on, my fine Red friend, I'm going to make some tea. In the morning, we'll go to Battalion together. They'll want to ask questions and write reports on both of us.

3.

The next morning Rokka rose in a happy mood, but his prisoner was sunk in gloom. And though he drank the tea Rokka made for him, he said hardly a word until at last Rokka broke the silence:

—Hey, don't be so sad. We'll go to the stockades together. We'll have a hell of a time there.

A little before nine Rokka arrived at the battalion orderly room with his prisoner. In Sarastie's dugout Lammio and a second lieutenant, who had been detailed to keep the record, were waiting. Rokka's case was of such importance that Sarastie had wanted to be present when he was being questioned.

The dugout was a modest place, for Sarastie had not been bitten by the architectural craze that had affected most of the commanding officers. As Rokka marched in behind Baranov, instead of saluting he said briskly:

—Good morning. Well, here I am. Koskela said you'd telephoned for me.

As always with Rokka, the officers were taken aback. They had been solemnly discussing the importance of maintaining discipline at a time like the present when pessimism was everywhere. And now here was the very object of their discussion bouncing in with a most unmilitary "good morning" accompanied by a stranger in Russian uniform.

—How . . . ? Who is that man?

—This one? His name's Baranov.

Sarastie alone was clever enough to grasp that Rokka was deliberately staging the scene. In fact, watching Rokka's face, he could hardly keep from laughing. The man was obviously weighing in his mind the strength of the impression he had made. Aside from that he was as calm as if this gathering was nothing in the least unusual.

—So that's Baranov, repeated Sarastie. —And why have you brought him here?

—I took him prisoner last night and I thought that since you're going to make a report, you could make one about him at the same time. They say you've been talking about handing me a prison sentence, so I thought maybe me and him could go together. Make one job out of two.

But the prisoner was so important that the officers hardly heard Rokka's jibes as they rushed to inquire how he had been taken.

—They came to fetch me to Russia. But I told 'em I couldn't come because I was up for a court-martial. Three of 'em got killed in the argument, but I saved this one. He's a fine upstanding chap. I spoiled his face a little when I kicked him, but he'll get his looks back soon. This Baranov's quite a gentleman. He's a captain.

Sarastie was more interested than ever.

—How do you know that?

—One of the men in the dugout talks Russian. He's a captain all right. He was in command of the raid.

Rokka gave a detailed description of the encounter, and Sarastie got Koskela on the telephone. As he replaced the receiver he eyed Rokka searchingly.

—What kind of a man are you?

—Me? You mean to say you don't know me? I'm Antti Rokka. A farmer from the Isthmus. At the moment I sell bullets.

The second lieutenant who was writing down the results of the interrogation tried to keep a straight face, not daring to laugh in the major's presence, until, seeing the major's self-control give way, he too burst out laughing. Only the two captains, Baranov and Lammio, remained grave. Rokka kept a solemn face but he was intently following the situation. He seemed bent on extracting all the amusement he could from it while still avoiding a court-martial.

—How did you turn the tables on them?

—By a little shooting, and a lot of kicking. That's how. They were tough boys. In fact, I only barely succeeded in getting here to be questioned and court-martialed.

Sarastie choked and beckoned to the stenographer.

—Take the prisoner out and send for the interpreter. He's a valuable prize. We've been wanting one like him for a long time.

The lieutenant left with Baranov, and as soon as they had gone, Rokka said:

—I don't think you'll get anything out of that fellow. He's hard as bone. It's a damn good thing I heard 'em coming. Who knows how it would have gone with the court-martial? Oh well, in this war you never know what's going to happen next. If you try to follow regulations you get into all sorts of trouble. It's a damn shame but what can you do?

Rokka spread his arms and raised his shoulders in a gesture of regret.

Sarastie sat silently trying to think. He found it most difficult to decide what to say, so many conflicting things were involved. He could not help admiring the man and being amused by his actions. But Sarastie knew now what Rokka had been trying to do.

—Tell me seriously, why do you find army discipline so frightening that you feel compelled to resist it at every turn?

—Why, I know all there is to know about discipline. And I've never resisted it. What I resisted was an order to lay stone borders for some paths. I've said all there is to say about that to Lammio there. He's the fellow who's to blame for everything. Ever since I came here he's been picking on me for all sorts of things, but never for anything that makes sense. We've never once quarreled about anything real; always over one of his fancy ideas. I'll tell you again, I came to fight willingly. I wanted to help win the Isthmus back. And I'm more than a match for any of you. Anybody but Antti Rokka would have been captured last night. What the hell am I expected to do beyond that? It wouldn't tire me to keep kowtowing, but it wouldn't help us the tiniest bit, so I don't kowtow. Let me tell you I'm not running about here for your sakes. I know damn well that we're going to lose this war, but the nearer we come to losing it, the sillier the jobs you set us to. Court-martial me, but it won't make me respect you. And there's half a million men here just like me. You seem to think the only reason we're here is so there's always someone standing before you with his heels together saying: Yes, sir, yes, sir . . .

Rokka fell silent and looked out of the window with the air of a man who knows that nothing that would be said from that moment on would be of any significance. At last, Sarastie said in a voice which he tried to make stern:

—That isn't the reason. But what you call kowtowing is the outward sign of discipline, and when it's lacking, then discipline too is lacking. And lack of discipline would mean that those half million men would be incapable of doing what they are here to do, which is to defend Finland. Remember they're not all like you—a lot of the old hands only have your negative qualities. And your statement that we've lost the war isn't true. No war was ever won without setbacks, and soldiers always tend to draw conclusions from circumstances whose real meaning they don't understand. Nothing decisive has occurred so far.

Rokka shrugged his shoulders impatiently, and his voice was bitter as he said:

—Understand! When hundreds of thousands of men are left

to die in a trap you don't need much brains to know what it means. Do you think such things are done except because they couldn't be helped? Everything's lost. I've known it for a long time . . . but you talk about stone borders to paths.

All this while Lammio had remained silent. But now he indicated he would like the major's permission to speak. It was an unnecessary request, but Lammio wished to emphasize his own willingness to observe the "rules."

—Rokka, tell me where you think you'd find another company commander who would take as much as I have taken from you? Think before you answer.

—Ha! Think. Now you're talking as though there was sense in the game you've been playing. Your own likes and dislikes are all you've been following and not any principles. So don't try that talk on me. . . . Call that lieutenant back and let's have the inquiry. Hell, I've had enough.

Lammio looked helplessly at Sarastie, waiting for his decision. Ponderously the major rose and drew himself up to his full height.

—The battalion can get along very well without you. An army is never dependent on one man no matter how good he may be. But I forgive you. Not because I feel compelled to do so but for other reasons. And on this condition. You are not to breathe a word of what we have said here nor boast of having got off. And from now on you will obey orders like the rest. If you start spreading information about this session, you will be injuring my prestige, and in that case I will see that you are punished. I trust you understand my position clearly. I hope so for your sake but also for my own and that of the army. I have no personal desire to break you, but if at any time I regard it as essential, I shall do so.

Sarastie drew air into his lungs and threw back his shoulders as if thus he made himself conscious of his might and, with that, of his power to forgive without harming himself.

Lammio, on the other hand, fancied that Rokka had been humbled, though he would have preferred an actual punishment. Rokka, however, was pleased, but he had no intention of submitting without conditions.

—I said I'd do what has to be done in war. But tell that Lammio to leave me in peace. I know damn well that if he keeps on as he's been, there'll always be trouble.

—You'll be granted no special privileges. As I said, what happens to you in the future will depend on your behavior. You may go.

Rokka went. But he got only as far as the open air before he turned back and, re-entering the dugout, began in an aggrieved voice:

—I've only just remembered. Men who bring in prisoners were promised leave. That means I've a right to an extra fourteen days. And I brought in a captain.

The major shook his head at the audacity of the man.

—If you're entitled to it, you'll get it. Put in your application as soon as you like. To tell the truth, I'm sorry you yourself have made it impossible for you to get a Mannerheim Cross.

—The fifty thousand marks'd be nice, but nothing so marvelous. Pretty soon I'll have made as much selling rings and lampstands.

This time Rokka left for good, striding along and whistling gaily. By the time he arrived at the dugout it was as if nothing unusual had happened.

—Well, what did they say to you?

—About what?

—About the prisoner and that other business.

—Nothing much. They just want me to go on leave. I've earned it.

Only to Koskela did Rokka disclose what had happened at the command post. But Lammio behaved with more restraint than formerly and nothing more was said about the whole matter—or of a Mannerheim Cross for that matter.

4.

During the autumn, far-off Italy finally collapsed, and as one of the reverberations the worst slackers among the battalion were singled out for disciplinary drill. Among those chosen was Honkajoki, for Lammio had always viewed his antics with a skeptical eye and now had decided they were a danger to morale. A captain had been detailed to supervise the drill, but already on the first day he perceived the hopelessness of his task. What could he do, for example, with that tall fellow who had shown up with a longbow over his shoulder and persisted in executing every maneuver incorrectly? Or with that one called Viirila, the very sight of whom was painful? And yet he had to admit that Viirila and an astoundingly high proportion of these black sheep were among the best fighting men of the battalion.

An order had been issued making the men's release dependent on their ability to drill properly. Actually, however, it depended more on willingness than ability, for there was not a man among them who did not know all the maneuvers. Nevertheless the captain was forced to ignore many faults or he would have been drilling them through all eternity. Now the last two men remaining were Honkajoki and Viirila who stood side by side displaying the the utmost indifference. Honkajoki had obeyed the captain's order and exchanged his bow for a rifle, but it was the only matter in which the captain's word had prevailed.

A sergeant gave the orders as the captain stood looking on.

—To the rear, fall out!

The two men turned and scurried to the rear as ordered. But instantly Honkajoki managed to run into a big spruce and with his chest against it went on frantically marking time at the double until, pretending to notice the tree for the first time, he retreated a little and then ran past it. Viirila charged away as fast as he could go, flattening juniper bushes beneath his big feet.

—Detachment, fall in! ordered the sergeant, and immediately Honkajoki turned and came running back to halt in front of the sergeant. Viirila, however, feigned not to hear and went on running.

—Halt! I gave the order to fall in, screamed the sergeant.

Viirila stopped, tossed his head like a horse champing at the bit and emitted a long neigh. Then he broke into a run once more, only to stop again and paw the ground, snorting like a nervous mount. At last, kicking and blowing, he made a sudden dash that brought him to Honkajoki's side.

—What do you think you're doing? Stop your clowning, said the captain in a voice which while stern echoed also his disgust with the hopelessness of his task.

Viirila's only answer was to paw the ground again and try to muzzle Honkajoki.

—Stop that!

Viirila neighed and lashed out backwards with his foot.

—Get on with the drill, the captain said to the sergeant, hoping thus to extricate himself from the situation. And indeed, Viirila did cease his play acting and for a few moments drilled with such surprising expertness that the captain promised to release him from further drilling. Immediately thereafter, however, he began to make wrong turn after wrong turn and to perform rifle exercises of his own invention which were so ludicrous that the sergeant burst out laughing and the captain had to turn away to hide his own unwilling smile.

After devoting a week to the two comrades, the captain quietly abandoned the project, fully aware that he had failed.

The extra drill, of course, did nothing to alter Honkajoki's habits. When not busy with his perpetual-motion machine, he roamed the camp as a self-appointed educational officer. For over a year he had succeeded in maintaining interest in his perpetual-motion device, and whenever he deemed that it had been forgotten long enough to again command attention he returned to it. He was often joined by Vanhala, despite the fact he had been made a corporal as a reward for single-handedly repelling a raid by an enemy patrol while on guard.

In the early winter Hietanen took a shell splinter in his thigh, but his wound was so slight that he was away for only a month. But on his return he was no longer his usual lively self, and gradually a new seriousness and gravity began to be discernible in him. By now he was in charge of the platoon a good part of the time when Koskela was either on leave or substituting for a company commander who was. But he and Maatta were still at the center of every card game, and the same outbursts occurred each time Hietanen gambled away his pay.

The man most upset by the impending inglorious end of the war was Wolf's Paw. For him, as for Rokka, defeat meant a very real personal loss, but while this realization merely made Rokka bitter, in Wolf it gave rise to a melancholy lassitude. Even Rokka found it hard to keep his comrade's spirits up, untiringly as he tried. In this one matter alone, Wolf failed to echo Rokka's moods and ideas as usual.

About Christmas time news came that the German battleship *Scharnhorst* had been sunk in the Arctic.

—The buttons are dropping off Adolf's coat one by one, boys.

It was a few days later that Honkajoki called at a neighboring dugout carrying his longbow.

—Peace to you all.

—What's the news, bowman?

—Thank you for asking. It looks as though we might have a bit of frost.

—Well, a little more cold can't harm us.

—Let us hope so. Taking a broader view, however, felt boots and padded coats seem to be the trump cards these days.

One of the soldiers sitting on his bunk looked up and, despite the lieutenant lying in another bunk, said:

—We've made a lot of fun of 'em, but we could use some of those warm clothes ourselves.

The man was as alone among his companions as Lahtinen had been, his very daring to venture such comments within the hearing of an officer seeming symptomatic. Honkajoki smiled.

—My esteemed comrade apparently refers to such articles in a material sense, and there I agree with him. But if he has carried their significance over into the ideological sphere, then I must part company with him.

—How's perpetual motion coming?

—In the final stages. Everything is solved, except for one last little detail. I have not yet succeeded in eliminating friction and the pull of the heavenly bodies. If we were in a vacuum I could demonstrate perpetual motion here on the spot. As matters are I have to find some other solution.

The men understood little of what Honkajoki was saying; what amused them was the exaggerated dignity of his tone.

After half an hour of such nonsense Honkajoki turned to go, but first he took off his cap and crossed his hands.

—As the hour is late, a prayer for this humble hut would not be amiss. Preserve us from our enemy's wiles and above all from his snipers and anti-tank guns. Our rations might be a little larger if Thou still hadst stores in hand for Thy children's needs. Give us bearable weather that we may the better stand guard over Thy cause. Protect all patrols, sentries and drivers—gunners don't matter so much. Protect our commander-in-chief and our chief of staff and lesser brass accordingly if Thou hast time to spare, and the other officers if Thou must. And finally and particularly, preserve the Finnish leaders from bashing their heads against a Karelian pine a second time. Amen.

If Honkajoki, before leaving the dugout, had caught the lieutenant's eye, he would have understood immediately why he was ordered to report to Lammio the next day.

Honkajoki was not a Rokka, so Lammio made no attempt to conceal his anger when his solemn figure reported, the longbow on his shoulder:

—Private Honkajoki reporting, Captain!

—I can see that. May I ask by what line of reasoning you arrived at the conclusion that you are an educational officer?

—Captain, any means of strengthening morale in these difficult times must be helpful.

—But you sow defeatism. Are you a Communist?

—Captain, my honor as a soldier prevents my answering that question.

—Your honor! I'll honor you with a court-martial if you don't stop maligning the army and its commanders. Do you know what the safety of the country depends upon?

—Captain, it depends on that great and noble man, Marshal Carl Gustaf Emil Mannerheim.

—Right. On him *and* on his army. And you are one of that army's parasites. A louse, at home only in dirt.

—Captain, in my opinion the louse cannot be accused of being responsible for dirt; it is only a consequence of it. But maybe my logic is at fault.

—Don't try to be clever. I repeat: are you a Communist?

—I am an inventor. My actual occupation has been the collection of conifer-tree cones, yet I have always regarded the advancement of science as my chief mission in life.

—Are you insane?

—Captain, that is a question the individual suspected can never himself decide. It is his actions that dictate the answer.

—My dictate to you is that you stop your clowning. I am giving you one last warning. Subversive activity must be stopped immediately. We cannot afford to let any enemy into our lines even if he wears the gray uniform of Finland, which by the way is too honorable to be worn by the likes of you.

—Captain, for a very long time one of my sincerest wishes has been to divest myself of it. Unfortunately through long experience I have discovered the futility of this desire. It is sad, very sad. But leaving that subject, I beg permission to offer my ideas on the present situation.

—Doubtless they are well worth hearing.

—As for the Russian's success, that I would say is temporary. Communism will ultimately collapse because of its inherent impossibility. Thus final peace terms will be dictated by Finland. From the very beginning I have never regarded Communism as a factor to be taken into account. Firstly, because for twenty years the surrender of grain by the collectives has been downright economic plundering. They didn't even leave seed for the peasants. As soon as the soldiers of the victorious Red Army return to their homes, revolution will break out. And the government will be powerless because, you see, the Germans will have stolen all the barbed wire.

—Get out.

—Certainly, Captain. I must still warn you, however, of another factor. The greatest danger of all to my mind is the Yellow Peril.

—Get out! Get out!

—As you say, Captain.

5.

For the third time skeletons clothed in rotting rags emerged from the snow. Water gushed in the trenches and sentries blinked as they looked into the flashing mirrors of their periscopes. And the front grew ever quieter although snipers still occasionally claimed a victim and Russian patrol activity increased.

Nevertheless, a feeling that great events were impending hung in the spring air, and once again the men sought comfort by clinging to forlorn hopes. Rommel would repel the landings in France and then:

—The Panzers will move east again, boys.

—If he can drive 'em back into the sea, everything will get better.

—You won't live to see that happen! It was Hietanen, now perhaps the most pessimistic of all, strange as it seemed to the others. Something else had also changed in him. He who had always been so full of life had begun to stare vacantly off into space. True, such moments were rare, and as soon as they were over he would be rushing from one end of the line to the other again, but in those moments he seemed to sense something. Perhaps it was simply the heavy fighting that all knew lay ahead, and the fact that many more of them would die, he perhaps included.

Koskela almost alone remained unchanged—except, of course, for Rahikainen. Business, however, had come to an end, for no one bought lampstands these days.

—Let's try making a few coffins, Rahikainen jokingly suggested one day to Rokka, only to have him wave away the suggestion.

—There's no money in that line. They'll bury you without one.

Then, while inspecting the positions on Million, Kariluoto caught a shell splinter in the shoulder and was carried off to the hospital. Now Koskela took temporary command of the Third Company and Hietanen took over the platoon.

At the end of May a fine new canteen was completed for the battalion, and its opening was celebrated by entertainment by a touring troupe of performers. A motion picture theater which was to be a model of its kind was also planned for the entire regiment's use. About the same time the men were assigned new wood-cutting tasks, and Hietanen fought a major psychological battle to get his men to work on them.

But before any of them had done much work, an order came that caused all wood cutting to cease.

Chapter XIII

1.

—You don't intend to leave that lovely girl on the wall to be raped by the Russkies, do you?

—Why not? She's just about worn out already.

The men were rolling their packs in silence, their faces solemn. Carefully Honkajoki took up his carved bits of wood, regarded them thoughtfully and put them in his pack.

—They may set Ivan on the right track. You never know, he may be as near to a solution as I am.

—Jesus Christ, so this is what it's come to. Back we go again, after we almost rotted to death here.

Sihvonen jerked the straps of his pack angrily as though it was their fault things had come to such a pass.

Hietanen stood in the middle of the dugout silently watching the others' preparations. Three years ago he had supervised their departure from the burned clearing with a great deal of cheerful chatter. Now he looked on silently. With Koskela in command of the Third Company, the responsibility for the entire platoon now lay on his shoulders.

The telephone had been dismantled, and they were waiting for the order to withdrew to arrive by runner. When at last it came, they took the machine guns from the trench and left. From a bend in the path they saw Devil's Peak outlined against the sky for the last time. Only a light screen of riflemen remained behind to cover the withdrawal.

Vehicles were drawn up beside the road, waiting, and as soon as the platoon arrived the machine guns were loaded and the men marched away.

The road to defeat began quietly. The bridgehead on the Svir was being abandoned without a fight, and they marched past deserted dugouts, fruits of two and a half years' pecking at the earth. Here and there empty artillery emplacements loomed as a silent bitter march brought them to the famous river.

—It just wasn't meant to be Finland's frontier, this little brook.

—Hell, what's it matter? There'll be an end to this blasted business sometime.

—Well, it isn't finished yet.

—In the Isthmus we're on the run with our tail between our legs.

—Just wait. We'll still have to pay for every tree we cut down for wood.

—Yes, and not only us but our grandchildren.

—I know one thing for sure, said Rokka. —With the war out of the trenches again, we'll know what it is to be hungry. Our rations are barely enough for lying around and keeping still. From now on we'll be hunting for crumbs, boys.

Day gave way to twilight and still the footsteps echoed on the road: Finnish soldiers on the march, each cap slanted at a different angle to suit a personal taste, blouses unbuttoned, and on each face a bitter expression. A man filled his lungs with air and began to sing. In the unprintable words of a soldier's song his soul cried out to the summer night its bitterness at three years of useless fighting, voicing in them his defiance of all those who opposed or sought to rule him.

2.

The smoky air was full of sound. Endless shelling and aerial bombardment kept the earth continuously vibrating, while from all points of the compass came the unbroken roar of aircraft formations. The whole world seemed charged with destructive power.

Sarastie's battalion was now part of a unit created during the withdrawal and known as Task Force Karjula. At first it withdrew rapidly along the poor forest roads until, having brought its front into line with the other units, it became engaged in constant, extremely heavy fighting.

Bit by bit they yielded up the East-Karelian fields they had captured three years ago at such bitter cost. Again they were hungry, resentful and tired. Heavy exertion called for plenty of food, but owing to the disordered state of the Finnish transport even their scanty regulation rations were usually hours late and often short. Occasionally they might be glutted with food, for several large army dumps had to be destroyed. Then the starving soldiers would seize all the food they could possibly carry. Now again Rahikainen placed his talents at the disposal of Hietanen's platoon and many times kept his comrades from going hungry. Once he even wormed his way into a barracks camp that was under heavy fire and at the risk of his life came back with ten pairs of brand-new army boots. He would, of course, never have volunteered for such a dangerous task on the battlefield. To Rahikainen the only unfortunate thing about the retreat was that since no one was carrying anything that could be bartered for, he had to give away the provisions he procured without receiving anything in return. Nor could he sell anything because few had any money.

The platoon completed the first part of its journey without loss, except for Honkajoki's longbow. He had faithfully carried it with him, but finally a day came when they were forced to abandon their positions in great haste. Honkajoki tried to grab the bow before leaving but a sniper shot a hole in his sleeve, and when they had stopped running, Honkajoki said regretfully:

—In spite of the gravity of the situation I feel like swearing. Indeed, I think I will. Damn that misbegotten Russian for making me abandon my personal weapon.

Otherwise Honkajoki was not embittered. Defeat seemed no more important to him than anything else in the world. Once he vanished for three days. On the same day four men disappeared from Number One Company, the evidence pointing to their having joined the Pine-cone Guards, as the deserters roaming the woods were called. Honkajoki, however, soon turned up again, saying he had merely been scouting for billets. Actually he had accompanied the deserters, but happening to stray from the little band he had thought it safest to rejoin his unit.

Yet the platoon's fighting spirit was better than most. Although Koskela was no longer with them his influence was ineffaceable, and Hietanen and Rokka were men no one would lightly desert. Hietanen never exhorted. He merely slung his tommy gun on his shoulder and went, and the others followed. But as the days passed he seemed to grow visibly older and gloomier. And with his gloominess his courage also grew. But now it contained an element of defiance, the cause of which could be guessed from the terse threatening order to shut up that put an end to any gloating of a political nature over their defeat.

His was not the care of any good officer for the morale of his men. It was the reaction of a man who in the face of defeat realizes that the patriotism he had formerly regarded so lightly was actually an integral part of his attitude toward life and that to strike at it was to strike at the very roots of his being. The man in him had let the boy be gay and carefree while everything went well, but in defeat came forth to shoulder the burden.

Rokka on the whole remained unchanged. He fought, if anything, even better than before but indulged in no heroics. When he saw a situation was hopeless, he ceased trying, knowing full well that if he stood firm someone else was bound to give way. He said more than once that to die unnecessarily was worse treason than to desert. But rumors that deserters were being shot moved him to fury. Luckily he had no occasion to meet high-ranking officers these days, or his anger might have involved him in serious trouble.

Only Salo remained firm, his faith in ultimate victory unbroken. Indeed, the fewer grounds he had for his belief, the stronger became his dogmatic assertions.

One day as they were withdrawing, a flight of Stormoviks thundered over.

—Run for cover!

—I expect we'll see our fighters up there soon, said Salo, when they had reached the shelter of a ditch. Immediately a shout of derision went up, the invisibility of the Finnish fighters having long been the reason for a great deal of complaint.

—See 'em! You damned fool, you saw plenty of 'em when they weren't needed, but where are they now? Those Russky bastards aren't afraid to show themselves.

Immediately Salo rose to the challenge.

—They show themselves as long as we let 'em. And as long as we go on running, what do you expect?

—Don't go setting yourself up as a hero, you ape. You're as quick on your feet as anybody.

The truth was that Salo was in every way the most average type of soldier, one of the mass of ordinary men which form the bulk of any army. He did his duty as he saw it as well as possible without in any sense being a hero. Thus in the present controversy he seemed out of character, for his comrades did not consider it his role to hint at cowardice in others. Salo lapsed into silence, but when the Stormoviks returned, instead of taking cover he rested his rifle against a tree and aimed at the approaching aircraft. He took no notice of the others nor of Hietanen's sharp order to take cover, but stayed where he was.

As the first swept into view, he fired and worked the bolt for another shot before the Stormovik opened fire. Bullets churned up the dust at his feet as he crumpled and fell. Then, as quickly as they had come, the planes disappeared, leaving the men to rush to Salo's aid. They found him pale but still conscious. A bullet had pierced his left leg, splintering the bones so thoroughly that it was obvious that he would walk for the rest of his life on an artificial limb, if he survived at all.

He bore up without a moan under what must have been frightful pain as the medical corpsmen removed his boot and dressed the leg. Beads of sweat stood out on his forehead, his body stiffened every now and again with the pain, but not a sound escaped him. It was as if he were trying to be braver than nature had ever intended him to be. In a strangely calm voice he said:

—What's the use of weeping over one leg? At least I won't ever run from those bastards again.

After he was placed in an ambulance the platoon one by one bade him farewell. And as they each uttered some worn platitude, their voices revealed the extent to which Salo by his unnecessary sacrifice had purchased their respect. None of them ever saw him again, but when they did happen to remember him it was as a good and brave fellow. The last impression covered all the earlier ones, and even his unwavering faith in victory, which had given rise to so much joking, was now seen not as stupidity but as indomitable courage.

Endlessly the retreat went on, and the ever fiercer fighting now left no room in their minds for anything more than fear, hunger and a never-satisfied longing for rest.

3.

The machine-gun company's command post was beside a twisting forest road. Firing could be heard from the front, and heavy shells were dropping between the post and the lines as Lammio and Sinkkonen interviewed a new draft and the clerk entered the men on the company roll. The clerk was a corporal now, and since the replacements included eight boyish recruits straight from training camp, he put his questions to them in the bullying tones of an officer. It tells enough of the sort of man he was to say that he had borrowed his tone and gestures from Lammio.

In addition to the boys, the draft included three *Landsturm* men in their fifties. The newcomers had already dug themselves foxholes to provide shelter from splinters, and each time the earth shook they looked longingly at the holes.

Lammio stood talking to the sergeant major, tapping his boot tops with his swagger stick:

—You'd better make drivers out of those old men and give rifles to the ones we've got now. Hietanen can have four of the youngsters since his need is greatest. By the way, I hear Kariluoto's back again, so Koskela will be returning to his platoon. It's only temporarily, though. He's being transferred to another company as C.O. Sarastie doesn't want to let him go, but the way things are I don't think what he wants will mean anything.

Sinkkonen turned to the *Landsturm* men:

—We're sending the younger drivers into the line, and you'll be taking their places. I suppose you can all drive a horse. You there—what's your name?

Sinkkonen pointed to a big swarthy man sitting dejectedly on the edge of his foxhole nervously chewing a straw. But instead of replying, the man looked away and grunted:

—What the hell does it matter what my name is?

Lammio tripped and almost fell in his hurry to get to the man.

—Answer that question properly! And never mind the acting.

—They ought to know my name, seeing as how they knew where to come to drag me from my home. Aye . . . that's the truth. Damned if it isn't.

Lammio could feel his temper rising, but fortunately he remembered Sarastie's stern warning not to stir up the men in time to control himself:

—Well, you do have a name?

—It's Korpela, if you must know, the man grunted surlily. —Aye. Private Korpela.

Korpela went on nervously chewing his straw, then suddenly jerked it out of his mouth and threw it angrily from him. But he continued sitting silently staring into space, lost in his own thoughts. Only when Sinkkonen led the rest off to eat did he shoulder his pack and follow, muttering unintelligibly to himself.

Sinkkonen did consult Makila about which of the drivers was to be sent into the line, but as usual left all the arrangements to him. However, Makila was having his own problems. It was almost impossible now to get supplies in the regular way, and, indeed, he rarely knew for how many men he had to provide. Very often, in addition to stragglers, he would have to feed whole units which had lost contact with their transport. Equipment had begun to disappear as drivers secretly lightened their loads, and many horses also were killed by the bombs of the Stormoviks which ruled the skies. And Makila reacted to all this by becoming ever stingier. The more equipment he saw destroyed, the closer he watched the rest, unlike most other supply sergeants who in the same situation let everything slide.

When, after feeding the new men, he detailed the oldest of them for duty as drivers, the one who had given his name as Korpela snapped angrily:

—Well, where are the damned horses we're supposed to drive? Let's move the supplies so the profiteers can sell more and make even more money.

But Makila had no time for such unimportant matters as profiteers. Pointing out the horse Korpela was to drive, he said with a cough:

—That's yours. Be sure you take good care of him. Feed him whenever you have a chance.

Korpela almost exploded.

—Holy Satan, I've been driving horses all my life! You take care of yourself. Aye, you just do that.

Now it was Makila's turn to turn red. And though he said no more to Korpela, his voice when he spoke to the others was tense. Meanwhile Korpela examined the harness, all the while keeping up his incomprehensible muttering. Makila watched him out of the corner of his eye, and when Korpela had finally left the carts he crossed to them and put the harness straight. Satisfied then, he turned to the drivers.

—Whose turn is it to take the soup up front?

Shells were bursting beside the road, so Makila was not surprised that it was nobody's turn.

—Uusitalo, I guess it's yours.

The soldier he had spoken to cursed angrily.

—Christ, you ought to go yourself just for once and see what it's like! It's always easy to order others.

Without a word Makila fetched a horse that had been tethered beneath the sheltering branches of a spruce, harnessed it and hoisted the soup kettle on the cart. But as he was about to drive it off Uusitalo slouched over and growled:

—Get the hell out of there and give me the reins.

Makila looked past him blankly and jerked the reins:

—Hrrm . . . errr . . . Never mind. I'm going this time since you're all so scared.

With a cluck of his tongue he got the horse in motion and set off walking beside the cart. He had several miles to go, the Stormoviks having made it necessary to disperse the supply dumps and move them as far as possible from the front lines. He had covered a considerable distance when he encountered a messenger on a bicycle who waved to him:

—Look out for yourself! Ivan's got the road bracketed. The shelling's real heavy just past the mortar positions.

Makila did not even bother to reply but continued his unhurried progress, looking neither right nor left. He passed the mortars and approached the sector under the heaviest fire, a swampy hollow lying at the bottom of a fairly steep hill. Reaching the top of the hill, Makila paused to wait for a lull, for the shells were falling at short intervals. The rumble of muzzle reports would be followed by a rasping shriek which aways stopped a second before the crash came. The horse snorted and trembled, and Makila moved to hold his bridle. Soon the interval between the shells lengthened and then for almost five minutes there was no new explosion.

Now at last Makila climbed into the cart. But before he was halfway down the hill the shelling began again. For the first time in his life Makila struck a horse, sending the beast into a startled gallop down the hill as the shells sent spouts of mud flying less than a score of paces away. Makila blessed himself as he realized that the soft soil appreciably reduced the danger of flying splinters, but abruptly the horse reared on its hind legs and began to push the cart backward. Quickly Makila got down to lead it by the bridle.

The next two shells crashed farther away, and the horse snorted, took a few prancing steps and tried to rear again. Makila patted it and spoke soothingly:

—Don't be afraid. Come on, old fellow, let's go. We're in God's hands now.

Makila spoke to the horse, but actually the words were intended for himself. Yet he was surprisingly calm. Only his eyes which blinked each time a shell crashed evidenced his fear. Again there came the crash of a muzzle report, but this time the shriek that followed was ominously short. Makila saw foam, green-flecked with grass, fly before his eyes as a red flame flashed before him on the road and opened a wide crater. He did not even have time to scream before his body was torn to shreds.

The horse fell in the shafts, then tried to rise on its forelegs. It gave a wild agonized scream, then, its head shaking once or twice, collapsed.

The next shell went wide and only slewed mud over both bodies.

4.

The machine gunners sat at the edge of the holes they had dug waiting for their food, bad-tempered and hence silent. A couple of days ago they had taken up their present positions along a brook. It was only one new line among many they had tried to hold, but it was exceptional in that the Russians had not yet tried to dislodge them. Heretofore they had almost immediately pierced each new Finnish line, and the retreat had been resumed. Bearded, dirty, their faces lined with weariness, the men stared down at the ground. An occasional stray bullet smacked into a tree, and from the other side of the brook came the growling of a tank. In the distance was the thunder of aerial bombardment, a sound rarely absent these days.

They were ravenously hungry. Two days before Rahikainen had brought an enormous load of food he had found in a truck that had been shattered by a bomb, but that had vanished all too quickly. They could not refuse the men, even those of other units, who came begging: —Give us a share, we haven't eaten for two days. As little as the phrase "comrades in arms" had come to mean to them, hunger was something they understood so well that they gave away their last crumbs.

Suddenly there was a commotion as a group of soldiers appeared lugging a badly battered soup kettle. Makila's body had been found by an anti-tank unit bringing up a new gun to replace one that had been destroyed. From the number on the kettle they had identified it and now had brought it back to the platoon. And so great was the hungry platoon's disappointment at the tiny bit of soup still left that they had hardly a thought for Makila. Rahikainen even said moodily:

—He was miserly while he was alive, and death hasn't improved him.

There was scarcely a ladleful for each of them, but into that they crumbled the last of their bread and slowly began to eat.

It was Rahikainen, however, who pronounced what would serve as Makila's eulogy!

—He was man enough to throw away all the officers' trash we'd have had to carry. Remember how he tossed away the icons that lieutenant in the first platoon was dragging with him?

—There's been lots of better stuff thrown away. The men over there said whole truckloads of flour were driven into the lake. Didn't I tell you the brass thought we'd be sitting here forever? They were still bringing up stuff when they ought to have been carting it away.

Rokka and Wolf's Paw now shared the same eating equipment, Wolf's pack having been abandoned after a skirmish.

—I told you not to take that pack off your back, Rokka growled. The men had indeed begun to throw their packs on their backs before doing anything else whenever an alarm was sounded, so poorly did they view their chances of repulsing the attack.

It was Rokka who first observed the group of men approaching and shouted:

—Look, damn it! Kariluoto's back. Now we'll get some real fighting . . . he's got some new men, too. What the hell am I talking about—they're only children.

It was indeed Kariluoto bringing a new draft to the battalion. He led his charges to the CP where, overjoyed at seeing Koskela again, he shouted from a distance:

—Greetings, old man! I see you've still got your feet under you. Nothing can kill a man like you. God doesn't want him and the

Devil's sure he's got him. I brought a few more lads with me. Four of 'em are for the machine guns.

Kariluoto was indeed a happy man. He had taken advantage of his leave to get married and was still up in the clouds. Reports of a retreat and of defeats, if they had reached his ears, had done so without his hearing them. Thin and with dark circles under his eyes, he laughed as he thought of his beautiful young bride.

With the egotism of a man in love he had managed to keep his mind free of the events that might shatter his happiness. Finland could not fall because that would make Captain Kariluoto unhappy, and why should anyone wish to do that? The whole world must know that he was newly married to a girl whose beauty and charm was truly unique.

Koskela stood waiting as Kariluoto hastened up to him. Then he seized the extended hand.

—Glad to have you back, and congratulations.

Kariluoto smiled in greeting, but already his high spirits were ebbing as he saw Koskela's protruding cheekbones, his red swollen eyelids, his forced smile.

—Thanks, he said, and then asked softly: —How are things?

—We're alive. But we've done some moving since you left.

—Yes, so I've noticed. Let's get these new men assigned, then we can go off somewhere. I've got a few things in my pack. I'll take over the company afterwards.

—That's all right. The Second Platoon's on the other side of the road, the First and Fourth on this, and the Third's in reserve. The battalion wanted it for its own reserves, but they let it stay when they heard that its strength was down to sixteen men. The Jaeger Platoon patrols our flanks, and that's the whole of our reserves. It seems damn little.

—Sarastie was hopeful about the defenses along the brook. He thinks the line will hold.

—It may. But both flanks are wide open. When you haven't the men, you haven't the men. If we had some reserves to hold the flanks . . . but it's been like this all along.

They doled out the new men and then took themselves away from the messengers and telephones so they could talk in peace. Kariluoto opened his pack and drew forth some dried-out sandwiches.

—Want a drink with it?

—I'd better not.

—Don't worry, there isn't enough left for more than one.

—Then it's not worth taking. Well, what's happening out in the world?

—Oh, nothing very much. But what's the situation here?

Koskela groaned softly. —It's all over for us. The thing's beyond hope.

Kariluoto's face mirrored his surprise at hearing Koskela speak this way. Then he laughed softly.

—Yes, I guess it is. Who would have thought the Germans wouldn't be able to pull it off? And we certainly can't hold out by ourselves.

Koskela did not reply, and Kariluoto began to think he was holding back something. But at last Koskela shook his head angrily.

—This isn't war. It's plain murder. I don't blame them for running away.

—You mean the deserters? said Kariluoto. —Are there very many?

—They're not of any real importance, and I don't mean the actual deserters. There aren't too many of them, and most are men who've lost their nerve and wouldn't be of any use if they stayed. But nobody wants to fight. Everybody's turned spineless.

Koskela's face took on its former stolid expression, and he fell silent. Nor did Kariluoto wish to continue the conversation, divining that Koskela had said more than he had wanted to.

For a while they chewed their sandwiches in silence. But at last Kariluoto asked:

—What's going to happen to us?

—The battalion, you mean?

—No, all of us. The whole of Finland.

—The things that always happen to the vanquished. We'll have Ivan's fist stuffed down our throats.

Kariluoto's jaw trembled as in a voice that hovered between tears and rage he said:

—No! No, by God! I couldn't stand it . . . I don't want to live to see it.

—There's no hope. Not the slightest.

—Then we'll fight on till we're all dead.

—We've been doing that right along, Koskela said wearily. And Kariluoto, seeing that the conversation troubled Koskela, said no more on the subject. Instead they discussed practical problems.

Koskela explained that for the time being he would still command his old platoon, but that his transfer was only a matter of time. The shortage of officers had become too acute for a lieutenant of his experience to be allowed to remain a mere platoon leader. Actually there had been two company commands vacated in the battalion which had been filled by younger men, but they had been appointed while he was in temporary command of the Third and both men were regulars. Koskela's interest in these matters had nothing to do with ambition; he would have preferred to stay with his old comrades, but he could do that only by being given a company in the battalion.

When they had finished their scant repast they went to inspect the positions together. Graphically Koskela explained the successive phases of the withdrawal, and gradually Kariluoto began to grasp how complete the Finnish collapse had been.

5.

The new men assigned to Hietanen's platoon were busy digging foxholes for themselves. There were four of them, and Hietanen had detailed all of them to the first squad which had fewer men than the other, though all the sections had been undermanned from the very beginning of the war. In the present situation the main hardship this inflicted on the men was that there was more guard duty for all of them, but during the retreat it had made the removal of equipment extremely difficult.

Now three of the men were taking matters most seriously, obeying Hietanen's instructions with a haste that betrayed their nervousness. The fourth, a sturdy blond youth, seemed to be at ease from the first minute. When he had dug his hole, he sat on the edge of it and asked jauntily:

—Well, where are the Russkies? I'm ready to try my hand at killing a few of 'em.

Rokka's head rose from his hole.

—Well, well, look what we have here. But don't talk so loud or they'll hear you, and when they find out it's you, they'll run away.

—How old are you? Hietanen scowled.

—Seventeen, sir, answered one of the lads.

—Christ! We were young when we started but not infants.

—Mother Finland tears the babe from its mother's breast and sends him out to defend her, snickered Rahikainen.

The ghost of a smile flickered over Hietanen's tired face.

—I just heard myself called "sir" for the first time. I trust all the rest of you heard it, too. Now you know the kind of man I am.

—By the greenest recruits right out of the training center with the fear of God still in them, Rahikainen said bitterly. —They're sending all the old men and children here.

Chapter XIV

I.

Voo . . . ooo . . . oooo . . .

Aircraft streaked over the front lines toward the command posts and the artillery positions, the sudden roar shattering the silence and sending the men diving into their holes. An unusual quiet had prevailed along the front, lulling them into a mood of self-deception born of hope in which they imagined that for some dim reason the fighting had come to an end. Two uneventful days had restored their nerves, but the tension within them was still so close to the surface that it took only an instant to return them to the blind panic which had characterized the withdrawal. When the planes had passed over, they began to climb out of their foxholes but quickly threw themselves down again as a continuous rumble came from the Russian lines.

For a few seconds they were permitted to hope that the barrage would not fall on them, then the crash of the first shells told them their hope was vain. The ground swayed and shook, the air screamed and howled, and in the midst of all this fury their hearts hammered until it seemed a wonder they did not burst. They tried to make themselves as small as possible, and fingernails clawed at the sandy bottoms of their foxholes.

Trees snapped like matches, tongues of flame and pillars of smoke rose to the treetops, splinters, branches and clods of earth fell in a continuous hail, and somewhere a humming shell splinter found a man and set him screaming:

—Help . . . I'm hit . . . I'm hit!

Hietanen pushed his face against the bottom of his hole, his eyes tightly closed, and counted every explosion in his vicinity:

—Again . . . again . . . again . . . again . . .

It was a means he had discovered of keeping the terror the crashes aroused in him under control. But now a disturbing new sound invaded his consciousness. Someone was moaning pitiably, crying for help. After wrestling briefly with his fear Hietanen raised his head and looked about. A few yards away one of the new recruits was dragging himself along the ground, screaming for help, his features distorted with terror and pain.

Hietanen sprang out of his foxhole, and seizing the man, began to drag him into his own hole, his face purple with rage.

—You bastard, didn't I tell you to stay in your hole? But no, you've got to go and leave it and get hit.

He had warned all the new men against exposing themselves, knowing from experience that when fear gained the upper hand a man was liable to rush senselessly out among the bursting shells just as this boy had.

Almost roughly he dragged the boy behind him. Shell splinters screamed by his ears and earth rained down on him as he crawled on all fours, pulling the wounded boy along by his belt and one hand. As he did, the boy continued to scream, but it was more in fear than pain for he was not seriously wounded.

Suddenly a blast of hot air struck Hietanen in the face at the same instant that a shell splinter tore through the cartilage of his nose, ripping out both his eyeballs. With a tortured cry, he collapsed on top of the recruit.

The boy tried to free himself from beneath Hietanen's weight but was too paralyzed by fear and the sight of that awful bleeding face to do so. When at last he gained control of his vocal chords, a long despairing wail burst from his lips.

This new cry brought Koskela and Vanhala crawling to their aid. Carefully they lifted Hietanen off the lad and pulled both into the nearest foxhole. As they did so the barrage passed over them, and Koskela shouted to the recruits:

—You there! Try and fix up these two, and if we have to leave, be damned sure you take them with you.

The rest of the men went scrambling to their battle stations, for already the growling of a tank and the rattle of small arms could be heard from the other side of the brook. A ragged cheer, too, was echoed on the breeze, but this apparently was a ruse for no attack came; the shouting ended and soon the firing also died. Grimly Kosekela concluded that the barrage had been intended only to upset their nerves in preparation for the real attack. It was a tactic the Russians had used before. Bidding Rokka keep an eye on the platoon he made his way to the rear to see how Hietanen was faring.

Hietanen was just regaining consciousness when Koskela arrived. He moved his hands, clumsily touched his bandaged face and muttered:

—What happened?

Gently Koskela drew Hietanen's hand away from his face.

—Don't worry. Keep as still as you can.

—Koskela?

—Yes. Don't move. You got a bash on the nose.

Koskela looked at the men, pointed to his eye and received a nod in reply. He held up two fingers, and again the nod. Blood was still dripping from Hietanen's sleeve, and they were dressing a small wound below his elbow with special care, fussing over it to distract Hietanen's attention from his eyes. He gasped:

—It hurts. Why's my forehead so numb?

—You were hit in the nose. It's not . . .

—I know. I've lost my eyes.

As consciousness returned to Hietanen, his pain grew worse. The blow had numbed his senses, but as the numbness wore off he began opening and clenching his fists. For a while he managed to keep from crying out. Then such a terrible scream broke from him that the recruits recoiled in fear. Carefully Koskela lifted the wounded man's head.

—Drink a little water. The stretcher bearers'll be here soon. I'll go along with you to the road.

—I don't want water. Where's the boys?

—Back on the firing line.

—Are we still there, right where we were?

—Of course.

Hietanen turned on his side and groaned. Then he collapsed onto his back again, his breath coming in tortured gasps.

—Is anyone else here?

—The new men.

—Give me a pistol.

—Don't worry. We'll be at the clearing station soon.

—I can't stand it. My head's on fire. Christ, it's terrible. Christ . . . Christ, help me . . . Give . . .

—Believe me, you'll be all right. You won't die. You're all right except for your nose. The bridge is broken, that's all.

But Kietanen began twisting frantically again and Koskela sent the recruits running to hurry the stretcher bearers.

Now that the Russians had quieted down the men began to drift back to say farewell to Hietanen. Silently, each in turn touched the hand that clutched the wooden pole of the stretcher. Then the medical orderlies arrived and, lifting the stretcher, set off with it. The last the men heard was a long cry of agony. Such a sound would not easily escape Hietanen, and from it they knew how severe his pain was.

Koskela accompanied the stretcher to the roadside where the half dozen other men who had been wounded in the barrage had already been gathered. Kariluoto had called the field dressing station for an ambulance, and for once one happened to be there.

The ambulance, a converted bus, came swaying along the bad road, and the driver, careless of what happened to his vehicle, turned it around on the rough, rocky road.

The badly wounded were placed in the front, but Hietanen, though he knew that the shaking was worse in the back, insisted on being put there so a man with a stomach wound could go up front. When at last all the wounded were aboard, Koskela seized Hietanen's arm.

—Take it easy. After all, life doesn't depend on seeing. I'll come see you as soon as I can.

But Hietanen was in such agony that he could pay little attention even to Koskela. Between moans he muttered:

—Goodbye, and give the best to the boys from me. Take care of yourself.

Long after the ambulance had vanished around a bend in the road Koskela stood motionless, staring after it. Then, lighting a cigarette, he made his way slowly back to his platoon, sunk in gloom. Despite his long absence from the platoon the men were still a part of him, and something of himself went with each one lost. The old platoon was still connected in his mind with the spirit and the victories of the early days of the war. Every man who left it took a part of that mood with him and left instead a sense of despair and of the senselessness of the struggle. And Hietanen was the one man with whom Koskela had felt himself most closely bound.

Koskela knew, however, what had to be done, for he had the ability to concentrate on the things he wanted to, to the exclusion of all unwanted thoughts. Once again he thrust away the tormenting feeling that watched like a ghost over all this crazy killing and suffering, the feeling which had sent him into a rage when Lehto had killed the Russian prisoner. There was no room here for humanity. Deliberately Koskela began to consider whether he could alter the placing of the machine guns to advantage.

2.

Major Sarastie sat on a bed of moss smoking cigarette after cigarette. Dark rings circled his eyes and the hand holding the cigarette shook nervously. His summer blouse was soiled and crumpled. In the swamps and brush the color had worn off his boots and been replaced by a pale greenish tint.

His was certainly not a distinguished command post, Sarastie mused. A field telephone, a campfire for making ersatz coffee, and messengers and signalers squatting on the ground a little distance away. He had no adjutant, for that officer had taken command of the Jaeger Platoon when it was left without a leader. No new Jaeger officer had arrived, and probably none would.

Shells screamed overhead, and planes roared past to worry the supply columns to the rear. A Finnish trench mortar coughed three times nearby. Ammunition was running too low for a greater show of strength, and the supply situation was growing worse with every passing day. The Stórmoviks were seeing to that.

Sarastie feared for his flanks. The Russians were now employing flanking tactics as successfully as the Finns had on their advance. But what could he do? Adequate reserves were essential if he was to protect his flanks, but where could he get them?

Instead the Jaeger Platoon had to patrol both flanks, and he had one platoon from the First Company in reserve close behind the front line if it gave at any point. No more men could be spared from the already dangerously weak front line. And of what use was it to station a few men everywhere and nowhere have enough? Nowadays one had to take risks. He had been promised an Engineer Company as a reserve when it had finished a road-building job, but from what he had heard the job was nowhere near finished. And all his commanding officer could say was: —We must take emergency measures.

In Sarastie's opinion his superior was a fool, and they were on bad terms. Theirs was the usual quarrel between a commander and a subordinate, the one demanding more than the other thought possible. Each time Sarastie failed to stop the Russians with his exhausted battalion, the commander felt that sufficient effort had not been made. What, thought Sarastie, can effort do when I have no men? And that's something a commander cannot remedy. Sarastie felt that he had done all he could. He had tried to treat the men right, had stressed to his officers the importance of their attitude toward the men, and bawled hell out of Lammio. There was to be no more playing the gentleman; an officer was henceforth no different from a tommy-gun man. Sarastie had read a great deal of military history and the present situation had made him remember Napoleon's words: "I have been too long the emperor. I must again become General Bonaparte." He had been stern where sternness was called for, but using his power to send his men to destruction he regarded as not only senseless but immoral.

There it was. If only their morale could be raised, the line would be that much stronger in proportion. It would be possible to do things whose consequences could be calculated beforehand. But now it was all a matter of luck; the line might hold or it might break. The effort of which the men were capable was less predictable than ever, for they seemed to have no will to fight. There might be an occasional flash of the old spirit, but it took very little to extinguish it.

A Jaeger patrol was just back from the right flank which was anchored on a large swamp. Sarastie, however, relied little on the swamp, for he himself had executed flanking movements through far worse terrain, and experience had shown that the Russians were just as good at that game. The patrol reported that all was quiet in that sector, but how much could one depend on such reports nowadays? The uncertain voice in which the report had been made gave him reason to suspect that the patrol had not been out as far as it was supposed to go.

He tried to swat a mosquito whining in his ear, but the insect easily sailed away from his hand. A dull gurgling sounded in his stomach, and a momentary spell of nausea brought perspiration to his brow. Dysentery was common among the troops.

Sarastie's fears were verified as a sentry came running out of the forest, panting for breath.

—Major, Russkies!

—Where?

—Over there. Hundreds of 'em! All with tommy guns.

Quickly Sarastie ordered the runners and signal men to form a firing line, then set off in the direction in which the sentry had pointed. Everything became clear to him as he saw the advancing Russians flitting among the spruce trees. He was being encircled.

Quickly he ran back and ordered the reluctant men to their stations. Already ragged firing was signaling the opening of the skirmish.

—I'll call the front lines and ask for help, he shouted. But instead of setting up defenses, the messengers and signalers fled. And as they ran, Sarastie saw a Russian soldier steadying his tommy gun against a spruce preparatory to firing. With an oath, he drew his pistol and emptied the magazine. He was just reaching for the telephone when the bullets thudded into his body. He died instantly.

3.

The ambulance rocked along the pitted road with its groaning cargo. The driver kept his eyes on the road, twisting the steering wheel in an effort to avoid the deepest holes. An orderly felt a wounded man's pulse, then rose and whispered to the driver:

—He won't last to the clearing station.

The driver made no reply for the road demanded the whole of his attention. Since he was driving as fast as he could, the news made no difference to him anyhow.

Hietanen tried with all his strength to hold the stretcher, for every bump sent a surge of pain careening through his skull. And yet he was half thankful for the pain which gave him no opportunity to think of what the future held in store for him. All he wanted now was to have the ride end or to die. Occasionally his despairing wail rose above the chorus of groans when the pain became unbearable.

As the ambulance approached the high ground on which the command post was situated, the sound of firing rose above the noise of the motor, but no one paid any special attention to it. Then as the car rounded a curve the windshield shattered. With a choking sob the driver collapsed over the steering wheel, then rolled off it onto the orderly who had fallen beside the switch. The ambulance lurched drunkenly into the ditch and stopped as bullets rattled through the metal sides, and a tongue of flame flickered from the hood.

Hietanen was the first to recover from the stunning effect of the crash and rise to his feet. All around him he heard cries and moans as he groped his way to the rear door and pushed it open. The result was a new shower of bullets. A man crawled at his feet crying:

—The car's on fire . . . it's on fire . . . help me out!

—Where's the driver and the orderly? shouted Hietanen.

—Dead. Help . . .

Cursing, Hietanen thrust the man out the door and groped his way back to the front of the car, shouting:

—Anyone who can't get out take hold of my hand. I'll pull you. But if you can walk get out by yourselves. Through the back door. Quick!

A hand grasped his outstretched arm, and although the effort sent waves of excruciating pain racing through his head, Hietanen pulled the man along the floor, ignoring his screams and groans as his shattered hip dragged on the floor. There had been six wounded but the two in front had been killed by the same burst as the driver and the orderly. As he pulled his man along Hietanen heard the last survivor in the car shouting for help:

—Come and help me . . . The car's on fire . . . I've no legs . . . I can't move . . .

The shouts ended in a fit of coughing, for the car was filling with smoke. But Hietanen had reached the back door with the man he was helping and now he shouted back:

—I'll come. Don't worry, I won't leave you . . .

The recruit Hietanen had been helping when he himself was wounded had been first out of the ambulance. But although he was much less severely wounded than Hietanen, he was too frightened to think of others. Instead he tried desperately to crawl away from the car until a Russian bullet ended his attempt.

Reaching the door with the second man, Hietanen jumped down to the road and began to pull him out. But suddenly a frightened cry broke from the man:

—Duck . . . get down . . . he sees you . . . there . . .

He had no time to say more for a burst struck the doorway and he lay still. Hietanen fell slowly on his side, his lifeless body shuddering as a machine gun hammered bullets into it.

The ambulance burned with a great roaring and crackling, and for a long time the sound of coughing could be heard from it and a voice crying:

—Come help me . . . Why did you leave me? Can't anybody hear? . . . Jesus help me! My blanket's on fire . . .

A fit of coughing followed the cries, to be succeeded by an animal-like scream. Then there was only the crackle of the flames.

In the clear blue of the summer afternoon bomber squadrons growled in the sky. To the south, toward Lake Ladoga, the air was filled with the rumble of a barrage.

4.

Kariluoto sat eating the last of the food he had brought with him from home. From the bliss of his marriage he had come straight into this misery, and his mind was overwhelmed with the horror of it all. He had heard of the withdrawal at home, but now he knew that the Finnish collapse was complete. Columns of fleeing soldiers were being harassed by the ever present Stormoviks as they fled, leaving behind their arms and supplies.

He felt sick to his stomach. To defeat was added shame. He had imagined the army withdrawing slowly, contesting every inch bitterly, but the rumors he had heard were true.

They had retreated before this, feared and run, but always later they had turned and tried to make up for it. Now nobody thought it shameful to run. Men spoke openly of running and turned the matter into a joke. True, there was nothing they would not joke about, yet Kariluoto squirmed inwardly when he heard them.

He did not condemn fear, for he had long ago confessed his own fears. In fact, he found himself wondering if he would not run as they did were he not a company commander.

He remembered the ghost that had haunted him: a gray-haired captain thrusting shoulder first into a tempest. And in his ears the ghostly echo of a voice still echoed: —Let's try, Lieutenant, let's get going. Each time he remembered, he gasped with pain and shame. Then, when he began to be aware that he understood his experience as Kaarna had, the ghost had forgiven him. He knew now exactly how Kaarna had felt at the time.

He could still envy men whose courage was an integnal part of their character. But how cunningly he had protected himself against feeling inferior! Such courage, he had thought, had no moral value, merely a practical one. Once when the talk had turned to Viirila's insensate bravery he had smiled sarcastically and said: —Yes, but I suppose the horses are least afraid of all here.

No, he could sympathize with fear. But indifference—that bitter, mocking jesting about catastrophe—that brought tears of mortification to his eyes.

It was moments before he heard the sound of firing in his rear and realized that fighting must be going on back there. An enemy patrol, perhaps.

He cranked the handle of his telephone, but no answer came from Battalion. Now he shouted for his runner, ordering him to fetch the officer in charge of the reserve platoon. When the young lieutenant came he ordered the platoon to secure the road leading to Battalion. But hardly had the man gone when the firing broke out again, and this time there was no mistaking the slow chatter of a Russian machine gun. A picture of the ambulance came into Kariluoto's mind; by now it must be somewhere near that firing. But still more significant was the presence there of a Russian machine gun; it meant that heavier forces than a patrol were on the road in their rear. Again he tried to establish contact by telephone, and again his effort was in vain.

Frantically he gathered together more men and sent them to the aid of the Third Platoon, then made his own way to the artillery observation post. A nervous lieutenant greeted him:

—Our telephone wire's cut. Same thing with the trench mortars. We're trying to radio.

—Ask them to get me Major Sarastie.

But when contact was made, the artillery positions reported that contact with the battalion CP had ceased. They had received information that men had come in saying Sarastie had been killed and the road cut. A Jaeger Platoon was at the moment setting up a roadblock on their side of the Russians.

Seconds later they reported that new information had just come in. The trench mortar positions had fallen into Russian hands; Captain Lammio had ordered the transport to withdraw and was collecting all the men he could lay hands on to reinforce the Jaeger Platoon.

Kariluoto's breath came faster. This was his hour of trial. He was the senior company commander in the battalion, save for Lammio who was on the other side of the break.

—Get me the task force commander.

Kariluoto lit a cigarette and drew the smoke deep into his lungs to steady his nerves. As he took the radio telephone in his hands, he tried to hide their trembling.

The commander's voice was crisp, and his orders brief:

—Pull all the men you can out of the line. I'm blocking the road in the west, but that won't help you. Your positions must be held. Do you understand?

—I can extricate myself by a detour.

—It's not a question of extricating but of holding your positions. I'm sure Ivan's not in great strength. One good blow will clear up the situation, so hit him as hard as you can. Use your own judgment as to where. That's all.

There was precious little on which to exercise judgment, Kariluoto reflected. The Second Company and the machine guns would have to hold the brook line. The First and Third would provide a striking force.

Having assembled the company commanders and Koskela whom he put in command of his own company, he explained the situation. Koskela studied the map.

—If we break off contact quietly and go around between those lakes we'll slip out of his hands like a dog through a gate. Ivan won't have covering parties very far from the road. As for the brook line, it can't be held. And I don't believe for a moment that he'll allow us to open up the road. We couldn't hold the line even as it's manned now, and with only the Second and the machine guns it's absolutely impossible. Anyway, we'd better be prepared to destroy both anti-tank guns.

—We've got our orders.

Koskela closed his map case with a bang.

—True. But they don't alter the situation.

—The commander knows the situation. There's no use trying to explain things to him.

—No. And that wasn't what I meant.

But despite Koskela's objection, the First and Third Companies were drawn out of the line and the Second Company spread out accordingly. Koskela took Rokka and Maatta with him, for although he knew that their machine guns would not be much use in an attack, he wanted the men, especially Rokka. And Rokka at once put Vanhala in charge of the machine gun and promised to join the riflemen in the firing line. Inspired by his example, the men behaved as in former days, with briskness and determination. There were no questions and no grumbling, for the gravity of the situation had brought out the steel in them. Briefly they had wondered what had become of Hietanen, knowing that the ambulance had been in the danger zone, but they had no time to think much of what had already happened. This evening their own lives hung too precariously in the balance. Many of the men scheduled to be left behind to hold the brook line even asked to be taken into the attacking force, and Kariluoto took a few of the best.

The deployment was completed: the Third Platoon on the left, the First on the right of the road and Kariluoto's former platoon in reserve.

Koskela had informed the company of the situation and added:

—The only thing that can get us out of this fix is our own guns and our own guts.

To Kariluoto, however, he said before setting off:

—When we start, Ivan'll start too. Speed doesn't matter much, he's been ahead of us all the time. That barrage during the day was to cover his movements. He's been there three hours, and you'll find him dug in up to his throat. The only way to save our hides is by making that pilgrimage through the woods.

—You know our orders.

—I know 'em. And I know the commander doesn't realize what he's asking. He should be opening the road from that end, but he's not doing a damn thing. It'll be even harder for us to do it. In a couple of hours you'll see what'll happen. The Second Company will be retreating onto our backs, and the First and Third will be strewn all over the woods.

Kariluoto looked away. He knew that Koskela was right, but though his courage sufficed for self-sacrifice, it stopped short of that required to ignore an order. His voice grated as he said harshly:

—Well, it's not hard to run away, but we can't. Just remember, it only hurts once.

Koskela smiled; this was the first time Kariluoto had ever spoken to him in the tone of a commander giving an order. Until now it had always been he himself who had led the way—which Koskela had often felt uncomfortable about, knowing it was still a legacy from those days at the beginning of the war.

He said no more, but when Kariluoto walked away a premonition filled Koskela's mind: That man is going to die today.

Rokka was busily stuffing his belt full of hand grenades from a half-filied box when Koskela approached him. He smiled up at the officer.

—A lot of Russkies are going to die today.

—Perhaps—and maybe a lot of us as well. But we've got to do our best.

—You don't have to try to build up my morale. I suppose you know some prayers.

—I've forgotten them.

—Well, start remembering, then. You'll be needing them soon. Vanhala's still going around laughing at the packs on everybody's back, but me, I don't feel like laughing any more.

—I think we've all got pretty long faces. By the way, it'll be up to you to choose your way. We ought to form a shock group to lead the way, but there isn't time so the best men'll have to lead and hope the rest follow.

—I'm as good a shock group as you'll have any need for, believe me.

Rokka went off humming gaily to himself. It was, of course, a pretense, for he could not help but realize how little chance they had of succeeding. But the fact that despite that he could still hum showed Koskela that here was one man whom the hopelessness of the situation would not prevent from doing his utmost.

5.

—Forward.

A soft shuffling filled the forest, but not a word was spoken, for these men knew their jobs without orders. Passing through the screen set out to cover their departure, they moved on, holding their breaths, expecting shots to ring out any minute.

Their watches showed 1900 hours. Perfect peace and quiet reigned in the forest, but farther ahead firing could be heard beyond where the road had been cut. Occasionally a dry spruce branch snapped under a boot. But no one took any notice of the twilight beauty of the forest, for all eyes were concentrated on discovering a sign of the enemy before he spotted them. A scout moved in front, twisting from tree to tree and bush to bush, trying to remain invisible. Suddenly those behind saw him fling himself down and at the same instant a nasty whine filled the air: Pee . . . peeuh . . . peeuh . . .

Prr . . . prr . . . prrrrrr . . . the scout's tommy gun replied.

—Russkies ahead. Russkies ahead . . . Dug in on the slope . . . Pass it on . . .

Silently the platoons spread out as the artillery observer called for a barrage. It came at once, but only feebly for the Stormoviks were harassing the batteries. And no sooner had it stopped than the Russian guns opened up behind them. They were so near the enemy, however, that the Russian observer dared not call for too close fire for fear of hitting his own troops, so the barrage fell about a hundred yards short. It was still rumbling behind them as Koskela yelled:

—Let's go get 'em, boys!

—Let's get 'em . . . Get 'em . . . Get 'em . . . !

The words appealed to the men and the order was passed down the line in the same words. They were determined this evening to try in earnest. Nor was this surprising, for their position was of just the sort to arouse a Finn's fighting spirit. A mighty cry echoed among the trees:

—Aaaaaah. . . . Get . . . the . . . bastards . . . hohlaaaa . . . Get 'em . . . aah . . . !

Viirila's voice rose above the rest, easily distinguishable by his private war cry. Kariluoto had once told the men that in the Thirty Years' War the Catholics' battle cry had been "Jesus Maria," and Viirila had given this a typical twist all his own. Hence, mingled with the cheering, his voice could be heard bellowing loudly: —Jesus the Bastard; Jesus the Bastard!

An ear-splitting crackling filled the forest as though an enormous bonfire had been lit and the sound magnified a hundred times over. At the foot of the slope three men fell in quick succession, and the rest were forced to take cover. The very tree trunks seemed to crackle and bang, pieces of bark flew over their heads, and short vicious hisses filled the air.

Koskela was just behind the firing line watching the situation develop. He realized at once from the Russian fire that they were entrenched along a front at least as wide and probably wider than the Finns. All that was possible, then, was a direct breakthrough. Straight ahead! But the volume of fire from the top of the gently rising slope seemed certain to doom the attempt to failure.

—Soften him up, boys, he shouted to the men nearest to him, who stepped up the tempo of their fire. Then Koskela himself spotted a machine gun, and the head behind it vanished as he sprayed it with his tommy gun. But a new head appeared almost at once and the machine gun resumed its tapping. Koskela fired again and though his bullets struck home, this time the machine gunner remained in sight. The corpse was not there long, however, and again a new helmet rose into sight. When that, too, vanished, no fourth head appeared, although Koskela was sure that the Russians on the hill knew what lay behind them if they turned to flee. Not a yard would be yielded without its dead. That much was certain from the beginning.

Things could not be allowed to stand long as they were, for it would be fatal to let the advance bog down. Something had to be done, and Koskela realized he would have to do it himself. But before he had time to plan his move, Rokka's voice rose on his right, a score of paces away:

—Hey, you with the automatic rifle! Take a crack at that pile of brush beside the pine over there. And give it hell.

—What for?

—Because there's an automatic rifle there. I'm going to try to get behind that uprooted stump, and I'll never make it if they spot me.

The automatic rifle opened up, something gray flashed, and Rokka was behind the stump he had indicated before a stream of bullets lashed the ground he had just crossed.

One glance sufficed to tell Rokka that the pile of dry alder twigs concealed a slit trench manned by three Russians—a tommy gunner and two comrades with an automatic rifle. Swiftly he took a hand grenade from his belt, feeling a schoolboyish glee, for he knew he couldn't miss. Then his eye fell on a spruce cone and he picked it up and threw it. The cone fell on the twigs and immediately one of the Russians leaped for it. But as he did so Rokka's hand grenade fell behind him. A startled cry came from the trench, the heads vanished, and the pile of twigs rose in a puff of smoke. Instantly Rokka dashed into the trench. A hand moved, and he fired downward without missing a stride.

Bullets began to fly around him, and he ducked, shouting:

—Come on now, boys . . . I'll cover you. . . . Do you know what's up ahead? Finland! . . . Come on, boys!

He estimated the direction from which the bullets were coming, and as soon as they stopped, raised his head and fired. A second trench was out of action. Then he glanced behind him, just in time to see the new platoon commander, Lieutenant Taskinen, spring to his feet shouting something and the next second crumple and fall. Then he saw the man who had covered his dash with the automatic rifle lying motionless, and farther back, another man on the ground wagging his head drunkenly.

He had just fired another burst when a body crashed into the hole beside him. It was Viirila. Viirila cleared space for himself among the dead and immediately began opening one of their packs. Finding a long uncut loaf of bread, he thrust it into his blouse.

Viirila's arrival had been noted, and bullets sent the dust flying from the rim of the slit trench. But Viirila merely drummed with his feet on the ground and roared:

—Ho, you out there . . . who the hell do you think you're shooting at? . . . Hey, you bastards . . . will you stop it, or shall I come and take your gun away from you?

—Listen, let's clear out a few of these trenches and make a hole. . . . Then we'll roll up the line. You take the right, and I'll take the left. Got any hand grenades? Rokka asked.

—I've got two or three potato mashers . . . Want some of this bread?

—We haven't time for that now.

Viirila raised his tommy gun, and a short burst felled a man who was just raising his helmeted head out of a foxhole. Then he peered out for a sight of the terrain and crouched down again. He mumbled as if giving himself orders:

—Private Viirila, you will man the hole of that Russky soldier you just executed, and then you will bring that machine-gun position at the foot of that pine under fire.

Rokka saw the machine-gun position his comrade meant; it was sheltered from their fire by a boulder. Because of that the machine gun was also unable to fire at them, but the hole Viirila intended to man lay in its line of fire. Rokka decided that when Viirila made his dash it would be up to him to make the machine gunners pull in their heads, and when Viirila rose he opened fire.

Viirila moved like a whirlwind. Under ordinary circumstances no one would have believed such a huge and slovenly fellow capable of such speed and strength. In fact his huge boots seemed to touch the ground only two or three times as he soared over the gap. And with the last stride came his war cry:

—Jesus the Bastard!

All the time Rokka kept splinters flying from the boulder with his bullets. The machine gun was silent, and that sealed its doom. Viirila's head rose from the foxhole, and his tommy gun rattled until it was empty. One of the machine gunners tried to crawl to shelter, but Viirila had already inserted a new drum, and the crawling figure fell.

Now Rokka made his dash and also reached a good firing position. Thus the two men had opened a breach in the Russian line. True, the gap was no more than thirty yards wide, but it was adequate. Koskela saw immediately that Rokka and Viirila had set the stage for an assault, and taking the lead himself, ordered his men to charge. It was precisely the right psychological moment for action. The men had seen what their two comrades had accomplished and rose to the charge cheered by that example.

Hand grenades crashed, foxholes and slit trenches were fiercely contested at close quarters, and a quarter of an hour later Koskela's company was on the crest of the ridge. But of the sixty-eight men who had started, only fifty-one still lived.

They reached Major Sarastie's command post to find his dead body stripped to his underwear. And here they were surprised by a heavy counterattack, which they repelled only by a desperate effort. Maatta and Vanhala had exhausted all the machine-gun belts they had with them by the time the attack ceased.

6.

Kariluoto crouched beside the wreck of the ambulance. The smell of the corpses was sickening. The two men caught inside had burned almost to cinders, but Hietanen's body and that of the recruit had only been singed enough to burn their clothes off.

The First Company had also succeeded in advancing a little as the Russians had had to draw back after Koskela's attack drove them from their positions on the other side of the road. But now their resistance had stiffened and both sides were locked in fierce exchange of fire.

Casualties were heavy, but for once the men could not be accused of lacking enterprise. The company commander, Lieutenant Pokki, fell almost at once. He had made the mistake of shouting to some of his men who had come to a halt:

—Go on, boys! There's damn few Russkies left out there—and they're sick of it.

—Then you go, damn you, if that's all there is to it, the reply came. Angrily the lieutenant had rushed to take the lead and within seconds fell with a bullet through his throat.

Now a decisive step had become essential. The firing was slackening noticeably and Kariluoto knew from experience what that meant: the men had sought cover and were firing at random, their initiative all but gone. A report had come in from Koskela that he was being counterattacked, and Kariluoto listened apprehensively to the savage shouting that mingled with the sharp crackle of small-arms fire.

Something had to be done. Should he withdraw? Assemble the battalion and break away into the forest? What about the colonel's order? And then there was the message just received from the commander of the Second Company saying that contrary to expectations the Russians were quiet all along the brook line. Yet it would be difficult to press the attack. Close beside him three corpses lay in a row, and a wounded man was shrieking as a stretcher bearer dragged him to shelter. And even as he looked, a man came creeping out of the line, holding his side from which blood was pouring.

Kariluoto felt the weight of his responsibility for his men hanging on him. But because he had to he swallowed his uncertainty and shouted his order:

—All right, men, we're going to chase the Russkies right into the lake. Fourth Platoon! Join the company.

To break off the attack would have rendered the sacrifices already made useless. And besides, Koskela needed support. Attack it had to be. There were but two alternatives: either master the situation, or else . . . no detour through the wilds but death.

The Fourth platoon spread out in open order and Kariluoto sent it straight ahead into the depleted line of the First Company in the hope that this reinforcement would help get the advance under way again.

Something of Kariluoto's mood must have infected the platoon, for, though the men had seen the slope devour their comrades, they seemed undaunted, as if they felt that they had no right to spare themselves. They knew that Kariluoto had held them in reserve because his link to them was closer than to the other units. They were the straw he clutched at last in desperation, and now everything depended on them. They would not fail him.

Kariluoto himself took his place in their line and a fierce yell rang out. Within seconds individual sounds were indistinguishable in the din.

Napoleon and the Old Guard at Waterloo—indeed the comparison was not as farfetched as it may seem. Three years ago this very platoon had stormed the first Russian bunker line, and there were still men here who had fought in that battle: Ukkola, Rekomaa, Lampioinen, Heikinaro and others.

The First Company swept to the attack, firing from the hip, keeping up a continuous roar though they had not yet seen the enemy. There was only the hail of lead whipping the ground and the foliage.

—That's the way, Ukkola! Kariluoto shouted, seeing the man bounding forward, firing as he went. Then he gave a startled cry as Ukkola dropped his tommy gun and fell heavily to his knees behind the shelter of a hummock.

—Ukkola.

—In the chest . . . I've had it . . . Oooh God, it hurts.

Within seconds the medical corpsmen were at this side, dragging Ukkola to cover. Cursing, Kariluoto pressed on again but soon even he had to take cover, for now they were in sight of the Russians and Rekomaa and Heikinaro fell in quick succession. The men hugged the ground, desperately seeking shelter until Kariluoto feared the advance had bogged down permanently. Shouting, he sprang to his feet and, dashing to the shelter of a pine, fired desperately but ineffectually at the well-entrenched Russians.

Around him more cries went up for stretcher bearers. A First Company man rose to his feet to hurl a hand grenade, and Kariluoto clearly saw the bullet strike him and heard the man gasp as he died. From the right came word that the section leader had fallen.

Desperately Kariluoto shouted exhortations, but the men remained motionless. What was the matter with them? Then he realized that in the past ten minutes the line had dwindled almost to extinction. No one was close to him on either side, and as he watched two more wounded men began to creep out of the line farther off.

Still the Russians fired, persisting even when not a Finn was in sight. Bullets drummed into the moss, and a sense of hopelessness swept over Kariluoto. The attack had failed. Even as he lowered his head in dejection a panting messenger came streaking through the trees: the First Company also had been unable to advance. Losses were exceedingly heavy.

The explosions echoed in Kariluoto's ears until they became one confused, bewildering din. Dimly he thought: I've killed off the company. I drove them to their deaths . . . I knew we couldn't succeed, but I sent them to die. . . .

Behind him the firing was desultory. God knows there were not many left to fire. Kariluoto was aghast. His old platoon was little more than a name, and the Second Platoon of the First Company which had attacked at the same spot was no better off.

The only consolation was the arrival of a messenger from Koskela reporting the repulse of the counterattack and describing the piles of Russian dead before Maatta's machine gun. But, Koskela added, he would not be able to advance any farther and thus regarded the operation as having failed. He advised Kariluoto to wait until they could join forces for a new attempt.

—Wait. For what?

Kariluoto gave way completely to despair. He could expect no aid from Koskela. Both faced equally strong forces and the Russians were everywhere strong enough so the Finns could not transfer troops from one sector to another. If they could not break through now, they would not be able to do so later either.

He withdrew a little ways and walked behind the line to the right. Perhaps he could still make one last try here with the Third Platoon. Its officer was wounded, and Kariluoto took command in person.

—Let's go, boys. One more try.

Not a voice answered, but the men began to prepare quietly for a charge.

—Forward.

Slowly the line moved forward, but the Russian fire rose again to full fury, and soon Kariluoto once again saw the advance come to a halt.

—We can't stop . . . We can't stop . . .

Blindly he stumbled forward, his face deathly white, his voice choked and stiff.

—Once more, boys . . .

When the bullet hit him he felt a strange and immense relief. For three seconds he was aware that he was dying, but during those seconds he feared death less than at any time in his life.

Chapter XV

I.

It fell to Koskela to report Kariluoto's death to the commander of the Second Company and ask him to take over. Nor was he surprised when the commander bade him take the post, for it was far from a tempting command.

—If you'll agree to pull back by the route between the ponds, I'll do it, Koskela bargained.

The commander, however, demurred. They would first have to get in touch with headquarters by radio.

Koskela was in a rage. He knew that his men could not continue the attack, but he also knew Colonel Karjula was easily capable of ordering them to keep it up. Left to himself, he would have disengaged the enemy and communicated with headquarters only when he knew that the men could no longer be sent to their deaths. He knew enough about Colonel Karjula to suspect that the colonel would instinctively declare a true account of the situation to be exaggerated.

Nor was he disappointed. But he stuck to his guns, saying bluntly that the battalion would not continue the attack, at any rate not under his command. Instantly Karjula exploded, screaming that he had a covering force out on the Russian's west flank which would be inundated if the battalion withdrew.

The argument was still in full swing when sounds of furious fighting came from the direction of the brook line. Within seconds the telephone rang and the Second Company reported it was under heavy attack. Koskela passed the information on to the colonel, and this time, though his voice was wrathful, the order came to withdraw:

—Bring all your equipment with you.

With a sigh of relief Koskela put down the radio telephone and called to the artillery second lieutenant:

That's that. But just in case, let's forget this thing for a while.

Then Koskela went to work. The orders he gave were clear and concise as he ordered the First Company back a short distance, withdrew the Third Company completely from the south side of the road and set it up to form a defensive line on its north side along a front which faced partly on the road, partly on the brook line. Having thus created a horseshoe line, he ordered all the wounded assembled.

One of Kariluoto's men asked hesitatingly:

—What about the dead? We brought the captain's body along.

—We've got enough to do to save the living.

Koskela did not even glance at Kariluoto's body, nor, indeed, at any of the dead. This was no time for pious thoughts. All that now concerned him was the battalion; he was determined to save what remained of it no matter what might happen.

He was frankly troubled over the situation of the Second Company. It seemed impossible that it could succeed in withdrawing under heavy Russian pressure. Koskela knew that in such circumstances an orderly withdrawal could easily degenerate into panicky flight. He could not even send help, for he had to hold a line of retreat open if the Second was to withdraw in peace.

Luckily the men on the south side of the road managed to extricate themselves and reach safety before Russian tanks swept aside the defenses along the road. The tanks destroyed one of the anti-tank guns along with its crew, but the other went flying through the air after its crew had piled everything explosive they could lay their hands on beneath it. A small charge in the barrel would have sufficed, but that would not have been as dramatic.

Four machine guns were left behind, and a few wounded, but considering the conditions Koskela was satisfied. He sent the Second Company north, to act as a spearhead, while the First and Third companies held the loop of the horseshoe around the machine gunners, the trench mortar and anti-tank gun crews and the artillery spotters.

—Four of you take each stretcher and we'll toss the machine guns in a pond. But we'll keep one as a memento.

Koskela glanced around and saw Maatta leaning on the barrel of his machine gun.

—Do you want to take yours along?

—It's all the same to me.

It was as if Maatta's machine gun were destined to be the one kept. From the first days of the war Maatta had tended it lovingly, first as gunner, then as NCO in charge. No one had ever heard him ask anyone else to carry it. And although Maatta's answer was noncommittal, Koskela knew that he had conferred on him an honor no decoration could equal. He had demonstrated before them all his belief that Maatta could carry a machine gun better than anyone else.

The men hesitated at first. The idea of throwing away the weapons they had lugged all through the war at the cost of so much despairing effort seemed incredible.

Finally Koskela angrily snatched up the nearest machine gun. A splash and the weapon vanished. Koskela's irritation was as unusual as his abandoning the machine guns, but it put an end to the men's hesitation and the guns went hurtling into the pond.

Russian tanks were rumbling on the road, and the rearguard was under fire from enemy infantry as Koskela set a course due north toward the cluster of nameless small ponds through which he had wanted Kariluoto to withdraw in the first place. A First Company patrol had established the presence of a large Russian force on the north side of the road, and Koskela wanted at all costs to avoid becoming engaged with it for the battalion was in no condition for action of any sort. His only desire was to lead the battalion to safety and that called for a long detour.

He knew, of course, that their escape would be only temporary, for they would soon have to fight again. But even so there was nothing to be gained by boldness today. The past three hours had been the bloodiest in the battalion's history. And for the first time most of their dead had had to be abandoned. Koskela remembered Hietanen's charred body. Even the bandage over his eyes had burned to ashes.

A groan broke from his clenched lips.

2.

Vanhala, Rahikainen, Honkajoki and Sihvonen carried Ukkola on a rough litter.

He was in severe pain. The bullet had entered through the breast pocket of his blouse, and though at first the wound had not seemed dangerous, as soon as they set off Ukkola began coughing and spitting blood. They tried to comfort him, but Ukkola refused to accept their reassuring words—more than once he himself had knelt beside a dying comrade whispering promises of speedy recovery. He was not really afraid of death; it was the continuous pain that was hard to bear.

To console him, Honkajoki described how he himself had been wounded and what a delight the military hospital had been. Heedless of his listener's restless movements and agonized breathing Honkajoki told his story.

—All the prettiest girls are there as nurses' aides. They want to be heroines. That's why they don't mind washing a soldier's behind. Haven't the boys risked their lives, too? That curly blond hair of yours will work miracles, so try to hold out a little while. Carefully, boys. Don't jar him.

—All right, let's take a rest.

Vanhala slumped on the grass and mopped his face with his cap. It was midnight, yet the sky was still not completely dark. A fine mist rose from the hollows. Vanhala's face twisted in a grimace as though, despite all the night's events, he found himself still able to smile.

—Having suffered slight losses but still triumphantly undefeated, our army withdraws to new defensive positions.

Now it was Ukkola's turn to smile. He had kept watch with Vanhala for hundreds of hours. He spoke in agonized gasps:

—Oooh . . . urrrh . . . While . . . aah . . . ooh . . . While . . . we can . . . go . . . go on . . . they'll keep saying . . . uun . . . aah . . . undefeated . . . aah . . .

—Don't try to talk. Try to rest.

—It's no use . . . uun . . . so long as there's . . . a man left . . . to slaughter . . . work . . . they'll say . . . undefeated . . . aah . . . When will they say . . . aah . . . defeated?

Honkajoki wiped the blood from Ukkola's lips.

Vanhala sensed that despite the great pain Ukkola wanted them to regard him as the same old Ukkola, so he said, giggling:

—Indomitable despite its losses, laughing proudly in the face of death, the army looks beyond immediate defeat to the day of ultimate victory. Khee-hee . . . Hear that? We can't lose.

They had heard the words a few days ago in a broadcast, and despite his pain Ukkola was amused at the faithfulness with which Vanhala had preserved the phrases in his memory.

They set off again, but they had not gone far when one of the wounded died. Carefully the stretcher bearers placed the body at the foot of a tree and went off to relieve other squads. The dead man had been hit in the stomach by a shell splinter and taken along although obviously dying.

Later another of the wounded began to rave wildly:

—Don't . . . don't leave me . . . If they attack . . . Promise you won't leave me . . . Don't leave me behind. . . .

But despite his screams the bearers gave him no assurances. They toiled on, gasping and puffing, and each time the terror-stricken man tried to rise on the stretcher they pushed him down again.

Ukkola seemed to be in greater pain, and Vanhala undid his greatcoat and carefully covered him with it. Ukkola hid his face with his arm, and every now and then a groan escaped him, followed usually by a curse. More and more blood came from his mouth, his breathing grew more labored, and he shivered more and more violently, until they had heaped everything that could serve as a blanket on him.

Four years of semi-starvation had failed to crush his vitality. Ukkola had been an outstanding athlete and had acquired a physique and stamina which even death found hard to overcome.

They reached their first objective and now at last Koskela established contact with the colonel, who was literally foaming at the mouth. No sooner had the battalion withdrawn from the road than Russian tanks had overwhelmed the roadblock and broken through. It meant the retreat had to be continued, and the battalion would have to prolong its detour. The colonel set the point at which Koskela was to arrive on the road and roared:

—This is an order! That little berrying jaunt you've been on ends there. Do you understand?

Koskela listened unperturbed. Karjula's rebukes seldom affected him, for though he was not given to vanity he was fully aware that few men could have brought the battalion back in as good condition as it was in now.

The march went on, but now the stretcher bearers were almost exhausted, for the uneven ground multiplied their task many times over. Once one of the men carrying the stretcher in front of Ukkola's fell, causing the wounded man to be thrown to the ground with a shriek of agony. The bearer rose, spat and angrily seized the shaft again and for a while his fury helped step up the pace.

Ukkola's bearers no longer spoke; they were too exhausted. Silent, intent solely on making progress, they struggled onward as Ukkola groaned and fought for breath in constantly increasing pain.

At three in the morning, as dawn was banishing the twilight, they paused to rest. The bearers were watching the scouts moving on their flank when a shot rang out almost beside them. Startled, they turned in time to see Ukkola's body fall back on the litter. He had shot himself with the rifle Sihvonen had left leaning on the stretcher.

They would have liked to take Ukkola's body to the road but were forced to abandon the idea because of the need to relieve exhausted bearers, and because Koskela insisted on haste. Instead, they hastily grubbed soil from the bottom of a small depression with entrenching tools, laid the canvas-wrapped body in the shallow grave and shoveled a little earth and moss over it.

Even Honkajoki was serious now. Death had been such a constant presence that night that nonsense seemed out of place. As they shoveled, Rahikainen said:

—He could have stood it. But every man adds up his balance sheet his own way.

—You know, Ukkola was the last of the boys in the Fourth Platoon who left training camp when we did, said Vanhala. —I remember one time when we were recruits Ukkola came back from a march with a big rock in his haversack. He'd cheated making up his pack, and Kariluoto put the rock in instead.

—He was a pisshead then, that Kariluoto, said Sihvonen. —But he turned out to be a man.

They left Ukkola's grave without even saying a prayer. But as he turned to go, Sihvonen burst out bitterly:

—Finns are dying everywhere now. It's all over for us.

3.

Transports streaming away from the front clogged every road.

It was not yet dawn but the light was already strong enough to make the drivers fear air attacks. The carts were camouflaged with foliage, and branches had been stuck into the horses' harness.

—Let's space out the intervals, shouted Sinkkonen, as he tried to ride his bicycle along the roadside to pass the carts. Lammio, too, was on the move. Karjula having entrusted to him the organization of the transport withdrawal.

Korpela, the new *Landsturm* man, walked beside the cart he was driving. He had ransacked the cart for officers' valises or other baggage, but the previous driver had thrown all such things away, leaving nothing on which he could vent his wrath.

Then Sinkkonen in passing bade him keep an eye out for aircraft, and instantly Korpela turned on him furiously:

—I suppose I've got lots of time for sky watching! Pedal your little bike, you bastard. Take good care of it, you'll need it to get away.

Some time later he passed a solitary Lotta standing beside the road. Raili Kotilainen had not found a husband on the campaign, but she had made up for this by taking an extraordinary number of lovers. It seemed years since the day the adjutant had taken a snapshot of her beside a captured Russian trench mortar in the early days of the war. Then Raili had still been a glowing maiden, but like everybody else she had been worn out by war. Bedraggled and dirty she had slid down the social ladder, ending up at last with an anti-tank private, and causing Sarastie to draw on his meager store of Latin to comment: *Sic transit gloria mundi.*

Now her bicycle had broken down, and she was feeling tired and sorry for herself. The passing men did not even bother to disguise their contempt, and she was forced to endure their scurrilous shouts. Then, seeing Korpela, she decided to beg his aid, feeling that a man as old as he was might show some fatherly sympathy. With an attempt at a smile she approached him.

—Please, I can't ride this and I'm so tired. Won't you take me on your cart?

A Lotta in the front lines! Her effect on Korpela was that of a red rag to a bull.

—I've never yet carted dung on Sunday. And sure as hell I'm not going to start now.

As luck would have it, Lammio overheard his words. Bidding the girl climb on the next cart, he screamed at the *Landsturm* man.

—Private Korpela!

—I hear you.

—What did you tell that girl just now?

—I said what I said. I've got enough of a load, without carting whores.

—Look out, Korpela! You'll go too far. One more word and it'll go badly for you.

—Don't worry that head of yours, you goddamned popinjay.

I've gotten along without your advice this long, and I can keep on doing without it.

Now at last Lammio's suppressed rage burst forth.

—You're under arrest! You there—a couple of you men get over here at once. Take this man's rifle.

There were no volunteers. Nor were any needed, for suddenly a cry came from the rear:

—Planes coming . . . Air raid . . . Stormoviks . . . Take cover!

Immediately horses were driven off the road into the forest and all traffic vanished. Except, that is, for Korpela. A wheel of his cart stuck in the ditch and the horse was unable to pull it out. The beast pulled and jerked dutifully, but the treacherous mud in the bottom of the ditch held the wheel ever tighter. Korpela pulled and lifted until his eyes bulged, but his efforts were in vain, and the cart remained mired in the ditch.

The explosions of bombs from the planes could now be heard plainly farther back on the road.

Vo . . . ow . . . rooommm . . .

A plane roared past, a burst from its machine guns stirring up dust along the road. Others followed swiftly behind.

— Help me lift it, you damn bastards.

But despite Korpela's shouts, no one came to his aid. Most of the drivers had, indeed, left their horses and plunged deeper into the forest.

—All right, run . . . go ahead and run. Run like hell! Leave the poor horse here to be killed . . .

Overhead the planes were circling for a new run. Bombs crashed and machine guns crackled unceasingly. The angry barking of an airplane cannon sounded and suddenly splinters flew from the backboard of Korpela's cart sending him diving for cover, only to rise as soon as the plane had passed. It was then that Lammio, having escorted the Lotta to safety, approached Korpela's cart. He held himself erect, seemingly oblivious to the attacking aircraft, and when Korpela saw this he was almost beside himself with rage. It was as if Lammio was challenging his own bravery.

— Keep away from here, you bastard! I don't need any help from the likes of you.

But Lammio continued to approach, until Korpela suddenly threw down the reins and stood in the officer's way.

— Get me transferred right away! I want to move to another unit.

— What the devil are you talking about?

— Jesus Christ, I'd dive into the earth to get away from you! I'd go all the way to Hell if only I was sure I wouldn't ever have to set eyes on you again.

— Korpela, I warn you for the last time. Defeat makes your kind of man bold, but don't make the mistake of thinking that the army will let anyone spit in its face even if it should lose the war.

— Ha! Who's spitting in whose face? You're the one who's been spitting in people's faces for years. And stop clutching at that pistol or I'll throw it and you after it into the forest . . .

Korpela turned away as another plane approached. As he walked back to his cart he fairly hissed:

— Now . . . now I know what a gentleman's like! I didn't quite believe it, but now I know.

He tore the harness off the horse, still raving:

— To hell with it, let the damn cart stay there. Torturing poor dumb beasts as though they'd done someone harm . . . Go on. Why should you stay here to be tortured? Go on.

The plane came roaring up from the rear, tongues of flame darting from it. Korpela stood alone in the ditch, shaking his fist and yelling up at the aircraft:

— Go on, you too, you bastard! Shoot like hell now you've got the chance. Get it off your chest, you son of a bitch.

The aircraft lifted, passed and swooped upward, its tail flashing. Below, the horse bolted in terror and galloped into the forest. Korpela was dragged along, his hands caught in the reins, until they slipped off and he lay motionless on his back. A pool of blood began to form beneath his body.

4.

The planes had disappeared by the time the battalion reached the road. Koskela had radioed for ambulances, and now they began arriving. Quickly the wounded were lifted into them, and they roared away.

And now Lieutenant Colonel Uuno Eemeli Karjula arrived on the scene. He was a bull-necked, stocky man who always seemed to be shouting. His face was deeply lined and from the corners of his mouth a hard, cruel line ran to his jaw.

He had gone into the Winter War a captain and won his promotion to major and then to lieutenant colonel by his personal bravery and irresistible energy. His deficiencies as a tactician were admitted, but the brass obviously felt his dominant personality made up for that. He had earned a reputation as a good officer, which he undoubtedly was, but no one ever worked with or under him without eventually hating or fearing him. Sarastie had once gone so far as to say to his adjutant after a quarrel with Karjula:

— He's the kind who if it weren't for the army would be a criminal. Just plain luck determines which side of the prison bars they stand on.

Lately defeat had demoralized him completely. He was angry not only because the entire army was retreating but because by withdrawing, the battalion had endangered his whole task force. If they withdrew only a few more miles, his position would be completely untenable. The dead Sarastie was therefore treated to a barrage of insults, whether he heard them or not.

—God damn him, where were the man's reserves? Sitting on his backside on a road without covering forces . . .

Karjula ignored the fact that he himself had approved Sarastie's dispositions and promised him a pioneer company as reserves, but had instead kept the company on road work. It was even now helping to block the highway along with other hastily scraped up forces which altogether were capable of no more than a weak delaying action.

Koskela made his report to Karjula, who could hardly wait for him to finish. Despite the many men within earshot the colonel shouted:

—And now, thanks to your hasty evaluation of the situation we're about to have our flank destroyed. And as if that wasn't enough, you brought the battalion out through the ponds for no reason whatever. You wasted two precious hours, and we lost our best positions.

Koskela tried to ignore Karjula's words, knowing that no amount of reason could dissipate the man's fury. But his calm voice seemed only to increase the colonel's rage.

—You have to remember that in the circumstances I could not afford to keep one flank of the battalion in touch with the enemy. The need to move the wounded to safety made our position too vulnerable for that. And, on top of that, the men were too demoralized by defeat to fight well.

— I know all about the situation and I don't need your explanations. But you must realize that the battalion lost out only when you admitted defeat. Now I want you to reorganize the battalion immediately and position it along the edge of the swamp. But this time keep a reserve strong enough to use on either flank. There'll be some new anti-tank guns coming up soon, and I'm doing my best to procure rockets. You'll be in charge of the battalion until Lammio has organized our supplies, then you can take command of the Third Company. Lieutenant Ovaska will take over the machine guns.

— I gave orders to dump the machine guns in a pond so the crews could carry the wounded. I only kept one.

Karjula's teeth gnashed. — In a pond? Dumped? The . . . mach . . . ine . . . guns . . . gone!

Karjula would not have been so enraged if one part of his brain had not been forced to admit that Koskela had acted correctly. But that was precisely what he did not want to admit, for it would imply recognition of defeat.

— By God, Lieutenant! . . . Deliberate aid to the enemy . . . I ordered you to bring out your equipment. Machine gunners are machine gunners, not litter bearers.

Then Karjula himself seemed to realize that he was saying what should be left unsaid. In an awkward effort to undo his words he said:

— Well, you can save your reputation by holding this line. Get some steel into your spine.

He had observed that there were witnesses to his outburst, and now he turned his anger on them, enraged that they had heard the stupid things he had said to Koskela.

— And you, you men—what are you, sheep or Finnish soldiers? Your duty is to hold a position or to die. Jesus Christ, you're wearing the same uniform as the men who defended Summa and Taipale! They knew how to die; all you know is how to run. Damn it, you ought to be ashamed of yourselves. Any man who leaves his post after this will find out that there's a paragraph in the military code that concerns him. No more playing about. We neither ask nor give quarter. Is that clear? . . . Then get to your positions.

Honkajoki rolled his eyes, his mouth open in feigned amazement. Then, mimicking the colonel's voice, he asked:

— Corporal Vanhala, are you a sheep or a Finnish soldier?

— I'm the world's best ram, kee-hee . . .

Abruptly they were interrupted as Koskela began making his defensive dispositions.

The men demanded food, but there was none although they had been promised new supplies. Silent and sullen, they set about digging foxholes as a covering force crept off through their lines. Pioneers mined the road and some of the ground on either side of it, but the mines were too few to make the minefield effective. There was far too much open space between the swamp and the road.

Soon Lammio returned to take command of the battalion, and Koskela returned to the Third Company. He was very reticent and seemed lost in thought as he gave his orders in a low voice that was tired and listless. Close beside the road Maatta's machine gun was in position beside a bog, while the rest of the platoon served as a regular rifle platoon, with Rokka in charge. As he came down the line, Koskela stopped behind Maatta's gun and sat on the ground, his back to a tree.

For a long time he sat as though petrified, his broad jaw and high cheekbones standing out beneath his tanned skin. He had lost weight, and there were deep circles beneath his eyes. The day before yesterday had been his thirty-first birthday. He had remembered it only yesterday. Not that it mattered.

The world had fallen silent for a moment as all sounds of fighting had died away. Such moments came only rarely of late, for the Russians had been redoubling their efforts during the past few days.

Koskela leaned his head against the tree and let his eyes close. The sun was warm on cheeks which weather and weariness had made tender and rough. His mouth was parched, and his empty stomach felt weak. Then a picture of Karjula began to form before his eyes. Koskela did not feel insulted by the berating he had received, for he knew perfectly well that it was impossible for Karjula to suffer a disappointment without taking it out on somebody else. If he hadn't been made the scapegoat someone else would have; Karjula would never lack pretexts. So he forgot all about it, and then he forgot everything else that was going on. He was conscious only of a sense of warmth and lassitude. The present faded and he lay in a state between sleep and waking. Dimly he heard voices coming from the direction of Maatta's machine gun. One of the voices was Hietanen's and Koskela felt vaguely troubled. Something was wrong but he could not think what. Then one voice said something, and Hietanen laughed. Koskela's puzzlement grew. What was there to laugh at? Something was certainly wrong. Hietanen's face was visible to him now, a charred and bloodied bandage covering the upper part of it.

— Have a smoke?

Koskela opened his eyes with a start. Why did Hietanen look so strange standing there, a cigarette pack in his hand? Maatta was surprised to see Koskela staring at him as though he had not understood his offer of a cigarette. Then Koskela relaxed with a sigh and took the proffered cigarette:

— Ah . . . Thanks. I guess I fell asleep.

— I saw that. But there's tanks prowling around out there. They don't intend to let us rest.

Maatta sat down beside him and Koskela leaned back against the tree again. His dream troubled him. What had made him mistake Maatta for Hietanen? His mind was full of an unrest for which he could find no reason.

— I wonder how long I'll last around here.

Now where did that thought come from? He did not ordinarily allow such thoughts to enter his mind. Then he remembered his thought the last time he saw Kariluoto alive: He's going to die today.

Had he almost reached the end of his own life? What put such thoughts in a man's mind? It was probably all fatigue. He'd been dreaming. Hietanen had been dead before the flames reached him. But the men inside the ambulance! It must have been horrible.

Pee peeoo peeoooooooo . . .

— Well, here we go. Let's keep our eyes open.

5.

Koskela lay in a foxhole as the ground shook and swayed. Something came humming through the air and thumped on the edge of the hole.

— How the hell do they manage to move their guns so quickly?

Koskela raised his head cautiously only to pull it down again as he saw a pillar of smoke rise nearby. Dirt fell rattling into his hole.

As soon as the explosions ceased, Koskela heard the familiar shouts of the attacking Russians. Rifles were already crackling, and on the left Maatta's machine gun hammered away. As he ran crouched behind their positions, Koskela saw three tanks approaching along the road, their machine guns lashing the ground beside the road this side of the mine barrier. Koskela passed men who were nervously shooting at the tanks as if their rifles could penetrate their armor. A man fell and from beyond him a distressed voice cried:

— They'll flatten us. Boys, they'll flatten us!

— Stay where you are! They'll flatten nothing. The road's mined.

Koskela shouted as loudly as his lungs permitted so he would be heard above the roar of battle. He knew that words that could not be clearly understood were liable to spread fear. A few anti-tank men were in the roadside ditch, and Koskela crawled to their side.

— Got your HE charges?

— Yes, but we can't get near enough . . .

— Let me give it a try. A couple of you come with me.

— You'd do better to wait in a slit trench. This ditch's too shallow.

Koskela knew the advice was sound, but he also knew that if he did so he would be too late. The men would be in full flight long before the tanks reached the trenches.

A high explosive charge was no longer a very effective means of dealing with a tank now that their armor protection had been improved, but there was no alternative.

Koskela set off, followed by two anti-tank men, as the first tank stopped and then turned off onto the roadside, its crew apparently certain that they would not encounter anti-tank weapons. And in fact they would have been used by now if there had been any. The tank drove ahead boldly, its machine guns raking both sides of the road.

Before it lay a bend in the ditch caused by a rock which it had to skirt. If only he could reach that bend. . . .

With a last breathless dash Koskela reached it and squeezed down to wait as the tank came on, firing steadily. He tried to keep as calm as possible, knowing from experience that in situations like this planning made all the difference. A man must not act too quickly. It was best to forget where he was and just throw the charge without thinking of the danger.

I can make it now, he thought. Then in one motion he jerked the fuse, rose to a crouch and threw with a swinging underhand toss which dropped the charge right at the base of the tank's turret. It rolled onto the armor protecting the track and then exploded with a roar. Instantly the tank made an awkward half-turn and stopped, its track broken. But Koskela never saw that. A tommy gunner on the other side of the road riddled him the second after the charge left his hand. Awkwardly Koskela tried once to raise himself on his elbows, then collapsed into the ditch.

The remaining two tanks stopped for a moment, then came rumbling past the wrecked one. The men in the firing line saw that Koskela had not risen, and as the tanks approached they began to fall back. That started it.

Karjula had not left Lammio's command post. He knew that somehow he had to get this road blocked or there would be nothing left of Task Force Karjula. Where in hell could that anti-tank gun be? The crew were probably all goddamn Reds. What have planes got to do with transporting a gun, he wondered. Aircraft are up in the air. They can't keep a road blocked.

His thoughts were interrupted as the telephone rang and an excited voice reported the positions overrun as well as Koskela's death. Most of the Third Company was in a panicky rout. With an oath Karjula hurried out, pausing only to order Lammio to organize a new defense line with the aid of the reserve.

By the time Karjula reached the battalion it was in full retreat. Stopping the first men he saw, he bellowed loudly:

— You goddamn flock of sheep, get back to your stations! I'll shoot any bastard who takes another step!

But the frightened men hardly paused in their flight. Only one even bothered to pant:

— What can we do? . : . There's no anti-tank guns. Koskela got himself killed trying to stop them.

Karjula's pistol was in his hand, and the men closest to him stopped fearfully and took cover in the ditch. Farther off, however, the men went on running.

— There're coming . . . the panzers are coming!

The cry gave new impetus to the panic, and one of the men Karjula had stopped took to his heels again, causing the colonel to lose his last shred of reason. Farther off still another man was walking off in defiance of his shout, a tommy gun slung over his shoulder.

— Halt! You there. Stop! For the last time. Halt!

The man was Viirila, who pretended not to hear and continued on his way. He was not running but walking, and slowly at that. And since he was not running, he felt the order did not concern him. He had left the positions with the rest, but his unhurried gait was intended to show that he was not afraid of the Russians, or of Karjula.

— Halt! Where do you think you're going, soldier?

— To Hell! And you can go there, too!

Viirila bellowed out his answer in a voice which added to Karjula's fury. A lust to kill seemed to sweep over the colonel. The violence within him that had always been seeking an outlet now rose to the surface, and he was powerless to control it.

Viirila transferred the tommy gun to the crook of his arm, certain that Karjula would not shoot. But his movement gave the final impetus that turned impulse into action, and Karjula deliberately shot him in the middle of the chest. Viirila sank slowly to his knees, then toppled over.

Karjula's breath came in sobs as he walked blindly to and fro. Then he gained control of his voice:

— Men. Under the articles of war I condemned a traitor to death. Men, Finland's fate depends on you . . . There's no time for play, now. Every man of you who runs will meet the same fate.

The men looked at each other aghast. Karjula's behavior had completely effaced the effect his deed might otherwise have had. And to crown it all, the victim had been Viirila, the company's best fighter.

Gradually the men's surprise turned to anger. Lips drew taut, and hands gripped the stocks of weapons. A little ways aw^v a man even aimed his rifle at Karjula but did not shoot. Instead, from the lips of yet another man came an agonized cry:

—Come on, you Red bastards . . . Come on, smash through and take over everything . . . we're murdering our own people here.

The man howled like a maniac, his voice that of a child beyond itself with terror.

His cries seemed at last to bring Karjula to his senses. But there was no other course open for him in the situation he had created except to go on. Viirila was the second man he had shot. The man who was shouting would certainly have been the third if the Russian tanks had not saved him. A shell hissed from behind the bend in the road and crashed at Karjula's feet, sending him sprawling on his back in the middle of the road.

The flight began again.

Karjula recovered consciousness almost at once. He tried desperately to rise to his feet, but fell again, for his left leg was almost torn off. He was on his stomach now, the upper part of his body supported by his arms, roaring:

— Back to your positions! Goddamn you all, halt! Help me, you goddamned cowards. Back to your positions, and give me a tommy gun.

There was no hint of weakness in his voice. It was as commanding and angry as ever as he continued to try to rise, cursing wildly, bellowing with rage and pain. His struggle was like that of a wounded beast of prey in its last extremity, full of an all-encompassing rage and a bottomless despair born of impotence.

Heedless of his bellowing the men streamed past until Rokka arrived, one of the last to leave. He had not seen what had happened, but he could guess it from the clues scattered around. Karjula was now barely conscious, and a Russian tank was sweeping the area with its machine gun as Rokka seized the colonel in his arms and bore him out of the zone of immediate danger. Carefully he laid him on the ground.

— I'll be damned if I'll do anything more for him. He's beyond human pity. As far as I'm concerned he can stay here.

Fortunately, two Second Company officers took charge of Karjula and carried him until they found two medical corpsmen whom they impressed to take over their burden. The corpsmen bore him away, loudly cursing all officers in general as they did so.

The battalion was in full retreat with Lammio's rearguard joining the rest after only a slight skirmish. Indeed, the entire task force had completely abandoned its positions. The men's morale was so low that the battalion might well have disintegrated completely if they had not reached the old frontier just then.

Across it, the men's spirits seemed magically to rise, and now at long last they had a chance to rest. Naturally no investigation of Viirila's death was ever held. And if one had been held, the only official result would have been rebukes for the men's complaints and their failure to go to Karjula's aid. But even this last could not be too seriously pressed, for during panics wounded had been left behind many times before this.

When, after a rest, the battalion was ordered to counterattack, it did so with remarkable vigor and sent the surprised Russians reeling back. Once again the men were full of energy and enterprise. This was Finnish soil under their feet now, and they would die before yielding it.

Fighting raged along the frontier defense line, and it did not take the Russian commanders long to realize that they were beating their heads against a stone wall.

Chapter XVI

I.

Rokka was afraid.

Ceaselessly he wandered from one flank of the platoon's positions to the other. The Third Platoon was no longer his, a new home-front second lieutenant having arrived that day to take command, but a sense of responsibility still weighed heavily on him, for a difficult situation lay ahead. The platoon had its back to a river across which defensive positions were being dug. Their task was to hold a bridgehead as long as possible to allow the positions to be fortified. The only remaining bridge across the river lay to their right.

Ever since the machine-gun company had dumped its weapons, it had been functioning as an ordinary rifle company with only Maatta's gun for support. A couple of days before, the platoon had received three more recruits as replacements, and two more men had been drawn from the kitchen staff. This, in Rokka's opinion, was too high a percentage of inexperienced soldiers. The recruits were no better nor worse than the older men, for a man acquires his nature at birth and not in the army, but an inexperienced man is always more liable to panic, and that was precisely what had to be avoided in the present situation at all costs.

Wolf's Paw lay in his foxhole puffing tobacco smoke to drive away the mosquitoes circling around his head, and Rokka called to him in passing:

— Hey, Wolf, remember how we used to go swimming in the Vuoksi when we were kids?

— Do I? We'll never see that place again, Antti. There's nothing but corpses swimming there now. I've heard the river runs red.

— We'll swim there again, yet.

Dry rations had been distributed for several days to come, and the recruits were wrapping up their sugar. Rokka winked as he said to them:

— Don't bother trying to save that sugar, boys. It'll get all wet because we'll be swimming soon.

— That's only a rumor. Why, we'll jump that brook if it comes to that.

The recruit who spoke was puffing manfully on a cigarette, his cap set at a jaunty angle. It was the youth who had asked on arriving where the Russians were, so he could start killing them. His name was Asumaniemi. Rokka had answered him sarcastically then, but now, though his tone was still bantering as he addressed the lad, there was no sarcasm in it. That first evening, in repelling the counterattack at Sarastie's command post, the boy had dropped three of the attackers.

After the battle the others had perhaps heard a little too much about these three fallen, but Asumaniemi was allowed the right to boast of his exploits since he had been completely unafraid under fire. And that first occasion had been only one of many. Asumaniemi had become one of the pillars of the platoon so that Rokka was joking as he warned him:

— Don't open that jaw of yours too wide, youngster. You'll swim like the rest of us, so eat your sugar and don't leave it to get wet.

Second Lieutenant Jalovaara arrived just then from the command post.

— What's all this talk about swimming?

— I told the boys to eat their sugar before it melted when we swam the river.

— You'll start a panic with that kind of talk.

— It seems to me it's the Russkies who send us galloping and not me. Wait a bit and you'll see us go dashing through that water like a flock of wild ducks.

— And what else should I expect when my second-in-command is the first to talk about running away?

Rokka had hardly met the new officer, but already from what he had said he knew the man had no idea of the real reasons for the change in the nature of the war. Jalovaara had been discharged from the army after the first big offensive because of the important civil post he held, and recalled only when heavy losses had decimated the ranks. And while Rokka was irritated by his comments, he was even more worried by the feeling that the man's innocence was dangerous.

—You've got no idea of what we're talking about. We've learned to take our Russky friends seriously. Ivan has his wants we have ours, and we haven't always been able to keep him from satisfying them. And I don't think we will now, either. The men are afraid, and I don't blame them for being ready to run.

— We'll retire over the bridge in good order when the order comes. You just do your duty and leave the rest to me.

The lieutenant's voice rang with resolution. He was determined to act bravely at the front, and he could not yet bring himself to believe the war lost. But no matter what happened, he would not let anything keep him from doing his duty. Of that he was certain.

His attitude annoyed Rokka who had begun to turn on him the same derisive smile which had always made Lammio lose his temper. Gently, as though speaking to a child, Rokka said:

— We'll all be lucky if the Third Company gets across by the bridge. The Russkies have tanks on the road, so we'll probably have to swim. But if you keep on making all that noise, we may not even have a chance to swim. Ivan'll hear us and be on our necks before we know it.

— You just mind your business and obey orders like everybody else. And right now your orders are to keep an eye on the positions. I've heard about you. In my platoon there's no room for malcontents—my command is going to carry out its orders without grumbling.

— It's never done anything yet without grumbling, and I don't think it'll start to now. You've got a lot to learn, and damned if I'm going to teach you. Cross the bridge if you can.

Rokka turned and stalked away angrily. Making his way to the positions, he sat down and began complaining:

— Why the devil can't I ever seem to get along with officers? Koskela was the only one I never quarreled with. What's wrong with the rest of them?

Vanhala laughed at Rokka's puzzled tone.

— Who knows. Has it ever struck you that it just might be your fault?

— Mine? Rokka was genuinely amazed. — How the hell could it be mine? I always talk sense to 'em, but all they do is to bleat about trifles. What have I ever said to any of them that could make 'em lose their temper? I try to keep things going as long as there's the tiniest chance, and they're at my throat for it. All I wanted was to make sure everything was set up so that we could pull out in good order if it was necessary. But instead he starts shouting, "Over the bridge." How the hell can we cross there when Ivan'll be there first? It's as if they wanted to get us killed.

Rokka stared angrily at his boots, then shrugged his shoulders.

— Let them all go to Hell, then. Karelia's gone. The war's lost. I've got nothing more to lose. All I'm trying to do now is make 'em pay for the Isthmus. I got a major the other day. Served the damn fool right for coming spying here with a patrol. The First Company's boys got his badges. You missed that chance, Rahikainen.

— I've stopped collecting 'em. They can have 'em for all I care—the badges, Karelia, the whole goddamn war. Good riddance.

— Come on, now. We're hitting back on the Isthmus. They're not advancing any more, said Sihvonen.

— Yes, but it doesn't help any. Sooner or later Ivan'll break through. We've lost the war. All we've been through hasn't done any good whatever.

Pee peeoooo . . .

— Look out, cried Asumaniemi.

They all settled deeper in their holes, except for Rokka who remained sitting where he was and spoke as though to himself:

— Bullets! That's all that's around here. But why not, when everybody in the world has nothing better to do than run around the woods banging away at each other?

— Get the hell into a foxhole, Wolf called anxiously.

— Even a man like Koskela, Rokka went on, ignoring his friend's warning. — If anybody knew that dying out here was useless, he did. But there he went, just as if he'd committed suicide. He didn't have a chance of getting away after he'd thrown the charge, and he knew it. Say, Vanhala, what did you say to the chaplain yesterday?

— Khee-hee-hee. He asked about the watch that boy in the First who got shot by a patrol had . . . I told him I supposed someone had taken it who needed a watch. . . . Funny what chaplains worry about nowadays. Men being killed on all sides like pigs in a slaughterhouse, but that doesn't interest a chaplain at all. To him stealing's worse than murder. To me it doesn't seem very awful to take a watch from a man who doesn't need one any more.

Vanhala chuckled heartily, sprawled on his back in his hole. But his merriment vanished as heavy firing broke out in the direction of the road. Grimly they prepared to repel the attack.

2.

Half an hour later the situation seemed to demand that the company's flanks be pulled back. But there was no enemy pressure on them, and no order came. Nevertheless the Third Company, which had been defending the road, was already in full retreat toward the bridge, closely pursued by the Russians. When at last the company commander's runner brought the order to withdraw, Rokka knew that the safest course was to swim the river. Again he suggested it to Jalovaara, but the lieutenant once more rejected the idea.

The platoon, therefore, began to withdraw toward the bridge, but as they approached it a ghastly sight met their eyes: crawling across the bridge were the Third Company's wounded while the Russians blazed away at them. Even as they watched the Third's new commander crumpled before a burst from a machine gun. Then a hoarse shout reached the watching men:

— It's going up!

The cry set off a chorus of screams, for there were still men on the bridge. Then a tremendous explosion shook the area, sending bodies high into the air along with the debris of the bridge.

The Third Platoon would have to swim after all. Pieces of timber were still raining down among them when Rokka shouted:

— Get the new men across first! Maatta, get the machine gun over. Rahikainen, Sihvonen, Honkajoki, help him. We'll keep them from getting down to the water.

The men directed waded into the river, which was too deep to ford only in the middle. A couple of strokes were enough, however, to take a man through the deep water.

Jalovaara, Rokka, Vanhala, Wolf and Asumaniemi stayed behind, firing as fast as they could at the approaching Russians. Once

Jalovaara motioned to Asumaniemi to leave, but the boy ignored him and went on emptying one magazine after another.

— Got one! Look—he's down beside that bush . . .

— Get going, you son of a bitch, Rokka shouted at him angrily.

Jalovaara heard him and, turning his head, beckoned to them all to leave.

— Get out of here, all of you. I'll cover you.

Rokka knew that the officer was trying to atone for his recent actions, but he saw no sense in that kind of behavior and said so:

— Not without you. What the hell good is one man? Come on, let's go.

They started down the bank, but as Wolf was about to enter the water he staggered and fell. In a resigned voice he said:

— I can't, Antti. I can't.

— What's the matter?

— Go on. Quick. I can't . . . run . . . I'm hit. Run, all of you. They're shooting from the bridge.

The bullet had indeed come from the wreckage of the bridge, for where they were now a bluff protected them from the shore. A machine-gun burst spattered the water. They had been sighted. The water was turning red around Wolf as he struggled to rise, only to slip on a stone and fall again. He gave a single cry of pain as Rokka swung him onto his shoulder. Wolf was a good-sized man, but Rokka bore him like a child as he plunged into the river.

— Head up! Keep your head up . . . here we go now.

The men already across the river tried to cover the five still in the water as they reached the bank and began to climb it. They were almost to the top when a crackle of fire came from the opposite bank. With a last spurt they tumbled headlong into the trench, but as Rokka was in midair a yell escaped his lips:

— Ow! God damn it.

The others lifted Wolf off Rokka's back. Wolf babbled excitedly:

— Antti . . . you're wounded . . . I heard it hit you . . .

— I know . . . in the shoulder . . . Goddamn, it hurts . . .

Quickly the medical corpsmen attached to the Jaeger Company which had manned the positions began to dress their wounds. Wolf's was bleeding profusely but the wouna was not serious. Rokka's shoulder, however, was worse. The bones had obviously been shattered, for when the orderlies moved his arm to remove his blouse he grimaced with pain.

Then Rokka remembered the lieutenant. Jalovaara had immediately begun to organize the men who had crossed the river first in support of the Frontier Jaegers, fearing that the Russians might try to cross the river without stopping.

— Hey, Lieutenant, Rokka shouted.

— Were you hit badly? asked Jalovaara walking up to him.

— In the shoulder, damn it. But say, are you ready to admit that we swam?

— I can't deny it. Not until I've changed into dry clothes, at least.

The lieutenant took the matter so well that Rokka's antagonism vanished. He said no more and Jalovaara, confident now that there was no immediate danger, went back to assembling his men who were being withdrawn behind the line to rest. They carried Rokka and Wolf with them as far as the road to wait there for the ambulance. All the way Rokka swore and complained from his stretcher:

— To think that I'd live to see myself carried like a cripple! All my life I've never had to be helped by anyone . . . Jesus, how my shoulder hurts. How's yours, Paw?

— Better if I keep still.

— Boys, do you know where Antti Rokka's going? To his wife Lyyti. And the brats. Ouch! I've only seen the youngest one on one leave. My father-in-law got them evacuated. I'm going to brew the old fellow some real beer for that . . . Antti's fought his war. I wonder what's going to happen to this arm.

— It'll be all right, an orderly offered. — The collarbone's broken, that's all.

— Well, it sure hurts like hell. Of all the goddamn things—three months at Taipale where it rained iron and nothing happens, then a measly little stream like this. But things are always happening . . . you can't stop 'em . . .

At last the ambulance arrived, and Jalovaara seized Rokka's hand and said seriously:

— Well, we'll be seeing you, I hope. We're going to need good men. And I hope you'll forget our disagreement. I was pretty green.

— That's all right, Lieutenant. You aren't the only officer I've quarreled with. I'll tell you a few things, though . . . in Maatta and Vanhala you've got two good men. And when young Asumaniemi learns to fight with his head, he's going to be a real devil. Honkajoki's a good man. He sounds like he's crazy, but don't let it bother you. And when you're hungry, put Rahikainen on the job and there'll always be something to eat. And that's what you'll always be—hungry, just like now.

When they all had said goodbye Rokka and Wolf were lifted into the ambulance.

— So long, boys. Wolf, see they don't separate us on the way. Hey, watch how you put me in. I'm not leaving here feet first. That's the way.

The ambulance drove off to the accompaniment of loud expostulations from within. The orderlies were being instructed as to how to handle wounded.

— He sounded just like that when he first came, said Vanhala, solemnly. The rest also felt very depressed. Within a very short period much had been torn from the platoon. Vanhala, Maatta, Honkajoki and Sihvonen felt orphaned amid all the new faces.

— Hietanen, Koskela, Rokka, Wolf. The gang's shrunk all of a sudden, said Sihvonen.

— Except for Wolf they all were the leaders, said Vanhala, looking at Maatta. — If that's the way it is, it's your turn next, kheehee. . . .

Maatta did not reply at once but a little later, as he walked off toward the rest of the platoon, they heard him mutter:

— A temporary sergeant's something even God would think too small a fish to fry.

3.

The sun had just risen.

Rifles crackled sharply in the clear air. A fine mist hung over the river as Lieutenant Jalovaara crawled laboriously up to Vanhala.

— Try that gully. See that body?

— I see it.

— Well, they've got an automatic rifle beside it. And over in that clump of fallen trees they've got at least two machine guns. But the bottom of the gully is out of their line of fire. Maatta will make them keep their heads down. If you can get into the trench and put them out of action, the rest'll be easy.

Vanhala examined the hill, his face solemn.

— I'll get into the trench all right. But keep that automatic rifle silenced.

— We'll be right behind you.

The lieutenant looked at Vanhala.

—If you don't want to, I'll go. You can bring the lads after me.

— I'm going to try, but I'd better take Asumaniemi and Honkajoki with me. . . . No others—any more'd only be in the way.

— All you need to do is put those machine guns out of action. That'll open the door. Honkajoki! Asumaniemi!

The two men crept nearer.

— Two or three men'll have to try to get into their trench through that gully. Any other way would cost too much. Vanhala's going ahead to clear the way. Are you willing to try?

— I will, said Asumaniemi eagerly.

—I will if you order me, Honkajoki said. —But I won't volunteer.

— Well, call it an order.

— Then I'll go.

— Good luck, then. You know, boys, we've got to push them back. If we let them broaden the breach, it'll be a big job to close it. Show them we aren't going to let them spit in our faces.

Having finished, Jalovaara crawled off to join the rest of the platoon, leaving the three volunteers to draw up their plan.

— They were a fine lot to let Ivan get right into our positions. And across the river. I'll bet they messed up their trousers when they heard him coming.

Asumaniemi cursed with masculine bravado, but Vanhala and Honkajoki were silent as they studied the ground. Honkajoki did say, however, in quiet reproach:

— Slow down, brother, slow down. Don't be so anxious.

— Yes, and there's eleven Finns lying out there. The boys didn't just run away, said Vanhala.

After he had been made section leader Vanhala had begun to take matters far more seriously than before. Of course, the heavy fighting might have made anyone disinclined to joke, but his new responsibility had played its part in the change.

A night or two before, the Russians had managed to cross the river under cover of darkness and had captured two strongpoints. The machine-gun company, which was being held in reserve, had been ordered to retake them, and Jalovaara's platoon was preparing to capture one. It was to be a surprise attack without artillery preparation, a feat which would indeed be risky with their own positions so close to the Russians. Vanhala, with the help of Honkajoki and Asumaniemi, was to gain the end of a communication trench leading to the Russian positions. It appeared possible because of the deep gully between the positions—if the automatic rifle dominating the gully could be put out of action. The three men were then to silence the two machine guns. This would enable Jalovaara to reach the positions with the rest of the platoon and then work his way down the trench.

Vanhala regarded the gully for a while before he said:

— There's no use gambling on it. Straight ahead, that's the only way. And we can't run or we'll be spotted for certain.

Asumaniemi shoved an egg-shaped hand grenade into each of his pockets, and the others did the same. Vanhala placed his extra tommy-gun magazines where he could get at them easily, then he looked at his watch.

— Eight minutes.

— Can't we get going earlier? Why wait for the rest? Let's the three of us get the thing over with.

Honkajoki rolled his eyes.

— Let's go home, Vanhala . . . the boy'll do everything that's needed.

— Sure, just say the word, and I'll go by myself.

4.

Jalovaara lay behind a tree as the time passed slowly. The platoon was ready, but still they had to wait for zero hour. He examined the gully along which the shock group was to advance. He would have liked to lead them in person, but there was no one to whom he could entrust the platoon. Maatta was incapable of commanding a unit of any size, for in spite of his bravery he lacked the qualities that made other men follow him. He would lead the way, but he wouldn't open his mouth if the others failed to follow him. How sorely he needed Rokka right now! The quality of the human material certainly was falling off. The drafted older men sent as replacements were of no use and the conscripts born in '25 were too young and green. Many of these latter were brave and enthusiastic but only after a number of weeks did they become good soldiers, and until then their casualty rate was extremely high.

A fortnight had wrought a great change in Jalovaara. Not only was he filthy and bearded, but his whole attitude had changed. He was not harsh as he had been, but firm in a quiet way. He was almost comradely with the men, and he addressed every member of his platoon by his first name. For two weeks now they had been engaged in bitter defensive fighting and during that period Jalovaara had become the officer to whom Lammio, now a major, entrusted the most difficult tasks.

The battalion had clung stubbornly to its positions until last night when, helped by mist and darkness, the Russians had overrun the two strongpoints. But even then the improvement in the men's fighting spirit had been evident. The Second Company had retreated only after bloody hand-to-hand fighting in the dark, and the already short-handed Third Platoon had left behind eleven dead.

— Those positions must be retaken. And not lost again. Even if it means death to all of us, we stay here.

A bitter defiance born of despair swelled in Jalovaara's mind. He realized that the war was indeed lost. But Jalovaara had never felt such hate for the Russians as now, when defeat was in sight. They would revel in their victory and destroy everything he, Jalovaara, valued. It was better to die first.

Jalovaara tensed as his eyes caught the flash of a gun barrel. He squeezed the trigger of his automatic rifle.

Immediately dozens of weapons opened up. Maatta's machine gun joined in at once, its tap-tapping easily distinguishable above the reports of other weapons.

Vanhala crept forward on all fours. Then, suddenly, Asumaniemi dashed past him, shooting from the hip. Instantly Vanhala also sprang to his feet, realizing that Asumaniemi's boldness had made concealment impossible and that the safest thing now was to trust to speed.

Pee-pee-ow . . . pee-peeoo-peeoo-peeoopeeoo.

Vanhala almost flew the fifty paces to the end of the communication trench. Someone had him in his sights, for he could hear bullets hissing spitefully past his head.

The communication trench began as a shallow ditch and for a stretch continued that way. It was not manned, but nevertheless it was under fire. Vanhala flopped down on the bottom, and, glancing back, saw that Honkajoki had not followed them. Beside him, Asumaniemi raised his head for a look ahead, and a hail of bullets drummed into the side of the trench.

— We did it! Well, here I go again. Follow me and keep those eggs ready.

— My God, there's only two of us!

— Don't worry, it'll be all right. . . . Here I go.

Asumaniemi sprang forward and Vanhala moved to follow. As he did so, a hand grenade dropped ahead of them and exploded. In a single motion Asumaniemi pulled one of his egg-shaped grenades from his belt, tore out the pin and threw.

It flew as only a ball thrown by a schoolboy can fly and dropped exactly on the desired spot. As it exploded the boy burst into motion, leaving Vanhala to follow at a weird gallop on all fours, his buttocks sticking up.

Peeoo-peeoo-peeoo-peeoo-peeoo . . .

The tempo of the firing increased as the platoon, having seen Asumaniemi and Vanhala reach the communication trench, fired as fast as they could. Jalovaara knew that the greatest danger still lay before them, for while the gully was only partially exposed to Russian fire, they now were actually in the Russian positions.

Jalovaara could see that Honkajoki still had not moved. But what was that? There he was, on the move at last.

It was a strange sight, for Honkajoki was moving along on all fours, bounding like a rabbit at astonishing speed. Within seconds he had vanished into the communication trench.

Around the first bend in the trench lay a Russian mangled by the hand grenade. A second was creeping away wounded, as two new men were coming along the trench to their aid. For but a second they halted, paralyzed, then both died without a cry. Asumaniemi shouted over his shoulder:

— The trench branches off. We need someone to hold one fork.

— He didn't come with us, panted Vanhala, but before he could finish his sentence, Honkajoki leaped into the trench in their rear.

— Quick, quick . . . this way.

Honkajoki scrambled up to them, his eyes like saucers.

— Over there's where the trench branches out . . . remember? One leads to dugout Number Two . . . You'll have to hold that while we go for the machine guns . . .

Keerraashh . . .

— Hand grenade!

Asumaniemi made his second throw and dashed to the fork. But three hand grenades flew toward them in quick succession and they had to leap back to shelter. Asumaniemi cursed and hurled another of his own grenades.

No more enemy hand grenades came after that, so they took the initiative again. Quickly Asumaniemi dashed to the next bend and disappeared around the corner. Seconds later Vanhala and Honkajoki sprinted after him and rounded the corner in time to see him emptying his tommy gun into a still-moving pile of bodies. Here the trench branched, and Vanhala threw two hand grenades one after the other in the direction of Number Two dugout and beckoned Honkajoki to station himself at the mouth of the trench leading there.

—And, by God, don't let 'em through . . . and don't go away. . . .

Then Vanhala threw his last hand grenade over Asumaniemi's head and after the crash they rounded the next bend, stepping on the bodies at the bottom of the trench, which yielded unpleasantly under their feet. Asumaniemi was almost bursting with enthusiasm and to his surprise Vanhala felt himself similarly exhilarated. Obviously they had succeeded beyond all expectations.

As they opened fire from the parapet to keep Russian heads down, they heard Jalovaara's voice in their rear, and saw him coming at a run, followed by Sihvonen and a few of the new men. Farther back the other section was approaching through the gully.

The two machine guns they had set out to put out of action lay silent on the trench parapet, their crews having abandoned them and fled when Vanhala threw his last grenade. And though the advancing men were still under fire from a distance, they pushed their attack nonetheless.

Jalovaara was the first to leap into the trench, and he immediately sent Vanhala back to lead the other section down the trench leading to Number Two dugout.

—All right now, boys, we've won a foothold and we're not going to lose it again. Asumaniemi . . . here we go.

Quickly they began to roll up the Russian defenses, Jalovaara in the lead, a tommy gun in the crook of his arm, and Asumaniemi pitching hand grenades over his head. Russian grenades came at them from every bend, but none of the Russians could match the length and accuracy of Asumaniemi's throws, and they were able to advance almost as fast as they could run.

The trench soon joined the one along the river which had been the Finns' front-line defense. Here a fierce hand grenade duel was waged until Jalovaara put a swift end to it by racing boldly to a bend in the trench and enfilading the section beyond. A Russian captain and a half dozen of his men fell here and the defense collapsed.

That was the decisive blow; the other strongpoint that had fallen into Rusisan hands could now be brought under fire from the retaken one. Jalovaara ordered Maatta's machine gun brought at all speed, and soon the neighboring strongpoint was under murderous fire. The Russian positions lay spread out below them. It was for this very reason that the second strongpoint had originally been abandoned by the Finns. Having first taken the high ground, it had been as easy for the Russians to rake the positions as it was now proving for the Finns.

While Maatta emptied belt after belt into the Russian positions, the others continued to mop up the trenches. Then came the moment for which Jalovaara had waited, the moment when the Russian survivors were forced to climb out of the trench and leave the positions to escape the murderous fire. A lone figure clambered onto the parapet in an attempt to dash down to the river. He fell after taking only a couple of steps.

Vanhala waved his arms excitedly.

— There they go . . . Hey, a dozen of 'em!

Now the Russians were fleeing the trench in bunches. Their position, however, was hopeless as the Finns opened fire. Even the most timid worked themselves into a fury now, for there was little danger and plenty of easy targets. Few were the Russians who reached the river, but even these died within seconds of entering the water.

Not a single Russian got across the river despite the heavy fire their comrades were keeping up from their bank in an effort to cover the retreat. A rumble as of thunder came from Number Two dugout and they guessed what had happened. A charge of high explosive had blown it up.

— Hey, I've used up all my cartridges. Who's got some more?

Asumaniemi half turned and stood up, momentarily exposing his head and shoulders above the parapet. The next second he staggered and fell, clutching his breast. When Vanhala turned him on his back they saw instantly that he was dead. The bullet must have hit him right in the heart.

Jalovaara turned away, tears in his eyes. He took two angry strides, then managed to control himself as he said:

— Always! Always the best go first . . .

The firing ceased, then men standing as though struck dumb. The easy slaughter and the successful counterattack in which they had not suffered a single casualty had made them feel almost superhuman. But Asumaniemi's death had smashed that mood like a sledgehammer blow.

He was one of the most beautiful corpses they had seen. His face still wore an expression of childlike surprise, but except for that it was quite peaceful, lacking the distorted grin that made most of the dead so unpleasant to look at.

Now Jalovaara left a few men behind to secure the river bank, and with Vanhala, Honkajoki, Sihvonen and one of the recruits made his way down the communication trench to Number Two dugout. And as they went five Russian soldiers surrendered to them, seeing their retreat cut off.

The strongpoint had been recaptured, at a cost to the Second Section of only two wounded. Three prisoners had been taken from the dugout, bringing the total to eight. Jalovaara sent them on immediately and hastily began to organize a defense, for as soon as the Russians became convinced that there were no more of their own men in the positions they would certainly lay down a terrific artillery barrage in revenge.

Quiet reigned also in the neighboring strongpoint. There, too, the Russians' attempt to escape across the river had been hopeless for Maatta's machine gun had the whole river bank under its sights.

Maatta himself was calmly smoking as Jalovaara approached. He seemed to pay no attention to Jalovaara's praise, saying as though he had not been listening at all:

— Guess I'd better get this contraption to one of the dugouts. There'll be a lot of iron coming over soon.

Jalovaara smiled and went along the trench to join the others who had gathered around Asumaniemi's body which now lay on a stretcher. When the stretcher bearers had gone, he said to Vanhala:

— Well, this means another stripe. But it's . . . it's . . . too bad. Jalovaara's voice shook: — Asumaniemi deserved better.

Then he looked at Honkajoki.

— And you did your share, too.

Honkajoki took off his cap and bowed, sending them off into gales of laughter. But it was a little too hearty. There was a note of hysteria in it now that the strain was past.

Then as one man they dived for shelter as from across the river came a hollow rumble like thunder.

5.

They lay in shelters dug into the walls of trenches and tried to make themselves as small as possible. Fire, earth, steel and smoke whirled in the air over them and they knew the old unalterable terror. Eyes shut, hearts pounding, muscles quivering, they tried to blend themselves into the soil. Today they were, if anything, more frightened than ever, for they knew that the end of the war was upon them.

— Don't let me die now. . . .

They had stopped firing yesterday, but the Russians were still at it.

Dazed from lack of sleep, weary in body, worn out in spirit, they waited for the thunderous crashing to cease. What use had their valiant stand along this river been? What good had their counterattack a few days ago done? Now they were to give up the positions without firing a shot.

They had lost, and their punishment was upon them. For what? It was a question to which many answers would doubtless be given, none of them satisfactory. In defeat they had but one consolation: in laying the whip of defeat to their backs Fate had released them from all responsibility. For victory would certainly have entailed responsibility—responsibility for acts which would have had to be accounted for one day. As long as human history is written, so long will one event be the cause of that which follows. And in cause lies responsibility. He in whose hands lay the power of cause, let him answer for the consequences. These men had paid for their sins with the skin off their backs. They had only one desire left: to preserve their wretched lives through these last minutes. Thereafter they would be free, pure and blameless. Happy men.

The thunder continued. Blending into one mighty roar the sound traveled far in the clear autumn morning. Up to the very last second it welled forth as though proclaiming, drunk with its own power: Woe to the vanquished!

They, however had no need to fear the voice mingling with the echoes: Woe to the victors!

6.

Maatta opened his eyes to see a man come into sight around a bend in the trench. It was one of the replacements, an oldish man who had been behaving strangely for some time. He was bareheaded and his eyes were rolling wildly.

— Take cover!

The man heard Maatta's warning, but instead of obeying stopped in front of his shelter.

— Get down.

The man stared into space, taking no notice of him until Maatta rose from his shelter and motioned him down.

— Get down. It's almost over.

The man looked wildly at Maatta with bulging eyes and then without further ado began to climb up the parapet. Instantly Maatta seized him, and though he struggled fiercely to be freed, Maatta dragged him down to the ground, where a furious struggle ensued. At that moment the firing ceased, leaving a silence broken only by Maatta's gasps and the lunatic's cries:

— Let go! Goddamned parachutists . . . Let me go . . . I'll decide everything . . . Land and money for all . . . And power, too, for everybody . . . Let me go, you bastard . . .

Now Vanhala, Sihvonen, Rahikainen and Honkajoki rushed to help Maatta who was having difficulty keeping the man down. Not until four men were holding him by an arm or leg and Maatta was sitting on his chest was he overcome. Even then he went on shouting and cursing, gnashing his teeth and foaming at the mouth. He babbled meaningless words and every now and again broke into a wild roar.

Men rose from their shelters. Silently, they watched with tired eyes as the maniac was taken away.

Finland's war was over.

Mess tins hung over campfires as Mielonen strode along the road shouting:

— Anyone who wants to can come to the CP to hear the broadcast. A minister'll be spouting.

The men were lying on the roadside, some asleep, others brewing ersatz coffee.

— We can hear him from here. And we know what he'll say.

— Who cares what those bastards say! Speeches aren't going to help anything. When your powder's all gone, it's better to keep your mouth shut than to go spouting about the rights of small nations. A dog raises his hind leg on them.

This last was from Rahikainen.

—Sure, we all know that. They're just stuffing a bone down the loser's throat . . .

That was Sihvonen: angry and tired, but still not quite certain whether he was angry with the Russians or the Finnish brass.

— . . . the achievement of good relations with our neighbors. Let friendly intercourse between all nations be our aim.

That was the voice of the cabinet member.

Honkajoki searched futilely in his pack for a bit of bread and brought up two strangely carved bits of wood which he tossed to Vanhala.

— Throw them in the fire, Vanahala. I've lost my inspiration.

Vanhala was on his knees beside the fire. He blew on it, and ash flew in his face. He rubbed his eyes with his fists, then looked at Honkajoki. Dirt and soot covered his face, which had lost its roundness, but a smile still creased the corners of his mouth as he said:

—Ah, if only we still had your longbow, khee-hee . . .

Soon they were all asleep. A solitary cart came along the road, the clumping of its wheels echoing among the pines. The load it bore was covered with tent canvas, but protruding from beneath it was a stiffened arm terminating in a clenched fist. The last dead were journeying homeward.

Deep in the forest Second Lieutenant Jalovaara sat dejectedly on a stump. He had gone their quietly, as though unaware where he was heading. Finding himself out of sight of everybody, he buried his face in his hands and for a long time stared at the ground without moving. From the distance came the sound of the cart on the road.

His eyes grew wet with tears, and his shoulders began to twitch. Then he shook with the bitter violent weeping of a grown man. Between sobs he murmured over and over, gritting his teeth:

—We heard . . . they told us . . . Finland is dead . . . and snow . . . hides her grave. . . .

Later the autumn sun warmed the ground and the men sleeping on it. Lingonberry plants glistened in the sunlight, and slowly the rumble of cart wheels faded into the all-embracing silence of the pine forest. The weary men slept and a benevolent sky looked down on them. It was by no means angry with them. It may even have felt a kind of sympathy for them.

These were good men.